PRAISE FOR *TO THE EDGE OF THE WORLD*

One of the *Washington Post*'s "Best Novels of 2006"

"Perhaps the best historical novel I have read…A stunning achievement of imagination and story-telling. In this novel Harry Thompson shows how the modern world was born, not in a laboratory, but on a storm-beset ship and out of a welter of ignorance, heroism and tragedy. A masterpiece."
—Bernard Cornwell, author of *The Last Kingdom, The Pale Horseman,* and the Richard Sharpe series

"…fascinating…Like O'Brian, Thompson gives us an entertaining grab bag of minor characters…this is good stuff indeed." —*Washington Post*

"[Thompson] used the artistic skills of a budding O'Brian and an astounding amount of research to tell the complicated story of the 1831 journey and its aftermath…[it] will delight O'Brian loyalists."
—*Chicago Tribune*

"Thompson's masterful storytelling brings all the shades of darkness and uncertainty of fate together with the flame of enlightenment and exploration. Recommended."
—*Library Journal*

"This is a fine, interesting and educational book, which I strongly recommend. It is nearly 800 pages long, but it maintains interest throughout the entire length."
—*The Roanoke Times*

"If you like seafaring adventure, then you'll want to travel the world in the almost 800 pages of *To the Edge of the World*…will fit well on the shelves of anyone who owns books by Patrick O'Brian…a thinking person's adventure."
—*Record-Courier*

"A master storyteller, Thompson tells the tale of two inquisitive men with irreconcilable world views." —*Pages Magazine*

MORE PRAISE FOR *TO THE EDGE OF THE WORLD*

"Deservedly Booker-longlisted, *To the Edge of the World* is by far the best historical novel I've read all year—an engrossing, thought-provoking page-turner that entertained me for hours on end and showed me many wonders."
—*Historical Novels Review* ("Editor's Pick")

"[Thompson] tracks the two men's paths with aplomb."
—*Publishers Weekly*

"A bestseller is born…an easy and picturesque yarn made muscular by historical fact and philosophical ideas." —*The Observer*

"A brilliant historical novel. An impressive book; something big that deserves attention." —*Mail on Sunday*

"Harry Thompson catches the atmosphere, and the language, of Victorian Britain with much skill and paints a vivid picture of the grim existence aboard … it's an excellent read, in the traditions of Patrick O'Brian."
—*Daily Telegraph*

"… a page turning action-adventure, combined with subtle intellectual arguments…[a] fascinating tale." —*Sunday Telegraph*

"Brilliant…terrifying, hilarious and uplifting…" —*Daily Mail*

"Thompson proves a master story-teller, whose vigorous command of character, period detail, weather conditions and fleeting emotions lifts the reader straight from his chair into the middle of a sudden storm."
—*Sunday Times*

"A ripping yarn…beautiful managed set-pieces, pacy, gripping and vividly chaotic."
—*Independent On Sunday*

"A fascinating read." —*The Times*

To the Edge of the World
—Book One—

HARRY THOMPSON

MACADAM CAGE

MacAdam Cage
155 Sansome Street, Suite 550
San Francisco, CA 94104
www.MacAdamCage.com

Cover painting by Raymond Massey,
Fellow in the American Society of Marine Artists and The Ship Store Galleries

Library of Congress Cataloging-in-Publication Data

Thomspson, Harry, 1960—
  [This thing of darkness]
  To the edge of the world / Harry Thompson.
    p.cm
  Previously published as: This thing of darkness.
  ISBN 1-59692-190-0 (alk. paper)
    1. Fitzroy, Robert, 1805-1865—Fiction. 2. Darwin, Charles, 1809-1882—
  Fiction. 3. Beagle Expedition (1831-1836)—Fiction. 4. Ship captains—
  Fiction. 5. Naturalists—Fiction 6. Patagonia (Argentina and Chile)—Fiction.
  I. Title.

PR6120.H664T48 2006
823'.92—dc22
                                                      2006044978

Book One Paperback edition: May 2007
ISBN 978-1-95692-225-9

TO MY FATHER

without whose help this

book could never have been written

'This thing of darkness I acknowledge mine'

The Tempest,

Act V, Scene 1

This novel is closely based upon real events
that took place between 1828 and 1865.

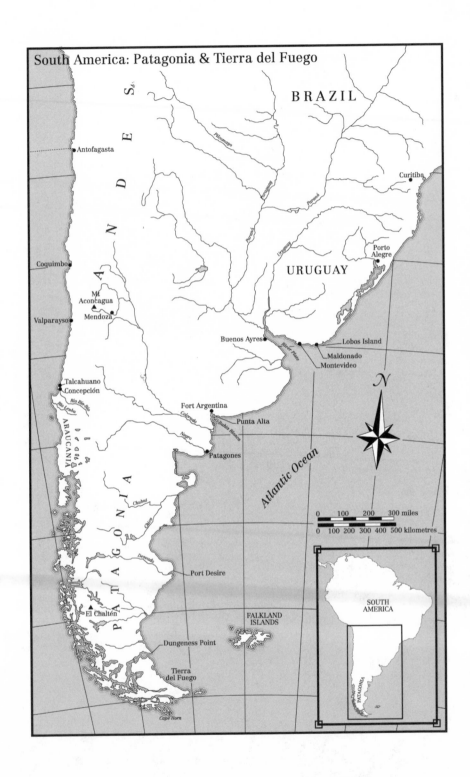

South America: Patagonia & Tierra del Fuego

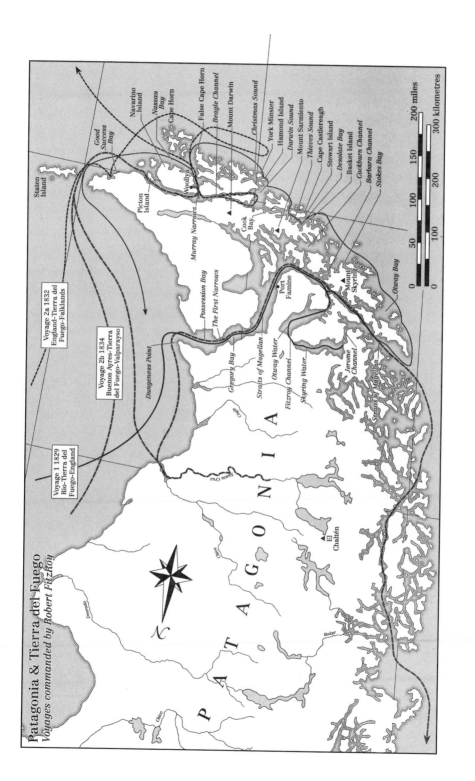

Patagonia & Tierra del Fuego
Voyages commanded by Robert FitzRoy

Voyage 1 1829
Rio–Tierra del
Fuego–England

Voyage 2a 1832
England–Tierra del
Fuego–Falklands

Voyage 2b 1834
Buenos Ayres–Tierra
del Fuego–Valparayso

Staten
Island

Good
Success
Bay

Navarino
Island

Nassau
Bay

Cape Horn

False Cape Horn

Beagle Channel

Mount Darwin

Christmas Sound

York Minster

Hamond Island

Darwin Sound

Mount Sarmiento

Thieves Sound

Cape Castlereagh

Stewart Island

Desolate Bay

Basket Island

Cockburn Channel

Barbara Channel

Stokes Bay

Picton Island

Murray Narrows

Woollya

Cook Bay

Possession Bay

The First Narrows

Dungeness Point

Gregory Bay

Straits of Magellan

Otway Water

Fitzroy Channel

Skyring Water

Port Famine

Jerome Channel

Mount Skyring

Otway Bay

Straits of Magellan

Santa Cruz

El Chaltén

Deseado

Chico

Chico

Baker

Coyle

PATAGONIA

N

0   50   100   150   200 miles

0   100   200   300 kilometres

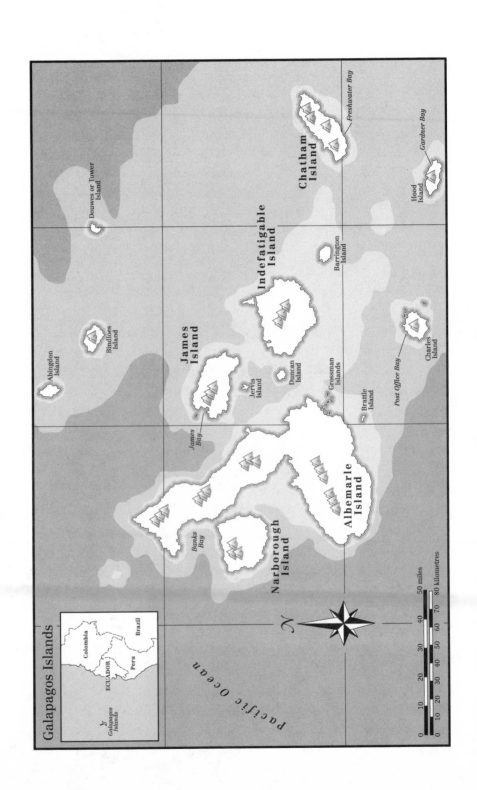

Galapagos Islands

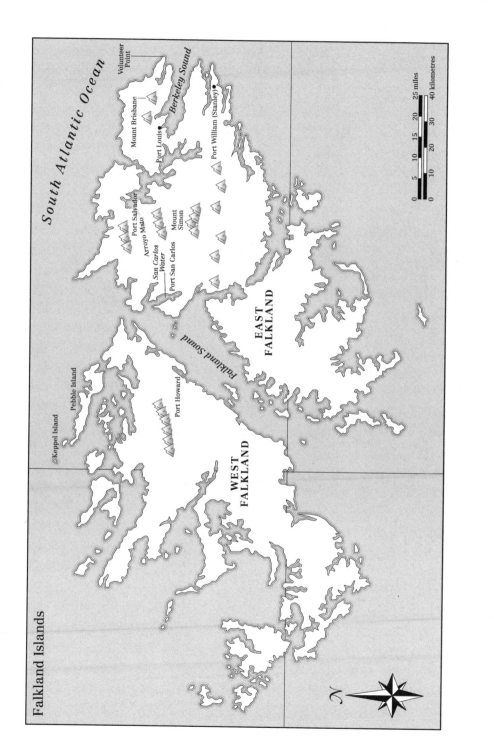

Falkland Islands

PREFACE

Port Famine, Patagonia, 1 August 1828

An icy wind shouldered its way into the Straits of Magellan from the west, pummelling the cliff walls and scouring the rocks as it passed. Its thirteen-thousand-mile journey across open ocean completed, it sought out the ancient glaciers of its birth in anger. As a grimy late-morning light ahead signalled the dawning of the brief southern day, it funnelled at speed through the narrows at York Road, before sweeping left into the bay of Port Famine. Darting and jinking as it hunted for a target, it picked out the solitary figure of Captain Pringle Stokes where he knelt. It buffeted him and tore at his clothes. It tugged at his thinning forelock in mock deference. It cut through the sodden wool of his coat, turning his skin to gooseflesh and congealing the blood in his veins.

Stokes shivered. *I am so emaciated,* he thought bitterly, *I can feel my shoulder-blades almost touching each other.* He shifted his weight as another furious gust did its best to hurl him to the ground. His knees jostled together in the cold gravel. His ceremonial scabbard, the badge of his rank, scratched uselessly at the smooth stones. He plastered the damp strands of hair back into place – a tiny, futile act of vanity – but the wind merely caught them again and flung them aside dismissively. *This place,* he thought. *This place constitutes the sum total of my achievement. This place is all that I amount to. This place is all that I am.*

Further down the beach, Bennet and his ratings, all drenched from the waist down, were still struggling to pull the cutter ashore; ants, going about their irrelevant business in the service of an unheeding monarch half a world away. *A curse on His Majesty,* thought Stokes, *and a curse on His Majesty's government,* in whose service they found themselves marooned in this wretched place. As he inspected them, the bent, sullen figures seemed to be winning their little war. They were probably wondering where he'd gone. Curiosity, he had learned, is one of the few feelings that boredom cannot kill. As soon as Bennet had the boat secured, they would follow him up the shingle. He did not have much time.

He had conceived his plan weeks ago, but today he would put it into practice. Why today? Nothing marked out this shoreline as different from any other. It was as wretched as the rest. Which was precisely why today was so apt. He had realized it, suddenly, when he had stepped out of the boat. *Today was the day.*

Stokes lifted his head heavenwards, as if seeking reassurance. As always, an obdurate black wall of rock met his gaze, shrouded in lifeless grey. Somewhere above him, hidden from view, was the snow-capped spur of Point St Ann, christened by one of his predecessors – Carteret, or Byron perhaps – in an attempt to imbue this place with spiritual familiarity, a sense of the proximity of God. Yet if ever God had abandoned a place, this was it. The ragged beech forest above the shoreline lay silent. There were no animals to start before a sudden footstep, no birds to soar and swoop, no insects even. Here was a scene of profound desolation. He and the men under his command were alone.

The only man with whom naval etiquette would allow him to converse, that damned fool Captain King, was a couple of miles away at least, another stupid speck in the wilderness. King had spent the winter beating up and down the east coast in the *Adventure*. At least the sun sometimes shone upon the east coast. This was truly a place where 'the soul of a man dies in him'. For if the sharp point of St Ann herself was unable to tear a hole in the suffocating blanket of cloud, then what chance did human beings have of living and breathing in such confines? A curse on King, and a curse on that fat buffoon Otway as well.

The time had come. His frail, icy fingers, lean from long months of low rations, reached down and grasped one of two pistols that hung from his belt. They were pre-loaded on board, of course, prior to any shore excursion, as per Admiralty orders. He couldn't even shit without following Admiralty orders. Would the lords care, he wondered, would they be secretly impressed by his gesture, or would they take offence? Or had he already been forgotten, he and his men, their futile labours destined to be mislaid for ever in the ledger of some consumptive little Admiralty clerk?

The pistol weighed heavy in his hand, and for the first time that day he felt nervous. For one tremulous instant he sought a friendly reflection in the gunmetal, but its dull gleam refused him even that consolation. Instead it offered only a reflection in time, of a sunlit September afternoon eight thousand miles ago, of himself in the doorway of Forsyth's gunshop at number eight Leicester Street. A day when the piece in his hand had shone handsomely, speaking to him of foreign travel, of exciting times ahead, before his life's path had narrowed and hemmed him in. The assistant had stepped out into the street to demonstrate the revolutionary copper-cap percussion system. Mock-aiming the weapon with (he had to admit) a dash of theatricality, the smartly attired young captain had attracted admiring glances from passers-by, or at least he had imagined so. What price those attentions now? It was half as reliable again as a flintlock, the assistant had said. Well, he would be needing that reliability today.

With a deep intake of breath, Stokes rested the barrel carefully against his front teeth, and curled a tapering finger round the trigger. His lips, suddenly dry, closed painfully around the freezing metal. A warm gush of fear welled in his bowels. Another gust plucked mockingly at his hair, daring him to go ahead. He had to do it, really, if he was any sort of man. To pull back now would be the ultimate, the crowning failure. So do it then. *Do it now.* His hand shook. Three. Two. One. *Now.*

Whether it was a last-second change of mind that caused his hand to jerk sideways, or a surge of fear, Stokes never knew. At the exact moment that the powder flashed and the iron ball smashed upward through the roof of his mouth, his hand dragged the barrel round to one side.

And suddenly, the wind was stilled. The crash of water on stone ceased. The clouds receded, and all the brutal discord of the Patagonian winter was gone, replaced by the purest, blinding agony. And then a tiny thought within made itself known: that if he could go through pain of such dazzling clarity and be conscious of it, he must still be alive.

PART ONE

CHAPTER ONE

Rio de Janeiro, 13 November 1828

'It took Stokes twelve days to die.'

Captain King's voice carried the faintest hint of accusation. He sat forward, his eyes fixed upon the admiral.

'The powder explosion blew away half of his brain. Never have I seen a man suffer so much. Such great agonies…and yet he bore his fate with fortitude. He had' – King paused, remembering the pitiful, mutilated creature brought squealing and snuffling back to the *Beagle* – 'He had no eyes. He made little sense; he merely cried out. He became lucid again on the fifth and sixth days, even philosophical as regards his fate, in spite of the pain. Thereafter he lapsed into incoherence once more. He died on the morning of the twelfth.'

Admiral Otway exhaled at last. 'Poor Pringle,' he murmured to himself, and sat back heavily. The manner of Stokes's death disturbed him, rather than the fact of it.

Sensing an advantage, King persisted. 'It had become clear to me, from reports in the days preceding his death, that the balance of his mind had become disturbed. For instance, he stopped for four days to survey the gulf of Estevan, when the *Beagle*'s supplies were very nearly exhausted, a survey that I had most emphatically not commissioned.'

'The south has the strangest effect on a man,' offered Otway apologetically.

King held his ground. 'I do not honestly believe, sir, that any of us had ever previously experienced such conditions. The weather was atrocious. The crew were incessantly employed. At Cape Upright, for instance, the *Beagle* was under way all night for four nights. Most of the crew were sick with rheumatic complaints. Four men drowned. Three died of scurvy.

Conditions were little better aboard the *Adventure*.'

The accusatory tone of his remarks, King knew, served no purpose other than to provoke Admiral Otway to mild discomfiture. It was mere sport on his part, his meagre reward for months of back-breaking toil. He had no reason to fear Otway, no need to seek the admiral's influence: this was his last commission, indivisible, unalterable, fashioned in Whitehall. His future was already out of Otway's hands. Both men were aware, too, that King had given Stokes the tougher task, ordering him west into the teeth of the gales that howled up the Straits of Magellan. The sad fact was that Stokes had been a bad appointment, a mediocre captain crushed by the pressure of his responsibilities. Goading his superior now, King realized, helped only to ease his own frustrations.

The close tropical atmosphere bore down stickily on both men, as Otway pondered how to put into words what he was going to say next.

King monitored a bead of sweat as it made its way down the admiral's neck, then dissipated suddenly into the stiff, high-necked woollen collar of his frock-coat. The contrast between Otway's immaculate, starched uniform and his own, battered and salt-bleached, struck him briefly as absurd. Instinctively he raised his fingers to the thick, grey-streaked beard that had kept him warm in the south. He had not shaved now for over six months.

Otway closed the book on King's accusations with an expansive gesture, as if to sweep aside the accumulated disasters of the preceding six months. His action prompted King to refocus, to widen his angle of vision. Rio de Janeiro harbour spread itself gloriously behind the admiral, filling the sternlights of the *Ganges*: white sails dotted everywhere like a field of cotton in the sun, cormorants skimming home sleek with their day's catch, the bright terracotta roofs of the new merchants' mansions climbing the steep hillsides alongside their crumbling, mildewed predecessors. Otway had the air of a circus impresario, thought King, installed before this magnificent panorama in his shiny coat, looking for all the world as if he was about to produce a dove from a handkerchief. Abruptly, he realized that this was no idle simile. Otway was indeed on the verge of making a big announcement. The admiral's fingertips met.

'Clearly the *Beagle* requires a commander of considerable qualities. Someone whose powers of leadership are, er, commensurate with your own.'

Don't bother flattering me, thought King. *We both know I'm going back because I have to.*

'She needs someone who can inspire the men to hitherto unsurpassed levels of courage, fortitude and determination. Were the Service blessed with two Phillip Parker Kings' – Otway squeezed out as much counterfeit sincerity as he dared – 'I should have no dilemma. You have taken so much upon your shoulders, with so little support, that my gratitude to you knows no bounds.'

King realized, uncomfortably, where the conversation was headed and decided to interject, although he knew as he did so that it would be futile. 'Lieutenant Skyring has commanded the *Beagle* these last four months, sir. Considering the morale of the men and the state of the ship when Captain Stokes met his end, the transformation that Skyring has wrought is little short of remarkable. I can think of no one better suited to this commission than Lieutenant Skyring.' *Who should have had the job in the first place*, he added to himself.

'Indeed, indeed.' Otway grimaced. 'I have no doubt that Skyring is an extremely capable officer, and I am delighted to hear that he has made such splendid headway. However, the candidate I have in mind is a man of considerable capabilities. He's my flag lieutenant here in the *Ganges*. Only twenty-three, but the most—'

'Twenty-three?' King blurted out. 'Forgive my interrupting, sir, but Lieutenant Skyring is one of my most experienced officers. He has knowledge of the area and the complete confidence of the men. I simply cannot recommend—'

A little wave of the hand from Otway silenced the captain. 'I have already made the appointment,' he stated flatly, picking up a handbell and ringing it to attract his steward's attention. The man entered. 'Would you kindly request Flag Lieutenant FitzRoy to present himself forthwith?'

The steward gave a slight nod and vanished.

'A ship's captain, at twenty-three?' queried King, in more measured tones than before. 'He must be a highly impressive young man.'

'I shall only make him commander, of course,' replied Otway. 'He shall be acting captain of the *Beagle*.'

'FitzRoy.' King let the name drip from his tongue. 'Commander FitzRoy would not, I wonder, be a relative of Admiral FitzRoy, or of the Duke of Grafton?'

Otway smiled, sensing that King was now in retreat. 'Let us simply confirm that Commander FitzRoy will have ample means to fit himself out. In answer to your question, Robert FitzRoy is in fact the son of General FitzRoy, the nephew of both Admiral FitzRoy and the Duke of Grafton, also of Castlereagh. He is a direct descendant of Charles the Second. But much, much more importantly, he is also the most successful graduate ever to pass out from the Royal Naval College in Portsmouth. Not only did he complete a three-year course in eighteen months, and take the first medal, he subsequently passed his lieutenant's exam with full numbers. *Full numbers.* The first man in the history of the Service to do so. And before you enquire about his practical experience, for I can see the question taking shape on your lips, he has been at sea for nine years, lately in the *Thetis*. Bingham had nothing but praise. His record is nothing short of exemplary. I commend him to you, Captain King.'

There was a sharp rap at the door. Even his timing is exemplary, thought King.

Otway bade the young man enter. A slender figure appeared in the doorway, moved silently across the threshold, and seemed to glide into place opposite the admiral, where he dispatched the appropriate courtesies speedily but respectfully. There was nothing foppish about his elegance; King could detect physical resilience beneath his graceful manner, allied to a firmness of purpose. The young man's features were fine-boned, his nose was sharp and his ears were too large, but the overall effect was a handsome one. His countenance was open and friendly, his long-lashed eyes dark and expressive.

'Do you know Captain Phillip Parker King?' Otway asked the new arrival.

'I have not had the pleasure of Captain King's acquaintance, sir,' replied

FitzRoy, meeting King's gaze squarely with what seemed to be a genuine smile of admiration, 'but few in the service could fail to be aware of his extraordinary achievements in mapping the western and northern coasts of Australia. Achievements for which' – he addressed King directly – 'I believe you have recently been awarded a fellowship of the Royal Society, sir. I am most honoured to make your acquaintance.' FitzRoy gave a little bow, and King knew instinctively that the tribute had been sincere.

'I have been discussing with Captain King your promotion to commander of the *Beagle*,' boomed Otway, no longer able to conceal the showman's grin plastered across his features, 'and I am pleased to make you his second-in-command.'

'You have obliged me very much by your kindness, sir,' replied FitzRoy, with a knowing nod to King. He's a bright boy, thought King. He's assessed the situation perfectly. Still, that's no reason to give him an easy ride.

'Admiral Otway informs me that you were a college volunteer. Sadly, the benefits of such a formal education were denied to me as a young man. So what precisely do they teach you in the classroom at Portsmouth?'

'A great many subjects, sir. The full list is an extensive one—'

King cut him off. 'I am eager to add to the stock of my own learning. Pray enlighten me.'

FitzRoy took a deep breath. 'I recollect, sir, that we studied fortifications, the doctrine of projectiles and its application to gunnery, hydrostatics, naval history and nautical discoveries—'

King raised a hand. 'Naval history,' he said. 'I'm interested in naval history. Tell me what you know of the history of your new command.'

'The previous *Beagle* was an eighteen-gun carrier,' began FitzRoy, cautiously, 'which won battle honours at San Sebastian and the Basque roads. Her replacement is a ten-gun brig, Cherokee class, two hundred and thirty-five tons burthen, three-masted. So she's strictly speaking a barque, but commonly known as a coffin brig.'

'Indeed she is,' cut in King warmly. 'And tell me, Commander, why the ten-gun brig is known throughout the service as a coffin brig.' All three knew the answer, that more ten-gun brigs were lost every year than any other class of ship, just as they knew that King was looking for more than that. This was a technical test.

'The ten-gun brig, sir, is a deep-waisted vessel – dangerously so, if I might venture to say so. The top of the rail, I apprehend, is just six feet out of the water, less when fully loaded. Without a forecastle to turn away a large bow wave, she's liable to ship water...large amounts of water, sir, which are then unable to escape on account of the high bulwarks. So she's prone to wallow, or turn broadside on to the weather. In which circumstances a second wave, shipped before the first has had time to clear, might well finish her off.'

'Absolutely, Commander,' agreed King with grim satisfaction. 'It's like trying to sail a spoon. So tell me, Commander FitzRoy, how you would modify the *Beagle* to address such limitations?'

'I'd build a poop cabin and a forecastle, sir, to deflect the heaviest seas.'

'An excellent answer, Commander. Indeed, the work has already been carried out by your predecessor. Captain Stokes added a poop deck and a forecastle deck level with the rail. Altogether I'd say he added a good sixty inches to the height of the ship. Then again, Commander, in the Southern Ocean it's not uncommon to encounter sixty-foot waves, whereupon the poop and the forecastle make damn-all difference.'

'Indeed sir.'

'Put bluntly, Commander, the greatest achievement of the late lamented Captain Stokes may well have been that the *Beagle* returned safely to Rio minus only one officer.'

'Yes sir.'

'Do you feel you are up to the task of leading a crew of exhausted, half-starved and demoralized men through such conditions?'

'I am determined, sir, that the men under my command will receive my full attention as regards to their physical and mental welfare,' said FitzRoy, calmly.

'The *Beagle* was also your predecessor's first command. The pressures of that command thrust Captain Stokes into such a profound despondency that he shot himself.'

'So I heard, sir. An awful incident.'

'And you are sure you will remain immune to such pressures?'

FitzRoy hesitated, and for the first time, King detected a note of uncertainty in his confident manner. To his irritation, Admiral Otway chose that moment to blunder to the young man's rescue.

'The south is a place "where the soul of a man dies in him". That was the last entry in Stokes's log. He was quoting Alexander Pope, I think – eh, FitzRoy?'

'Indeed sir.'

'But then poor Stokes was a melancholy sort. Not like yourself. Hardly suited for such a lonely post. I blame myself,' he added, in a manner that implied he did no such thing.

'The men are convinced that Captain Stokes's ghost still haunts the ship,' King informed FitzRoy. 'You have an interesting task on your hands, Commander.'

'I'm beginning to see that, sir.'

'A familiar face or two wouldn't go amiss,' offered Otway, 'if you have any requests.'

'I'd like to take Midshipman Sulivan from the *Thetis*, sir, if that's possible. We were together in the *Glendower* as well. He's a capital fellow, and has the best eyesight of any seaman I've ever known.'

'I see no reason why not – provided Bingham has no objections.'

'You'll need a new master as well,' put in King.

'May I take Murray, sir? He's a fine navigator, and ready for his chance.'

'Of course, of course,' replied Otway generously. 'You may take Mr Murray with you. Murray and Sulivan it is.' The admiral produced a sealed package from his desk drawer. 'I have your orders here. You are to complete the survey of the South American coast from Cape St Antonio around to Chiloé in the west, as directed by Captain King. You are to take particular note of all safe harbours, and all suitable refuelling and watering places. You are to observe weather patterns, tides and currents, the nature of the country inland and the people therein, remembering at all times that you are the official representative of His Majesty's government. You and your officers are to avail yourselves of every opportunity of collecting and preserving specimens of natural history, such as may be new, rare or interesting.' Otway slid the package across the table. 'You can read the details at your leisure, Commander, but I would draw your attention to one significant instruction: the naming of topographical features. Grateful as I am to find myself honoured in perpetuity by the title "Port Otway", there has been a tendency of late to ascribe names of a more frivolous nature. I'm thinking in particular of "Soapsuds Cove", where you presumably did your washing. And "Curious Peak". What the devil was curious about it?'

'I have no idea,' replied King drily. 'You'd have to ask Stokes.'

'Admiralty orders are quite specific on this point. The maps you are updating were compiled by Byron, Wallis and Carteret back in the 1760s, since when it has been something of an embarrassment that English charts contain such trivial identifications as "Point Shut-up". The site of some unseemly squabble, no doubt. Try to confine yourself to practical descriptions, or if you must commemorate someone, I would recommend members of the government or the Royal Family. Of course you can commemorate yourselves, but I would suggest a limit for ship's officers of one or two place names each. Understood?'

FitzRoy nodded.

Otway's brisk tone softened. 'The *Beagle* is on her way up from Monte Video. When she arrives, she will be hove down and repaired. Before then I would pay her a visit. Unannounced. That is to say, I think you should make your presence felt.' He grinned conspiratorially, and gestured to indicate that the interview was over.

Formalities completed, FitzRoy and King took their leave of the admiral's cabin, stooping with the instinct of years to avoid cracking their heads as they crossed the threshold. Outside, King paused at the top of the companionway. 'So tell me, Mr FitzRoy. Of all the captains under whom you have served, whom did you admire the most?'

'Sir John Phillimore, sir,' replied FitzRoy without hesitation. The ensuing pause made it clear that King meant him to go on.

'We were escorting Lord Ponsonby to Rio as ambassador, sir. One of the younger midshipmen suffered a terrible injury to his arm, and was in danger of losing it. Sir John gave the Ponsonbys' cabin to the boy, and himself slept in a cot outside the cabin door, giving instructions that he should be wakened immediately if anything were to befall the lad. We were all much impressed. It was Sir John who reduced the men's daily rum ration from half a pint to a quarter. Which, I must confess, improved the efficiency of the ship considerably.'

King raised both eyebrows. 'Good luck with the rum ration.'

FitzRoy smiled back, and King could not help but like his new second-in-command.

'Skyring's disappointment will be bitter, I confess. But he is not the sort to pay this off on you. He is a generous type. I will give him our supply schooner, the *Adelaide*, which should help soften the blow.'

'I hope so, sir.'

'One more thing, Mr FitzRoy. That quotation in Stokes's log – "the soul of a man dies in him". Who really wrote it?'

'Thomson, sir. It's from *The Seasons*.'

'You'll go far, Mr FitzRoy. I think you'll go very far indeed.'

CHAPTER TWO

Rio de Janeiro, 15 December 1828

With a brisk, matter-of-fact breeze behind her, the little cutter slid easily through the choppy blue of Rio bay, a curious petrel or two in pursuit. Enlivened by the sunshine, the crew put their backs into it. Occasional flecks of foam from the oars flung themselves gaily into Robert FitzRoy's face as he sat in the stern, but on such a day as this, the odd splash was hardly an imposition. It was a glorious morning to be alive; and, as it was certain to be one of the last such days he would see for a year or more, he should really have been able to enjoy it to the full. King's challenge, though, continued to perturb him.

They raced past a fisherman's skiff, its silvery catch glinting in the sun. A large, muscly black stood balanced in the prow, holding aloft the pick of his fish as enticingly as he could, while the cutter skimmed by unregarding. FitzRoy felt a flash of pity for the man, who could never know the world and all it offered, who had not the opportunities provided by modern civilization to make whatever he wanted of his own life.

Dropping behind them, resplendent, the *Ganges* lay at anchor, the pride of the South American station, her jet-black pitch contrasting smartly with her blinding white sails, the Union flag fluttering from her jackstaff, the blue ensign rippling square from her mainmast. Ahead in the distance, dwarfed by the rounded symmetry of the Sugarloaf mountain, the squat shape of the *Beagle* could just be made out, low in the water like a lost barrel. His first commission. It was hard to keep the butterflies subdued. Make your presence felt, Otway had said.

By his side in the cutter's stern, Midshipman Bartholomew Sulivan, just turned eighteen years of age, chattered away about home, about matters naval, about the task ahead of them, about anything. He really did take the palm for talk sometimes, but a cheerier, more optimistic companion was not to be found anywhere. Guiltily, FitzRoy realized that he had not been paying attention for some minutes.

'...and do you remember that Danish fellow, Pritz, who pressed three of our men for the Brazilian navy? And old Bingham telling him' – here he adopted Bingham's fruity tones – '"I hear my boat's oars. You had better give me back my men." And the look on the Dane's face when we climbed over the rail and he realized he must knock under! And do you recall him all crimson, shouting at us as we rowed off? "Remember Copenhagen! Remember Copenhagen!"' Sulivan's face flushed with excitement at the memory.

'We raced each other over the rail, as I recall,' admonished FitzRoy, 'and you were first over, even though you were supposed to be in the sick list that day.'

'It was the devil of a spree!' said Sulivan, and the ratings at the nearest oars grinned discreetly at the youngster's high spirits.

FitzRoy's mind, though, could not settle. *I am now responsible for this young man's life. His life and the lives of more than sixty others. Every decision I take affects their survival. Any misjudgement I make could kill us all.*

Had the commission been his four months earlier, this golden morning would have found FitzRoy his usual confident self, speeding across the waves towards his future. The depression that had overwhelmed Stokes would have seemed as distant a prospect as the wild channel where the poor fellow had surrendered himself to it. Four months earlier, however, there had occurred a...disturbance: that was the only word for it. An isolated incident, which had filled FitzRoy with disquiet, and which now refused to be forgotten.

It had been just such a day as this, the air at its sweetest, the sunshine clean and clear, and he had felt a sudden surge of elation as he prepared to order the signal to Wait for Dispatches. A kind of giddy excitement had seized him, a wild happiness, which led him in a whirling, mischievous dance. Glowing with joy, he had been struck by a tremendous idea. Why not run up all the flags in the locker in a splendid array? What a fine sight it would make! How in keeping with everyone's mood on such a blessing of a day! Then, why not add all the night signals, the white lights, guns, horns, bells and flares, in a magnificent celebration?

The midshipmen had laughed when he had described his plan, taking their cue from his own merry countenance, but their smiles had slackened and disappeared at the realization that he was not joking. He had tried to persuade them, pumping their hands, invoking their Christian names, urging them excitably to join in the entertainment. They had failed to understand, had assumed him to be drunk. There had been a scuffle – a vulgar push-and-pull, his uniform ripped – which had culminated in them locking him in his cabin, still flushed with fatuous excitement. The incident had been hushed up – Bingham had been told he was sick – and quickly forgotten by the others, but what the devil had he been thinking of? What malign spirit had taken control of his mind?

The next morning had been even more inexplicable. He had woken in a state of what could only be called fear. A black despondency had suffocated him, squeezing all other thoughts from his mind, isolating him from the world outside his cabin. He had lain alone in his cot, shivering and frightened. In this state of overwhelming helplessness, there had seemed no point to his life, no point to his work, no point even to existence itself.

Gradually, the darkness had seemed to take shape in his mind. As he was still in the sick list, his friends had presumed him to be battling the dog of a hangover, but this was a much fiercer beast. It slavered at him, mocked him. *You are completely in my power*, it seemed to say, *should I ever deign to visit you again.*

Within a few hours, however, the creature had stirred itself and padded away. He had emerged from his cabin shaken, cowed and deeply embarrassed. Since that day, everything had been as it should, but the incident continued to loom large in his consciousness. Had the creature really departed? Or was it merely biding its time, toying with him, waiting to return at a moment when men's lives depended on his skill and judgement?

He had thrown himself at phrenology, had turned himself into an expert on the subject, staying up late to study Gall and Spurzheim, had spent hours in front of the mirror feeling the bumps and hollows on the surface of his skull, but to no avail. He thought of his uncle: a formidable intellect, one of the foremost statesmen of his age. Castlereagh had taken his own life. He thought, too, of Stokes. Had he, Robert FitzRoy, come face to face with whatever those men had encountered in their final moments?

Profoundly troubled, he realized that Sulivan had stopped chattering, and was looking at him with an expression of concern. 'I say, FitzRoy, is everything all right?'

'Of course. My dear Sulivan, you must forgive my inattention. It is not every day one is given a vessel of one's own to fret about.'

'And three cheers to that!'

'Even so, my rudeness is quite inexcusable.'

'Not a bit of it, old fellow, not a bit of it.'

FitzRoy sat up in the boat. Loath as he was to dampen the young man's enthusiasm, he felt obliged to make a little speech. 'Look here, Sulivan... now they've sewn a couple of stripes on my sleeve, we shall still be the best of friends, of course – the very best of friends – but you do understand that it would not be fair on the other officers, the other midshipmen especially, if I were to show any sign of special friendship towards you? A ship's captain eats alone, reads alone, even thinks alone. I have to be fair and just. I'm determined to do the right thing, Sulivan, the right thing by everyone, even if I end up the loneliest old man on the ocean. I hope you understand.'

'Oh absolutely, old chap, absolutely. I mean, it couldn't be any other way. It will be a privilege to serve with you, sir.' Sulivan looked up at his new commander, and could only see everything that he wanted to be.

By now they were close enough to the *Beagle* to hear the water's slap against her sides, and to see the welcoming party gathering at the rail. Whatever Otway's recommendations of surprise, King was not the sort to leave Skyring and his men caught unawares by the visit. FitzRoy could make out Skyring by his uniform now, taller than the others, perhaps thirty years of age, his face dominated by a Wellingtonian nose and topped by a shock of dark hair. As the cutter pulled alongside, the lieutenant's leaning gait seemed to suggest that the fierce southern winds had left him bent permanently at an alarming angle.

FitzRoy climbed gracefully up the battens, waving away offers of help, and shook hands enthusiastically with Skyring. His predecessor's rueful smile indicated that no more needed to be said by either man, and that FitzRoy could consider the matter of his leapfrog promotion closed.

'How do, Lieutenant?' said FitzRoy, warmly.

'Your servant, sir,' replied Skyring. 'May I introduce to you Lieutenant Kempe?'

Kempe, a cadaverous, unsmiling man, whose teeth seemed to be fighting to escape his mouth, stepped forward and offered a calloused hand. On closer inspection the crew, like the ship, had a weatherbeaten aspect. Skyring had obviously done a good job during his brief tenure: the Beagle was freshly caulked, her decks white, her sails free of the tropical mildew that could take hold seemingly in hours – but there was no disguising the beating she had taken. Everywhere there was evidence of running repairs, in her rebuilt masts, repaired rigging and the fragile patchwork of her sails.

'This is Mr Bynoe, our surgeon.' A dark-haired, clean-shaven young man with a friendly countenance stepped forward and pumped FitzRoy's hand rather more encouragingly. 'At least, he has been acting as surgeon. He'll be resuming his duties as assistant surgeon when Mr Wilson arrives,' added Skyring, in wry acknowledgement of the parallel. A broad grin from Bynoe, to whom FitzRoy instinctively warmed.

'This is Midshipman King,' went on Skyring. 'Midshipman Phillip King.'

FitzRoy had no need of the warning, although he was grateful for Skyring's gesture. The boy before him, no more than a child, was a scaled-down replica of Phillip Parker King. 'I take it that you are related to the captain of the Adventure?'

'He's my father, sir.'

'Your father is a great man and a fine captain, Mr King.'

'Yes sir. He is, sir.'

The younger King seemed harmless enough at first encounter, but this was an unexpected handicap all the same.

'And this is Midshipman John Lort Stokes.' Skyring indicated a robust-looking youth with a military air and a correspondingly firm handshake.

FitzRoy raised a quizzical eyebrow.

'No relation to the late captain, sir,' explained Stokes, briskly.

'Mr Stokes hails from Yorkshire,' said Skyring, as if that clarified the situation.

FitzRoy breathed an inward sigh of relief.

Further introductions were made between the two midshipmen and Sulivan, Stokes being deputized to show the new man the ropes, before Skyring moved on to the warrant officers.

'Bos'n Sorrell, sir.'

Sorrell, a square-framed man with thinning hair, who looked as if he had been fat in a former life, was clearly eager to talk. 'The late captain was a fine man, if I may say so, sir, a fine man. He saved my life, sir, and many others.' He bobbed uncomfortably before FitzRoy, as if in need of an urgent visit to the heads.

'Mr Sorrell was formerly in the *Saxe-Cobourg*, a whaler that was wrecked in Fury Harbour,' explained Skyring.

'The captain, sir, he sent two boats to row eighty miles down the Barbara Channel to look for survivors, sir,' said Sorrell, sweating with gratitude. 'If it hadn't have been for him, I wouldn't be alive today. A fine man he was, sir.'

'Well, Mr Sorrell, I hope I will be able to live up to Captain Stokes's many achievements,' said FitzRoy. *All except the last one.*

Coxswain Bennet, a ruddy-faced, flaxen-haired young man, was the final member of the welcoming party. He had preferred to keep his counsel throughout the previous exchange, and his blank expression, FitzRoy guessed, betokened an instinctive sense of diplomacy rather than any intellectual shortcomings. Skyring's introduction of Bennet had been almost an afterthought.

The formalities over, Skyring came straight to the point. 'I'm afraid the damage below is far worse than anyone thought. The forefoot and the false keel have been torn clean off. A little run-in we had with the rocks at Cape Tamar. It'll take at least two weeks to put right.'

'Two weeks? My orders are to turn her straight round and head south again. The *Adventure* and the *Adelaide* are to leave in four days' time, and we are to sail with them.' A collective groan escaped the assembled officers. 'Mr Skyring here is to command the *Adelaide*.'

'Then it would appear I shall be leaving you behind. The copper bottom is absolutely shot to pieces and will need replacing. It appears you will be enjoying Christmas in Rio.'

The officers' expressions brightened a little. FitzRoy did his best to join in with the smiles, but levity did not come easily at this point. His first order as captain, and he would be unable to fulfil it promptly.

'Shall we take the grand tour?' offered Skyring, and motioned the others towards the rear of the tiny main deck. With the ship at anchor, the deck watch were mostly idle: sailors slouched here and there playing cards, or lay curled up asleep in coils of rope. They were a ragged lot, dressed in a battered mixture of slops and ducks, threadbare blue pea-jackets and patched-up canvas blouses. There was no singing, no laughter, no animation. These were hollow-eyed, exhausted, sullen men, observed FitzRoy, malnourished in body and soul. They observed him too, suspiciously and with barely concealed contempt. FitzRoy thought he heard the derisive whisper as he passed, 'College boy.' *That's all I am to them,* he thought, *a boy just out of school. Nine tough years in the* Glendower, *the* Thetis *and the* Ganges *mean nothing to them. I must prove myself from scratch. Perhaps they are right. Perhaps that is how it should be. I have experienced nothing like the ordeal they have been through. It is my duty to win them over.*

Sorrell blustered ineffectually, lashing out left and right with his rattan. 'Look lively, lads! Jump up now! Make way for Captain FitzRoy!'

The men shifted, but their movements were lifeless and perfunctory. After a few short steps the party arrived at Stokes's new raised poop deck, in the centre of which stood a solitary door.

'This is the poop cabin,' said Skyring. 'Captain Stokes preferred it to the captain's cabin so he used it as his own. He built it himself, which may account.'

FitzRoy lowered his head gravely, and stepped into the room where Stokes had died. It was cramped, extremely so, which was not unusual for a coffin brig: the distance from floor to ceiling could not have been more than four foot six. This cabin, though, appeared to be more uncomfortable than was strictly necessary. Not only did the mizzen-mast run straight through the middle of the room, but the steering gear was stashed under the chart table, taking up all the available legroom. A tell-tale noise from the other side of the wall informed FitzRoy that the officers' water closet was right next door. A sparse selection of water-damaged volumes occupied the shelves that lined the back wall, for the cabin had also doubled as Stokes's library. His cot still hung from the ceiling in memoriam, directly above the table and immediately beneath the skylight, as if spreading itself to absorb every ray of sunshine that filtered through the greasy glass. *That was why he wanted this cabin,* FitzRoy realized instinctively. *He was reaching towards the light.*

'Sometimes there are only two or three hours of it,' said Skyring, who had followed his gaze. 'Daylight. Down south. In winter.'

His eyes met FitzRoy's. 'Will you be wishing to keep this cabin? The men suppose it to be haunted.'

'I presume the captain's cabin is still below decks?'

Skyring nodded.

'Then I shall take the captain's cabin as normal. Irrespective of any ghosts.'

With Stokes's spectre thus dismissed, they stepped back into the warm Brazilian sunshine, where the other officers stood waiting, then all proceeded down the dark hole of the after companionway to the lower deck. A familiar reek assaulted FitzRoy's nostrils there: the concentrated smell of men who have not washed themselves in several months, mixed in a treacly stew with the wet scent produced by holystones, sand, water and wood, as the below-decks watch scrubbed half-heartedly on their hands and knees. Sorrell again tried to whip up some enthusiasm with his rattan, and one of the men, a grinning, red-haired Cornishman, wished FitzRoy a polite good morning that could have been either friendly or mocking, he could not tell which.

The captain's cabin, at the bottom of the companionway, proved marginally roomier than Stokes's berth in the poop, but no taller and a good deal more gloomy. Despite the presence of a small skylight, it was impossible to see into the corners. On the wall in the half-light, like religious artefacts, hung Stokes's three chronometers: scientific icons, without which measurements of longitude could not be taken, without which there could be no expedition, without which the world could not be captured on paper, tamed and subjugated in the name of God and King George. They were obviously government-issue chronometers, their glass foggy, their metal housing battered, and one of the dials disfigured by a deep, vertical crack, but they did at least appear to function. FitzRoy made a mental note to dismantle them, clean, oil and reassemble them before the ship headed south once more. *This tiny cabin*, he thought, *will be your home for the next two years*; and for a brief moment he allowed himself the indulgent realization that the flag lieutenant's quarters on the *Ganges* had been utterly luxurious by comparison.

Having acquired a lantern, which seemed to make no difference whatsoever to the gloom, the party inspected the gunroom and the midshipmen's berth, and peered into the chain locker. FitzRoy could hear Sulivan chattering away behind him, befriending his fellow midshipmen with characteristic ease and rapidity, even though they could barely see each other. As they moved past a line of neatly spaced hammock hooks, however, FitzRoy was brought up short by the sight of two unstowed hammocks and their contents, a pair of ample Brazilian whores sleeping off their night's exertions. For the first time in their tour of inspection, Skyring began to struggle. 'The men have been away since the end of 1826. They haven't seen a woman in two years – with the exception of a brief leave period last December. I thought...well, you know, Admiralty regulations do permit women on board in port.'

'Married women.'

Skyring grimaced and indicated a cheap wedding ring, which adorned the fat hand spilling out of the nearest hammock. 'It doesn't actually state whom they should be married to,' he offered.

'Mr Bennet,' said FitzRoy, 'perhaps you would be kind enough to wake the two...ladies, and arrange for them to be escorted back ashore in the jolly-boat.'

'It'll be a pleasure, sir.'

Skyring attempted to look at the ceiling, but was already forced to stoop so low by the lack of headroom that he found himself staring instead at the back of Bennet's head.

FitzRoy said no more, and the party finally emerged, blinking, through the fore hatchway. As they arrived on deck and straightened their backs for the first time in a quarter-hour, FitzRoy turned, to be greeted by another unexpected sight. 'What in heaven,' he enquired, 'has happened to your yawl?'

Where the largest of the surveying boats should have been, bridging the gap between the foremast and the mainmast, was a crude, white-painted vessel cut from twisted timber. Inside it, where a smaller cutter should have resided, lay only a few tools.

'Our original yawl was dashed to pieces by waves in the Gulf of Estevan,' explained Skyring. 'The one you see here was constructed by May, the carpenter, from driftwood. The cutter was stolen.'

'Driftwood? Stolen by whom?'

'The Indians. They'd steal the *Beagle* herself if you turned your back for an instant. The Fuegian Indians are the most degraded creatures on God's earth – little better than animals.' There was a murmur of assent from the company. 'And if the Indians don't take the boats then the elements will. Between the three ships we've lost eleven boats, all told. I'd say that of all the men on board –' Skyring leaned further over than usual, and confided in FitzRoy '– May is the one indispensable man on the manifest. Lose May and you might as well set sail for home.'

'I should very much like to meet him.'

May was duly summoned, and proved to be a short Bristolian whose hair had apparently been cut by a blind man. His cheeks were permanently flushed and reddened by scores of tiny broken veins.

'I must compliment you on your ingenuity, May.'

'Sir.'

'This boat of yours is a remarkable achievement.'

Silence from May, who appeared taciturn to the point of mulishness.

'Don't worry about him,' said Skyring, when May had returned to his duties. 'He rarely obliges any of us with conversation.'

FitzRoy shifted his attention to the nearby rigging, which enmeshed the foremast in a thick tracery of blackened rope. He gave it a spirited tug. First impressions were encouraging, but then he took a closer look at what appeared to be a repair and picked at the tar covering with a fingernail. Something caught his eye. 'Would you come here a moment, Mr Sorrell?'

The boatswain bobbed forward uncertainly.

'Take a look at this, please.' Sorrell peered at the exposed fibres. 'Now tell me what you see.'

'It – it's not hemp, is it, sir?'

'No, Mr Sorrell, it's not. It's sisal.'

'Yes sir. Most definitely sisal. God's my life, sir, I have no idea how this happened.'

Skyring and Kempe exchanged glances.

'Who carried out this repair?' asked FitzRoy.

'Able Seaman Gilly, sir.'

'Fetch him here.'

Within a few seconds Sorrell had scurried back with a reluctant Gilly, who proved to be an oldster, as grimy and wiry as any of the crewmen FitzRoy had seen so far. Gilly eyed his new commander suspiciously.

'Did you carry out this repair, Gilly?'

'Aye aye sir.'

'How long have you been in the Service?'

'Nine year or thereabouts.'

'And how many years an able seaman?'

'Six.'

'And have all those years not taught you that sisal is insufficiently strong for rigging?'

'Couldn't find no hemp, could I?'

FitzRoy's voice was iron. 'I cannot look over this, Gilly. You have endangered your fellow crewmen's lives. Once my commission has been read, you will be flogged at the gangway at six bells of the forenoon watch.'

Gilly said nothing, but gave FitzRoy a look of contempt.

'You may return to your duties.'

The man turned on his heel without a word and walked away.

'Shall I make it a batty, sir?' Sorrell, relieved to have escaped a tongue-lashing, was now attempting to distance himself further from the crime by recommending a severe punishment.

'Mr Sorrell, you know as well as I do that more than a dozen lashes are expressly forbidden, and have been for as long as you or I have been in the Service.'

'I know, sir, but Captain Stokes always—'

'Captain Stokes, God rest his soul, is no longer with us. You will carry out a sentence of a half-dozen lashes at six bells. Furthermore, Mr Sorrell, when the *Beagle* is hove down, you will personally inspect every rope, every inch of her rigging and every link in her chains. Is that clear?'

'Aye aye, sir. I'll do it most zealous, sir,' said Sorrell, shifting his weight from one foot to the other and back again.

'Tell me, Mr Sorrell, how many minutes does it take the *Beagle* to make all sail?'

'In good conditions, sir? From reefed? I'd say about a quarter-hour, sir.'

'Well, Mr Sorrell, let's see if you and I can get that down below twelve minutes, shall we?'

Sorrell, who had not dared breathe for the past minute or so, emptied his lungs at the prospect.

'And now, if you will oblige me by mustering the ship's company aft, with Lieutenant Skyring's permission I should like to address them.'

The order was piped and men began to emerge, from the lower deck, from the hold, from the magazine, from coalholes, lockers, storerooms and even – limping – from the sick bay, until it seemed impossible that the narrow deck would hold them all. They formed themselves into a ragged square, the red-coated ship's marines to the left, while Skyring read FitzRoy's commission.

FitzRoy himself stood on the poop, flanked by his officers in their peaked caps, dark coats and white trousers, until Skyring had finished. Then he stepped forward. He placed his hands on either side of the compass housing as if it were a lectern and spoke in a clear, firm voice. 'My name is Robert FitzRoy. I am directed by my lords commissioners of the Admiralty to take charge of this vessel. My orders are to complete the survey of the South American coast begun by Captain Stokes, from Cape St Antonio in the east to Chiloé Island in the west, under the direction of Captain King in the *Adventure*. Lieutenant Skyring is to accompany us in the *Adelaide*. We shall make sail in approximately two weeks, after the ship has been hove down and repaired. Most of you, I know, will not relish so hasty a return to the south, but we may consider ourselves fortunate in some respects. The service is decreasing in size every day, as the war becomes no more than a memory. Ships are being broken up, commissions are not being renewed. The ports and taverns of England are packed with men who clamour for a berth. I know – I have been home recently. We are the lucky ones. And we have an opportunity not just to sail one of His Majesty's ships, but to do so for the benefit of future generations. To survey unexplored territory, to map it and to name it, is to contribute to history. This is the chance offered us today.

'I have learned from Captain King and Lieutenant Skyring of the hardships borne on your first voyage, of the inclement conditions, the sickness and the lack of food. The weather that we encounter will, of course, be a matter for our maker. But I give you my word, as God is my witness, that the health of every man on board, and the sufficiency of victuals and provisions, shall be my prime concern.

'There shall – as a consequence – be new regulations. For the avoidance of ship fever, every man is to wash himself thoroughly a minimum of once a week. All clothing is to be boiled every two weeks. All decks are to be scrubbed with vinegar every two weeks.

'For the avoidance of scurvy, there will be an antiscorbutic diet, which will be compulsory for all those on board. No man is to go more than three days without fresh food caught locally. Hard tack, salt meat and canisters of preserved food are not sufficient. Every man is to take a daily dose of lemon juice. Lime juice is not sufficient. I shall also be asking Mr Bynoe to supply extra rations of pickles, dried fruit, vinegar and wintersbark. The daily wine ration is to remain at one pint, while supplies can be maintained. But for the avoidance of drunkenness, the daily rum ration is to be reduced from half a pint to a quarter of a pint.'

FitzRoy paused to let this sink in. The shocked gasp at the prospect of weakened grog was audible across the deck.

'No man under the age of sixteen is to receive a rum ration.'

Another pause, punctuated this time by a smaller, higher-pitched gasp.

'There will be no gambling. There will be no women in port. Before divine service on Sundays, all officers and men who can read and write, and I include myself in this, will be expected to contribute to the education of those who cannot. This will be a modern ship, run along modern lines. But the punishment for anyone who disobeys any of the new regulations, or any order for that matter, will be of the most old-fashioned sort. In particular, anyone who by his laxity endangers the ship, or the life of anyone aboard, will be flogged, as Able Seaman Gilly has discovered.

'The refit will make the next two weeks a busy time for all of us. Nonetheless I shall ensure that every man is granted a period of shore leave. I trust that you will enjoy yourselves ashore. I trust also that you are all familiar with the penalty for desertion.

'When you return to the ship, your work will begin in earnest. I intend to make the *Beagle* the best-drilled, best-handled vessel on the ocean. My object is that every one of her people shall be proud of her. That is my task, and yours too. Thank you for your time. You may go about your business.'

The crew milled about for a few seconds, murmuring among themselves, then disappeared back into the myriad hatchways and crevices of the ship. FitzRoy released his grip on the compass housing.

'Well done sir,' breathed Sulivan.

'At least they didn't come charging up the quarter-deck waving cutlasses and crying, "Liberty,"' said Skyring. 'Now, if you will permit me, Commander, I'll go and gather my effects. The very best of luck to you. They're not the best crew that ever sailed the ocean, but they're not the worst either. There is potential in them. I am sure you will unlock it.'

'You oblige me with your kindness,' smiled FitzRoy politely, and the two men shook hands once more.

There remained only the matter of Able Seaman Gilly. As was normal custom, the ship's company reassembled before the gangway at six bells to witness the flogging. Gilly was stripped of his rough canvas jacket and tied down. It was clear from the scars that laced his back that he had aroused the ire of Captain Stokes – and, no doubt, various predecessors – on numerous occasions. Sorrell, eager to impress, laid it on thick from the first blow, but Gilly clamped his teeth fast together, determined not to make a sound.

As the second blow fell, FitzRoy's gaze shifted from the errant sailor towards the shore. In the distance, proceeding slowly away from the ship as it lifted and fell on a freshening breeze, he could just make out the jolly-boat, and in it, Bennet's distinctive flaxen mop, almost hidden behind the wide backs of the two plump Brazilian women seated side by side. He turned back to observe the deck again, and the sea of watching faces under his command; only to become aware, uncomfortably, that every man jack of them was staring not at the flogging, but directly at him.

CHAPTER THREE

Maldonado Bay, Uruguay, 30 January 1829

It was a glorious evening. A damp tropical breeze behind the *Beagle* nudged her softly towards the south-west. She slid silently into the mighty estuary of the river Plate, where the fifty-mile-wide sweep of warm brown river water gushes into the dark, welcoming depths of the Atlantic. A sliver of black-and-white on a shining sea, she navigated the divide between river and ocean, milky tea to her right side, port wine to her left. Giant columns of cloud marched across the landward horizon, golden shafts of sunlight angling between them, as if someone had lit a fire in the temple of heaven.

Robert FitzRoy stood by the wheel, Lieutenant Kempe a mute presence at his shoulder, and allowed his senses to bathe in the grandeur of the scene. In the distance ahead he could see the sharply curved promontory of Maldonado Island, the only interruption in the otherwise level plane of the horizon, jabbing up like a thorn from the flat stem of a rose; and in the shelter of Maldonado Bay beyond, he could just make out the spars of the *Adventure* at anchor. The glimpse of stitched canvas and carved wood promised friendly faces and welcome reunions for the *Beagle's* crew after a month alone at sea. FitzRoy's orders were to rendezvous with King in the *Adventure*, Skyring in the *Adelaide* and Admiral Otway in the *Ganges* at Maldonado before the day was out. The *Beagle* was only just on schedule, but she had been handling increasingly well for such an ungainly little vessel, and would arrive before dusk. He could take justifiable pride in the changes he had wrought during the preceding weeks.

They had hove her down off Botafogo beach, to the south of Rio de Janeiro, the crew camped along the shore in tents. Naturally enough it was Sulivan who had volunteered to inspect the damage to her false keel, who had dived again and again into the shimmering water. Finally he had been hauled back aboard exhausted, the skin on his back lacerated by the jagged copper below. FitzRoy had been forced to take over the task himself, to prevent his shattered subordinate flinging himself back into the sea. The youngster had paid for his exertions, though, with a bout of dysentery, and now lay weak in a sick-bay cot with a high fever and a chamber pot for company.

They had hauled the *Beagle* out of the water using ropes, her fat belly ripped and encrusted with barnacles, gasping and glistening like a landed whale as the seawater streamed off her in a hundred cascades. They had laid her down by hand on a platform constructed from four large market-boats. They had re-payed the cracked pitch in her seams and sealed it with hot irons; they had cleaned out her bilges, oiled her blocks, blacked her meagre armaments and painted the gun-carriages; they had polished her brightwork to a mirror finish with brick dust. And then she had been lowered snugly into the water again, to be welcomed back by the warm waves lapping around her hull.

Between Rio de Janeiro and the river Plate he had drilled the men relentlessly: reefing and furling sail in all weathers, sending down sails and yards for imaginary repairs, or waking the crew in the middle of the night to fix non-existent leaks. They had performed gun drill at all hours, summoned to action stations without warning by the drums pounding out the rhythm of 'Heart of Oak'. Piped orders were practised again and again. Orders that had needed to be yelled through the speaking trumpet at first were now kept to a minimum. The boatswain had only to bark, 'Make sail!' and the bare trees of the *Beagle*'s masts would bloom white within minutes. She would always be an ungainly little brig, her decks awash even in the lightest seas; she would never dance adroitly to the tune of her captain like one of the elegant ships-of-the-line. But she was at last assuming a sturdy reliability that did her company credit. FitzRoy was beginning to feel proud of his sailing-spoon.

'It begins to look very dirty to leeward, sir.' Lieutenant Kempe was one of those perverse customers whose smile – half grin, half grimace – carried a hint of satisfaction at unfortunate developments. But he was unquestionably correct. The giant pillars of cloud on the western horizon were filling and darkening, and appeared to be increasing in size – which did not make sense, as the warm, gentle breeze that half filled the *Beagle*'s sails was blowing from the north-east.

'Barometer reading?'

'Steady sir, 30.20. That's up from 30.10 half an hour ago.'

Everything was as it should be. The barometer said so. But tiny alarm bells rang in FitzRoy's mind. Most of the crew didn't hold with barometers – he'd had a hard job, in fact, persuading his officers that such gadgets had any part to play in modern seamanship – preferring their captain to handle the ship by instinct. A good captain, of course, was capable of marrying science and nature in his deliberations. The barometer may indeed have been adamant that nothing was wrong, and the nor'-easterly behind them may have contained barely enough vigour to ruffle the milky sheen of the estuary, but this, he was keenly aware, was no ordinary estuary. More than twice as wide as the English Channel at Dover, the river Plate was notorious for its sudden *pampero* storms. None of the crew had ever seen one, but they had heard the stories. Their instincts tensed like violin strings.

A long dark roll of cloud had curled into being on the horizon, filling the spaces between the vapour columns and blotting out the setting sun. Should they cut and run for the shore, he wondered? Or should they drive ahead to the sanctuary of Maldonado Bay? The former would involve disobeying orders. The latter risked being caught in the open, if this was indeed a *pampero*.

'Barometer reading?'

'Steady sir, 30.20.'

This simply didn't make sense. If a storm was indeed in the offing, the barometer should have been sharing his alarm. He resolved to stay on course for Maldonado.

'No, wait a minute, sir. The quicksilver is dipping. 30.10 sir…it's dipping fast sir. It's dipping really fast sir. 30 dead sir. It's dipping really fast sir.'

Even as the master relayed the bad news, the nor'-easterly wind behind them dropped away to nothing. The sails fell slack against the masts. Only the creaking of the rigging betrayed the *Beagle*'s presence in a world of silence. There was a moment of hush on deck, as officers and crew stood in awe and watched the cloud columns grow, thousands of feet high now, grotesque black billows at the core of each pillar like the smoke from a cannonade.

FitzRoy's ribcage constricted. *It's so easy to know what action to take when you are only the subordinate. I have to take charge. Now.*

'Barometer reading 29.90 sir. The temperature's dropping too sir.'

'Take her into the shore, Mr Murray. Any shelter you can find.'

Murray made a quick calculation. 'Lobos Island is only a few miles off the coast, sir, but there's no breeze.'

'I believe we shall have a sufficiency of wind before very long, Mr Murray.'

'Aye aye sir.'

The master relayed the instructions to the helmsman. 'Larboard – I mean, port – a hundred and thirty-five degrees.'

The cadaverous half-smile continued to divide Lieutenant Kempe's bony features. The crew were still learning to use the word 'port' instead of 'larboard', at FitzRoy's insistence: 'larboard' could sound uncommonly like 'starboard' in the middle of a storm.

The helmsman swung the wheel down smoothly with his right hand, and the ship inched slowly to starboard, reluctantly answering the call of her rudder.

'Double-reefed topsails, Mr Sorrell, and double-reefed foresail. Batten the hatches and put the galley fires out.'

The boatswain piped the orders to the crew, and within seconds the rigging swarmed with figures: younger, lighter hands in the tops and out on the yard-arms, burlier sailors in the centre, wrestling with the heavier, more uncooperative shrouds of canvas.

A few seconds, and the adjustments were made. Now all they could do was wait like sitting ducks, and hope that the storm, when it came, would fill their reduced sails sufficiently to drive them towards the darkening shore.

'Barometer reading 29 dead sir.'

'That's impossible,' breathed FitzRoy. He had never known the quick-silver fall so far so fast. Swiftly, he crossed the deck to check for himself. There was no mistake. You could actually see it falling with the naked eye.

'Hold on to your hats,' murmured little King, somewhat unnecessarily. They were clearly in for the blow of their lives. Hands closed silently around ropes, rails and brass fittings – anything that looked securely screwed down.

'Look sir,' said Bennet, ruddy-faced under his flaxen mop. He'd come up on deck as the ship had changed course, and was now leaning over the port rail and squinting upriver to the west. All eyes followed the direction of his gaze. Before the rolling black cloud lay a lower bank of what appeared to be white dust, skimming across the silken brown waters towards them at incredible speed.

'What is it? A sandstorm?'

FitzRoy reached for his spyglass. Even at closer quarters, the white band across the horizon was difficult to make out. 'Great heavens...I think it may be...*insects*.'

As he breathed the last word, the vanguard was upon them. Butter-flies, moths, dragonflies and beetles arrived by the thousands, a charging, panic-stricken battalion, driven helplessly by the surging winds at their back. They flew into blinking eyes and spluttering mouths, snagging in hair and ears, taking refuge up nostrils and down necks. They clung to the rigging and turned the masts white. The sails disappeared beneath a seething mass of tiny legs and wings.

Even as the crew fought to clear their faces of these unwanted guests, the sea did it for them. Thick spume arrived in a volley, borne on a wall of wind that smacked into the port side of the *Beagle* with a shudder. Suddenly the sails filled to bursting, the wind squealed through the rigging, and the little brig darted forward as if released from a trap, keeling violently to starboard as she did so. The spume thickened into dense white streaks of flying water, the ocean itself shredded and torn as the elements launched their frenzied attack, raking the ship's side like grapeshot. The sound of the wind raised itself into an indignant shriek, and then, beneath it, came something FitzRoy had never heard before: a low moan like a cathedral organ. *How appropriate*, he thought – for this was indeed shaping up to be a storm of Old Testament proportions.

Straining under the press of sail, and foaming in her course, the little brig drove crazily forward, her masts bent like coach whips.

'Another hand to the wheel!' shouted FitzRoy. No one heard him, but no one needed to: already two or three men were moving forward to assist the helmsman, who grappled with the wheel as it bucked first to port and then to starboard in his grasp. Like a burst of artillery fire, the fore staysail, the thick white triangle of sturdy English canvas that led the ship's charge, flayed itself to ribbons as if it had been a mere pocket handkerchief.

'Storm trysails, close-reefed!' FitzRoy screamed from an inch away into Sorrell's ear. Again, the crew barely needed the boatswain's frantic attempts to relay the instruction. Figures swarmed back up the masts like monkeys, into the rigging and out on to the violently swaying yards. Even though they were close-reefed, the sails flapped madly, fighting like wild animals to cast aside their handlers, but gradually, steadily, they were brought under control. The storm trysails were FitzRoy's only remaining option. Too much sail and the wind would rip the canvas to pieces. Too little and the ship would lose steerage, leaving the elements free to batter her to destruction.

The sea was heavy now, the ship rolling, the decks swept every few seconds by several feet of thick, foamy water. The sky had turned black, but incessant lightning flashes were now illuminating the scene, both from above and below. *It's like an immense metal foundry*, thought FitzRoy. *God's machine room. If just one of these lightning bolts strikes a mast, we're all dead men.* A flash illuminated Kempe's skeletal face to his left, and he could read the fear written there. The lieutenant's smile was frozen mirthlessly on his face. *I must not give in to my own fear. If I do they will smell it. They will know.*

Hanging grimly to the taffrail behind them, Midshipman King stood open-mouthed in wonder. *Even during two years in the south, he's never seen a storm like this*, FitzRoy marvelled. Then he followed King's gaze. Then he saw the wave. And then all of them saw it, illuminated in a white sheet of electricity. A wall of water as big as a house – forty feet high? Fifty? Sixty? – towering above the port beam, a sheer brown cliff frozen in the lightning's flash.

'All hands down from aloft!' he tried to shout, but the words died in his throat as he realized there wasn't time. Every man on deck slid his arms and legs deep into the rigging, each desperately trying to sew himself into the very fabric of the ship, muttering prayers that the ropes would hold fast. FitzRoy looked up and saw the topmen scrambling in from the yards to the crosstrees on the mast. Another lightning flash, and his eyes locked with the terrified gaze of the Cornishman who had greeted him on his first day aboard. The man was clutching for dear life to the main-topmast cap.

A moment later, and the wave took the weather quarter-boat, effortlessly crumpling the little cutter to matchwood. Four brisk rifle shots snapping across the wind indicated that the windward gunports had blown in. Then the wave slammed across the deck, illuminated stroboscopically by the lightning, bulldozing into the men tangled in the rigging, pulverizing everything in its path. It felt like being hit by an oxcart. The *Beagle* tipped at an alarming angle, the whaleboat on the lee side dipped momentarily under the surface, instantly filled to the brim with water and was gone. *She's going over on her beam-ends. Dear Lord, we're going down.*

As the wave passed, FitzRoy looked back up for the Cornishman, but the entire main-topmast was gone, the main-topsail and the crewman with it. The fore-topmast was gone too, and the jib-boom, while the main-deck bow gun, which had been lashed abreast of the mainmast, had jack-knifed in its lashings, carriage upwards. Most of the remaining sails were flying free of their stays, flapping insanely. The lee side of the deck was still under water. The ship sagged helplessly, seemingly uncertain as to whether to right herself or give up the ghost and slide silently into the depths. FitzRoy could see the drenched figure of Midshipman Stokes, up to his waist at the lee rail, hurling the life-buoy into the surging waves. Beyond him two figures in the surf struck out powerfully for the *Beagle's* side, only to be swallowed by the darkness. When the lightning flared again, there was no sign of either man.

Even as Stokes performed his vain rescue act, FitzRoy screamed and gestured to Murray, who had lashed himself to the wheel, to bring the stern round into the wind; but it was clear from the helpless look in the master's eyes that the *Beagle* would no longer answer her helm. And yet agonizingly, unwillingly, the natural buoyancy of the little ship began to assert itself over the weight of water that had flooded her below decks. Like a cask she rose, and slowly regained her trim. As she climbed gradually towards safety, a second big wave cascaded across the decks. Stokes, caught in the open, slipped to the floor and was slammed against the lee rail, a mass of broken spars and tangled ropes piling after him, but somehow the water pouring through the sluices pinned him there, bruised and bloodied. Again the *Beagle* fought to right herself.

This is my ship. I must do something, before the next wave destroys us. FitzRoy slithered across the incline of the deck, grabbed a hatchet and hacked through the stern anchor-rope. Kempe, frozen to the compass-housing, looked on in horrified confusion, clearly thinking his captain had gone mad – but one or two of the seamen cottoned on, and stumbled across to help him. Between them, they grabbed the biggest fallen spar, lashed it to the rope-end, and hurled it overboard. Then FitzRoy hauled the dazed and bleeding Stokes back up the planking by his collar, just as the third wave made its pulverizing way across the deck. The waves were coming every thirty to forty seconds now, the crest of each peak level with the centre of the *Beagle*'s mainyard as she floundered her way through the troughs.

Curled in a dysentery-racked ball of pain in his cot below decks, Bartholomew Sulivan was shaken by the sight of the sick-bay door slamming open, forced off its catch by a waist-high tide of green water, even as the ship lurched and threatened to pitch him into it. Outside the door he could see crewmen, those who would normally have been resting between watches, bailing furiously for their lives. There was no time to feel for his uniform in the guttering flame from the oil-lamp, so he plunged through the cabin door in nightshirt and bare feet, and waded towards the companionway leading to the upper deck.

Gradually, the *Beagle* began to slew round. The anchor cable had run right out to the clink, and the lashed-on spar, acting as a huge rudder, was pulling her stern round into the wind. Sulivan took in the scene at a glance, his white nightshirt flapping madly in the wind. One or two crewmen froze in astonishment. Was this the ghost of their former captain, come to claim their souls?

FitzRoy froze too, but for different reasons. *I'm not running a damned kindergarten here, you young idiot! Get back inside!* He gestured angrily for Sulivan to retreat, but the youngster was not to be deterred. He had the best eyesight of any on the ship, and a lookout was needed. Barefooted, adrenalin dulling the vicious pain in the pit of his stomach, he sprang into the mizzen-mast rigging, and clambered up into the wildly swaying tops. Shorter and stouter than the other two masts, the mizzenmast was the only intact vertical remaining on the *Beagle*'s deck. With the ship's stern into the wind, it would now be taking the brunt of the waves. In the circumstances, it was an almost suicidal place in which to locate oneself.

Sulivan did not have long to wait. The first really big sea to approach from the stern thundered up underneath the rudder, like a horse trying to unseat its rider. As the little brig's stern climbed towards the crest, her bow wallowed drunkenly in the trough. Broken spars and torn canvas shrouds cascaded down towards the bowsprit, some fifteen feet below the wheel. Then, with a smack, the wave broke over them from behind, punching the air from the sailors' lungs and flooding the maindeck to waist height. Such was the weight of water that the *Beagle* slewed off course, her stern drifting to starboard; and FitzRoy, Bennet and Murray fought the wheel, every sinew straining, to prevent her broaching. FitzRoy barely dared look up at the mizzen-mast, but look he did, and there, sheened by lightning, was the wild, drenched figure of Sulivan, his face flushed with excitement, punching the air by way of a return greeting.

Another mighty sea came billowing over the stern, and another, and it became clear to the exhausted men at the wheel that they must soon lose their battle to keep the ship in line with the wind and the waves. All but one of the storm trysails were gone now, ripped into convulsing shreds by the banshee winds. With insufficient sail to guide her, it was only a matter of time before the *Beagle* slewed beam-on to the weather again.

FitzRoy fought to clear his mind. *If the steering chains or the rudder quadrant snap we're finished anyway.* He gripped the wheel ever more tightly with cold, shaking fingers. *We'll have to bring her head round into the wind. It's our only way out of this. I'll have to take a gamble with our lives.*

There must, he calculated, be about thirty-five seconds on average between waves. To bring the *Beagle*'s head right round would take longer than that. If she was caught beam-to between waves in her battered state, she would certainly be rolled over. But if she stayed where she was, with big seas breaking repeatedly over her stern, the end would only be a matter of time. FitzRoy took a decision. Prising his fingers from the wheel, he grasped the hatchet once more, fell upon the anchor rope, and severed the rudimentary rudder that was keeping her in position. Then he seized the wheel from the bewildered Murray and waited for the next wave. Lieutenant Kempe, long past understanding, stood like a statue, clinging bedraggled to one of the uprights of the poop rail. Little King, open-mouthed, sea-battered and frozen in shock, no longer a naval officer but a stunned child, seemed barely to know where he was.

Another big breaker reared up behind them. FitzRoy could not see it, but he felt his knees give way as the deck surged up beneath his feet. As it did so he swung the wheel down violently to his right. The ship yawed to starboard, surfing down the rising face of the wave as the wind caught the tattered remnants of her canvas.

Of course, thought Murray, who suddenly understood. FitzRoy had used the force of the wave to accelerate the *Beagle*'s about turn to gain her a few vital extra seconds. It was an extraordinary gamble, for as she swung round, she rolled exaggeratedly to port, almost on her beam-ends once more. The lee bulwark dipped three feet under water, all the way from the cat-head to the stern davit. Foaming eddies of water barrelled across the deck, thumping into the chests of the crew, grabbing at their clothing, inviting them down into the depths. *The skipper's mistimed it. She's going down.* The main-topsail yard blew right up to what remained of the masthead, like a crossbow fired by a drunkard who'd forgotten to insert a bolt. Incredibly, tiny figures still hung from each yard-arm, tossed about like rag dolls but somehow still clinging to braces and shrouds. Up on the mizzen-mast, like a gesticulating lunatic on the roof of Bedlam, Sulivan swung far out above the boiling sea, the mast dipping so low over the water it seemed as if he would be pulled under by the next wave.

But somehow, slowly, ever so slowly, the *Beagle* rose again, her prow swinging, inch by inch, round into the gale. Water sluiced through her ports as her decks emerged once more from the angry foam. A flash of lightning illuminated the next monstrous peak. It was some way off, but it was coming in fast. The little ship seemed to be taking an age to manoeuvre herself into the wind. FitzRoy could only pray now. *Come round faster. For God's sake, come round faster.* It was as if the little brig herself was rooted to the spot in fear. Imperceptibly, she felt her way by degrees to port, painstakingly precise in her movements, a frail, unwilling challenger turning to face a champion prizefighter.

The lower slopes of the wave slid under her bow, feeling her weakness, hungrily seeking the leverage to roll her over. The *Beagle* began to climb, but she began to roll too. Higher and higher she climbed; further and further she rolled to port. And then the peak of the wave furled over the prow, to deliver the final, killer punch. The *Beagle's* bowsprit pierced the wave's face at an insane, impossible angle; then she took the full impact three-quarters on, a foaming maelstrom powering unstoppably across her decks.

FitzRoy could see nothing. Surging white water filled his eyes and mouth. He no longer knew whether he was facing upwards or downwards. He merely fought for life, the breath sucked from his lungs by the thundering impact of the wave. Was this it? Was this to be his death, here, off the South American coast, at the age of twenty-three? Then, suddenly, there was air, and with a wild surge of elation he knew that she was through, that the *Beagle* had gone through the wave, that she had come round into the wind.

And then he saw Sulivan, like an extra sail tangled in the mizzen-tops, screaming soundlessly and pointing to the stern. He followed the line of Sulivan's jabbing finger but there was nothing there, only blackness. Another big sea furled over the prow. The *Beagle* shuddered and backed

off, but she had ridden the wave sufficiently to hold her course. By now
Sulivan was positively frantic. FitzRoy's eyes tried to follow his wild
signalling once again, and there, framed by an encompassing sheet of
lightning, he saw what Sulivan had been trying to warn them of: the sheer
rock face of Lobos Island, not eighty yards off the stern. Gesticulating for
all hands to follow him, he lunged across the deck and fell upon the larger
of the two remaining bower anchors, still attached to the ship by thick
iron cables. Other crewmen fought with the second anchor, and with a
clanking rush that in ordinary circumstances would have been deafening,
but could barely be heard above the crash of the storm, several hundred
pounds of cast iron disappeared over the side and into the water. The
anchors bit immediately. Just how shallow the water was became apparent
as another wave slammed into the prow, and the *Beagle* juddered back
again, her hull actually scraping across the smaller of the two anchors as
she did so. The chains began to pay out, and they could all now see the
face of the island rearing behind them, maddened white surf thrashing
about the rocks at its base. It was a matter of yards now. The *Beagle*
shipped another towering sea, which forced them to give yet more ground,
towards the solid wall at their backs. To have come this far, to have fought
against such odds, only to be dashed to pieces against the shore!

Then, a shuddering sensation, which ran the length of the deck,
announced that the cable had run to the end of its scope. Now it was up
to the anchors to hold them. FitzRoy thanked God he had ordered the
boatswain to inspect every link of her chains, and hoped to Christ that
Sorrell had done his job properly. Another wave thumped into the prow,
and all of them felt the rudder scrape against shingle; but the *Beagle* gave
no more ground. As long as the cables did not part, they might yet be
safe from destruction. FitzRoy stared back up into the mizzen-tops once
more, hoping to acknowledge Sulivan's presence, hoping to let him know
that he had saved them all, but there was no sign of life from the young
midshipman.

Exhausted, every drop of energy spent, Sulivan clung, barely conscious,
to the swaying rigging, a shapeless white bundle of rags flapping against
the night sky.

*

'By the looks of it you were knocked about like peas in a rattle.'

Admiral Otway chuckled to himself, while FitzRoy wished he had moored somewhere else. Once more, he found himself standing to attention in the admiral's cabin, this time with the *Beagle* clearly visible through the sternlights. She did, he had to admit, look a sorry sight: not only was she battered almost beyond recognition, but what remained of her rigging was festooned with drying clothes and hammocks. Ragged wet sails hung limp from her booms.

'The locals say it was the worst storm for twenty years. You must have enjoyed a pretty half-hour.'

Half an hour? FitzRoy's mind reeled. It had felt like eternity.

'If you ask me, it's your own deuced fault, Mr FitzRoy, for cutting matters so fine.'

'Yes sir.'

'So, what damage to report?'

'Both topmasts were carried away, with the jib-boom and all the small spars. I didn't even hear them break. We lost the jib and all the topsails, even though they were in the gaskets. Two boats were blown to atoms – just shivered to pieces – and…and two men were drowned. Another two were crushed by a falling yard, and another badly cut by a snapped bowline.'

'A couple of matlows are neither here nor there. You can have some of mine. But the damage to the ship is more serious. You'll have to put into Monte Video for new boats and running repairs.'

Otway's tone mellowed, as he sensed FitzRoy's distress. 'Would you care for a glass of madeira? It's a devilish fine wine.'

FitzRoy demurred.

'Don't censure yourself unduly, FitzRoy. The *Adventure* was laid right over on her side and lost her jolly-boat, and she was safe in harbour. The *Adelaide* didn't go undamaged either. Sailors die all the time.'

'I don't understand it though, sir. The barometer gave no indication there was going to be such a blow.'

Otway grunted. 'Still taking the advice of the little gentleman and lady in the weather-box? That machine of yours is little more than a novelty, and the sooner you appreciate it the better.

"When rain comes before the wind,
Halyard, sheets and braces mind,
But if wind comes before rain,
Set and trim your sails again."

'That's the only wisdom I've ever needed in thirty years.'

FitzRoy remained silent.

'Now. One other matter. This Midshipman Sulivan of yours. What sort of fellow is he?'

'He's a trump, sir. I never saw his equal for pluck and daring. He can be eager and hasty, it's true, and he is, well, not the neatest of draughtsmen. But I'd say there's not a finer fellow in the service, sir.'

'Excellent, excellent.'

'He's a Cornishman, from Tregew, near Falmouth. He has the most extraordinary powers of eyesight. He can see the satellites of Jupiter with the naked eye. He's also an exceptionally devout officer, sir.'

'What sort of "devout"?'

'Midshipman Sulivan is a sabbatarian, sir.'

A harrumph from Otway. 'Can't say I hold with evangelicals myself. The Church of England should be good enough for any civilized man. Still, he sounds just the fellow. A vacancy has arisen for an officer of the South American station to study for a lieutenant's examination back in Portsmouth. He can join the *Ganges* for a week or two, then transfer to the *North Star* under Arabin. She'll give him passage home. It's a splendid opportunity for the boy.'

FitzRoy bit his lip. 'Yes sir. Yes it is.' As weary and exhausted as he felt, the spirit drained from FitzRoy more profoundly than it had at any point during the previous evening's ordeal. They were taking away his only friend.

Sulivan found FitzRoy seated at the table of his tiny, sopping cabin, adrift on a sea of home-made charts and diagrams scribbled across salt-damp paper. The young man ducked his head to enter and rested his hand on the washstand; his body was still weak from the effects of dysentery.

FitzRoy gestured for him to sit. 'You are supposed to be in the sick list, Mr Sulivan. I'm surprised the surgeon has allowed you up and about.'

'He...I didn't really feel it necessary to tell him, sir. I'm really very much better.'

'You don't look it. But, as it happens, it was necessary for me to pay you a visit. The entire vessel owes you a vote of thanks for your bravery. Your foolhardy bravery, I should attest.'

Sulivan coloured. 'Not a bit of it, sir. That's why I came to see you...I felt you should know that the crew are saying you saved their lives. The officers and the men. Nobody else could have navigated us through that maelstrom.'

'I didn't save anybody's life. I cost two sailors theirs by my own incompetence.'

'That's not true!' Sulivan blurted out.

'At the first sign of those unusual cloud formations, I should have stood in to the shore, reefed the sails, struck the yards on deck and sat tight. I made a serious mistake.'

'You had orders to follow!'

'Orders set out a month previous, with no foreknowledge of the weather that was to befall us. I should have had the courage to act by my own initiative.'

'Orders must be obeyed. You know that – sir. You did the only thing you could do.'

'Did I? I misread all the meteorological signs. The state of the air foretold the coming weather, but I did not have the experience to diagnose it.'

'Nobody can foretell the weather, sir. It's impossible.'

'Come, come, Midshipman Sulivan. Every shepherd knows the value of a red sky at night.'

'Those are old wives' tales, surely.'

'I grant you they have little obvious basis in natural philosophy. But they are valid observations all the same. Look at this.' FitzRoy indicated a pencil sketch of what looked like a small white cheese wedged beneath a large black one. 'Remember the conditions before the storm hit us? Warm air blowing from the north-east, barometric pressure high, temperature high. Then the conditions when the tempest began – cold air from the south-west, the temperature right down, pressure collapsing. This white wedge is the warm tropical air from the north. The black wedge is the cold polar air from the south. The cold air was moving so fast it dragged against the surface of the land, so the forward edge of it actually flowed *over* the warm air and trapped it underneath. Hence all those giant clouds. And it trapped us underneath with it.'

Sulivan's mind raced to keep up.

FitzRoy's eyes were alight with enthusiasm. He flung out a question. 'What causes storms?'

'High winds.'

'No. High winds are the *result* of storms, not the cause of them. That storm was caused by warm air colliding with cold air. Where are the stormiest locations on earth?'

'The Roaring Forties. The South Atlantic. The North Atlantic...'

FitzRoy let Sulivan arrive at his own conclusion.

'...The latitudes where the cold air from the poles meets the warm air from the tropics?'

'Exactly. The barometer didn't get it wrong yesterday. I did. The barometer stayed high because we were at the front of the heated air flow just before it was overwhelmed by the colder air above.' Excited now, FitzRoy warmed to his theme. 'What if *every* storm is caused in the same way? What if every storm is an eddy, a whirl, but on an immense scale, either horizontal or vertical, between a current of warm air and another of cold air?'

'I don't know...What if?'

'Then it could theoretically be possible to predict the weather – by locating the air currents before they collide.'

'But, FitzRoy – sir, there must be a myriad uncountable breezes...The Lord does not make the winds blow to order.'

'Every experienced captain knows where to find a fair wind or a favourable current. Do you think the winds blow at random? Those two poor souls who died yesterday – was that God's punishment or the result of my blunder?'

'I know it was God's will.'

'Mr Sulivan, if God created this world to a purpose, would He have left the winds and currents to chance? What if the weather is actually a gigantic machine created by God? What if the whole of creation is ordered and comprehensible? What if we could analyse how His machine works and foretell its every move? No one need ever die in a storm again.'

'It is too fantastical an idea.'

'What if the elements could be tamed by natural philosophy? What if the weather is really no more than a huge panopticon? It's not a new idea. The ancients believed there was a discernible pattern to the weather. Aristotle called meteorology the "sublime science".'

Sulivan looked amiably sceptical at the notion that pre-Christian thinkers might have had anything valid to say about the Lord's work. 'But even if you could predict these…these air currents, how could you communicate with the vessels in their path?'

'What is the prevailing direction of storms?'

'From the west.'

'Why?'

'I don't know.'

'Neither do I. Perhaps it is something to do with the rotation of the globe. But if the winds and currents in one place could be logged and analysed, and the results sent hundreds of miles to the east…Think about it. The Admiralty can get a message from Whitehall to Portsmouth in thirty minutes by semaphore telegraph. Surely it might be possible to get a message to every fishing fleet in Britain in advance of any impending storm. Think of the lives that could be saved!'

'From the middle of the Atlantic? How?'

The runaway carriage of FitzRoy's enthusiasm came to a juddering halt. He laughed, and released his grip on the pencil that he had been waving about like a magic wand. 'I don't know.'

Sulivan grinned too, and despite his objections FitzRoy could see the excitement in the boy's eyes, dark and shining in his pale, drawn face. Not the excitement of discovery, but the excitement of friendship.

And then he remembered what he had to say to him. 'Mr Sulivan, I've been across to the *Ganges* to see Admiral Otway.'

The youngster grinned conspiratorially. It was as if their old friendship had been revived, refreshed, allowed to resurrect itself here in the private confines of FitzRoy's cabin. 'What did the old goose want?'

'The "old goose" wants to send you to England, to make of you a lieutenant.'

Silence. Sulivan froze in his seat as if a dagger had been plunged into his back. Eventually, he spoke. 'How did you respond?'

'I coincided with him. It is an opportunity you cannot afford to turn down.'

Sulivan's eyes filled with tears. 'No, you cannot. Hang me if I shall go—'

FitzRoy interrupted softly: 'Sulivan, I don't set up to disappoint you – I am as wounded as you are. But this is the best step for you, as we are both well aware. I would not have acceded to his request without it were so.'

'I will not go.'

'Orders must be obeyed. You know that.'

Sulivan's face was sheened with wet. He dragged back his chair, raised himself to his feet and fled, the door slamming shut behind him.

With a heavy heart, FitzRoy returned to his meteorological calculations. The clouds that had advanced so menacingly on the *Beagle* had been hard-edged, like Indian-ink rubbed on an oily plate...Hard-edged clouds always seemed to presage wind...It was no use. He could not concentrate. He thought of putting down his pencil, and going in search of Sulivan. He need not have bothered, however, because a moment later a gentle knock announced that Sulivan had returned. 'Commander FitzRoy, sir. I wondered...' Sulivan hesitated. 'When I first went to sea, sir, my mother made me promise to read from the psalms daily, and to pray the collect. I have never omitted that duty. She also gave me this. I have read from it every day.' He pushed a battered red copy of the scriptures across the captain's table. 'I'd like you to have it.'

'I cannot accept. Your mother meant for you to have it.'

'I'd like you to have it, sir. It would mean a deal to me.'

'My dear fellow, every lonely old captain on the seas turns to God or the bottle. It is considerate of you to drive me away from the latter prospect but…' FitzRoy tailed off.

Sulivan summoned up all his resolve, more than he had required to climb the mizzen-mast during the previous night's storm, and addressed his captain. '"Be strong and of good courage; be not afraid, neither be thou dismayed: for the Lord thy God is with thee whithersoever thou goest." Joshua one, verse nine.'

And with that, tears stinging his eyes, he turned and left FitzRoy's cabin for the last time.

CHAPTER FOUR

Dungeness Point, Patagonia, 1 April 1829

The three motionless figures stood sentinel on the shore, drawn up on horseback in line abreast. Some twenty feet up the beach, a lone horse stood to attention, riderless, without a saddle, but perfectly still.

'They're Horse Indians. Patagonians.'

FitzRoy took the spyglass from Lieutenant Kempe. It was difficult to make out many details of the distant trio and their solitary companion, but it was clear from their attitude that they were an advance guard, posted to greet the ships.

'Whoever named this place Dungeness was spot on,' piped up Midshipman King. 'I've been to the real Dungeness with my father. This is the living spit.'

It was indeed. A deep indigo sea smeared against a beach of rounded shingle, backed by a low, thorny scrub. The sky was a pale cornflower blue. It could easily have been a beautiful, breezy autumn day on the Kentish coast, except for two crucial differences. First, the beach was dotted with penguins: fat, fluffy ones moulting in the sunshine, downy feathers floating off them like dandelion seeds puffed in the wind; and sleek, more confident black-and-white birds, slithering down to the sea on their bellies and launching themselves into the surf. The shallows were thick with bobbing penguin heads. The three statuesque sentries and the riderless horse, who provided the second aberrant note, now came into focus.

'Either their horses are very small, or the Indians are extremely big,' observed FitzRoy, squinting through the lens. 'The giants of Patagonia, perhaps?' he murmured.

'I beg your pardon, sir?' enquired Kempe.

'I've been reading about the Patagonians in one of Captain Stokes's books. A Jesuit missionary called Faulkner met one chief who was seven and a half feet high. Admiral Byron apparently met a man so tall he couldn't reach the top of the fellow's head. And Magellan reported giants here too. When he saw their footprints in the sand he exclaimed, *"Que patagones!"* What big feet. Hence the name of the place.'

'I can't say we ever encountered any that big, sir, but they certainly average more than six feet. You should converse with Mr Bynoe, sir. He's interested in the savages.' Kempe's tone made it clear that he found Bynoe's interest a trifle eccentric.

Midshipman Stokes attracted FitzRoy's attention. 'The *Adventure* is signalling, sir.'

All hands looked across to King's vessel, a hundred yards away across a field of white horses, where a line of little flags was in the process of being hoisted. King was back in charge now, with the admiral gone to do His Majesty's business at Monte Video, and would remain so for the rest of the expedition.

'Captain King wants you to lead a shore party, sir.'

'Very well. Mr Bennet, if you'd care to prepare the whaleboat and select six men. We'll need firearms and ammunition. And ask Mr Bynoe if he would be good enough to join us.'

'I'll go below and get the medals ready, sir,' offered Kempe.

'Medals?'

'Presents for the savages. They have a moulding of Britannia on one side, and His Majesty on the other. Savages love shiny things, sir.'

'I am told you are something of an anthropologist.'

Bynoe's earnest young face flushed slightly. They were bouncing towards the shore in the *Beagle*'s whaleboat, pulled along by six pairs of wiry arms. 'I wouldn't say that, sir. That is, I'm interested in all areas of natural philosophy but I have no great learning. Stratigraphy is what really interests me, sir, but I know so little.'

'Well, you've had ample opportunity to study the coast of Patagonia as it hasn't changed one whit these last thousand miles. How would you diagnose it?'

Bynoe stared across at the featureless plain that stretched hundreds of miles into the interior, which found its end here at the southern tip of Dungeness Point. There were no hills to break the monotony, no trees, not even a solitary thicket. There had been only salt flats, low, spiny bushes and tufts of wiry, parched grass since the last white settlement at the Rio Negro; and no sign of life either, other than a few grazing herds of guanaco and the occasional disturbed, flapping ibis. 'It's not very interesting, is it, sir? Well, not to the other officers. They don't reckon it much of a hobby to have the steam up about a lot of rocks.'

'Is it not part of the officers' duties to take a keen interest in the surrounding landscape?'

'Well, yes, I suppose so, sir, but that rather became pushed to one side when we reached Tierra del Fuego. Conditions are so tough there. It's just me interested now, sir – and Mr Bennet, of course, sometimes.' Bynoe hastily added the last part, having noticed a cloud of panic pass over the coxswain's normally sunny countenance.

'And your stratigraphic diagnosis?'

'I'd say there were three layers to the coastline, sir. Gravel on top, then some sort of white stone – maybe a pumice, I don't know – then a layer of shells in the ground. I've had a look on a shore expedition. I couldn't identify the white stone but I'll tell you a curious thing about the shells. They're mostly oyster shells, but there are no oysters hereabouts. So it looks as if the oysters have become extinct since the shell beds were laid down.'

'That's very good, Mr Bynoe, very good indeed. Has it occurred to you that the central white layer might also consist of shells, but shells that have been crushed to a powder and compressed into stone?'

'Crushed by what, sir? There's only a thin covering of gravel above.'

'By the action of the water, perhaps. Why is the land hereabouts covered in salt flats? I would hazard a guess that this country was once submerged under a great many feet of seawater. A sudden inundation, perhaps, that deprived the oysters of the oxygen needed to sustain their life.'

'By Jove, sir, I do believe you've got it!'

'I wouldn't go that far, Mr Bynoe. I am only hazarding a guess, but tell me what you know of our friends on the shore there.'

'They'll be from the settlement at Gregory Bay, sir. We stopped there in 'twenty-seven. They're led by a woman called Maria, who speaks a little Spanish. The Horse Indians have been trading with the sealing-ships for hundreds of years, so they're well used to Europeans. I doubt we'll be needing those.' He indicated the Sea Service pistols, the bag of shot, the wad cutters, rammers and the box of flints in the bottom of the boat.

'A few hundred years ago they were hostile, and armed with bows and arrows. Sarmiento built two settlements, called San Felipe and Jesus. I believe there were three hundred settlers at Jesus, but the Indians left no survivors. Then in San Felipe there were about two hundred settlers, who starved to death for the most part. There were only fifteen left when Thomas Cavendish sailed by. They being Spaniards, he...well, he put the rest to death. He renamed the bay Port Famine. You can still find a few ruined walls in the beech forest. It's where Captain Stokes took his life, God rest his soul.'

'We must thank God that we live in civilized times.'

'Absolutely, sir.'

FitzRoy sat back. Inquisitive penguin heads surrounded the boat now, craning to look over the side as it passed, then darting forward to the prow to get another look. On the beach, the three sentries were close enough to examine in more detail. There were two men and a woman, tall, muscular and broad-shouldered, each over six foot in height, with long, luxuriant black hair divided into two streams by metal fillets at the neck. What was visible of their skin was dark copper, but their faces were daubed with red pigment and divided in four by white crosses, like the flag of St George reversed. Their flesh was further ornamented by cuts and perforations. Their noses were aquiline, their foreheads broad and low beneath rough black fringes. The woman's eyebrows were plucked bald. About their shoulders they wore rough guanaco-skin mantles, the fur turned inwards. They were armed with bolas and long, tapering lances pointed with iron. They carried an air of lean strength and wary pride. Their horses, by contrast, were small, woebegone, shaggy creatures, controlled by single reins attached to driftwood bits. Rough saddles and spurs cut from lumps of wood completed the rudimentary trappings. For FitzRoy, the comparison with Don Quixote was irresistible.

As the whaleboat scrunched into the shingle, scattering penguins, he stepped lightly ashore. One of the horsemen broke ranks, trotted forward and gravely handed him a stained piece of paper. He unfolded it with what he hoped was comparable gravity and read:

'To any shipmaster:
From Mr Low, master of the *Unicorn* sealer.
I write hereunder to emphasize to him the friendly
disposition of the Indians, and to impress him
with the necessity of treating them well, and not
deceiving them; for they have good memories,
and would seriously resent it.
I beg to remain Sir
Wm. Low
Master, the *Unicorn*
6 February 1826'

FitzRoy refolded the paper and returned it with a nod that indicated he had understood. The horseman spoke in a low, guttural language – rather as if his mouth was full of hot pudding, thought FitzRoy – and produced a spare guanaco skin from under his saddle. Leaning forward, he proffered it to the Englishman. FitzRoy could smell him at close quarters, a deep, pungent animal smell.

'*¿Agua ardiente?*' the man asked, in Spanish. FitzRoy shrugged his shoulders to indicate that he had none. '*Bueno es boracho.*'

'*¿Habla español?*' FitzRoy asked.

'*Bueno es boracho,*' the man repeated. *It's good to get drunk.* With that he turned and galloped away with his two companions. The lone, riderless horse further up the beach remained, as before, utterly motionless. Only then did FitzRoy and Bynoe notice that the animal was quite dead. And, furthermore, that it had been stuffed.

'They've gone without their medals,' murmured Bynoe.

*

Dungeness was drawing round to the *Beagle*'s quarter when the ship caught the first gust of the howling gale that blows perpetually through the Straits of Magellan. Funnelling through the narrows, where the rocky banks are so close that it seems as if a passing vessel cannot but scrape her spars against one side or the other, the winds exploded from their constricting bottleneck and swept at high speed across the shoals and sandbanks of Possession Bay. Windbound, with topmasts struck, the *Beagle*, the *Adventure* and the *Adelaide* approached the narrows in tight formation, jinking delicately between the underwater obstacles: not just sand and rock, but huge tangled gardens of giant kelp, whose strands can grow to twenty fathoms long in just fifty feet of water.

'Apart from the westerlies, there's an opposing tidal stream of eight knots,' explained Kempe. 'The tide here is above seven fathoms. Last time out it took us more than a week to get through the first narrows.'

FitzRoy was painfully aware that, as the lead vessel of the formation, the *Beagle* must be first to attempt the narrows. She was already making ever shorter tacks in an attempt to zigzag against the headwind and the current. It was hard to see how she could possibly manoeuvre through the pinched opening ahead in the face of such a gale. At least the crew were putting their backs into the process of tacking. The lower sails were clewed up and the lee braces slackened, while the weather braces became the lee braces and vice versa, and the whole process began again. It was back-breaking and repetitive work, and for every ten yards they gained against the wind, nine were lost to the current. The sailors sang as they hauled.

'When beating off Magellan Straits, the wind blew strong and hard,
While short'ning sail two gallant tars fell from the topsail yard;
By angry seas the lines we threw from their weak hands was torn,
We had to leave them to the sharks that prowl around Cape Horn.'

'I do wish they wouldn't sing that particular shanty,' FitzRoy murmured. 'They have a song for every occasion,' said Lieutenant Kempe, with his death's head smile.

'Would it please you if I started off a different one, sir?' offered Boatswain Sorrell.

'No, thank you, Mr Bos'n. I do believe I should be well advised not to interfere in such a matter.' FitzRoy made a mental vow. *I will not let the elements dictate to me this time around. I will make my own luck.*

As the afternoon wore on the *Beagle* made repeated attempts to tack through the narrows, but a breakthrough proved impossible, and eventually the weary afternoon watch had to admit defeat. During the dog-watches of the early evening the *Beagle* stood off the narrows instead, making short tacks merely to stand still, the wind too strong for her to heave to and drift. As the sun settled, the breeze finally fell away, and the dusk was dotted like starlight by the fires of the Indians along the northern shore. The curious shrill neighs of the guanaco herds sounded from far off in the darkness. Where the deck had earlier been a scene of frantic, sweaty activity, now the dim light from the binnacle illuminated only the men at the wheel. The night lookouts took up their positions at the four corners of the ship. FitzRoy, frustrated, stalked the starboard side of the poop deck. 'We could have made it through the narrows in this light breeze.'

'It's too dark now sir,' said Bennet, self-evidently, eager to please. It was his turn at the wheel.

'If there's a seven-fathom tide flowing eastward through the narrows during the afternoon,' pondered FitzRoy, 'then presumably it flows back west during the night.'

'I suppose so sir.'

'And this dip in the wind speed. Does it occur every night or is it an aberration? Last time you were here, trying to fight your way through for a week, did the wind speed drop every evening?'

'I can't rightly remember, sir.'

'Mr King, fetch me Captain Stokes's weather book, if you please.'

The youngster scurried off importantly, and returned with the volume. The late captain's weather book did not really do justice to its title. It was supposed to contain all the readings of the day and the hour – wind direction and force, sympiesometer and barometer values, air and water temperatures, latitude and longitude readings – but the details recorded were sporadic at best. On this occasion, however, fate had been kind. There, in the entry for December 1826, with early-voyage enthusiasm, Captain Stokes had recorded calm evening after calm evening at the blustery exit of the First Narrows.

'Pass the word for the bos'n,' ordered FitzRoy. Duly summoned, Sorrell scurried on deck. 'Mr Sorrell, bare poles, if you please.'

'B-bare poles?' Sorrell could hardly believe his ears.

'You heard me, Mr Sorrell. Furl all the sails. We are going to ware through the narrows under bare poles. There's eight knots of tidal stream that will take us through.'

'But it's pitch black, sir.'

'The current can see where it's going, Mr Sorrell.'

'But we could hit a shoal, sir, or – or—'

'Surely you are not questioning Mr Bennet's skill at the wheel?' A grin from Bennet found an answering smile. 'Those who never run any risk, who sail only when the wind is fair, are doubtless extremely prudent officers, Mr Sorrell, but their names will be forgotten. I do not intend the name of the *Beagle* to be forgotten.'

'Lord preserve us. Aye aye sir.'

Sorrell piped the order to a disbelieving crew. There was activity, too, on the *Adventure*, where King and his officers came to the side with nightglasses to try to make out what was afoot on board the *Beagle*. Across the water came the characteristic creaks of the capstan turning, as the soaking anchor cable began its journey up the maindeck and back into the cable tier, the ship's nippers darting here and there to straighten its passage as royal pages would shepherd home a sozzled master. Almost silently by comparison, the great dark sheets of the sails were furled up into the yards, revealing a mass of glittering stars through the *Beagle*'s rigging. And then, slowly, she began to drift on the tide, gliding between the shoals, riding the stream towards the dark gate ahead.

Nobody made a sound on the *Beagle*'s decks as she slid through the chasm, the coxswain at the helm applying the deftest touch here and there to keep her aligned with the current. The rocks to either side appeared as misshapen silhouettes, black spaces where the starlight had been sucked away into nothingness. All ears were strained for the sound of tearing copper or splintering wood that would presage disaster. It never came. The *Beagle* ghosted through the narrows with some elegance, as if guided by an invisible pilot.

After perhaps twenty minutes the hemming rocks on either side took a step back, conceding defeat, and the channel widened out into the flat bowl of Gregory Bay. As the narrows gradually fell astern, it seemed that nobody would dare be the first to speak. Finally, Bennet broke the silence. 'Well *done* sir,' he breathed.

'What *will* my father say?' wondered King.

Out on the gloom of the maindeck, some unknown voice raised a hurrah.

'Three cheers for Captain FitzRoy!' And the crew gave a rousing hip-hip hurrah that brought a broad smile of relief to FitzRoy's face, and set the dogs barking out by the campfires on the northern shore.

A week later, the *Adventure* and the *Adelaide*, their crews no doubt flogged with exhaustion, were still battling miserably to break the wind's stranglehold on the narrows. From the maindeck of the *Beagle* it was possible to catch occasional glimpses of them tacking back and forth at the entrance, desperate to force a passage but unwilling to emulate FitzRoy's risky experiment. The delay was becoming a matter for concern, as only two days' supply of fresh water was left on the *Beagle*, the rest being sealed and stored in the *Adelaide*'s barrels. There would be plenty of fresh water further south, amid the glacial streams of Tierra del Fuego, but here there was precious little: water was the one commodity that the Horse Indians were reluctant to trade. There was no shortage of food, however, and the crew had dined on fresh guanaco meat, mussels and limpets, and an unfortunate pig brought from Monte Video, which had been killed and roasted. The cook had even proudly announced the preparation of a special feast for the captain, of baked shell-pig, in honour of his navigational daring: FitzRoy had eaten the entire baby armadillo upside-down in its carapace. To ward off scurvy, the men had been sent to gather cranberries and wild celery, much to the mystification of the Indians, who seemed to subsist entirely on a diet of lukewarm guanaco meat without suffering the slightest ill effects.

FitzRoy had also dispatched the officers to record their surroundings, dividing them rather arbitrarily by subject on the basis of any slight inclination or aptitude he had been able to discern. Bynoe had been appointed ship's stratigrapher; Midshipman Stokes, who was revealed to have been a keen huntsman in his native Yorkshire, became the *Beagle*'s naturalist; the new surgeon, Wilson, rather reluctantly took on the role of collecting and recording sea life; Kempe was put in charge of all meteorological observations; FitzRoy himself concentrated on the anthropology of the native peoples. Midshipman King, desperate to become involved, was appointed general assistant to everybody. No animal, fish or shellfish could be eaten until it had been logged, examined and recorded on paper, preferably in colour. FitzRoy's cabin was already disappearing under piles of King's badly illustrated fish. Stokes had made the startling conjecture that the two types of penguin they had seen, distinguished as Patagonian and Magellanic penguins under the 'Aptenodytes' section of the ship's natural encyclopedia, were actually adult and young forms of the same bird. The Indians of the Gregory Bay settlement were becoming used to the sight of FitzRoy and his officers poking about their tents and asking questions using sign language: strange, inquisitive white men, quite unlike the sealcatchers, who only wanted to trade, or purchase women. The investigators from the *Beagle* had also solved the riddle of the stuffed horse: the animal marked the grave of a *cacique*, or chief. All great men, it was discovered, were buried sitting up in the sand, with their favourite horse stuffed and mounted facing the spot, to watch over them.

'Mr Kempe says that the savages are a different species from us. On account of their dark skin.'

'Does he, indeed.'

FitzRoy had taken Bynoe, who seemed to be the most intelligent and eager of the officers, on another tour of the Indian camp.

'Whereas Mr Wilson says they are the same as us. They are only brown because of the smoke and ochre particles incorporated into their skin.'

'With all due respect to the surgeon, I feel that the absence of a qualified natural philosopher on board leaves us all somewhat in the dark.' Really, this was too much. Even King's fish paintings put such nonsense to shame. But the racial origins of the Patagonian tribes presented a conundrum: why were the Horse Indians such wiry giants, while a few miles to the south, across the water in Tierra del Fuego – the *Beagle*'s eventual destination – the Canoe Indians were by all accounts sleek, fat midgets? Every day posed new questions that FitzRoy was desperate to answer.

The Gregory Bay encampment smelt like a penguin colony. Groups of Indians sat amid their tents, spindly affairs constructed from brushwood stakes and guanaco skin, which shuddered in the strong breeze that gusted off the bay yet somehow managed to stay upright. One circle of men passed round a clay pipe; another group played cards with painted squares of guanaco skin; a woman, naked but for decorative smears of clay, grease and animal blood, breast-fed an eight-year-old child. All ignored the two white men. FitzRoy selected an isolated group of three, whom he found sitting in a huddle, combing each other's hair and munching any lice they found. He reached into his pocket and drew out three of the fruits of European technology: a whistle, a small music-box and his pocket watch. The whistle produced delight; the music-box, curiously, was of little interest; the ticking of the watch, however, left the Indians both fascinated and thunderstruck.

Good relations established, Bynoe produced a notebook and pen from his satchel.

'*¿Habla español?*' asked FitzRoy.

The men looked blank. The sailors had found few people at the camp who spoke any Spanish. The celebrated Maria appeared to be absent.

FitzRoy resorted once again to sign language. 'Englishmen.' He pointed to himself and Bynoe. One of the Indians heaved himself on to his haunches. His face was dramatically daubed with animal blood and charcoal streaks, an apparently martial design offset by the laconic manner with which its owner now produced a fist-sized block of salt and helped himself to a large bite. Eventually he spoke. '*Cubba.*'

'*Cubba?*'

Another bite of salt.

'*Cubba.*' White men.

They had the first entry for FitzRoy's dictionary. 'Indians.' He gestured to the trio.

'*Yacana.*'

Bynoe made another entry. The Indians were incurious about this: they appeared to know no system of writing or hieroglyphics. FitzRoy pointed at the tents. These were '*cau*'. A dog was a '*wachin*'. A fur mantle was a '*chorillio*'. And so on, until Bynoe had some fifty everyday words listed.

Now FitzRoy changed tack, and pointed across the bay to the southern horizon where a heaving swirl of grey cloud masked the rain-soaked mountains of Tierra del Fuego.

'Oscherri.'

With a flat hand, he gestured to indicate a short man from 'Oscherri'. A Canoe Indian. The men laughed derisively. '*Sapallios.*'

One spat into the dust. Others of the tribe had gathered round to watch now, and FitzRoy noticed that one individual wore a tiny crucifix on a chain round his neck, presumably a gift or trade from the sealers. He pointed it out, and gestured at the sky. It was time to widen his linguistic horizons.

'God,' he said, adding a quick mime of thunder and lightning for good measure.

The man nodded that he understood.

'Setebos.'

FitzRoy gripped Bynoe's arm in excitement.

'*"His art is of such power*
It would control my dam's God Setebos."'

'Mr Bynoe – that's Caliban, from *The Tempest*! If Shakespeare employed such a word in 1611, it must have been furnished by a matlow from Drake's expedition – perhaps even by Drake himself!'

The Indian with the crucifix began to speak, jabbing a finger at FitzRoy, then indicating the heavens to the west. Bynoe offered a diagnosis. 'I think he's asking if we've been sent by God. Or if we know God.'

FitzRoy shook his head at the man, but it seemed to make no difference. The Indian beckoned for the two Englishmen to follow him, and the crowd parted to show them a way through.

'Let us follow this Caliban, and see where he takes us,' suggested FitzRoy.

And so, obligingly, they allowed themselves to be led across to a nearby tent. The flap was pulled aside, releasing a thick plume of smoke, and they crawled in. A brushwood fire occupied one corner, which poured smoke into the interior of the tent, although there appeared to be no means for it to escape. Through red eyes they made out a frightened, naked woman crouched over the prone figure of a sweating baby, which was daubed with clay. On the other side of the sick child, a priest or medicine man was waving a rattle in the air, and muttering prayers or incantations over a neat pile of dried bird sinews. He looked at the new arrivals with resentment.

'They want us to cure the child,' breathed Bynoe.

'Then by good fortune they have invited the appropriate person into their tent. What can you do?'

Bynoe placed his palm across the child's forehead.

'It seems to be a simple fever, sir. Normally I'd recommend a calomel purgative. Failing that, a draught of hot port wine and a wintersbark tonic. I have tonic and wine with me – the port is cold, but it could be heated easily enough over the fire.'

The young assistant surgeon decanted a measure of port into a small glass vessel, which he laid briefly in the embers, before administering it to the shivering patient. Then he slid the draught of wintersbark down the child's throat. It was accepted with a hiccuping cough. Coughing himself at the thickness of the woodsmoke, and wiping his streaming eyes on his sleeve, FitzRoy gave quiet thanks for the efficacy of modern medicine. The two phials were passed round the crowd of Indians which had assembled at the tent flap, most of whom took an exploratory sniff. A faint murmur of scepticism seemed to pass among them. Finally, the owner of the crucifix – the father, perhaps? – indicated that he would like to borrow the captain's pocket watch. FitzRoy obliged. The man took the watch reverentially, and passed it back and forth across the child's face. The loud ticking filled the tent, seeming to still the buffeting breeze outside, and a whisper of approval passed between the Indians. *If only they knew how useless that is*, thought FitzRoy.

A steady, sleeting rain had set in by afternoon, persisting into the evening, and blotchy watercolour clouds obscured the fires on the shore. As usual the breeze died with the passing of daylight, enabling the *Beagle* to let go its anchors; the hustle and bustle of the afternoon was replaced by the ceaseless, soothing rattle of the chain cable as it passed back and forth over the rocks below. The officers had spent the afternoon teaching the alphabet to the illiterate men. Then FitzRoy had ordered painted canvas awnings to be set up to keep the decks dry, for the official 'song and skylark' period during the last dog-watch. Conducted by the ship's fiddler, this was a compulsory session of hornpipes and sarabands for the entire company, by order of the Admiralty. As Bynoe earnestly explained, the increased blood-flow generated by dancing helped to combat scurvy.

A perfunctory divine service had rounded off the afternoon's activities. FitzRoy's prayer was a standard fair-weather imprecation, but the theme of the Noachian flood had served to bring together the concerns that occupied his mind:

'O Almighty Lord God, who for the sin of man didst once drown all the world, except eight persons, and afterward of thy great mercy didst promise never to destroy it so again: we humbly beseech thee that, although we for our iniquities have worthily deserved a plague of rain and waters, yet upon our true repentance thou wilt send us such weather as that we may receive the fruits of the earth in due season; and learn both by thy punishment to amend our lives, and for thy clemency to give thee praise and glory; through Jesus Christ our Lord. Amen.'

Now FitzRoy paced the damp decks, a solitary figure, trying to thread together the Patagonians, the beds of extinct shells and the events of the Old Testament into a coherent whole. *Who for the sin of man didst once drown all the world.* Was this the deluge that had crushed a million shells to white powder on the Patagonian shore?

The night watches had been colder of late, as the freezing Falklands current brought the sea temperatures plunging, and he pulled his oilskin about him. Below decks, everything had been battened down to keep the warm tobacco fug trapped inside. Through the streaming skylights, smoky oil-lamps swung invitingly on their gimbals. In the fetid, sweaty atmosphere, the men talked about life and drowning and money and women. FitzRoy paused as he paced by the messroom skylight where the sound of Master Murray telling a joke issued forth clearly into the night.

'So Smith, who stutters, is on the tops'lyard. And he shouts to the mate below, "Me w-w-whatnots are j-j-jammed in the block of the reefing tackle." "Yer what?" shouts the mate. "I said me w-w-whatnots are j-j-jammed in the block of the reefing tackle." So the mate shouts, "If yer can't speak it, me bucko, sing it." So Smith sings out, clear as you like,

'"Slack away yer reefy tackle, reefy tackle, reefy tackle,
Slack away yer reefy tackle, me whatnots are jammed!"'

A pent-up explosion of masculine laughter greeted the final lines, and FitzRoy was overcome with a desire to join in, to bathe in the atmosphere of camaraderie and warmth. He descended the after companionway and opened the messroom door; but the instant he did so, the atmosphere died as if asphyxiated.

'Good evening, sir,' said Murray politely.

'Evening, sir,' from Bynoe.

Drinks were hastily put down, and pipes and snuff were laid on the table. Stokes was there too, and Wilson and Kempe.

FitzRoy did his best to muster an urbane smile. 'Good evening, men.'

'Anything we can do for you, sir?'

'No, thank you, Mr Stokes. I am much obliged. I merely came by to thank you most kindly for all your efforts today, and to bid you all goodnight.'

'Thank you, sir. Goodnight, sir.'

'Goodnight.'

And with that FitzRoy withdrew, outwardly unruffled, but inwardly smarting that he could make such a fool of himself. On the *Thetis* or the *Ganges*, of course, he would have been part of such an evening's entertainment; not by any means the most gregarious part but an integral part nonetheless. Now he was excluded by his rank. That was the way of the world, and he must accept it. Never again must he entertain such absurd emotional disarray. *I may guide them and shepherd them through difficulty and help them learn, but I cannot engage with them. I am not allowed to be their friend.* He shut the messroom door, crossed the planks, and made his way into his own cramped cabin. There he sat at his table, lit a lantern and drew the salt-stained volume of Admiral Byron's voyages from the shelf.

Byron had been shipwrecked in Tierra del Fuego on the *Wager* half a century before, one of four to make it home to England from a ship's company of some two hundred men. Something FitzRoy had read in Byron's account stirred in his memory now, and he leafed restlessly through the pages to find it. There it was:

'What we thought strange, upon the summits of the highest hills were found beds of shells, a foot or two thick.'

Beds of shells. On the summits of hills. Higher than those on the Patagonian shoreline. Higher than the salt crystals of the inshore salinas. Shell beds actually on the summits of hills. He took down the copy of the scriptures that Sulivan had presented him, and turned to Genesis 6:7: 'And the Lord said, I will destroy man whom I have created from the face of the earth; both man, and beast, and the creeping thing, and the fowls of the air; for it repenteth me that I have made them.' Was this not proof, then, of Genesis? How else did shell beds come to be on mountaintops, unless the mountains themselves had been inundated by floodwaters? There had been just eight survivors, according to the weather prayer. Had eight survivors really repopulated the entire planet? His eyes were drawn across the page, as if invisibly guided, to Genesis 6:4:

'There were giants in the earth in those days…mighty men which were of old, men of renown.'

Giants in the earth in those days. The giants of Patagonia? Eagerly, he began to devour the verses that followed, dealing with the repopulation of the earth by Noah's sons Shem, Ham and Japheth: how Shem begat the Semitic people, how Ham begat the Egyptians and Libyans and Cushites – the blacks – and how Japheth begat the Greeks, Parthians, Persians, Medes and Romans. How, a generation or two later, Esau married a daughter of Ishmael and begat the copper-coloured men. The red men of Patagonia and Tierra del Fuego.

Why, then, the disparity in height between the seven-foot Patagonians and the tiny fat Fuegians they so despised? The Fuegians apparently resembled the Esquimaux and Laplanders of the north. Perhaps the exposure to cold, wet and wind, the long winters cocooned in their tents, had shortened the legs of the Fuegians and increased their body fat. Perhaps the Patagonians, like the Swahili tribesmen of Africa, had grown tall and wiry because of the fine climate, the flat terrain and the enormous distances they had to cover in following the herds. Was it really possible that humans, originally cut from the same divine template, had adapted into a score of different varieties at the behest of the climate and of their surroundings? He had so much to discuss, and no one to discuss it with. He would have given so much, at that moment, to engage in conversation with a skilled anthropologist, mineralogist, or even a priest. Did Noah, he wondered, have anyone to converse with? How unimaginably great would have been the pressures of a divine command!

A commotion outside woke him from his reverie, and there was a knock at the cabin door. It was Boatswain Sorrell, perspiring slightly. 'If you please, sir, I think you may care to come up on deck.'

FitzRoy ducked out of his cabin and leaped up the companionway to the maindeck. It took his eyes a moment or two to adjust to the darkness, but he could already guess what had transpired from the sounds of cheering about him. Across the bay to the east, two small dark shapes had emerged from the gloom and the drizzle of the first narrows. After a week of fruitless, back-breaking toil, the *Adventure* and the *Adelaide* had taken a leaf out of FitzRoy's book, and had slithered through the rocky gates – thankfully unscathed – on the tidal current.

CHAPTER FIVE

Desolate Bay, Tierra del Fuego, 4 February 1830

'Are there any news, Mr Kempe?'

'None, sir. The search parties have found no traces.'

FitzRoy clamped his teeth in exasperation. Murray was now more than a week overdue. He had taken a party in one of the two whaleboats to survey Cape Desolation and the south-western side of the bay. Their provisions would have run out four days ago. It was a wild, surf-pounded coast, exposed to all the moods and frustrations of the Pacific Ocean, which made it all the more dangerous for men in a small open boat.

Up to this point, everything had gone as smoothly as FitzRoy could have hoped. The ships had sailed south from Gregory Bay towards Tierra del Fuego, the scenery changing dramatically as they did so. Ahead of them stood a battalion of sombre mountains, their sides plunging sheer into the sea, their summits white-capped, shrouded by mists and swirling storms. Gloomy beech forests, some of the trunks a good twelve or thirteen feet across at the base, clung in a tangled, yellow-green mass to the leeward shores. Wherever one looked, the mountain wall was riven with inlets; islands dotted its feet, mere crumbs of stone, as if the cliffs had been hewn by a giant with an axe. Here and there, in isolated coves, slender crescents of shingle provided the only flat land. Low clouds raced and tore themselves into strips against the bare rock. Once, just once, through a ripped coverlet of grey, a glittering, frosty peak had revealed itself, towering above its fellows. This was the awesome 'Volcan Nevado' recorded by Pedro Sarmiento in the sixteenth century. Captain King had seen it too, in the early days of the expedition, and had renamed it Mount Sarmiento. Nowhere in all this forbidding vista was there any sign of life. If the inhabitants of Tierra del Fuego were observing the ships, they gave no indication as yet of their presence. Instead, the dark channels that sliced through the mountains appeared to lead beyond the confines of the world of men, to the far ends of the earth.

King had split the three ships up. He had turned east in the *Adventure*. Skyring in the *Adelaide* had been sent into the labyrinth ahead, to explore and map the Cockburn channel as it wound between sheer rock walls to the south coast. FitzRoy in the *Beagle* had been ordered to follow the Straits of Magellan, turning west at Point Shut-up, then beating north-west towards the Pacific. There were inlets and channels leading off the north side of the straits, recorded a half-century before by Byron, Wallis and Carteret, that still had not been explored, surveyed or named; or, as in the case of Point Shut-up, renamed. They would keep the mountain wall of Tierra del Fuego to their port side, tacking up into the westerlies, while they explored the flatter, barren tundra of southern Patagonia to starboard. FitzRoy was looking forward to the task with enthusiasm; the only sour note was that King had transferred Bynoe to the *Adelaide*, where Skyring was in want of a surgeon, leaving FitzRoy to the conversational mercies of Mr Wilson in his place. Once again he had been denied the company of a potential kindred spirit.

He had sought solace in the solid efficiency of Midshipman Stokes. Crop-haired, compact and muscular, the Yorkshireman belied his eighteen years with a performance of almost metronomic reliability. Once an order had been given to Stokes, it could be safely forgotten. Swiftly, he became FitzRoy's most trusted surveyor. Although taciturn by nature – he was not one for a messroom chat about the finer aspects of stratigraphy or anthropology – he was unfailingly even-tempered, and stuck by his captain through thick and thin.

As autumn had turned to winter, FitzRoy and Stokes – the former commanding the whaleboat, the latter towed behind in the yawl – had set out with a month's supplies to investigate the Jerome Channel, a narrow opening on the north side of the strait. They were well prepared: every man in their party carried a painted canvas cloak and a south-wester hat like a coal-heaver's cap. In the absence of fresh food they packed the boats with tin canisters of Donkin's preserved meats, which made an agreeable mess when mixed with the occasional wildfowl – any bird unlucky enough to have delayed its winter migration found Stokes an unerring marksman. But despite all FitzRoy's precautions the weather tested their powers of endurance to the limit. Sometimes icy rain would set in for days; in the mornings their cloaks would be frozen hard about them. The winds whipped up short, awkward seas, which frequently threatened to capsize them, and made it impossible to land in the high-breaking surf; on occasions they had to row all night just to keep the two boats aligned with the waves.

Then there was the time-consuming, exhaustive work of the survey itself. This was modern, scientific map-making, not the broad guesswork of old. Soundings had to be made in every bay using the yawl's leadline, while the whaleboat foraged in the shallows rudder up, making transects with the lead line at various angles. At every land station, heavy theodolites had to be manhandled up hills, small portable observatories had to be set up, and the ship's chronometers had to be rated. It was a thankless task, but the men set to it with vigour.

And what discoveries they made. To their astonishment, the Jerome Channel widened out into a vast inland sea some sixty miles wide, hitherto unsuspected, which FitzRoy named Otway Water. A side-channel was named Sulivan Sound in honour of his departed friend; the celebrated Mr Donkin's preserved meats were commemorated at Donkin Cove, while bays were named after Lieutenant Wickham of the *Adventure* and FitzRoy's sister Fanny. At the far end of Otway Water, a narrow, twisting passage opened in the hills, which led, astonishingly, to another vast inland sea sixty miles long by twenty miles across. Frozen blue Niagaras of ice marked its western terminus, riven by serrated channels, where improbably shaped icebergs barged and jostled each other with silent grace. FitzRoy named this second reach Skyring Water, in honour of that gentleman's steadfast good humour in accepting his situation. Their provisions ran low before they could ascertain whether or not there was any exit from Skyring Water to the sea; so they made their way back to the *Beagle*, their thick winter beards streaked with ice. FitzRoy himself had lost two toes through frostbite; but no man had uttered a word of complaint, and their commander burned inside with a fierce pride. He would turn the *Beagle* into the best, the most efficient survey packet the Royal Navy had ever sent forth.

The rest of the winter had been taken up with following the straits to their conclusion, searching for channels in the cold rain and sparse daylight. Sulivan had been remembered again at Cape Bartholomew; King had been commemorated thrice in one vista at Cape Philip, Cape Parker and King Island. They had seen seals teaching their pups to swim, supporting them with one flipper, then gently pushing them away into deep water to fend for themselves. At a dark reach lined by black cliffs, now for ever entered into posterity as Whale Sound, Boatswain Sorrell had screamed 'Hard a-port! There are rocks under the bows!' which had revealed themselves instead to be a passing school of humpback whales. The beasts had accompanied the ship for some miles before peeling off to the south, at which juncture one had performed a graceful leap of farewell across the *Beagle*'s stern.

The human inhabitants of the straits had revealed themselves rather more cautiously at first. Not that they could hope to hide themselves from the strangers – far from it. The continuous fires – the most precious possessions of each Fuegian family, which were never allowed to go out – signalled their presence on the hillsides in the dark of night, like ascending banks of church candles. Theirs was a world revealed by darkness, when their dogs barked and their drums spoke. In the daytime the Indians fell silent, and followed at a careful distance in their boats. These canoes were curious, collapsible little vessels, sewn together from tree bark and invariably split into three sections: women, children and dogs in the rear, the women paddling; men at the front, armed with sticks, stones, wooden spears or daggers, the points beaten from shipwrecked iron; and taking pride of place in the centre, the divine, unceasing fire on its bed of clay. Alongside the fire, invariably, green leaves would be piled high for making smoke signals, so that the *Beagle*'s progress was tracked and monitored by all as she passed slowly up the straits. Occasionally, naked men would come to the shore in brave little clusters, shouting the single word '*Yammerschooner!*' and waving ragged pieces of skin at the strangers; but whenever FitzRoy put down boats to establish contact, the Indians would flee into the trees long before the shore party made the beach.

These men were nothing like the 'noble savages' of Patagonia. They were short, round, oily creatures, four feet fully grown, who seemed to spend as much time in the icy water – which could not have been more than a degree or two above freezing – as they did on land. They could hold their breath for several minutes at a time, before emerging from the cold black depths with the mussels and sea-eggs that seemed to comprise the bulk of their diet. It was hard to connect them with any other tribe on earth. Indeed, they seemed more like porpoises than men. They were, thought FitzRoy, like a satire on humanity.

At Mount de la Cruz, in that part of the western straits that Cook had christened 'The Land of Desolation', they made contact. A group of men appeared furtively on the shore, waving skins and shouting, '*Yammerschooner!*' as ever. One was painted white all over, another blue, another bright red. The rest were daubed with white streaks. FitzRoy gave orders for the ship to pull in to shore. It had been sleeting heavily for days, her yards and rigging were icebound, and the men's fingers were blue with cold. The *Beagle* pirouetted slowly round, like a fat ballerina. Despite the temperature, the natives on the shore were quite naked, except for the occasional tattered fox pelt thrown about their shoulders.

Bennet squinted through a spyglass as the Indians began to jabber and gesticulate excitedly.

'My eye! That crimson fellow reminds me of the sign of the Red Lion on Holborn Hill.'

'Red, white and blue,' pointed out Kempe. 'They've run up the Union flag to greet us.'

'It looks a regular crush on that beach, my boys,' laughed Murray. 'Do you reckon that shore is Terra del's equivalent of a fashionable saloon?'

'And what would you know of fashionable saloons, Mr Murray, hailing from Glasgow?'

A chuckle ran around the poop deck.

'Do you think I could hit him from here?' pondered King, raising his gun to the port rail. 'That would light a fire under the red savage's tail!'

'Put that down!' snapped FitzRoy. He strode across the deck, eyes blazing, and grabbed the weapon. 'What the deuce do you think you're about?'

'I'm sorry, sir.' King was smarting, bewildered. 'I was only going to fire over his head, sir. You should see the savages scoot, sir, like ducks. It's funny, sir. Captain Stokes always permitted gun amusements, sir. I wasn't really going to shoot him, sir.'

'So I should think not. They are not animals, put on God's earth for our sport! I'm ashamed of you, Mr King.'

'But – but they ain't human, sir.'

'They most certainly are men, just as you or I. Unfortunate men, maybe, forced by accident of circumstance to inhabit this Godforsaken spot, but they are our brothers nonetheless. They do not look like us because their physiognomy has adapted itself to the cold and rain. Were I to cast you ashore, Mr King, and were the good Lord to take pity on your soul and spare your life, then within a generation or two your progeny would very likely be short, plump and jabbering away like the lowliest Fuegian.'

'But it doesn't mean anything – does it, sir? Those noises they make?'

'How do you know? To the best of my knowledge, no Dr Johnson has ever taken the trouble to compile a dictionary of their language. An omission I intend to remedy personally. Instead of waving a loaded gun about the maindeck, Mr King, you would be better advised to improve your intelligence of such matters. I suggest you consult the scriptures, commencing with the Book of Genesis.'

With that, FitzRoy turned on his heel and stalked away, leaving a silence both uneasy and amused in his wake.

'They say the bottle is a strict master,' murmured Lieutenant Kempe, 'but the good Lord is far stricter, and no easier to turn aside from.'

They put the boats down, but by the time they reached the shingle, the natives had fled. In a clearing amid the first few trees of the wood, they found abandoned wigwams: not the spindly, elegant constructions of the Patagonians, but clumsy, squat affairs made from branches, leaves, dung and rotten sealskins piled into rounds. Carefully, FitzRoy positioned two empty preserved meat canisters at the entrance to one of the tents, then withdrew.

The next few hours, all that remained of the short southern day, were spent climbing to the frost-shattered summit of Mount de la Cruz to survey the land around. Even though the peak was only two thousand feet above the shore, it was a hard slog. All of Tierra del Fuego's lowlands seemed to be covered by a deep bed of swampy peat: even in the forest, the ground was a thick, putrefying bog, overlaid with spongy moss and fallen trees, into which the party frequently sank up to their knees. Finally, they reached the sleet-scoured rock above the treeline, took their round of angles, and left a soldered canister – containing a crew list and a handful of British coins – beneath a cairn for posterity.

When they clambered back down to the beach, there was still no sign of the Fuegians, but the canisters were gone. FitzRoy took another two, placed them in the same location, and retreated to the edge of the clearing. Then, with the exception of Midshipman King, he sent the sailors back to the boats. With precautionary pistols loaded, he and King sat on their haunches, their breath condensing in the evening gloom, and waited silently for night to fall.

After a long, cold half-hour, the dark rectangles between the tree trunks were brought into focus by smoky torches. There was a whispering in the forest, a strange, guttural confection of clicks and throat-clearings. King, nervous, edged closer to FitzRoy. Finally, the red-painted man appeared at the far edge of the clearing, tentative, wary. They could see him better now. He had the eyes of a Chinee, black, slanted at an oblique angle to his nose, which was narrow at the bridge but flattened at the point, where his nostrils flared against his face. Beneath these two black holes his face was split in two by an exceptionally wide, full-lipped mouth. His teeth, bared in his nervousness, were flat and rotten, like those of a badly tended horse; no sharp canine points disturbed their even brown line. His chin was weak and small, and retreated into the thick muscular trunk of his neck. His shoulders were square, his upper body tremendously powerful under its broad coating of fat, weighing down on the short bow legs beneath it; his feet were turned inward, his toes levelled off in a perfect rectangle. As the Indian paused, considering flight, FitzRoy could see that the backs of his thighs were wrinkled like an old man's; presumably from a lifetime of squatting on his haunches. He was like no other creature, man or beast, that FitzRoy had ever seen.

The Fuegian advanced slowly and cautiously towards the two canisters, keeping his eyes on FitzRoy and King throughout, inching forward until his fingers closed on his prize. His fellows watched from behind tree trunks and flaming brands, poised for a general evacuation. But just as he was about to dart for the safety of the woods clutching his reward, FitzRoy spoke in a calm, clear voice: '*Yammerschooner*.'

The man bared his horse-teeth again, not from nerves, this time, but in a smile. Then he seized the two canisters and darted back a pace or two, but stayed poised there, half lit on the edge of the clearing.

Slowly FitzRoy extracted a box of Promethean matches from his pocket, with a small glass bottle containing the ignition mixture of asbestos and sulphuric acid. He unscrewed the lid and dipped the match head into the liquid. It ignited instantly, and a gasp ran round the clearing to see fire flare so mysteriously from one end of a tiny wooden stick. FitzRoy held the flaming Promethean aloft.

'*Yammerschooner*,' he repeated.

Curiosity overcame the red-painted man's fear, and he edged forward.

'Mr King,' whispered FitzRoy, 'do you have any tobacco about your person?'

'Yes sir.'

'Slowly now.'

Gingerly, King removed his tobacco pouch from his pocket, extracted a pinch and held it forward.

'*Tabac, tabac*,' said FitzRoy. It was a word the Patagonians had learned. Perhaps it had filtered this far south as well. Certainly the sight of the dried leaves seemed to interest the Fuegian. A few clicks with his tongue and he beckoned the white-painted man and his blue colleague into the clearing.

'He's got something in a sack, sir.'

The white-daubed Indian was indeed holding a sack sewn from animal skin, which appeared to be wriggling in his grasp. The man edged forward, gestured eagerly at King's full tobacco pouch, then opened the sack to reveal the wet eyes and bemused face of a month-old puppy. From the Indian's gestures it was clear that he wanted to trade.

'Shall I give him the tobacco, sir?'

'Well, we might benefit from a ship's dog. Why not?'

King poured the tobacco into the proffered sack, keeping the leather pouch back for himself, and took the puppy from the Fuegian by the scruff of its neck. There were friendly grins all round.

King, however, wrinkled his nose in disgust. 'The stench is frightful, sir.'

It was indeed. On close inspection, it became clear that the Indians, as well as decorating themselves in outlandishly bright colours, had smeared their naked bodies from head to toe with an insulating coat of rancid seal fat. King had to restrain the puppy from licking its former owners.

'Keep smiling, if you can bear to,' said FitzRoy, through a fixed grin.

The white-painted man gestured for the pair to enter the wigwam. King looked enquiringly at FitzRoy, who nodded, and they crawled beneath the tent-flap, into a close, dark world, which reeked of stale smoke and rotting sealskin. The men followed, extinguishing their flaming brands, and more men after them, then women and children, until the tent was heaving with Indians, and curious faces filled the triangle left at the open flap. Brushwood was brought, and before long the wigwam was filled with leaping flames and eye-watering clouds of smoke. Again, FitzRoy mounted a match-lighting demonstration to the amazed crowd, before making a present of box and bottle to the red-painted man.

'Prometheans,' he said.

'Prometheans,' repeated the Fuegian, remarkably accurately. FitzRoy placed a finger to his own chest.

'I am Captain FitzRoy.'

The red man pointed to his own chest and repeated gravely: 'I am Captain FitzRoy.' The watching crowd in turn indicated themselves and murmured that they, too, were Captain FitzRoy.

FitzRoy smiled, genuinely this time, and gestured to indicate King and himself. 'Englishmen,' he announced, and then, pointing to the red man, he added: 'Indian.'

'Englishmen,' repeated most of the Fuegians, each indicating his or her fellow, before pointing out FitzRoy and announcing, 'Indian.'

'Did you fetch the notebook?' FitzRoy asked King, whereupon a chorus of Fuegians also enquired whether King had fetched the notebook.

'They're first-rate mimics, sir. It's why nobody has ever learned their language,' King explained, handing the book across.

'Why nobody has ever learned their language,' added a small boy.

'They're first-rate mimics, sir. It's,' said a fat lady helpfully.

'Look,' said King, shoving a finger up one nostril and crossing his eyes.

'Look,' repeated the Fuegians, and every Indian in the tent pulled the same face.

'This is getting us nowhere,' sighed FitzRoy.

'This is getting us nowhere,' sighed the blue man.

So FitzRoy took the pen, and started to sketch a nearby woman instead. Eagerly, the Indians gathered round to look. A reverential silence settled upon the tent. Emboldened, FitzRoy produced his handkerchief and wiped the white streaks from the woman's face. She did not object, but adopted the air of a dignified hospital patient. When the sketch was finished, to general approbation, FitzRoy was rewarded by his model, who orna-mented his face with white streaks in turn. There were murmurs of approval all round.

Food was brought: mussels, sea-eggs, yellow tree-fungus and a huge slab of putrid elephant seal blubber two and a half inches thick. This last item reeked more fiercely – if such a thing were possible – than any of the inhabitants of the tent. The Fuegians took it in turns to heat the blubber on the fire until it crackled and bubbled, before drawing it through their teeth and squeezing out the rancid oil. Then the slab was passed on so that the next person might repeat the process, all of them expressing exaggerated delight at the richness of this delicacy. Finally, the blubber was offered to King.

'I would refrain from trying that if I were you, unless you wish to spend the next fortnight clutching your stomach in the heads,' remarked FitzRoy, to a chorus of imitations.

Both men politely declined the offer, which seemed to cause not the slightest offence. The blubber slab was passed instead to a small child, whose mother tried ineffectively to hack off a piece with a sharpened mussel shell. FitzRoy drew his knife and came to her assistance, an action that drew gasps of admiration – not for his gallantry but for the razor-sharp blade he had produced. Making beseeching noises, the white-painted Fuegian who had traded the dog for King's tobacco now indicated that he wished to have the knife as a gift. FitzRoy demurred: it would not do, he reasoned, to start arming the natives.

A general consultation followed, and with great reverence a wicker basket was produced for FitzRoy's benefit. He opened it. Inside was a sailor's old mitten, and a fragment of Guernsey frock.

'These are regular museum pieces,' breathed FitzRoy. 'They must be all of a century old.'

'I wouldn't give a farthing for them,' snorted King under his breath.

Encouraged by the apparent show of interest, the white-painted Indian patted his stomach enthusiastically, then patted FitzRoy's stomach and chest in a show of friendship, but to no avail. Still the Englishman would not trade. Rebuffed, the Indian left the tent in some dudgeon, whereupon the nocturnal silence outside was interrupted by curious thrashing and beating sounds, as if the would-be trader was laying about the nearby vegetation with a switch. After a minute or two he returned, flushed but evidently pleased with whatever he had done. FitzRoy and King were on the point of dismissing the episode as just one more of the evening's inexplicable curiosities, when the man suddenly lunged forward, grasped the knife from its sheath on FitzRoy's belt, and hurled himself at one wall of the tent. The skins on that side gave way immediately, and the white-painted man was gone, away into the night air by means of the passage he had just created. *Of course. How could I have been so foolish?* FitzRoy admonished himself. *He has built himself an escape route while we sat here like two idiots.*

The other Fuegians in the tent now flinched in fear, as if afraid that the Europeans might lash out and strike them, as a punishment for the misdeeds of their fellow. But so nonsensical was the whole episode that FitzRoy burst out laughing instead, as much at his own stupidity as at the antics of the thief.

'I think we can overlook the loss of one case-knife in the circumstances,' he conceded, and King concurred gratefully.

The evening had not delivered its last surprise, however. Within a quarter-hour the man had returned, painted black this time, his hair fluffed up wildly, and without a grass pleat that had previously functioned as a headband. FitzRoy, astonished, jutted out a hand to demand the return of his knife. Assuming an expression of aggrieved innocence, and with much headshaking and shoulder-shrugging, the Indian endeavoured to indicate that he had no idea what the Englishman was talking about.

'Extraordinary,' murmured FitzRoy to King. 'He thinks that this disguise – for such we must presume it – has fooled us thoroughly.'

'Extraordinary,' agreed a nearby woman.

'Fooled us thoroughly,' added the blue-painted man.

'They're like a crowd of little kids,' scoffed King.

The newly blackened Indian went on the attack now, shouting angrily at King, pointing at the puppy and demanding its return. He was sweating profusely in the fire-heat, FitzRoy noticed, as were all the Indians, even though they were naked and the outside temperature had dropped below freezing.

'I feel it would be best if you returned the dog,' he whispered to King.

'But the savage has got all my tobacco, sir.'

'On this occasion, the better part of valour is discretion. Let us take our leave.'

So they bade farewell to the assembled throng, and made their way down to the boats by moonlight, expertly parroted quotations from *Henry VI Part 2* ringing in their ears.

As winter had given way imperceptibly to spring, the *Beagle* had finally battled its way up to the Pacific, where the three boats had made a rendezvous once more. This time King had ordered the *Adelaide* north, to explore the galaxy of tiny islands which constituted the coast of Araucania, while the *Beagle* had been sent south, down the storm-beaten west coast of Tierra del Fuego, a maze of islets, rocks, cliffs and fierce breakers. Ceaselessly they probed for channels, close-working against the wind and tide amid howling blizzards; it was, as FitzRoy wrote in his log, 'like trying to do a jig-saw through a key-hole'. He had become as bearded, wiry and weatherbeaten as his crew, but he prided himself that their morale had stayed high, and that not one man had been lost to disease or sickness.

After the disaster of the Maldonado storm, the barometer and sympiesometer had proved reliable watchdogs, warning them to find sheltered anchorage ahead of the worst gales, and no further crew members had been lost to the elements. It was not the same, he knew, on board the other ships. Mr Alexander Millar of the *Adelaide* had died of inflammation of the bowels, and both vessels had as many as a quarter of their people in the sick lists. The *Beagle*'s only casualty had been Mr Murray, who had slipped on a wet deck and dislocated his shoulder, in a bay that had subsequently been named Dislocation Harbour; the master had since made a complete recovery.

Slowly the map of the west coast had taken shape. They had discovered Otway Bay, Stokes Bay, Lort Island, Kempe Island and Murray Passage, and had successfully climbed Mount Skyring, a peak discovered by the *Adelaide* in the Barbara Channel the previous winter. The rocks on the summit had been so magnetic as to render FitzRoy's compass useless; he had reason once more to regret the absence of a stratigrapher on board. What if there was mineral wealth waiting to be discovered in the mountains of Tierra del Fuego? There had been shell beds, too, on Mount Skyring. Was this further proof of the Biblical flood? As he dined in his cabin on soup and duff, the rain lashing against the skylight, he wrestled alone with these great questions.

January – high summer, although it was hard to discern any difference from the southern winter – had found the *Beagle* warping in and out of Desolate Bay; a risky process, with the ever-present danger of losing an anchor, but nonetheless safer than trying to close-manoeuvre a square-rigger in such a confined space. She had anchored at last in a narrow road, and boats had been sent out to survey the barren granite hills of Cape Desolation. FitzRoy and Stokes, their work done, had made it safely back to the ship. Now Murray and his men were missing. The search parties had found no sign of a sail. Had Murray struck a rock and drowned? To lose so many men…It simply did not bear thinking about. FitzRoy shivered, turned up his collar against the rain, shut his eyes momentarily against the stress, and steadied himself instinctively against the pitching of the deck. He headed for the companionway and the sanctuary of his cabin.

He was awakened just after six bells of the middle watch by his steward pounding on the door. 'By your leave, you'd better come quickly, sir. There's a sail.'

FitzRoy fumbled for his watch. Ten past three in the morning. He grabbed his uniform, struggled into it and made his way up on deck. On the port side of the ship, lookouts with lanterns were straining their eyes towards a tiny, indistinct shape in the water. It most certainly wasn't the whaleboat. It wasn't a native canoe either.

Boatswain Sorrell, who had charge of the middle watch, was directing operations with more agitation than ever; he seized upon the advent of FitzRoy's authority with conspicuous relief.

'I called, "What ship?" sir, but the wind was too loud for them to hear – leastways, they never replied.'

'Send up a night signal, Mr Sorrell. A flare.'

'Aye aye sir. Which signal, sir?'

'*Any* signal, Mr Sorrell. Something we can see them by,' said FitzRoy, exasperated.

A moment later, the flare went up.

'Bless my soul,' exclaimed FitzRoy.

There, fifty yards off the port bow in a choppy sea, was some kind of…basket, roughly assembled from branches, canvas and mud, half full of filthy water. Inside, drenched, emaciated and shaking with cold, were three white-clad figures. The man at the paddle FitzRoy recognized from his hair as Coxswain Bennet. The other men, bailing furiously with their south-westers, were two of the sailors – Morgan and Rix, by the look of it. They were clad only in their flimsy cotton undershirts. How the ramshackle vessel had ever made it on to water at all, let alone half a mile out into the bay, was a complete mystery.

'Hoist out the cutter at once!'

'Aye aye sir!'

A burst of frenzied activity followed, and within five minutes FitzRoy was lifting the sodden, exhausted men aboard personally. Blankets were furled round them, and hot soup forced between chattering teeth. Concerned as he was, it was clear that FitzRoy could not afford to waste a second.

'What happened, Mr Bennet? Where is Mr Murray?'

'We were attacked, sir, by the savages. They stole the whaleboat in the night, with its masts, sails and all our provisions and weapons. Their vicinity was not at all suspected.'

'Were not lookouts posted, as I ordered?'

'I repeat, sir, that their vicinity was not at all suspected. Cape Desolation is a most remote location. They showed a most dexterous cunning, sir.'

'And this – this basket?'

'Morgan is from Wales, sir. They sail such baskets on the rivers there.'

'We call it a coracle, sir,' chipped in Morgan.

'Morgan constructed it from a canvas tent and some branches and mud. We volunteered to paddle it back to the *Beagle*, sir, but we were attacked by more savages – maybe the same ones, I don't know. They were armed with spears, and took our clothes. We have been two days and nights on our passage, sir, with only one biscuit each.'

'Good God, you poor wretches. But where are Mr Murray and the rest of the men?'

'Still at Cape Desolation, sir.'

'Then they must be rescued at once. Morgan, you have my congratulations and my heartiest thanks. And now we must get the three of you to the surgeon forthwith.'

Within a quarter-hour, the cutter had been fitted out with a fortnight's provisions, two tents, six armed marines and five hand-picked sailors: Robinson, Borsworthwick, Elsmore, White and Gilly, who had become the stoutest of loyalists since his first-day flogging. They pushed off at once, just as a few early grey streaks pointed up the horizon, into a dreary maze of splintered islets and black, surf-battered headlands. The wind being against them, they did not even try running up a sail: instead, seven hours' hard pull found them off the Cape, where the stranded survey party was easily spotted, huddled together on a cheerless beach. An almighty roar went up from the rescued men at the familiar sight of the cutter, and within a few minutes they, too, were being treated to soup and blankets.

The marines, meanwhile, fanned out and searched the island for the stolen whaleboat. They found deserted wigwams, a smouldering fire and half of the whaleboat's mast, which appeared to have been chopped apart with the boat's own axe. Perhaps inevitably, they found no other trace of the thieves or their prize.

'I'll order the surveying equipment stowed on board the cutter, shall I, sir?' enquired Murray cautiously, still unsure whether or not any blame was to be apportioned.

'That won't be necessary. The second whaleboat will be here soon, to furnish your passage back to the *Beagle*.'

'But what about the cutter, sir?'

'The cutter and its full complement, Mr Murray, is to go in search of the whaleboat that you have mislaid.'

Sarcasm aside, FitzRoy had decided not to pursue Murray's failure to post sentries. The missing whaleboat, however, was not a matter he could easily overlook.

'But it could be anywhere, sir. You may never find it in such a labyrinth. It may well have been scuttled until we've gone, or chopped up for firewood.'

'It is our duty to try. That boat is the property of His Majesty, which has been entrusted to our safe-keeping. Without it our surveying capacity is cut by one-third. Furthermore, it is our duty as emissaries of a civilized nation to teach these people the difference between right and wrong. We cannot simply sail away and let them keep it.'

'But there must be upwards of a hundred islands hereabouts, sir. We haven't even named most of them.'

'Then we shall remedy that omission on our passage. Have you christened this island yet?'

'No, sir.'

'Then we shall call it "Basket Island", in honour of Morgan's ingenuity.'

'Right sir. If you please sir – may I have your permission to accompany the search party?'

Murray was clearly exhausted, but if he wanted to atone for losing the whaleboat, fair enough.

'Permission granted, Mr Murray.'

Late afternoon found FitzRoy's party heading north-east across Desolate Bay, in the direction taken by Bennet's attackers. They made good progress, the sail filled out by a blustery breeze chasing in from the sea behind them. Ahead in the distance, the bay narrowed into a sound, a line of islands marking its north-western boundary. Behind these to the north rose ranks of snow-capped peaks, smothered for the most part by cloud; hidden somewhere among them was the mighty southern face of Mount Sarmiento. The cutter headed for the northern shore. The thieves were unlikely to hide on one of the outlying islands, FitzRoy reasoned, because their retreat might be cut off. More likely, they would have taken refuge in some cove or inlet. Murray and some of the others might have been sceptical of his plan, but with the cold spray biting his face, FitzRoy felt seized with optimism. The anxiety that the survey party might be dead had given way to a burst of exhilaration. This was, after all, why he had joined the Service as a child. Mapmaking was all very well, but he was twenty-four years old and – if one did not count the boarding of a rotting Brazilian gunship – he had never seen action. This might be his chance. His fingers closed instinctively around the pistol handle at his belt.

'There's a canoe up ahead, sir. They're making a run for it.'

The small black shape of a native canoe was visible against the grey hummocks of the islands off the port side. It was paddling for the safety of the shore with all haste; but the cutter's full sail and six enthusiastic oarsmen made for an unequal contest. The fact that the canoe was fleeing suggested to the pursuers that they had struck lucky right away. Within twenty minutes they had run her down, guns and swords arrayed in a powerful display, and had made the flimsy bark vessel fast to their own.

Inside the canoe sat a Fuegian family, sullen, unmoving, staring at the European sailors. One of the women in the rear section was breastfeeding. It had begun to snow, thick white crystals whipping in on the breeze and melting against the sailors' faces. FitzRoy noticed that the snow did not dissolve on the Fuegians' skins: mother and child sat in a mute tableau, a white mantle slowly forming on the woman's breasts and the child's face.

'Search the vessel, Serjeant Baxter.'

Baxter and two of his marines stepped into the canoe, sending it wildly rocking, and poked with their rifles into mounds of mussel shells, brushwood and rotten seal meat. One sent the fireside pile of green leaves flying.

Silently intimidated, the Indians did not move. Hidden in the base of the leaf-pile was a curled section of the whaleboat's leadline.

'Well, well, well,' said FitzRoy.

'Well, well, well,' said one of the Fuegians helpfully, the first time that any of them had spoken. FitzRoy ignored him.

'We will take a hostage, Serjeant Baxter. It is what Captain Cook did when his cutter was stolen in the Pacific, and the boat was returned. Take one of the young men, who has no dependent wife or children.' He pointed out the youth on the near side of the canoe. 'Let him be given to understand that he must lead us to the whaleboat, if he values his liberty.'

With various gestures, mainly of the cut-throat variety, and much waving of the severed end of the leadline, the young man was given to understand that he had better co-operate. With a disarming eagerness, he climbed aboard and waved his captors north, between the row of islands, to a narrower, more confined sound that ran parallel to the first.

As they sailed into the unknown, a rough map began to assemble itself in their wake, its legends bearing hasty and literal witness to their passage: Whaleboat Sound, Cape Long Chase, Leadline Island, Thieves Sound. Finally, in the gloom of the mid-evening, spurred on by their eager hostage guide, they rounded a promontory and found themselves in full view of a small Indian village: a cluster of wigwams, men warming seal blubber around a circle of glowing embers, a woman carrying water in a bark bucket, another sewing together two sealskins, children playing naked in the icy shallows. The cutter was upon the unwitting villagers almost before they had realized it. The men round the fire were first to react, jumping to their feet and fleeing into the beech forest. A small child ran terrified towards its mother, who seemed torn between flight and the pull of maternity. As the boat slid rapidly through the shallows, the red-jacketed marines were already over the side and splashing through the low breakers in pursuit. The woman fled. The child began to scream, incessantly, standing forlornly in six inches of cold water.

'Are they not going in too heavy-handed, sir?' said Murray, who looked worried. 'We don't even know if these people had anything to do with the theft.'

There was a warning glint in FitzRoy's eye. 'Justice is not always pretty, Mr Murray. One of the reasons these people live in such a degraded state is that they seem to have no laws. Not even the law of God – any sort of god. If we do not teach them the difference between right and wrong, then who will do so?'

Murray remained silent. There was something odd about the captain – something not quite right.

After five minutes, the marines had secured the beach, their final tally of prisoners totted up at six women, three children – including the screaming infant – and a man apprehended sleeping in his tent. They had also discovered part of the whaleboat's sail, the boat's axe and tool-bag, an oar – already refashioned into a short paddle – and the loom, roughly carved now into a seal club. FitzRoy indicated the lone male, who was squatting on his haunches, cowed and unsure.

'We appear to have apprehended one of the miscreants, and six of their wives. Take that man hostage. He is to be our second guide. We shall embark immediately.'

'Don't you think we should pitch camp ourselves, sir? It is practically dark.'

'You would do well to keep your counsel, Mr Murray.'

Again Murray saw the strange light in FitzRoy's eye, and did as he was bidden.

Led now by two mysteriously enthusiastic guides instead of one, both grinning and gesticulating to the sailors to continue rowing north-east, the exhausted party reached the head of Thieves Sound just after night-fall. They had been battling the elements now for almost eighteen hours. Two tents were wearily improvised using the boat's sails, oars and a boat hook. The two hostages were invited to sleep on the shingle, under a tarpaulin that Murray had given them. FitzRoy, though, could not sleep: he felt alert and alive and suffused with excitement. Odd sensations stirred through his muscles and across his skin, as if his body was no longer his own. He paced the beach until dawn broke, listening to the waves lapping loud against the stones, turning over possible courses of action in his mind. At five o'clock, as the western hills took on the faintest rosy halo, he ordered the marine sentries to wake the sleeping sailors and the two hostages.

A moment or two later, as he stood staring fixedly out into the sound, there was an embarrassed cough behind him. It was one of the marine sentries. 'Sir. The prisoners have escaped, sir.'

'What?'

'The prisoners. They've escaped, sir.'

'I heard you the first time.'

FitzRoy strode angrily up the beach and threw back the tarpaulin. Two roughly human-sized mounds of stones were positioned where the two Fuegians had lain the previous night. Murray and Serjeant Baxter emerged blearily from the tent, just in time to inspect the damage.

'Serjeant Baxter, I thought I gave orders for night sentries to be posted.'

'I posted them, sir.'

'Then why were two Indians able to get up and walk away under their very noses, after first constructing these – these simulacrums?'

'I don't know, sir.'

Baxter looked daggers at the two sentries.

'And as for your confounded tarpaulin, Mr Murray, it became a cloak for all evils.'

'Were you not awake yourself, sir? Did you see nothing during the night?'

'You are insolent, Mr Murray!' snapped FitzRoy, eyeball to eyeball with the master. 'Hold your tongue or I shall have you flogged like a common sailor!'

There was a shocked silence. The wind tugged mischievously at the corner of the tarpaulin. The captain, it seemed, was a changed man.

'Pack and stow the tents. We shall embark in ten minutes. We shall return to the village forthwith.'

After four hours' hard rowing, the hungry sailors found themselves back at the Indian settlement, but it was deserted. FitzRoy himself felt no hunger, no exhaustion. He felt guided by instinct now, or by some unseen force, as if the world itself was leading him. It was as if he could see himself from the air, moving forward decisively, with conviction. Optimism roared within him. *It is my duty to do the right thing. My sacred duty. I must not fail. I simply must not fail in my duty.*

Three canoes lay drawn up on the beach.

'Burn their canoes. Then spread out and search the vicinity. We must find them.'

Silently, the odd exchanged glance their only sign of apprehension, the sailors and marines fanned out through the ragged beech forest.

After twenty minutes' walk, the trees thinned and gave way to a slope of rain-soaked bare rock criss-crossed with crevices and gullies. By signals and gestures, one of the marines indicated that he had seen something ahead. About eighty yards in front, a thin plume of smoke was drifting from a fissure in the rock. FitzRoy felt all his senses tensed, intensified, accelerated. *Others will one day see the path we have taken. They will chart the angles and shapes our footsteps have made, as surely as we chart the bays and islands. They will see that we have followed the only path.*

He called the search party together. 'They have taken refuge in that cave. We will attack them immediately. Robinson, Borsworthwick and Gilly, make your way to the right of the cave. Elsmore, White and Murray to the left. When you are in position, you will lay down an enfilade, whereupon the marines will launch a frontal assault. Make all haste.'

With pistols and cutlasses drawn, the sailors moved forward in their two groups, keeping to the concealment of the forest edge as closely as possible. About fifty yards on, however, a ferocious barking announced that they had been spotted, by the Fuegians' dogs if not by the Fuegians themselves. Some of the sailors shot questioning glances across to FitzRoy, who beckoned them urgently to proceed. Still there was no sign of life from the mouth of the cave. Fifty yards further, and the left-hand party found their progress blocked by a rushing stream some ten feet across, edged with muddy banks. FitzRoy beckoned them to cross. Seaman Elsmore, who was the foremost of the party, took a running jump in an effort to clear the stream at one bound, but lost his footing on the far bank and slithered back into the water. As he tried to claw himself back up the slope, his fingers dug helplessly into the slippery mud. Suddenly two squat figures appeared from behind nearby rocks, then another, and another. Clutching large, sharp stones as weapons, they fell upon Elsmore, raining blows upon his head. As he fought to free himself, a huge stone was brought down two-handed into his eye-socket, which disappeared in a welter of blood. Insensible, his body was held under water by two of the Indians. The others continued to batter him, crimson bubbles marking the last of the air leaving his lungs.

At the moment that Elsmore had been attacked, FitzRoy had raised his loaded pistol and fired. *God has brought us here. This is our destiny. We must not fail Him.* But the weapon had missed fire: the powder, soaked through on the journey, had failed to burn. The Fuegian with the large rock raised it above his head again, ready to administer the fatal blow. Then, there was a deafening powder explosion and the man staggered back, a look of complete astonishment on his face. Murray had shot him clean through the heart. But he did not drop his rock. Somehow, with speed, precision and a strength that appeared positively superhuman to his European adversaries, he hurled the stone straight at Murray. The blow knocked the master off his feet, and shattered the powder-horn that hung from his neck. It was the Fuegian's last act: abruptly, he pitched forward into the stream, dead before he hit the water. White was the first to arrive on the scene, pulling Elsmore back up the bank, cushioning his shattered face in his lap. Murray, only seconds behind, lifted the head of the dead Fuegian from the water by his hair. It was the second of the two hostages to whom he had given the tarpaulin the previous evening.

By now the other Indians were streaming out of the cave in fear, having witnessed the inexplicable and sudden death of one of their number. FitzRoy urged the marines forward, their weapons no longer necessary. Instead they fought to subdue the terrified Fuegians, who struggled with extraordinary strength. FitzRoy and Serjeant Baxter grappled with one slippery, brawny, barrel-bodied specimen, who – upon finally being manhandled to the ground, face flushed, eyes blazing – turned out to be a young woman of some seventeen years. Within a few minutes the contest was over, the majority of the Fuegians fleeing unhindered into the beech forest. There were eleven prisoners: two men, three women, and six children. The trophy count was far less impressive than before: merely a piece of the whaleboat's tarpaulin, vandalized into small squares to no discernible purpose.

Breathing hard, his uniform ripped, FitzRoy ordered the prisoners to be frogmarched down to the cutter.

'We will take the women and children on board the *Beagle* as hostages. Then the men will guide us to our missing whaleboat. The custody of their families will act as a security far stronger than rope or iron.'

The next morning the *Beagle* headed back south, out through the jaws of Desolate Bay, and round to Cape Castlereagh on the wave-lashed tip of Stewart Island. Fat, placid and apparently unperturbed in the sleeting rain, a gaggle of Fuegian women and children sat on the maindeck, gorging themselves on fatty pork and shellfish, swaddled in woollen blankets. They seemed profoundly undisturbed by the change in their surroundings, be it the staring Europeans or the waves that occasionally swirled among them, soaking their legs and haunches. At the prow the two male 'guides', as eager as their predecessors, urged the ship on with enthusiastic gestures and hand signals, apparently oblivious of the glorious mass of billowing sails above their heads. Crew members stood around bemused, unsure how to react to the invasion. Surveying operations, which had been carried out by Stokes in FitzRoy's absence, had now been suspended. Both the cutter and the remaining whaleboat were provisioned for a week, and ready to embark at a moment's notice. Lieutenant Kempe, who had charge of the forenoon watch, had assumed control of the *Beagle*'s steerage. FitzRoy, isolated, seemingly unable to communicate with anyone, paced the poop deck, a lonely figure grappling with his thoughts. *I must do the right thing by God. He has brought me to this place to do His will. I am not of Him, but He has created me. It is my duty to administer justice. To distinguish between right and wrong.*

They put the cutter and the whaleboat into the water in bitter drizzle at Cape Castlereagh, FitzRoy and Bennet in the former, Murray commanding the latter. Led by their two willing guides they came upon a scattering of deserted wigwams just before nightfall, the native fires still smouldering, and were rewarded with a small prize in the shape of the remaining half of the leadline. They erected their makeshift tents on the shore once more, their Indian guides wrapped in blankets on the beach beneath the open sky. This time FitzRoy did not pace the shoreline, but lay awake in one of the makeshift tents, wrestling with his disembodied thoughts. *I am doing the right thing. I am the only one who realizes this.*

At three o'clock he rose and left the tent, knowing that the Indians would be gone. Sure enough, two mounds of round stones lay under the blankets on the beach. He stood there, staring at the piles of stones and the thrown-back blankets, his senses crackling like sheet-lightning, every nerve-end tingling. The end of his journey to salvation was near now. He could sense it. Gradually, he became aware of a presence behind him. It was Murray.

'Mr Murray. Did I not order a watch to be posted over the prisoners?'

'No...you did not, sir.'

Neither man said a word. Finally, after a long interval, FitzRoy spoke: 'We must return to the *Beagle*.'

'Aye aye sir.'

Murray was looking at him oddly, FitzRoy could see that. Did the man not understand? Could he not see God's holy truth, staring him in the face?

The journey back passed in silence. The men at the oars were going through the motions now, rowing blindly and mechanically. Visibility was poor, and rain drove horizontally and ceaselessly into their backs and down their necks. It was a tired, sad and confused party that sighted the

Beagle late on in the forenoon watch, a day after they had left it. Boatswain Sorrell came to the side, a look of woe on his face.

'Mr Bos'n. What news of your prisoners?'

'They are gone, sir. All except one, sir.'

'Gone? Gone where? We are in the middle of the ocean!'

'Gone over the side, sir. All three women and five of the children. Gone over the side like porpoises in the night, sir.'

FitzRoy grasped a manrope in each hand, and scaled the wooden battens on the *Beagle's* heaving flank with uncommon agility. He hauled himself on to the deck and stood face to face with the quivering boatswain.

Lieutenant Kempe came across to intervene. 'There was nothing anyone could do to stop them, sir.'

FitzRoy looked at Kempe, and realized that his eyesight had become crystal clear. He could see the skin on Kempe's cheek, and the tiny lines on its surface in all their minute detail. All around him, the colours of the world were now so rich and deep that they seemed to resonate inside him.

'Don't you understand?' said FitzRoy.

Don't you understand? God has brought us here and announced to me my destiny. He has re-created me, an ordinary man, in His image. He has re-created me after His likeness. Can you not see that, Mr Kempe? Can you not see that?

The inside of the cabin was dark and silent. A faint rattling and creaking indicated that the ship was still at anchor. FitzRoy stirred. The worst of the night's terror had drained away now. Fear and dread had come in the dark, had choked him and mocked him, tugging his emotions this way and that, playing with him like a bird of prey with a mouse. But now they were gone, and shame and embarrassment flooded his mind, together with a terrible, crushing disappointment that the tiny glimpse he had been given, of something infinitely strange and wonderful, was now snatched away from him for ever. He opened half an eye, and the grimy skylight blurred into focus. He realized that a blanket had been laid over the outside, to keep his cabin dark. How long had he been lying there?

How long had his madness lasted? The events of the previous days came flooding back now in all their hideous detail. *Dear Lord, what sickness possessed me? Please, God, what damage have I done?*

There was a knock at the door, and Stokes came in with a bowl of soup. FitzRoy shifted in the fusty darkness, uncoiling his stiff limbs within the frame of his tiny cot. After a moment or two he tried to speak. 'I have not been well.'

'No, you haven't.'

FitzRoy was glad that Stokes had abandoned the due military formalities for the moment.

'How came I here?'

'The coxswain and I fetched you. You was not right in yourself.'

'How long have I been here?'

'About thirty hours.'

'Is everything under control?'

'Everything is under control.'

'What news of Seaman Elsmore?'

'He will lose the sight of one eye, but he will not drop off the hooks. He is recovering of his wounds.'

'And the whaleboat?'

'We shall never see it again.'

What madness to think otherwise, FitzRoy realized.

'Am I better now?'

'I can fetch the surgeon if you so wish, but I would reason from your questioning that, yes, you are better now.'

'To whom do I owe apologies?'

'You are the captain. You do not *owe* apologies to anyone. If you so prefer it, you might have conciliatory words with Mr Murray, Mr Kempe, the bos'n...'

'Thank you.'

FitzRoy swung his feet gingerly to the floor. Every muscle in his body ached as if it had been pummelled repeatedly. Stokes raised a hand in mild protest. 'Do you not think it would be better to rest further? This kind of delusional fit...the surgeon seemed to think you might need a considerable period of rest.'

'No...no thank you, Mr Stokes. I feel that the madness is now behind me. But thank you most humbly for your kindness.'

Feeling grubby and sticky-eyed, FitzRoy pushed past Stokes and opened his cabin door. A marine sentry stood to attention, his expressionless face speaking volumes. FitzRoy inched unsteadily up the companionway and out on to the maindeck. A hushed silence greeted his appearance. Crewmen seemed to give ground imperceptibly as he made his way forward to the cluster of officers gathered at the wheel. Kempe was there, and King, and Murray, and Boatswain Sorrell.

'Mr Bos'n. It seems I owe you an apology.'

Sorrell bobbed unhappily. 'Not a bit of it, sir, not a bit of it. You was just unwell, that's all.'

'Mr Murray.'

'No trouble sir. As the bos'n said, sir. The south is tough on a man, sir.'

'Mr Kempe.'

'Please don't mention it, sir.' Kempe smiled his half-smile.

'I understand, Mr Kempe, that you have been in control of the *Beagle* during my absence. I am much obliged. I owe you a vote of thanks.'

'My privilege sir.'

'She has handled well?'

'She has handled well, sir.' Kempe paused. Whether he was enjoying the moment or was disturbed by it, FitzRoy could not tell. But there was evidently something more. 'Just one small matter to be resolved, sir.'

'Yes, Mr Kempe?'

'What are we to do with *her*, sir?'

Kempe gestured towards the binnacle box. There, playing happily with a makeshift rag doll, a wide, appealing smile on her face, sat the rotund figure of an eleven-year-old Indian girl.

CHAPTER SIX

York Minster, Tierra del Fuego, 3 March 1830

'How are you feeling?' Surgeon Wilson leaned forward, narrowing the gap between them, shepherding as much sympathy and confidentiality as he could into the intervening space.

FitzRoy thought hard about the question. 'This morning...not very bad.'

Not very bad? Not very bad, when I must consider making an invalid of myself and resigning my command? Not very bad, when I have taken leave of my senses, when I have endangered my ship and risked the lives of its crew? Not very bad?

'Well, physically, Commander, I would say you are in extremely good keep.'

Indeed he was. FitzRoy's physical strength had never been in doubt. But it was no sort of weapon against whatever had assailed him, first a year and a half ago in the Brazilian sunshine and now here in the Stygian south. The original attack, back in his flag officer days, had been allowed to slip unlamented into the past, dismissed as an isolated incident, a mere oddity. But the wheels of time had now crunched suddenly to a halt, as if paralysed by fear: not just the constricting, terrifying panic that had served as the climax to each of the two attacks, but a groundswell of dread in the pit of his stomach that he knew would remain with him as long as he lived. Something primeval lurked inside him, something that frightened him because he did not know if he could ever exert authority over it. He had travelled to Tierra del Fuego to chart the wilderness, to list it and catalogue it, that it might be tamed and civilized; to bring the primordial darkness under control. But what of the darkness inside him, which waxed and waned and flexed its strength seemingly at will? Was that to be tamed? And what of the good Lord? Would God be his beacon against the darkness? Or was God punishing him for his presumption? Was this perhaps some sort of test, an examination of his faith? Had the darkness indeed been created by the light? He wondered if this was how Captain Stokes had felt, alone and afraid at the *Beagle*'s helm, rendered small and puny in the face of the mute, prehistoric wilderness all around, the deep-tangled forest that threatened to envelop him and pull him down into its consuming maw. *Please help me. Please help me, God. If not for me then for the sake of my men.*

'And you say you had no warning of the attack?'

'None. It took me quite by the lee.'

Wilson pursed his lips in a suitably diagnostic manner. A column of smoke from his pipe spiralled aristocratically towards the low ceiling of FitzRoy's cabin. But despite the surgeon's stiff-backed manner and the prematurely greying hair that lent an air of dignity to his prognostications, his rumpled and frayed uniform gave away the fact that he was anything but a medical expert at the top of his profession. This was a career naval surgeon going through the motions. FitzRoy did not hold out much hope of a cure. He felt, nonetheless, that he should ask the question that mattered most. 'I wonder if my illness will not unfit me for my command.'

'My goodness, no. This kind of morbid depression of the spirits is not unheard-of here in the south. Why, only last week one of the crew thought he had seen the devil. It turned out to be a horned owl. I have been a surgeon since ten years, and if I had a guinea for every time a man found himself in the dismals I'd be a rich man. No, Commander, we'll soon have you right as a trivet.' Wilson held his pipe at what he hoped was a reassuring angle to his teeth.

He hasn't got a clue how to deal with this, any more than I have. 'Well, Mr Wilson, I've dipped into my phrenology manual and tried a little self-examination in the mirror, but it's an infernally difficult and delicate business.'

The surgeon digested this information with a condescending smile. 'Ah, yes. They do say craniology is all the rage in London. I've never been a bumpologist myself. Bone up on this or that, and before one knows it, some other technique is in fashion. You know, I prefer to rely on more tried and tested prescriptions. My recommendation, Commander, is that you drink a glass of hot wine well qualified with brandy and spice twice a day, once upon waking and once before sleeping. Then I'd like you to take a Seidlitz powder with calomel after every meal. In due course, I think you'll find the purgative effect will rid you of all the impurities that have accumulated in your blood vessels during the course of the voyage.'

Seidlitz powders. Calomel. The basic, unthinking cure-alls in the top drawer of every journeyman apothecary.

'Will that be all, sir?'

'Yes, thank you, Mr Wilson. You oblige me with your kindness. I am most grateful to enjoy the benefits of your medical wisdom.'

Wilson ushered himself out. FitzRoy stood for a moment by the skylight, pensively. Then, in a moment of decision, he took the purgative powders and the companion phial of liquid that Wilson had left behind and emptied them into the icy shallows of the wash-hand basin.

The immense perpendicular tower of rock, named York Minster by Captain Cook for its uncanny resemblance to the celebrated cathedral, loomed threateningly over the port bow. Eight hundred feet high, jet black and guarded by lesser spires, it reared out of the sea, devouring all the dismal daylight it could and reflecting nothing back by return. FitzRoy took care to stand the *Beagle* well out to sea, despite the invitingly calm look of the waters at the base of the tower. Experience had taught him to avoid 'williwaws', the sudden hurricane squalls that could rush over the edge of a precipice, carrying with them a dense flurry of spray, leaves and dirt. Before one had time to react, a ship could be over on her beam ends, in the middle of a previously placid harbour. In fact they had lost their best bower anchor in yet another gale in Adventure Passage, the ship pitching bows under; but this storm had been accurately foretold by the barometer, so they had shortened sail by degrees in the face of its advance. The topmasts and yards had been struck well before the worst of the weather had hit, and there had been no further damage. The quietly ingen-ious carpenter, May, had even moulded a replacement anchor, in a home-made forge below decks. Subsequently, upon finding a large shipwreck spar thrown up on the shoreline, the carpenter had demanded to be left on a beach in Christmas Sound with a party of sailors, where he intended to construct a replacement whaleboat too – the local beechwood apparently leaving much to be desired as a boat-building material. FitzRoy could only marvel at the man's craftsmanship and utility.

Standing now on the raised poop, the captain scrutinized the torn, choppy sea in their path. About a hundred yards dead ahead, there sat a solitary Indian canoe, seemingly impervious to the waves that tossed it up and down, to all intents and purposes waiting calmly for the *Beagle* to run it down. He could just make out the occupants as they rose and fell, by turns visible and invisible behind the grey ridges of seawater. Was this to be a sequel to the episode of the stolen whaleboat? Or had the eighty miles of close-worked sailing they had put in since Desolate Bay taken them into another part of the Fuegian nation, where news of their running battles with the Indians had yet to percolate?

Any sense of relief that FitzRoy might have entertained at the prospect of putting that episode behind him were promptly punctured by the sound of a childish giggle at his feet. There, smiling coyly up at him, was the little round Fuegian girl, an ever-present reminder of his aberration. Her face was freshly scrubbed, her hair had been cleaned and tied in two neat bunches, and she wore a rather fetching patchwork dress, which had been fashioned by one of the seamen from rags found at the bottom of the slops basket.

'Shall I carry her below, sir? Is she getting in your way?' Boatswain Sorrell reached a hand down affectionately to the little girl.

'No, no, thank you, she's fine where she is. It is no trouble.'

'She's become a regular pet on the lower deck, sir. The men call her Fuegia Basket, sir, on account of Morgan's sailing basket.'

'Yes, I had heard that. It rather suits her. Has she picked up any English yet?'

'Not so as I could say, sir, but she can repeat anything you like straight back at you. She knows her lines as regular as a prayer-and-response.'

'Make sure everybody keeps trying. Then I'm sure she will soon get in the way of it.'

'Very good sir. She's a sweet little thing, sir, seeing as how them's little more than animals.'

'Quite so, Mr Bos'n.'

FitzRoy decided to let the comment pass. He had in fact been side-tracked by a sudden blinding realization: that in all his dealings with the Fuegian race, stretching back the better part of a year now, he had not seen a single old man or woman. Every Fuegian they had encountered was young, strong and fit. Where were all the elderly people? Where were all the cripples, the invalids, the mental defectives? Were they simply unable to survive the harsh southern winters? Or was the answer more sinister than that? He glanced down at the gurgling, happy little girl at his feet once more, as if to read her mind, but she just beamed sweetly back at him.

By now the lone canoe was no more than ten yards ahead of the *Beagle*'s prow. With a few deft paddle-strokes the natives within brought her along-side, hauling on the *Beagle*'s manropes to make her fast. The sturdiest and tallest of the Fuegians, a relative giant at some five feet tall, climbed out of the canoe, scaled the battens on the ship's side and stepped on to the deck. At once his fellows detached their grip on the ropes, and their canoe sheered off to starboard. The man stood stock still, the cynosure of all eyes, a primitive, feral visitation in the centre of the maindeck. Powerful, brooding and quite naked, with arms and legs like tree trunks, he stared around him through narrowed eyes. He exuded physical confidence. FitzRoy felt the hairs at the nape of his neck rise instinctively. *Who is the animal now?* he thought.

'Do we take paying passengers, then?' asked King, coolly.

'Place is turning into a regular menagerie,' mumbled the boatswain to himself, disapprovingly.

Fuegia Basket was the first person to move. Clutching up her skirts, she skittered across the maindeck and presented herself to the visitor. Giggling with delight she spoke, the first time she had done so in her own language, with the now-familiar concoction of guttural clicks and throaty noises. Poised motionless, holding himself rigid with a solemn muscular reserve, the stranger replied: a slow, low, brutal voice, the words obviously selected with caution and delivered with exactitude. Fuegia Basket's eyes widened in response, and there was a second's pause. Then, suddenly, she threw back her head and erupted in a peal of laughter, turning delightedly to share her merriment with the watching crew.

FitzRoy kept his eyes on the new arrival. The man's expression remained as unmoving as stone.

On a height above Christmas Sound, reading angles, FitzRoy was able to take in the sheer impossibility of his task: a hundred peaks, a thousand caves, a million tiny shards of rock flung into the sea. The subtle undulations of the land were obscured by thick beech forest, no riot of vegetation but a slow, dull march, close-ranked and impenetrable. Metronomically accurate now in his map-making observations, not so much immune to the cold as habituated to it, he allowed his thoughts to drift to the *Beagle*'s two new acquisitions. The male Indian, named York Minster by the crew after the location where he had boarded the ship, could not have been more different from little Fuegia. Sullen and taciturn, he continued to say nothing, but FitzRoy could tell that he was watchful. His eyes were as restless as his posture was immobile. In particular he watched after the girl, his narrow gaze never once leaving her as she skipped about the decks. She would dance merrily with the crew in the evenings, or play with her makeshift dolls, a whole family now sewn together from rags by some kind soul. All the while his eyes would bore into her back from his squatting position up by the foremast chimney grating, where he stored his uneaten food like some big cat back from the prowl. It seemed to FitzRoy that York's was an intelligent gaze; whether this was conventional intelligence of the European kind, or merely low animal cunning, it was hard to tell. Certainly, dressed as he was now in the slops and ducks of the common sailor, York Minster could have passed at first glance for an unusually short and stout member of the crew. His immense physical strength, though, marked him out from the others. Challenged to arm-wrestling matches, he was – once he understood what was required of him – easily a match for any two of the sailors put together.

FitzRoy could tell from York and Fuegia's chatter, from the way that new sensations stimulated them to communicate with each other in their strange clicking language, that some kind of shared reasoning power united these two disparate characters. He felt enormously frustrated by the limits to his understanding. *There is less difference between most nations or tribes than exists between these two individuals. If I could help to prove that all men are of one blood, what a difference it would make.*

He had consulted Captain Stokes's copy of the *Dictionnaire Classique*, which divided men into thirteen distinct races, but to no purpose. The book marked Tierra del Fuego down, quite erroneously, as a Negroid area. Nobody, it seemed, had ever deigned to study the curious inhabitants of South America's southern tip. Cracking the code of language, FitzRoy knew, would be the key. Unfortunately, York would not talk to any of the sailors. Fuegia would only parrot English with a wide, beaming smile. But they did speak to each other: already he had identified a noise like the clucking of a hen as 'no'.

So long as we are ignorant of the Fuegian language, and so long as the natives are equally ignorant of ours, we will never know about them, or their society, or their culture. Without such an understanding, there is not the slightest chance of their being raised one step above the low place which they currently hold in our imaginations.

And then, on that wild, lonely peak above Christmas Sound, FitzRoy was struck by a big, beautiful idea.

If I carry a party of Fuegians to England, if I acquaint them with our language, and our habits and customs, if I procure for them a suitable education, and equip them with a stock of articles useful to them, if I return them safely to their own country; then they and their fellows will surely be raised from the brute condition in which they find themselves. They can spread their knowledge among their countrymen – the use of tools, clothes, the wheel! It could even be the start of a friendly Fuegian nation. They could facilitate the supply of fresh provisions and wood and water to ships rounding from one ocean to another. And if I could go further, and form them in the ways of polite society, then it would prove to the world that all men are created equal in the eyes of God.

The idea whirled in his brain, simple but fabulous. He would need Admiralty permission, of course, and both King and Otway would have to give their blessing, but if the Fuegians were educated at his own expense, then the Admiralty could hardly complain. The next survey ship could return the party to Tierra del Fuego. What could possibly go wrong?

A crack of gunfire from the beach below jolted him from his reverie. May's boat-building party, hard at work on the replacement whaleboat, were under attack. Most of the sailors, armed only with tools, were rushing to take cover behind one end of the half-built boat. One of the crew, who must have been caught out in the open, lay face down in a pool of blood on the shingle, apparently dead. Two Fuegian women, who had apparently attacked him with sharpened rocks, were retreating from his body towards the far end of the beach, where a further ten or so of their number now gathered, chanting. They wore the white-feathered grass bands about their heads that, FitzRoy had come to learn, denoted hostility. Alone in the middle of this panorama, walking calmly up the beach towards them, firing into the air, reloading, walking a little further and then firing once more, moved the figure of Surgeon Wilson, a most unlikely hero. Perhaps Wilson's apparent lack of imagination really betokened a serene inner strength after all, wondered FitzRoy. He ran forward down the hillside, Stokes at his heels, both men already drawing their pistols.

By the time they reached the beach it was all over. Wilson, normally one of the more invisible officers, had been fêted as a hero, and was now engaged in trying to save the life of the injured man, whose skull was fractured. The Indians had taken to their canoes, but had been swiftly overhauled by a party of sailors in the cutter. All but one of the pursued Fuegians had dived over the side to escape capture, the exception being a frightened, slender youth, who now stood bewildered and shivering in the rough grasp of Davis, one of the crew. Beside him on the shingle was a length of the leadline (identifiable by its white five-fathom marker), a few tools and several empty beer bottles from the missing whaleboat. Shaking with rage, Davis pressed the muzzle of a loaded pistol to the boy's temple. 'Shall I shoot him now, sir?'

'No! Put your gun down. This man is drunk.'

'They've buzzed all the beer from the whaleboat sir. Every last drop sir.'

'Let go of his arm.'

The boy fell slack on his back, looking up at FitzRoy, his unfocused eyes white with fear, his feathered headband limp with seawater.

Mortal fear is the only manner in which these people can be kept peaceable. It is a state of affairs I have to change, if I can. I must do everything in my power to bring about a mutual understanding between our two races.

'Shall I just let him go then, sir?' asked Davis, confused.

'No. Bring him on board. Let him join his fellows on the *Beagle*.'

The newcomer was quickly christened 'Boat Memory' by the crew, as their last potential link to the vanished whaleboat. He seemed eager to help out around the ship, as if to atone for his part in the murderous attack at the beach, but for that very reason he found it difficult to gain acceptance. Furthermore his slender physique, most unusual for a Fuegian Indian, made him unsuited to physical tasks that – had he been similarly amenable – York Minster could have carried out without breaking sweat. York treated the new arrival with the utmost contempt, perhaps on account of his status as a defeated warrior, refusing to speak to him or even acknowledge him. They took to squatting at opposite ends of the ship, staring at each other through the thickets of rigging, the one baleful and contemptuous, the other cowed and frightened. It was left to Fuegia, inevitably, to act as go-between: unaware of any such nuances, she treated Boat Memory to the same winning display of affection that she served up to everybody else. FitzRoy felt the boy's sense of isolation keenly, and realized that this might provide him with the opening he needed. He found Boat Memory sitting forlornly by the poop cabin skylight, playing with a length of rope. FitzRoy stood ten yards away from him, and spoke in a loud, clear voice: '*Yammerschooner*.'

Without a word, obediently, Boat got to his feet, walked forward and presented himself humbly to the captain, holding out the length of rope.

FitzRoy could hardly contain himself. 'It means "Give to me,"' he breathed excitedly. '"*Yammerschooner*" means "Give to me."'

'By Jove sir, you've got it!' squeaked King over his shoulder, a delighted grin plastered across his puppyish face.

FitzRoy wiped any trace of levity from his own features. He stared directly and unwaveringly at the Indian, and pointed a finger at his own eyes. 'Eyes,' he announced.

'*Telkh*,' replied Boat Memory, without hesitation.

'Fetch your notebook, Mr King,' murmured FitzRoy, relief mingled with pleasure. The other officers began to gather round, interested despite themselves.

'Forehead,' tried FitzRoy, moving his finger upward.

'*Tel'che*.'

'Eyebrows.'

'*Teth'liu*.'

'Nose.'

'*Nol*.'

King scurried back breathless, notebook and pen in hand. FitzRoy ignored him and kept going.

'Mouth.'

'*Uf'fe'are*.'

'Teeth.'

'*Cau'wash*.'

'Tongue.'

'*Luc'kin*.'

'Chin.'

'*Uf'ca*.'

'Neck.'

'*Chah'likha*.'

King scribbled away, desperately trying to transliterate Boat Memory's words and make sense of all the tongue-clicks. FitzRoy kept it slow, his eyes trained on his subject.

'Shoulder.'

'*Cho'uks*.'

'Arm.'

'*To'quim'be*.'

'Elbow.'

'*Yoc'ke.*'

'Wrist.'

'*Acc'al'la'ba.*'

'Hand.'

'*Yuc'ca'ba.*'

'Fingers.'

'*Skul'la.*'

'Have you got them all, Mr King? Tell me you have translated them all so far?'

'I think so sir, except for a couple when I was getting the book.'

FitzRoy took the notebook from his midshipman and read out the first entry as best he could. Pointing to his own eyes once more, he tried out: '*Telkh.*'

Without averting his gaze, the young man pointed to the same spot on his own face and said, clear as day: 'Eyes.'

Then pointing to each body part accurately in turn, he continued without hesitation: 'Forehead. Eyebrows. Nose. Mouth. Teeth. Tongue. Chin. Neck. Shoulder. Arm. Elbow. Wrist. Hand. Fingers.'

There was a complete silence for at least ten seconds on the upper deck. Quite simply, nobody dared breathe. Finally, FitzRoy spoke.

'My God,' he exclaimed.

May's new boat was finished on the twenty-third. Kempe, meanwhile, had supervised the watering of the ship, and the stitching of new topmast rigging. As soon as the work was over, the *Beagle* weighed anchor, warped to windward and made sail out of Christmas Sound, steering small amid the profusion of rocks and islets. She made her way south-east along the coast to False Cape Horn, that cunning natural replica that lies some fifty miles up the coast from the real thing. There she turned north into Nassau Bay, her binnacle lamp a lonely pinpoint of light in the darkening winter evenings. The sick list was lengthening now, an untidy catalogue of colds, pulmonic complaints, catarrhal and rheumatic afflictions, not to mention two badly injured men. The fresh food of summer – the seabird meals of redbill, shag and bittern – had become a rarity. Anything they could catch or shoot now was offered first to the sick, and then to the Indians, on FitzRoy's orders. Nassau Bay, long known but long unexplored, was to be their final 'boat service' of the trip, for which the captain was duly grateful. Surgeon Wilson had impressed upon him that the crew's health was in dire need of recruiting. FitzRoy was all too painfully aware that this decline had begun following the episode with the whaleboat. Even though there had been no sign of any relapse on his part, it was as if the crew took its communal health – silently, invisibly – from him, as if damage to the head was reflected in the spirits of the body corporate.

The education of Boat Memory was now coming on so fast that FitzRoy could hardly bear to break off to recommence surveying operations. Fuegia, too, amazed to find that FitzRoy could suddenly communicate with her in her own tongue, had started to learn English with an astounding rapidity. Only York Minster, a brooding, intimidating presence to all but Fuegia, stayed silent. He sat in his berth up by the chimney grating in all weathers, surrounded by his secreted piles of food, oblivious of the cold and rain. Some among the crew thought he brought bad luck, or wished storms upon them, but none dared to confront him. To approach York felt like walking towards the entrance of a bear cave.

'I'm afraid the water in the wash-hand basin is a mask of ice, sir.'

FitzRoy's steward had arrived to waken him, bearing a bowl of steaming skillygalee porridge, but he had already been roused to half-sleep by the rattle of the anchor chain below. It was just before six o'clock, halfway through the morning watch, and it would not become light for a good couple of hours yet. Snow lay dark and thick on the skylight above. In terms of personal discomfort this was no more than FitzRoy was used to, but it did mean that much of the day would be taken up with the tiresome business of de-icing the rigging. He wolfed his breakfast, struggling into his uniform as he did so, and left his cabin, unwashed, as the sentry rang four bells. It was too cold to clean the decks, so the ship's company were already busy lashing up and stowing their hammocks. A tired-looking Murray, who was on duty at the wheel, seemed relieved to see a friendly face. 'I think it's going to be a fine day, sir. The stars are out and we have a good anchorage – one of the few on this coast fit for a squadron of line-of-battle ships.'

'Excellent.'

Murray paused. 'I'm afraid we lost the small bower anchor in the night, sir. The seaward cable parted through frost. It froze right through, sir. I had the remainder of the small bower cable shackled to the best bower, and rode with two-thirds of a cable on the sheet, and a cable and a half on the bower. I've had the men keep the cables constantly streaming wet at the hawse-holes with seawater all night, sir, to prevent any more icing up.'

'Well, it's a pity about the small bower, but you've done well, Mr Murray. I am grateful to you for your quick thinking.'

'Thank you sir.'

As FitzRoy's eyes became accustomed to the gloom, he became aware of a dim column of warm breath beyond the foremast, which signalled the solitary presence of York Minster, shrouded in a blanket in his accustomed spot. Boat and Fuegia had been persuaded to sleep below decks, but York chose to keep guard out in the open.

'He's been there all night, sir. As usual.'

The *Beagle* had anchored in darkness, but the emerging moon now illuminated steep wooded hillsides, hemming in the ship on three sides. Towards the northern end of the bay these slopes converged in a mess of islands. Here, as so often, FitzRoy, Stokes and Murray would have to hunt for channels, short-cuts and hidden routes into the interior of Tierra del Fuego.

A sudden commotion arose at the far end of the deck. York had sprung to his feet, all his senses alert like a hunted animal's. His eyes scanned the darkness intently, and then he began to shout. The head of Boat Memory soon appeared at the companionway, and behind him Fuegia Basket scampered on deck. All three began to run about agitatedly, dashing up to the rail where they would scream derisively and pull faces into the darkness, before shuttling back again, as if afraid to show themselves for too long.

'What the deuce are they shouting at?' wondered FitzRoy.

Neither he nor any of the lookouts could see anything, even with a nightglass. But then, conducted like electricity through the clear black air, came faint answering shouts and catcalls. At first they came by the score, and then, as they came closer, by the century. Screwing up his eyes and squinting into the gloom, FitzRoy could see tiny silhouettes, black shapes cut in the moonlit sheen of the distant channels. Canoes, a good hundred of them. Boat Memory ran past waving his arms and shouting, 'Yamana! Yamana!' Even the normally solemn York was running about in agitated circles. Fuegia, FitzRoy noticed, was in tears.

'What is it, Boat? Who are they?'

Boat was too panicked to answer. FitzRoy grabbed his arm roughly as he hurtled past and spun him round. 'Boat. Who are these men?'

'Bad men. Yamana! Kill Boat Memory!' He gestured to two scars on his arm as proof of the strangers' murderous intentions.

'Yamana?'

'Yamana! Bad men. Kill Alik'hoo'lip.'

'You are Alikhoolip? You and York and Fuegia?'

'Yes. Yamana kill Alik'hoo'lip! Bad men!'

'Nobody will kill you here. Understand? Nobody will kill you here.'

But Boat was already charging to the starboard rail to deliver another volley of insults into the darkness.

FitzRoy gave the order to beat to quarters, and the Beagle's drums thundered out into the blackness of the sound. Locks were produced for the guns, along with trigger lines, priming wires and powder, handspikes and rammers. The decks around the guns were wetted and liberally sanded. After a minute of frantic activity the men were standing by, waiting for the order to load.

'Are you going to give the order to open fire, sir?' asked Murray.

'I hope to God it will not be necessary. The recoil could play merry hell with the chronometers.'

A great flotilla of canoes was converging on the Beagle now, from more than one direction. Silhouetted figures stood in the little boats, waving otterskin mantles the size of large pocket handkerchiefs, or holding what appeared to be substantial wooden clubs in their fists. The shouts of the men in the canoes jostled and competed with each other to cross the gap between them and the ship. Now that they were closer, the jeers of Boat and York, and the wails of Fuegia, seemed suddenly pathetic by comparison. Steadily, the Yamana canoes converged into a tight ring around the *Beagle*, but still no attack was launched. The sailors stood tense and nervous by the guns; FitzRoy, pistol drawn, held himself in readiness to give the order to fire.

'Sir! Sir!' It was Coxswain Bennet who had shouted. 'They're not clubs, sir, they're fish!'

'I beg your pardon, Mr Bennet?'

The coxswain wore a huge grin of relief. 'Those aren't clubs they're holding, sir, they're fish. They've come to sell us fresh fish!'

At first light, leaving Kempe in charge of the *Beagle*, FitzRoy sent Murray east to map the open end of Nassau Bay, and Stokes west to explore the side-channels there. He, Bennet and King, fortified with plenty of fresh-cooked fish, headed north, where the walls of the bay narrowed. Strange, bright green conical structures lined the shore, which proved on closer inspection to be huge mounds of discarded sea shells, turned emerald by mould, and a profusion of wild celery shoots twisting through and around them. Despite the cold, this was the most heavily populated area they had visited: it was dotted with ramshackle, cone-shaped, brush wigwams, which looked like badly tended haycocks. The people seemed even poorer, muddier and more degraded than those to the west, having no sealskins, but their manner – in spite of Boat, York and Fuegia's terror – was unquestionably friendlier and more tractable. As soon as they saw the cutter they would rush to their canoes to trade fish and shellfish, waving their tiny ragged otterskins to attract attention. They would shout for a '*cuchilla*', the Spanish for 'knife': evidently, at some point in history, a party of Spaniards had passed this way. Miles of stubbly shingle beach fringed this end of the bay, guanaco hoofprints showing in the muddy banks of streams; after a year in the storm-battered depths of Tierra del Fuego, even the knowledge that a herd of guanaco was nearby felt like a friendly harbinger of civilization.

They sailed the cutter up into the northern arm of the bay, where it narrowed to a twisting channel barely wide enough for two ships to pass. Here, they came across an obstacle: three native canoes in line abreast, blocking their way.

'They don't wish us to go any further,' said King.

'They're trying to protect something,' said Bennet, realizing.

'Proceed slowly.'

The cutter pushed forward and, without a sound, the three native canoes parted to let it pass. The morning sun shone brilliantly for the first time in months; the water was glass. The sailors' breath rose and condensed frostily in their overgrown hair. At a quarter speed, the cutter drifted inch by inch along the final hundred yards of the narrows, to the place where the rock walls opened out once more. There it stopped; some of the men stared to the west, and some stared to the east, but in whichever direction they chose to look, the sight before them took their breath away.

'Well hang me,' murmured King.

'Great heavens,' said FitzRoy.

They were sitting in a channel between the mountains, except that the word 'channel' hardly sufficed. This was a ravine, a chasm, an axe-cut running through the heart of the continent, straight as an arrow, for perhaps sixty miles in either direction. It was about a mile or two in width, with snow-capped mountains three or four thousand feet in height ranged on either side, their sunny summits apparently suspended verti-cally over the deep blue water. Beneath the mantle of white, countless magnificent azure glaciers gushed cascading meltwater from side valleys balanced hundreds of feet in the air. Every arm of the sea in view was also terminated by a tremendous glacier; occasionally a steepling tower of ice would crumble from one of these cliffs into a distant corner of the sound. The far-off crash would reverberate through the lonely channels like the broadside of a man-of-war, or the distant rumble of a volcano. Hundred-foot ice blocks would bob gently through the water, like polar icebergs in miniature, and when the ripples reached the cutter, dazzling light flung itself out from their surface and broke into stars. Along the entire length of the ravine, the treeline ran absolutely level, as if drawn by a child with a ruler. The beech leaves clinging to the cliffs glowed an autumnal red at the base, merging into the customary yellow-green further up, where the cold had retarded the action of the seasons. Not for the first time, FitzRoy wished that an official ship's artist had been retained aboard the *Beagle*.

'This is unbelievable, sir. It's incredible. We have found a channel to rival the Straits of Magellan.'

'Indeed we have, Mr Bennet. If its two ends can be located and are joined to the sea, as they surely must be, then we have found a navigable channel that escapes the necessity of rounding the Horn.'

'What should we call it?'

'The narrows that brought us here will be named after Mr Murray. This channel is too important to be named after any one man. I think we should call it the Beagle Channel.'

'Are we to survey it ourselves, sir?' asked King.

'It would take a month at least. We are in want of provisions – we have only a few weeks' aliment left – and we are ordered to reach the Brazils by June. No, this is a task for some future expedition.'

They sat in silent awe for some twenty minutes further before finally setting to work. They surveyed the immediate locality of the channel and the Murray Narrows, climbed a nearby summit (which they named Mount King) by following the guanaco trails, collected greenstone samples for stratigraphic analysis, and gathered specimens of local barnacles and other shellfish. They camped that night on a narrow shelf of shingle, close-packed and shivering in their makeshift tent.

On their return through the narrows the next morning, the three silent canoes, each containing its own family, lay strung across the channel exactly as before, like guards of honour to an invisible potentate. A gentle breeze had sprung up, presaging the end of the precious clear spell, so the crew of the cutter tacked back down the narrows, a judicious oar here and there helping to keep them on course.

'Pull alongside that canoe.'

'Sir?'

'We have three of the western tribe aboard the *Beagle* – the Alikhoolip. We do not have any of the Yamana.'

'We are to take them with us? As specimens?'

'Not as specimens, Mr Bennet. As fellow men, to share in our civilization, that we may form them in the ways of our society. Besides, the die is now cast. We have not the provisions to return to the west, but if we release our three Indian guests here I suspect they will be torn limb from limb. So, yes, we are to take them with us.'

As bidden, the cutter slid alongside the middle canoe, over which a man in his mid-thirties appeared to preside. His face was crossed laterally by two painted stripes: a red one, running from ear to ear across his upper lip, and a white one that ran above and parallel, linking the eyelids. FitzRoy stood up and gestured to the man, suggesting that he, or one of his family, might like to join him in the cutter. The man grunted suspiciously, but a short, round youth alongside him, plucked by curiosity, stood up and peered at the strangers. A low, clicking conversation ensued, and the boy finally clambered into the cutter alongside the waiting FitzRoy. The older man, who was presumably the boy's father, held his hands outstretched and essayed a beseeching look, to indicate that he ought to be given something for his trouble. It was an awkward dilemma. FitzRoy had wanted a volunteer; he had not wanted to purchase another human being. But this was not a transaction, he told himself, merely a consideration paid out of respect to an elder of the tribe. He was here to help these people, not exploit them. He rummaged in his pocket and found a solitary mother-of-pearl button, which he tossed, not entirely convinced by his own argument, to the Indian in the canoe.

The rotund boy alongside him seemed placidly unperturbed by the exchange, but the older Indian gasped as if he had been showered with gold doubloons. He held up the shining button to the sunlight in wonderment and then, gesturing to the rest of his family, indicated to FitzRoy that for another button he might take whomever he wanted. His wife? His daughter?

'All hands to the oars. Let us make for the *Beagle*.'

And so the cutter set off back down the channel, tacking to port and then to starboard against the breeze. The Indian's canoe, presumably mistaking the zigzagging of the cutter for evasive action, clung gently in its wake, striving to follow its movements. The putative salesman stood in the bow throughout, now grinning and gesticulating enthusiastically to indicate that his entire family was for sale, if only the Europeans could provide another shiny object; the family in question, meanwhile, paddled calmly but energetically in pursuit of their reluctant purchaser.

'I can't say I care for this fellow overmuch,' observed FitzRoy, casting another embarrassed glance over his shoulder.

The boy alongside him grinned delightedly at the chase, urging the sailors via sign language to redouble their efforts, but it was to be a good hour before they shook off the enthusiastic salesman. In the meantime, FitzRoy endeavoured to distract his new charge's attention by producing a looking-glass, as much for his own interest as for the boy's entertainment. The young Indian took it in astonishment, gazing first at his reflection, then over and over again behind the looking-glass in search of his imaginary twin, then even behind himself in confusion. Finally he arrived at the stage of pulling faces, testing his reflection, pushing the *Doppelgänger* in the glass to extremes in the hope that it could be provoked into nonconformity. Relieved to have so captured the boy's interest, FitzRoy indicated to him that he could keep the looking-glass for himself.

In the early afternoon, as the crisp autumnal light began to fail, they arrived back at the *Beagle* to find a scene of pandemonium. The ship was still at the centre of a flotilla of canoes, packed with Indians eagerly trying to trade fresh fish, shellfish and ragged otterskins. York, Boat and Fuegia appeared to have taken charge of the trading, and were hurtling about the deck collecting worthless scraps – strips of cloth, rusty nails, glass beads and so forth – which they were exchanging for food. They appeared to have overcome their fears of the previous morning, and had adopted the swagger of stallholders at a country fair.

FitzRoy was first out of the cutter. 'What is going on here, Mr Kempe?'

'Your savages, sir' – Kempe was careful to put the stress on the *your* – 'are trading with the other savages. Your only orders were that they were not to leave the *Beagle*. As they are not part of the chain of command, sir, I confined myself to implementing precisely those orders I received from yourself.'

Boat Memory ran past at this moment, laughing all over his face. 'Capp'en! Capp'en! Yamana, *foolish* man! Yamana, *foolish* man! Boat give Yamana button! Yamana give Boat fish! *Foolish* man! *Foolish* man!' And he ran off excitedly to find another button, having used up all those on his own jacket. How excited would Boat have been just a few weeks ago, FitzRoy pondered, to exchange a fish for a button? At least they were learning.

A moment later, Coxswain Bennet escorted the Yamana boy over the rail. The effect was instantaneous. Seized with shock, York, Boat and Fuegia froze to the spot.

The youth, overcome with fear, began to cry. York strode forward, jabbed a finger at him, and shouted, 'Yamana! Yamana!'

The boy quailed in terror, and began to shake with sobs. FitzRoy stepped between them. Boat ran up and jeered at the new arrival over FitzRoy's shoulder. 'Yamana! No clothes! No clothes! Yamana *foolish* man!'

'No clothes! No clothes!' yelled Fuegia excitedly.

Unable to understand, the frightened youth blurted a few words back, through his tears.

'What does he say, Boat? What does he say?'

'Boat no understand. Boat no talk Yamana talk.'

My God. Of course. They do not have one language. Theirs is not one nation. These two do not understand a single word the other says.

Fuegia ran up and spat in the boy's face. 'No clothes! No clothes!' she screamed.

CHAPTER SEVEN

Rio de Janeiro, 1 August 1830

The sun stole down behind the dark, high mountains that threw a protective arm over the city to the west. The sea was quite smooth, but a freshening breeze on the *Beagle*'s quarter carried her on, at an exhilarating thirteen knots an hour, towards the harbour entrance. Behind, her foaming wake glowed with a pale, sparkling light, and before her bows, two milky billows of liquid phosphorus parted to let her through. Sheet lightning played incessantly on the northern horizon, and sometimes the whole surface of the sea was illuminated. As the daylight faded, the *Beagle* hauled her wind and stood in the offing for the night. Her sails were clewed up and stored, the anchors were let go, and a light was hoisted to the fore yard-arm, shining like a lone star against the setting sun.

'It's a beautiful evening, isn't it, Jemmy?' said FitzRoy.

Jemmy Button, as some wag had christened the Yamana boy, glanced up from the looking-glass that had become his constant companion.

'It's a beautiful evening, isn't it, Capp'en Fitz'oy? God make stars, God make sun, God make sea. God make Jemmy,' he grinned.

Humour and vanity were combined in Jemmy in equal measure. Sporting an ever-present smile, he would pick his way across the deck with a delicacy that belied his pot-bellied proportions, never taking his eyes off his own reflection, but never once tripping over a block or coil of rope. He looked after his new clothes with a fastidiousness bordering on obsession. The months since he had joined the ship had seen his relations with Boat Memory and Fuegia Basket cautiously advance towards the cordial; as for York Minster, Jemmy had established the same warily mute relationship with which everyone but Fuegia had to content themselves. The language barrier separating Jemmy, Boat and Fuegia had forced them to converse in English, which had lent unexpected impetus to their education. Jemmy's ready tongue and constant grin had made him even more popular with the crew than the little girl was, and FitzRoy sensed that the sailors had become proud of their human cargo. They were making a difference, they felt, helping to bring light to the darkness. The next survey ship that returned the four Indians would be like an arrow fired into the heart of the savage nation, an arrow tipped with the elixir of Christian civilization, which would spread through that country's bloodstream until all Tierra del Fuego was suffused with the word of God.

'Look, Jemmy! The sun is drowning!'

The passing sailor who offered this cheery greeting was none other than Elias Davis, who had been so ready to blow Boat Memory's brains out on the beach not a few months before.

'Gammon!' replied Jemmy, who relished English slang words. 'Sun no *drowning*. Tomorrow morning get up again. Sun go round earth, come again tomorrow. Earth is round.'

'Your people know this, Jemmy?' enquired FitzRoy. 'That the earth is round?'

'My people know this, Capp'en Fitz'oy. Climb mountain, you see far. Earth not flat. Earth round.'

These people are very, very far indeed from deserving to be called savages, thought FitzRoy.

'Do your people have a God, Jemmy?'

'All people have God, Capp'en Fitz'oy. God love everybody.'

'No, Jemmy. I mean, do your people have their *own* God?'

'No, no. My people not know God. My people *foolish* people.'

'Do your people think somebody made them? Who made you, Jemmy?'

'Jemmy's mother and father make Jemmy.'

FitzRoy laughed. 'Who made the mountains, Jemmy? Who makes the weather? Who makes it rain?'

'A big black man in the woods.'

The voice was not Jemmy's. Boat Memory had materialized at FitzRoy's shoulder, slender and earnest, his fine-boned features caught in the glare of the distant lightning sheets. As ever, his expression held a serious aspect, in contrast to the beaming cherub at FitzRoy's left.

'A big black man in the woods?'

'Yes. My people believe such man makes the rain and the snow. If food is wasted, he becomes angry and makes the storm.'

Boat Memory's English had advanced by incredible leaps and bounds since he had come aboard, but FitzRoy continued to be taken unawares by the sheer agility of the Indian's intelligence. He feared that his own contributions to their conversations were all too frequently mundane and unimaginative by comparison.

'There are no black men in the woods, Boat. You will see black men in London. You will see black men in Rio. Many black men.'

Boat looked longingly at FitzRoy, his eyes two inkwells. 'I dream to see London, Capp'en Fitz'oy. See St Paul's. See Wes'minster Abbey. See Temple Bar.'

Jemmy chipped in: 'My people say white man from the moon. White man white like moon. When white man take off clothes, wash in river, body white like moon.'

'I'm not from the moon, Jemmy,' smiled FitzRoy, 'I'm from England.'

'Englan' not on the *moon*. Foolish Indians think Englan' on the *moon*. This is bosh.'

'My people thought Mr King was English woman,' revealed Boat Memory. 'They don't know he is boy because he has no hair on his face.'

'Because he has no beard,' said FitzRoy, highly amused.

'Because he has no *beard*,' said Boat, savouring the new word, rolling it around his tongue and storing it away for future use.

'Beard look like tree on face,' giggled Jemmy. 'Jemmy no like beard.' And he glanced admiringly into the looking-glass once more.

FitzRoy caught sight of his own beard momentarily in Jemmy's glass. He would be shaving it off the next morning before he reported to Admiral Otway. It sat oddly here, a wild intruder on his face, in some ways more redolent of the savage south than the two Fuegian tribesmen leaning against the rail to either side.

He had written to the Admiralty back in early May, requesting permission to bring the four Fuegians home with him, hoping to secure the guarantee that His Majesty's Navy would return them to their own country the following year. The *Beagle* had spoke the packet *Caroline* off Good Success Bay, bound from Valparayso to Falmouth, and had consigned the letter to her. It was now August, so with luck the Admiralty's reply would be waiting for him at Rio; although what he was supposed to do if the answer was in the negative was beyond him. There were, in fact, five Fuegians on board, as Wilson had preserved the body of the attacker shot down by Murray in ice below decks; he intended to present it to the Royal College of Surgeons for scientific study. Wilson's own post mortem had discovered a thick fatty layer of insulation below the skin, closer to that of a seal than a human being. Both Wilson and FitzRoy thought that this subcutaneous layer, and the distinctively top-heavy body structure of the Fuegians, were adaptations, created by the harsh climate and the Indians' peculiar mode of life; it would be interesting to see whether or not the experts of the Royal College concurred.

None of the other Fuegians seemed remotely concerned by the presence of their fellow countryman's corpse. His death apparently failed to concern them at all. Indeed, the only disturbance of an otherwise uneventful return journey had been Jemmy's white-eyed terror on catching sight of some distant horsemen on the Patagonian shore. These, he explained, were the 'Oens-men', who would cross the mountains when the leaf was red, to kill or enslave the Yamana and steal their food. The three Alikhoolip, who had neither encountered nor even heard of the Patagonians, ignored Jemmy's wild, quivering fear with a calmness and equanimity verging on the perverse. Jemmy, meanwhile, took an enormous amount of soothing and convincing that he was safe from the mounted Oens-men, even half a mile out at sea; he was so terrified that he soiled his precious breeches. But the episode did not appear to linger in his mind. The next day, he was back to his old, prancing, chuckling self.

Empty of all her supplies now, the *Beagle* was hard to handle; she was too easily pushed around by the wind, and worked badly. But she had been making good time, until she became becalmed in a patch of constantly shifting light air just south of Monte Video. The endless hauling on the braces wearied the crew, and it was only the knowledge that they were nearing journey's end that kept the men focused on the task in hand. FitzRoy was determined that their mental discipline should not slacken. He did not want their arrival in port to be the equivalent of slumping wearily into an armchair after a long march. So the *Beagle* was given a new coat of black and white paint, the masts were scraped and repainted, as were the boats, the serving on the rigging, and the tips of the booms. The deck was scrubbed until it was spotless. Even the anchor cables were hove up on deck, to be chipped and checked.

They had finally arrived at Monte Video two weeks late, only to be informed by Captain Talbot of the *Algerie* that both the *Adventure* and the *Adelaide* had been and gone, and that they were now to rendezvous at Rio instead. Again, it was a moment when the crew's instincts would have been to slacken their efforts, but again FitzRoy refused to let this happen. And now, some nineteen months after their departure, the *Beagle* prepared to enter Rio harbour, in a palpably better condition than that in which she had left. Admiral Otway, FitzRoy knew, would be watching.

The following morning dawned dead calm, the ship marooned in banks of fog, which the sun drew upwards and slowly dispersed as the day wore on. At noon the midshipmen had trouble measuring the position of the sun, so harsh was its image as reflected by their quadrants. Soon after midday the Port Health Officer came aboard, to issue the 'Pratique' certificate of health. Black, curling ripples were already stealing across the glossy surface of the water as the *Beagle* weighed anchor and steered proudly for the harbour entrance.

'Away, bullies, away! Away for Rio!' exulted the crew, as they made sail.

Blue through the haze to port rose the mighty ridge that curled round the city, punctuated by the sharp spurs of the Corcovado and the Tijuca, and the flat-topped Gavia. To starboard the Organ Mountains stabbed upwards with their curious needle-points, and there, within the harbour itself, slumped the familiar hummock of the Sugar Loaf. Beyond that, a dazzling world of white sails awaited, clustered together at the feet of the great metropolis. Even among this wonderful constellation of ships there was no mistaking the *Ganges*, and just behind her, the *Samarang*, crossing the harbour in full sail, two of His Majesty's ships-of-the-line, imperious and haughty, towering over the little *Beagle* as she skated slowly towards them. A squabbling, barging rabble of masked boobies plunged for fish in the *Beagle*'s wake, as if to emphasize her inferior social status. FitzRoy ran up the numbered signal to identify himself.

'Keep a sharp eye open for any returning signals, Mr King.'

'Aye aye sir.'

King did not have long to wait. Grasping the signal book so tightly with excitement that his fingers practically turned white, he was rewarded by a line of signal flags fluttering into position in the lofty heights of the *Ganges*. 'The admiral's ordering us to moor alongside the *Samarang*, sir,' he gasped.

'That's unusually specific, isn't it?' queried Lieutenant Kempe.

FitzRoy grinned. 'Why, the old devil...It's a contest! He wishes us to compete with the *Samarang* in furling sail. He wishes to see how close we can run her. Well, we shall see about that! Mr Bos'n, make it known to the crew, would you?'

Sorrell marched down the deck, bawling at the top of his voice. 'All right, boys! Seems the admiral wants a set-to between us and the *Samarang*! Wants to see us put in our place at furling sail! Well? Are we going to be made fools of by a crowd of jumped-up fancies? What do you say, boys?'

A huge answering roar came back in the negative.

There were only a couple of hundred yards before the two ships would be abeam of each other. A state of high excitement obtained aboard the *Beagle*.

'I want every man in position, Mr Bos'n, but nobody is to move until I give the order.'

'Aye aye sir.'

The gap halved. There were just a hundred yards to go. And now fifty. Thirty. Twenty. Ten. *Now*.

Both ships began to turn into the wind at the same time. Figures swarmed simultaneously on to the yards of both the *Beagle* and the *Samarang*, hauling frantically on the clew lines, pulling the corners of the sails upwards into the masts. At breakneck speed, the courses, topsails and topgallants lost their billowing contours. The foretopsail, meanwhile, pressed against the mast, acting as a brake, slowing the *Beagle* to just a few knots. FitzRoy gave the order and the main bower anchor thundered into the water, sparks flying as the chain rattled deafeningly through the hawse. Almost at the same time, the foretopsail – its job done – began to curl up into the yards as well. FitzRoy stood tense on the poop deck, his pocket watch apparently ticking faster than normal.

'Ten minutes…ten minutes fifteen seconds…'

'Has a sounding ship ever beaten a man-of-war?' murmured Kempe.

'Not to my knowledge,' replied FitzRoy calmly. The *Beagle* was winning. It would be a close-run thing, but even across a hundred yards of water he could feel a creeping sense of panic enveloping the *Samarang*.

'Eleven minutes twenty seconds…eleven minutes thirty seconds.'

And then it was done. There was no doubt about it. The last inch of the *Beagle*'s sail was taken in. Across on the *Samarang* there were still corners flapping, edges of sail here and there still being drawn diagonally upwards by the topmen. An almighty cheer went up from one end of the *Beagle* to the other, which was immediately answered by another huge cheer from the crew of the *Ganges*, delighted to see their rivals on the *Samarang* humiliated in this way. Not just humiliated, but humiliated by a surveying brig!

'I wouldn't care to be on the *Samarang* tonight!' squealed King, dancing around the binnacle box for joy.

'They say old Paget is a real tartar,' said Bennet. 'Heads will roll!'

'Mr Bos'n, that was immaculate – quite immaculate,' said FitzRoy, with profound gratitude.

Sorrell, stilled at last, hung his head and blushed scarlet.

'And now, Mr Bos'n, when every last sail is taken in aboard the *Samarang*, I'd like every inch of canvas on the *Beagle* set.'

'You want me to *set* sail, sir?'

'Well, we wouldn't wish our colleagues on board the *Samarang* to think that was just a flash in the pan, would we?'

'Right you are, sir!'

Sorrell was grinning like a small boy on Christmas morning as he beetled off. The order to set sail again took the *Samarang* by surprise, but only for a few seconds. Paget's exhausted crew were back in the rigging only a moment later, but they were already beaten men. The momentum was with the *Beagle*'s crew now; heads had dropped, fatally, aboard the man-of-war. Midshipman King was leaping about the poop deck so delightedly that he was practically bouncing off the rails, but nobody was in the mood to rein him in. 'We're rubbing their noses in it! We're rubbing their deuced noses in it!' he declared.

Another massive cheer, echoing across the harbour, announced that the *Beagle* had defeated the *Samarang* not once but twice. Unchristian though it was to show off, FitzRoy simply could not resist this moment of triumph. 'Mr Bos'n, give the order to furl sail once more.'

'Aye aye *sir*,' purred Sorrell.

And so, for a third time, the crew poured into the rigging and out on to the yards, all their tiredness long since evaporated, their movements smooth and well drilled, confidence and exhilaration written on every face. The *Samarang*'s second attempt at furling sail, by contrast, was ragged and lacklustre. The contest, what remained of it, was a foregone conclusion. Suddenly, a crash of cannon echoed across the harbour. The men on the *Beagle* were taken by surprise, but only for a moment.

'They're saluting us, sir! The *Ganges* is saluting us!'

Indeed they were. The admiral's flagship was saluting a surveying vessel. All her crew stood in the rigging, waving their hats and cheering for all they were worth.

'My God, this must be a first in the history of the Service,' said Murray. 'Well *done*, sir.'

'Well done sir,' echoed Kempe, cautiously. 'And may I say it's been a pleasure serving with you, sir. A real pleasure.'

'Why thank you, Mr Kempe. Thank you very much indeed.'

'Marvellous! Simply marvellous! Commander FitzRoy, you have my congratulations.'

Admiral Otway, thumbs hooked into his waistcoat pockets, leaned back in his chair with ill-concealed delight. 'I had Paget across for supper last night, otherwise I'd have seen you sooner. He didn't say one word all evening. Beaten by a surveying brig! Priceless!' Otway roared with laughter at the memory.

It was the following morning. King and FitzRoy were reporting to the admiral's staterooms on the *Ganges*, just as they had nearly two years previously. This time, FitzRoy too wore the grizzled, salt-bleached aspect that had characterized King on the previous occasion.

'I have with me Captain King's official report as to your conduct, Commander. Would you care to hear the conclusion?'

FitzRoy glanced at King. 'I'd be delighted, sir.'

Otway paused briefly for effect, then began his performance. '"Commander FitzRoy, not only from the important service he has rendered, but from the zealous and perfect manner in which he has effected it, merits their lordships' distinction and patronage; most particularly in the discovery of the Otway and Skyring waters, and of the Beagle Channel, made by Commander FitzRoy himself, in the depths of the severe winter of that climate; and I beg leave, as his senior officer, to recommend him in the strongest manner to their favourable consideration. The difficulties under which this service was performed, from the tempestuous and exposed nature of the coast, the fatigues and privations endured by the officers and crew, as well as the meritorious and cheerful conduct of every individual, which is mainly attributable to the excellent example and unflinching activity of the commander, can only be mentioned by me in terms of the highest approbation." Pretty damned good, eh, Mr FitzRoy?'

'You oblige me with your kindness, sir,' said FitzRoy warmly to King.

'I wrote that, Commander, before I had an opportunity to speak to my son. He paid a visit to the *Adventure* last evening, and was most forthcoming about your voyage.'

'Indeed, sir?'

A cold hand reached round FitzRoy's heart and held it still for a moment. Had Midshipman King confided to his father the episode of the stolen whaleboat, and all that had followed? There was an awful pause, as Captain King's eyes seemed to bore into those of his subordinate.

'According to my son, Commander, it would appear that you are the finest commanding officer in the history of the service. A position, I should add, that I formerly held myself. It seems I have been utterly supplanted in the young man's affections – an achievement for which I suppose I should congratulate you.'

'Midshipman King is most unaccountably generous, sir.' Relief streamed from FitzRoy like water pouring from the *Beagle*'s prow in a heavy sea. King caught his gaze for a moment longer. Was there something else in it, something unspoken? He could not tell.

'Now, Commander, these savages of yours,' boomed Otway.

'Yes, sir.'

'Personally I can't imagine what you were thinking of, cluttering up the maindeck with those benighted creatures, but it seems the Admiralty sees things differently. I have a reply to your letter from Barrow in the Admiralty office:

"Having laid before my lords commissioners of the Admiralty the letter from Commander FitzRoy of the *Beagle*, relative to the four Indians whom he has brought from Tierra del Fuego under the circumstances therein stated, I am commanded to acquaint you that their lordships will not interfere with Commander FitzRoy's personal superintendence of, or benevolent intentions towards these four people, but they will afford him any facilities towards maintaining and educating them in England, and will give them a passage home again."

Et cetera, et cetera.'

'That's wonderful, sir.'

Otway harrumphed. 'Well, I can't see any good coming of it myself, but each to his own.'

'I have the four Fuegians present, sir, on the *Ganges*. If you please, I thought perhaps you might care for them to be presented to you.'

'They are here on the *Ganges*? Good Lord! Well, I can't say I've ever met a Fuegian. Very well, bring the brutes in.'

Boat Memory, Jemmy Button, York Minster and Fuegia Basket were ushered in and introduced to the admiral. Boat and Jemmy bowed, as they had been trained to do, and Fuegia lifted her skirts and performed a perfect curtsy.

'Most impressive, FitzRoy, most impressive. Their manners would do credit to many a matlow.'

'Thank you, Capp'en Admiral, sir. It is a great pleasure to make your acquaintance.' The speaker was Boat Memory.

Otway practically jumped out of his skin. 'Good grief, FitzRoy. It speaks English.'

'You have very beautiful cabin,' chipped in Jemmy. 'One day Jemmy have very beautiful cabin like you have.'

'Three of them speak excellent English, sir. We are making slower progress with York Minster here, whose real name is Elleparu. Jemmy here was born Orundellico. Fuegia's name is Yokushin. And Boat here—'

Boat Memory cut in: 'Please. My name is Boat Memory. I wish to have proper English name.'

'Well, quite. Absolutely. Who wouldn't?' said Otway, almost at a loss.

Fuegia broke ranks and charged up to the admiral, beaming from ear to ear. 'My name is Fuegia Basket. I have a pretty dress.'

Otway was on the point of shooing her away when, overcoming his prejudices, he found himself seized with a sudden impulse of generosity. 'Come here, my little creature, and sit on Admiral Otway's lap. Do not be afraid.' And he reached out a beckoning hand.

As Fuegia skipped forward, Otway felt sure he heard a low animal growl in the stateroom, but there were no animals to be seen, and no one present appeared to have made a sound. Perhaps he had imagined it. But – there was no denying it – the hairs on the back of his neck were standing on end. Looking about him he could see no rational reason for this, but some primitive instinct told him to beware the big, silent one, the muscular Indian who had yet to speak. Somehow, innately, Otway knew that York Minster was the source of the tangible sense of threat that now assailed him.

FitzRoy and King observed a curious expression steal across the admiral's face, rather as if a fly had settled on the tip of his nose. He halted Fuegia, just as she was about to clamber aboard his lap.

'Yes...well...quite...Anyway, FitzRoy...I'm sure you have plenty to be occupying yourself, what with refitting and such.'

'By your leave, sir, the *Beagle* has no need for refitting. She is in a first-class state of repair.'

'Really? Good heavens. Well, I'm sure, nonetheless, you have much to do.'

'Yes sir.'

Otway turned Fuegia about and propelled her gently towards the others. The big Indian was still staring intently at him, but the brute was saying nothing. As Fuegia toddled back across the stateroom carpet, Otway felt the hairs on his neck lose their charge and fall slack. He was still unsure what had happened, but as FitzRoy and his Indians disappeared through the door, his body gave a little shiver, and a feeling of relief washed through him.

Riding back to the *Beagle* with the mail sack, FitzRoy resisted the temptation to investigate its contents. All the crew, he knew, would be hanging by the rail, as eager as hungry dogs for the slightest titbit. He did, however, allow himself a glance at the latest newspapers, which were full of talk of reform, the successful trials of the Rocket and the Lancashire Witch, and the forthcoming opening of the Bolton and Leigh goods railway. What, he wondered, would the Fuegians make of a railway, or a steam ferry, or all the other appurtenances of the modern world? What, for that matter, would they make of the bustle of Rio de Janeiro? He would find out on the morrow.

Back at the *Beagle* he found himself surrounded by a pushing, shoving crowd of seamen, naval discipline hanging by the merest thread. Boatswain Sorrell fought gamely to restore order. FitzRoy had the letters distributed in the order that they came out of the sack, regardless of rank. *As cold waters to a thirsty soul, so is good news from a far country.* Of course, some poor souls would always go without mail, even after four years at sea: orphans, perhaps, or once-pressed men whose families had no idea of their whereabouts, or those whose wives had simply abandoned them.

He, at least, would be sure to have received a letter from his elder sister Fanny, who had yet to let him down. And sure enough, there, towards the bottom of the sack, was a letter addressed in her hand, affording him a familiar glow of love and nostalgia. Only when he turned it over did he see the black seal, as did everyone else present, and a hush fell over the deck. The nearest crewmen moved almost imperceptibly backwards and away from him.

FitzRoy was quiet. 'Mr Kempe, would you complete the distribution of the mail, please?'

'Aye aye sir.'

He took the letter from Fanny into his cabin, and leaned back against the bookshelves, his heart pounding against his chest wall, and he broke the black seal, and read what she had written.

His father was dead.

In a rush, all the air was forced out of his lungs, as if he had been kicked in the gut. His head swam. A wave of nausea rose in his throat, and he thought he would be sick there and then. Everything he had become, everything he had achieved, he had done with the purpose of his father's approval at the back of his mind. Why? He had barely seen his father since he had been sent away to school at six, and only twice since he had joined the Service at twelve. His father never wrote to him. His memories of his mother, who had died when he was five, were richer and more tangible than even his most recent recollections of his father. It was not as if he could ever have confided in his father, or opened his heart to him. And yet...*and yet I looked to his approbation as the true reward of any hard times I might pass. I have been influenced throughout everything by the thought that I might give him satisfaction. I always valued his slightest word.*

He wanted to confide in somebody now, to sit one of the officers down and tell them all about his father. The way his father spoke, the way he smiled, the way he sat on his favourite horse, the way he had once held his little boy. But it was out of the question. Even if naval etiquette had not forbidden it, he knew that any potential listener would be paralysed by rank, any sympathy they had to offer lost in the abyss between the two pillars of their respective status. A captain simply did not invite his subordinates to explore his personal grief.

FitzRoy looked up as the door of his cabin creaked open slowly. He was about to upbraid his visitor for failing to knock, and the marine sentry for failing to see that such formalities were observed, when he saw the reason for it. The visitor was Fuegia Basket, who peered wide-eyed past the door jamb. She wore a bright yellow home-made dress, like a single flower against the dark wood of the little cabin.

'Capp'en Fitz'oy,' she said. She crossed the floor and climbed into FitzRoy's lap. 'Fuegia love Capp'en Fitz'oy,' she said. And he put his arm round her, and he held her as tightly as he possibly could.

They made the *Beagle* fast to the quay with the anchor cable, which was unshackled and heaved around a quayside bollard, then lashed to the bitts. FitzRoy went ashore with Bennet and the four Fuegians, who were dressed as inconspicuously as possible, their hats pulled down over their eyes. He need not have worried. In their European clothes they passed easily for local Indians, and did not merit even a passing glance.

The reactions of the four Fuegians themselves were not so incurious, however; as the party made slow progress through the sweating crowds thronging the mole, and across the *praça* before the palace and the cathedral, lines of half-naked blacks carrying huge bundles atop their heads passed glistening in the other direction. Boat, Jemmy and Fuegia quailed visibly, the little girl clinging to York's breeches for protection, no doubt mindful of the black man in the woods who controlled the weather. Even York himself, FitzRoy thought, appeared less assured than normal: an air of tension pervaded his usually rock-like calm. Then, the sight of an ox-cart before the cathedral pulled them up in their tracks. All the sculpted baroque wonders above their heads were of scant interest compared to this fascinating horned beast, which set the three Alikhoolip chattering eagerly among themselves. FitzRoy had to pull them away before a crowd could gather to see what was so riveting.

He decided they should take the Rua do Ouvidor, where ox-cart traffic had been banned, to avoid any further zoological confrontations. It was, as Bennet remarked, 'precious warm', and even without the usual farm-yard-deep carpet of ox dung, the stench in the city centre almost made the officers gag after two years at sea. A babbling brown brook of human effluent ran down the cobbled gutter in the middle of the street, naked children paddling and splashing therein with happy abandon. Crooked, maimed blacks stared at the little group, leaning pitifully on their sticks, the offensively poor, unemployable detritus of the slave trade. Others peered through rusty wrought-iron balconies that seemed to imprison them behind pastel walls of mildewed, peeling stucco. FitzRoy felt faintly ashamed that the modern civilization to which he had brought the Fuegians appeared even more desperate than their own.

A padre with a long coat and a square hat bade them good day, and a handsome West African woman sailed by in muslin turban and long shawl, dripping with amulets and bracelets. At the mighty door of the Church of São Francisco de Paula they headed south, past the magnificent arched aqueduct that fetched the city's water down from the mountains, climbing now towards the more respectable suburbs of Santa Tereza and Laranjeiras. Imported trees grew everywhere here, plum and banana and breadfruit trees by the roadside, and long stands of bamboo transplanted from the East Indies. The houses were bigger, with tumbling vines and verandahs, each one a barrack square for a platoon of potted poinsettias. There were glimpses of olive-skinned children playing in back gardens, under the care of black nurses. FitzRoy took the piece of paper with the address from his pocket to check it once more. They ascended two more narrow cobbled streets, the roads here too steep and twisting for carriages, the Fuegians sweating copiously now in the heat, until eventually a sign in Portuguese indicated that they had arrived at their destination: the premises of Dr Carson Figueira, physician.

FitzRoy pulled the bell, and a silent black serving-girl came to the gate. She showed them through a terracotta-coloured patio lined with potted palms, into a dark, cool, empty room containing only a wall cabinet and a scratched mahogany desk, where she left them to themselves. A few minutes later Dr Figueira himself, a man as colourless as his office walls, appeared in the doorway.

'You must be Captain FitzRoy. I am pleased to make your acquaintance. I am Dr Figueira.'

The physician's accent was novel to say the least: it was flat and buttery like that of a New Englander, but it had also been dipped in the dark honeypot of Brazilian Portuguese. It was hard to equate such a rich, dominating voice with its undistinguished-looking, world-weary owner. 'My mother was American,' added Dr Figueira, in response to FitzRoy's unspoken question.

FitzRoy introduced himself, the coxswain and the four Fuegians, and wondered privately about the bareness of Figueira's consulting room.

'So these are the Indians your message spoke about?'

Figueira opened York's mouth and began to inspect his teeth as if he were a horse. York's eyes bored into the physician's, but otherwise he reacted with diffidence to being manhandled.

'My name is Boat Memory, sir. This is my friend Mr York Minster, whose teeth you are making inspection of.'

'*Nossa Senhora.* You've been teaching them English, Captain.'

Dr Figueira ignored Boat Memory's greeting, and it occurred to FitzRoy that he did not entirely take to the Brazilian physician.

'It is my belief, Dr Figueira, that the Fuegian nation shows a considerable potential to be elevated above its savage state. That is why I am bringing them to Europe. It is why I have brought them here.'

'You'll need to make uncommon haste, then. The Buenos Ayreans are heading further south every day. When they reach Tierra del Fuego, the Indians will go the way of the blacks, and be fit only for slaves.'

'Do you believe that blacks are fit only for slaves, sir? This very afternoon we have encountered most handsomely dressed black gentlewomen, habited in turbans and shawls, who had nothing whatsoever of the slave about them.'

'Those will be Mina Negroes from West Africa. Handsome they may be, but they're quite unfit for domestic service. They're too wild, too independent. But they are less than slaves, Commander. Lusheys, for the most part.'

Figueira had completed his cursory examination.

'The inoculation for smallpox is an expensive business, Commander. If you wish me to inoculate four savages I will, as long as your money is as good as the bank.'

'I shall have no trouble meeting your settlement here and now,' said FitzRoy coldly.

Figueira produced a metal tray, upon which lay a lancet, a cloth, a jar of vinegar and a glass phial containing a clear liquid. Dipping the cloth in the vinegar he cleaned a spot on Boat Memory's upper left arm, and prepared to make a small incision with the lancet. Boat's eyes widened. 'It's just a variolation,' explained the surgeon. 'A series of small cuts with a lancet dipped in the cowpox vaccine.'

'It's all right, Boat,' said Bennet softly. 'We've all had the same treatment.'

'It's medicine, Boat,' FitzRoy added. 'It will keep you safe from illness in England. You must have it done now, because it takes some weeks to work. If you like, I will take it first.'

'No, Capp'en Fitz'oy. I believe you.'

And he shut his eyes and submitted to Dr Figueira's ministrations.

Jemmy, who was quaking like a jelly, came next. He winced and gasped in fear as Figueira cut into both arms, then promptly smiled again the moment it was all over. Fuegia Basket, who was third, had seemed unconcernedly braver than the other two until the physician had her in his grasp, whereupon she began to whimper loudly. Both FitzRoy and Bennet started forward instinctively to comfort her, but Figueira was there first, placing his hands squarely on her shoulders. 'Do not fret, little miss. I will not hurt you, I promise.'

And with that he cut into her arm. Fuegia squealed and burst into tears. Before anybody could move, York was across the room, and had slammed Figueira up against the wall by the throat. FitzRoy and Bennet tried to pull him off, but York's arm was as rigid as gunmetal. Now it was Figueira's turn to widen his eyes in fear. York's fingers squeezed gently into the physician's neck; and then, to everyone's surprise, he spoke, in a low, harsh voice that came up from the depths of his throat: 'Hurt her, I will kill you.'

FitzRoy and Bennet slackened their futile grasp in sheer astonishment. Figueira, whose windpipe was too constricted to speak, shook his head as best as he could to indicate that nothing could be further from his mind.

'York...you can speak English!' gasped Bennet redundantly.

'He! He! He!' Jemmy, in the corner, was laughing. 'Mr York, he learn English all time! Fool Capp'en Fitz'oy, fool everybody. He! He! He!'

The packet *Ariadne* sailed into Rio de Janeiro harbour the next morning with the news that George IV was dead. The King had passed away at Windsor six weeks previously, on 26 June. It took some time for the news to percolate through the South American fleet, as there was no actual signal to indicate the King's death – it having been decided by Sir Home Popham some time previously that it would demoralize the men to include such a communication in the signal vocabulary. In fact, most of those on the *Beagle* were secretly delighted at the news: the new king, William IV, was a Navy man, who had served as Lord High Admiral in Rio. He had been known as a drinking man, a no-nonsense officer and a good sport. There was a general consensus among the crew that – as a former matlow – King Billy would see the Service all right.

An official period of mourning was declared throughout the fleet, as per regulations, and FitzRoy sat down to prepare the divine service that must be held in memory of His Majesty. His mind, though, was still reeling with its own grief, too consumed by its own misery to care about the death, six thousand miles away, of the man he had served so assiduously for two years. He had to force himself to concentrate. *I must throw myself fully into my employment. Only through forced occupation will I get through the days. I must not allow myself to be unemployed and alone, or the demons will come again.*

He remained stunned, too, by the revelation of the afternoon before. He had been obliged to part with a handsome sum to placate the aggrieved Dr Carson Figueira, but not before both Fuegia Basket and York Minster had consented to be inoculated; this after a nice speech in their own language by Boat Memory, who had – he later explained – urged them to put their trust in Capp'en Fitz'oy. The capp'en had given them his word, he said, that the white man's medicine would protect them against ill health in the future, and the capp'en's word was his bond. The momentarily loquacious York Minster had not uttered a single word since.

FitzRoy opened the battered copy of the scriptures that Sulivan had given him, and leafed through it. Whether he found the text of chapter fourteen of the Book of Job by accident, or whether he had read so much of the Old Testament by now that the chapter lay buried in his subconscious, he did not know. *As the waters fail from the sea, and the flood decayeth and drieth up; so man lieth down, and riseth not.*

He felt suddenly weary in himself, and at that moment he saw life as a struggle to placate an uncompromising Old Testament God; a God who could wipe out most of the earth's population in an instant with a mighty deluge, or take the life of one defenceless man, however good, however powerful, as was His wont.

The waters wear the stones: thou washest away the things which grow out of the dust of the earth; and thou destroyest the hope of man. Thou prevailest for ever against him, and he passeth: thou changest his countenance, and sendest him away. His sons come to honour, and he knoweth it not; and they are brought low, but he perceiveth it not of them.

It was not the most immaculately turned-out group of men that had ever bidden farewell to a monarch. The crew had been drawn up in two rectangles on either side of the upside-down whaleboat, which bisected the maindeck on its skids, its keel slicing the air like a half-submerged shark. They were as smartly dressed as they could manage, but the innumerable repairs and patchings-up that quilted their motley garments testified to the constant needlework required on a long voyage south. The file of red-jacketed marines to the left, their drummer boy at the far end, did lend the occasion an air of formality, although their uniforms would hardly have borne close inspection either. The officers at least presented a dignified prospect, a row of peaked caps behind their commander on the raised poop, their formal black frock-coats and white stockings cleaned and crisply pressed by their servants.

'Caps off!' commanded Lieutenant Kempe.

For a moment there was silence on board the *Beagle*, broken only by the creaking of the rigging as she rode, windlessly, at anchor. FitzRoy stepped forward to the azimuth compass, which had come to serve as his lectern whenever he needed to address the men. The creaking of the ship seemed more insistent now; almost rhythmic. He fought hard to keep thoughts of his own father from overwhelming his mind. 'We are gathered to give thanks for the life of His Gracious Majesty King George the Fourth.'

The rhythmic creaking was coming faster now, not loudly but insistently, from somewhere close by. King and Stokes exchanged questioning glances. Kempe glared inquisitively at Sorrell, who shrugged his shoulders in mystification.

'I shall read from the Book of Job, chapter fourteen. "Man that is born of a woman is of few days, and full of trouble. He cometh forth like a flower, and is cut down: he fleeth also as a shadow and continueth not."'

Even FitzRoy was forced to take note now. The creaking, accompanied by a gentle knocking noise, insinuated itself relentlessly into his concentration. He paused, and murmured to Sorrell, 'Mr Bos'n, is every member of the crew present?'

'Yes sir, excepting those in the sick list, sir.'

The sound was coming from one of the tiny cabins under the poop deck companionways, the one to the starboard side, which was occupied by Midshipman Stokes. Now it was Stokes's turn to shrug his shoulders with bemused innocence.

FitzRoy cleared his throat and began to read: '"And dost thou open thine eyes upon such an one, and bringest me into judgement with thee?"' He broke off. There seemed to be a jaunty, almost enthusiastic quality to the creaking and knocking now.

He strode briskly down the companionway, turned sharply at the bottom and flung open the door to Stokes's cabin. Stokes's hammock, the source of the creaking, was up on its hooks, stretched from one wall to the other. In it, his face a mask of furious concentration, his breeches about his ankles, lay York Minster. Bouncing astride York, her skirts gathered about her waist, her head bent against the ceiling, sat Fuegia Basket. Still bouncing, she turned delightedly and favoured FitzRoy with her most beaming smile. 'Fuegia love Capp'en Fitz'oy,' she said.

CHAPTER EIGHT

Plymouth Sound, 13 October 1830

'They must be married at the earliest convenience.'

'Married? How can she be married, sir? She is not yet thirteen.'

'I mean, they must be betrothed. At the very least, we must have the banns published in Plymouth, or I shall obtain a marriage licence from Doctors' Commons when we reach London.'

The issue of York and Fuegia continued to vex FitzRoy. As her legal guardian – for such he surely was, ever since the Admiralty's acknowledgement of his letter – he was responsible for the child's welfare. To allow her relationship with York Minster to continue unchallenged was out of the question. But to separate the Fuegians from each other would surely go against the purpose of his scheme, as well as being an interesting physical proposition, given York's frankly superhuman strength. The only answer FitzRoy could find was to legitimize their union. How he wished for spiritual guidance on the matter, but as there was no chaplain aboard such a small ship, he himself was the sole source of spiritual authority on the *Beagle*. Instead he had turned for solace to the wholly inadequate figure of Wilson, the surgeon, whose reaction to FitzRoy's concerns was predictably dismissive.

'Sir, these people, if they are indeed such, are of the lowest rung on God's ladder. Such behaviour is hardly unexpected at the basest levels of society. Take a carriage ride up the Haymarket and you will see girls of the lowest class, girls as young as eight or nine, offering themselves to the highest bidder. When the famines bit in Kent and Sussex and Hampshire, poor farmers sold their daughters at market, some, I have heard tell, in a halter like a cow. These savages are lower still, barely a step above the brute creation. To behave in this manner is in their nature.'

'Mr Wilson, I have given my word that these people will be raised from their base condition, and given every advantage of polite society. That is the purpose of their sojourn in England. If the girl finds herself with child when she is in my care, I will have failed in my duty before their visit has even begun.'

'But if they are betrothed, sir, how will they even know it? One is no more than a child, the other keeps his counsel like a simpleton.'

'You would do well not to underestimate their intelligence, Mr Wilson. York Minster may be a displeasing specimen of humanity in many respects, but stupidity is not one of his vices. Fuegia, too, is sharp of mind. I shall put the proposition to him, and to her, over dinner.'

'Over *dinner*, sir?'

'Over dinner, Mr Wilson. I intend to invite them to dinner, if the four of them can squeeze into my cabin. It will not be the noblest repast, as we are down to hard biscuit, salt pig and salt horse, but I have asked the cook to keep back the last few canisters of Donkin's soup and preserved vegetables. Even if a formal betrothal does not result, we may at least educate them in the way of a few table manners.'

The Fuegians filed into FitzRoy's cabin just after midday, their naturally crouching gait a useful attribute in view of the low ceiling. Suspicion was etched across all their faces at the sight of the captain's formal linen and glassware, even more so than when faced with Dr Figueira's tray of medical instruments. They had become accustomed to meals below decks, where food was eaten by hand or with a single knife, and drink was slurped from an open bowl; here, a veritable obstacle course was arrayed on the tablecloth. Coxswain Bennet – whom FitzRoy had also invited, as he had somehow drifted into the role of unofficial nursemaid to the Fuegians – entered with them, his burly form bent practically double in the tiny cabin, cheerily ushering his charges to their seats. FitzRoy's steward became the seventh person to try to insinuate himself into the tiny space, in a desperate attempt to pour water into the guests' glasses, but as a lesson in etiquette this got the afternoon off to a bad start: he was compelled by the lack of standing room to hover in the doorway and reach over the heads of those nearest to him.

Barely had York Minster's crystal goblet been filled with water than he grabbed it, and threw the contents down his throat in one swift move.

'York,' said FitzRoy gently, 'today I wish to teach you how to behave at dinner in England. It is thought polite to wait until everybody has their food or their drink before starting.'

York said nothing, but leaned towards the unlit candelabra in the centre of the table and sniffed at the candles.

'These are "candles". They give light from a little flame. At a polite dinner in England they would be made from beeswax. At a simpler meal, or here on a naval vessel, they are made from beef tallow.'

Once more York sniffed at the candles, which sat plumply in their twisted silver cradles, then abruptly grabbed and ate all three, cramming them into a capacious mouth. FitzRoy sighed. It was shaping up to be a long afternoon.

Jemmy, meanwhile, was holding each item of silver cutlery to the skylight in turn, an expression of wonderment on his face. 'Beautiful. Many beautiful knifes.'

Bennet, who was about to enlighten him, checked himself. He had only dined with a senior officer once before in his young life, when Admiral Bartlett had invited all his junior officers to dinner in groups aboard the *Persephone*. It had been, he remembered, a terrifying and painfully silent affair: officers were strictly forbidden to broach any topic of conversation until it had first been raised by their commander. Fortunately FitzRoy spotted his hesitation and gave him the nod.

'The spoon on the outside is for the soup course, Jemmy. Then the fork and knife on the inside are for the second course. With each course, you move in to the next two pieces of cutlery. Finally, your pudding cutlery is at the top of your place setting.'

'When Jemmy is rich man in Englan' he will have many courses, many cutleries.' Jemmy's eyes swam delightedly at this suggestion, and he bared his teeth with pleasure. 'Many beautiful knifes.'

'When a man and a woman are married in England, Jemmy, they are given presents for their home. This is how most people obtain their cutlery, and linen, and crockery.' FitzRoy indicated the three items in turn.

'Please, Capp'en Fitz'oy, what is married?' asked Boat.

'"Married" is when a man and a woman come together in the sight of God.' FitzRoy cut to the chase. 'When we reach England I believe York and Fuegia must be married.'

'Please, Capp'en Fitz'oy, York and Fuegia are already come together.'

'I believe York and Fuegia must be married!' squeaked Fuegia.

'They are together, yes, Boat, but their union has yet to be blessed by God.'

'God is late,' protested Jemmy. 'York and Fuegia come together many months ago.'

The servant began distributing ladlefuls of Donkin's soup, a thin, evil, green liquid, among the dinner guests. York lowered his head into the steam and sniffed warily.

'Remember, the outside spoon,' said Bennet helpfully.

York gave him a scornful sidelong look, lowered his face into the scalding fluid and began to slurp loudly. Jemmy, meanwhile, held a spoonful of bright green liquid to his lips, his grasp awkward but his technique surprisingly dainty. 'York is rough fellow. Very rough fellow,' he observed, down the length of his nose. York's green face rose bubbling from the steam, and silenced him with a glare.

'Do you not have marriage in your country, Boat?' enquired FitzRoy hastily. 'When the two families come together and celebrate?'

'Oh yes Capp'en Fitz'oy. When a man is old enough to hunt and a woman is old enough to bear childs. The family of girl will sell her to family of young man. But my people do not understand God's mercy. This is not a proper English married.'

'I believe York and Fuegia must be married!' squealed Fuegia, once more.

'We have a big celebrate, Capp'en Fitz'oy. It goes on for many days. We kill seal. Everybody come from many miles. Everybody celebrate – young people, old people.'

FitzRoy's memory was jogged. 'There is something I have been meaning to ask you, Boat. You speak of old people. But I saw no old people in

Tierra del Fuego. No grey-haired men or women.'

'There are old people in my country, Capp'en sir.' Boat looked unhappy.

'But not many. I saw none in a year and a half.'

'You did not look for them well, Capp'en Fitz'oy.'

There was something wrong now, FitzRoy could tell. Boat Memory was staring fixedly into the emerald depths of his soup bowl.

Jemmy, immune to the gathering crisis, chattered on obliviously. 'Sometimes my people very hungry, in winter. No food!' He gesticulated eagerly, rubbing his pot belly to indicate the unimaginable awfulness of not being able to fill it. 'Then we eat old people. Put head in smoke, they die quick. Women eat arms, men eat legs. Leave rest. Sometimes old people run away. Sometimes we catch, bring back. Sometimes no find, die in woods.'

Fuegia giggled.

FitzRoy became aware that Bennet had dropped his spoon, his ruddy countenance frozen in horror. A single virulent green rivulet was making its way purposefully down the starched white of his napkin. FitzRoy felt his gut seize and tighten at the revelation he had unleashed, but he ploughed on with grim anthropological fascination: 'But Jemmy, you have dogs. If your people are starving – hungry – do you not eat the dogs first?'

'Oh no Capp'en Fitz'oy!' laughed Jemmy. 'Doggies catch otters! Old women no!'

Boat Memory continued to stare red-faced at the tablecloth. Fuegia Basket suppressed another giggle. A strange snorting guffaw bubbled up through the shallows of York Minster's soup plate. It was the first time, FitzRoy realized, that he had ever heard York Minster laugh.

*   *   *

It was a very English dawn that broke over the Royal Dockyard at Devonport as the *Beagle* and the *Adventure* made their final approach: grey, featureless and nondescript, and therefore all the more welcome to the men, who had dreamed of such an English morning for the last four years. Here was the familiar heartland of His Majesty's Navy. Even the statuesque ships of Rio de Janeiro harbour would have paled alongside the mighty men-of-war that towered above the Devonport quays and, indeed, over the town itself. But there was no hammering or banging to be heard as one would expect in a naval dockyard, no vibrancy, few signs of life, even. The men-of-war lay deserted, painted bright yellow against the elements, their yard-arms, masts and rigging stripped. The war was long since finished. The titans that had defeated Napoleon and wrested control of all Europe from the dictator lay chained up, silent but proud, reduced to this sorry state by clinical economic necessity. HMS *Bellerophon*, heroine of Trafalgar and the Nile, wallowed rotting and unpainted, the cramped and sweating quarters below her decks packed with convicts due for transportation to Australia. The *Beagle* and the *Adventure* trod a silent path between these fallen giants, the men lining the rail navigating their own path between pride, regret and the simple thrill of homecoming. Alone on the grey wharf, a small crowd had gathered to meet the ships, for news of their arrival had travelled rapidly up the coast from Falmouth.

The four Fuegians crowded alongside the sailors, eager for a glimpse of the land about which they had heard so much.

'This is Englan', Capp'en Fitz'oy?' asked Boat Memory, for the third time, as if unable to believe the evidence of his eyes.

'This is England, Boat.'

'By the deuce, it may not look up to much, but this is old England all right,' enthused King, who had not seen England since he was ten.

Indeed, it did not look up to much. The flat grey-green landscape; the uninteresting little town, wreathed in wisps of smoke, that stumbled down the eastern bank of the river; the broad, deserted avenue paved with marble chips that ran white and lifeless from the dockyard gates; none of these could be compared with the sights and sounds that the *Beagle*'s crew had encountered over the previous four years. But this was home, and the gaggle of wellwishers crowding the quayside was made up of friends and family.

'I have dreamed of this day,' breathed Boat Memory, and he looked at FitzRoy, his eyes a wet slick.

'Jemmy too have dreamed of this day,' said Jemmy, as convincingly as he could, although – in all truth – this was not the shiny golden England of his imagination.

And then the hush was broken, suddenly, by a monstrous, clanking, belching sound, which took everybody on board by surprise. The Fuegians reacted first, their self-preserving instincts honed, Boat, Jemmy and Fuegia diving for cover, the little girl whimpering in terror as she curled herself into a ball inside a coil of rope. York, undecided between flight and furious resistance, bent down to the deck and shouldered a massive spar that two crewmen would have been hard put to lift. Brandishing it like a colossal spear he stood, nostrils flaring, cheeks flushed, legs braced apart, ready to confront his adversary.

'Good God,' said Kempe in amazement at this physical feat.

'He's a ruddy marvel,' said Stokes.

'It's a steam-ship, York,' said FitzRoy, soothingly. 'It's just a steam-ship. A ship powered by steam.'

York, unsure whether to trust FitzRoy, stood rigid and transfixed, a perfect physical specimen poised to face down his enemy in mortal combat. But the steamer waddled past unconcernedly in the opposite direction, its big side paddle-wheels clunking ineffectually at the water, coal smoke belching filthily from its two chimneys.

'They've witnessed the future and they don't like it,' scoffed King.

'Have you ever seen a railway train, Midshipman King?'

'No sir,' said King, addressing his own feet.

'Fuming like a grist mill and clanking like a blacksmith's shop? When you have seen one such run smoking past you, then I venture you may understand what it is to see your first steam-ship.'

'Yes sir,' muttered King, suitably chastened.

It was not difficult to spot Sulivan in the reunion crowd, mainly because he towered over most of them. FitzRoy had to pinch himself to equate this giant with the slender eighteen-year-old midshipman who had bidden him such a tearful farewell two years previously. And then, of course, there was the conspicuous white stripe on his sleeve, which indicated that this was now Lieutenant Sulivan. The two men navigated through the throng and pumped each other's hands so delightedly and so vigorously it seemed they must do themselves an injury.

'My dear Sulivan – my dear *Lieutenant* Sulivan.'

'It's wonderful to see you safe and sound, sir – and not a scratch on the *Beagle*! Oh, but I am being remiss in my manners. Miss Young, may I have the honour of presenting to your acquaintance Commander FitzRoy of HMS *Beagle*. Commander, this is Miss Young of Barton End, and her companion Miss Tregarron.'

FitzRoy became aware of two young ladies, waiting patiently arm in arm at Sulivan's elbow, and immediately swept off his cap. 'The pleasure is entirely mine, ladies.'

'Will you accompany us, Commander?'

'I would be delighted, Miss Young. And might I be so forward as to enquire of your Christian names?'

'Of course – I am Sophia. Miss Tregarron's Christian name is Arabella.'

'Do not Miss Young and her companion look well this morning?' beamed Sulivan, although the rapt way he pronounced the words 'Miss Young' left no room for doubt as to where the compliment was aimed.

'After four years at sea, my homecoming has been doubly blessed that I should find myself in the presence of such delightful company.'

The two women blushed prettily.

Like matching peacocks, they were arrayed in identical dresses of bright turquoise silk trimmed with broderie anglaise, their waists fashionably constricted, the outlines of their hips and legs concealed by a demure gathering of petticoats. Miss Tregarron, the chaperone, dipped the brim of her bonnet faintly and took a discreet step back into the crowd. Miss Young, round-faced and fresh with the beauty of youth, continued to gaze up adoringly at Sulivan. FitzRoy, too, stared up at his former midshipman, who had grown by at least three inches.

'When I last saw Mr Sulivan he was but a middie, and very much a boy. Now he has grown into a fine figure of a man.'

'He is five foot and eleven inches tall,' glowed Miss Young, so close now to her beau that they were almost touching. 'But I fear, Commander, that Mr Sulivan is demonstrating undue modesty this morning. Will you not tell the commander of your remarkable accomplishment in the lieutenant's examination?'

Sulivan's face suffused with scarlet. 'I passed for lieutenant with full numbers,' he confessed.

'Only the second person in the history of the Service to do so!' said Miss Young, so overwhelmed with affection it seemed she must burst. 'Following yourself, of course, Commander FitzRoy.'

'These are the most marvellous news!' FitzRoy would have thrown his arms around Sulivan and hugged him then and there, except it did not do for naval commanders to hug lieutenants in the middle of the Royal Dockyard.

'But it is you, sir, who must take all the credit. Everything I have learned about handling a ship, Miss Young, and I mean everything, I have learned from Commander FitzRoy here. Many is the hour that the commander gave of his free time in the *Thetis* to pass on his exhaustive knowledge of seamanship, from box-hauling to flatting in, from French shroud knots to selvagees—'

'Mr Sulivan talks about you continuously, Commander, in the most glowing terms.'

'Mr Sulivan talks continuously, Miss Young, but not always accurately. All that he has achieved, he has achieved by his own hard work and intelligence – I will not accept one iota of credit. Do you have a ship yet, Lieutenant Sulivan?'

'Not yet.'

'Then we shall exert all our influence to rectify the omission. At least with full numbers you will not go to the back of the mates' list.'

'Thank goodness for that! Of course I do not have a handle to my name, and they say that some who are without must wait ten years for a berth—' FitzRoy smiled, and Sulivan coloured at the realization of what he had just said. It would be hard to find a more useful 'handle' than 'FitzRoy'. Sulivan stumbled on, 'That is, my father has a large family, therefore it was a great object to him to achieve so good an education for me free of cost—'

'Pray excuse me.' This time it was Miss Young who had interrupted, her widening eyes fixed on the *Beagle*. 'But is that...a *little girl* I see on the deck of your ship?'

FitzRoy turned, just in time to see Fuegia dart behind the mizzen-mast with a cheeky grin. She was playing hide-and-seek with him.

'It is, indeed.' He laughed. 'That is Fuegia Basket. Come aboard and I will introduce her to you.' He proceeded to relate the story of the four Fuegians. 'It is my intention,' he concluded, as Sulivan helped Miss Young up the accommodation ladder, 'to secure for them a Christian education in this country before returning them to their own, so that they might draw benefit as a nation from the advanced condition of our society.'

'How wonderful, Commander – and how provident that the Lord has delivered you into our hands today! For I am acquainted with the Reverend Mr Harris, the vicar of Plymstock – he is the most prodigious friend of my father. He is also the local representative of the Church Missionary Society, whose very purpose is the provision of religious instruction to savages.'

'Then we must effect an introduction this very afternoon – that is, if you are amenable to the suggestion, sir.'

'Capital, my dear Sulivan – that would be capital!'

Fuegia ran up and hurled herself into Sophia Young's turquoise skirts.

'Pretty dress! Fuegia want pretty dress like this one! Fuegia be pretty lady too!'

'Why, Commander FitzRoy, she is delightful,' smiled Miss Young, stroking Fuegia's wild tresses, 'and it is to her great good fortune, I am sure, that the Lord has appointed you guardian angel to these poor unfortunate creatures. You have the power to give them life – eternal life – where once there was only misery and suffering.'

I hope so, thought FitzRoy. *I only hope so.*

* * *

The savages have been removed to Castle Farm outside Plymouth, in order to enjoy more freedom and fresh air, where they are said to be satisfied with their present situation. As soon as they are sufficiently acquainted with the language, and familiarized with the

manners of this country, they will begin a course of education
adapted to their future residence in their native country.

FitzRoy put down the *Hampshire Telegraph and Sussex Chronicle* in
irritation. How the deuce had the journalist tracked them down to Castle
Farm? And how did he presume to comment on the Fuegians' satisfaction or otherwise, when he had yet to make their acquaintance? The
Morning Post was even worse.

The *Beagle* has brought to England four natives of Tierra del Fuego,
taken prisoner during the time that the ship was employed on the
south-west coast of that country. Captain FitzRoy hopes that by their
assistance the condition of the savages habituating the Fuegian Archipelago may be in some measure improved, and that they may be
rendered less hostile to strangers. At present they are the lowest of
mankind, and, without a doubt, cannibals.

FitzRoy tossed down the paper in disgust. '"Taken prisoner"? What do
they mean, "taken prisoner"?'
Bennet felt it wiser to keep his counsel. Morrish, the phrenologist,
looked up from under beetling brows but said nothing, and continued
to unpack his Gladstone bag.
'Please, what is "taken prisoner"?' asked Boat Memory nervously.
'It means you do not wish to be here.'
'This is not true. This is a bad man who does not speak the truth. Boat
Memory is happy to be here in Englan'. One day Englan' and my country
will be frien's. Good frien's, like Boat Memory and Capp'en Fitz'oy.'
'That's right, Boat. One day our two countries will be friends.'
But how had the journalists discovered so much? FitzRoy was inclined
to suspect the Reverend J. C. Harris, vicar of Plymstock, a fat, fussy, fluttering cleric, whose appeal to the Church Missionary Society had more
or less come to naught: the clergyman had returned after a fortnight's
absence wearing a woebegone face and bearing bad news, a letter which
declared brusquely that 'The Committee do not conceive it to be in the

province of this Society to take charge of these individuals.' They had, at least, referred FitzRoy to the National Society for Providing the Education of the Poor in the Principles of the Established Church; an appointment had been fixed with the secretary, the Reverend Joseph Wigram, who was assistant preacher at St James's, Westminster, when the *Beagle* reached journey's end in London. She was due to set sail from Devonport on the day after the morrow. In the meantime, he had taken a vacant cottage in Castle Farm as a billet for the Fuegians, in an effort to protect them from prying eyes and from the international assortment of diseases for which Plymouth, as the hub of the country's naval activity, was justly famous. He had also written to the First Secretary of the Admiralty, Sir John Croker, requesting special leave for Murray and Bennet to accompany the Fuegians onshore. It would be no great travail to navigate his way up the Channel to the Port of London without a master and a coxswain.

The three officers and the four Fuegians were now arranged in the front parlour of Castle Farm cottage, watching the drizzle fleck the panes of the little windows embedded in the thick walls. The officers, especially, were not used to inactivity. FitzRoy had hired the phrenologist – which he had been meaning to do for some while – from the extremely limited selection available in the Plymouth area, in order to kill time. Boat Memory, who was to be the object of study, remained wary. 'Will it hurt, Capp'en Fitz'oy? Like Dr Figueira and his medicine?'

York Minster wore a contemptuous expression.

'No, Boat, it won't hurt. Dr Morrish is a phrenologist. He surveys the human head, just as I survey the seabed and the coast. He will feel your head, and make a map of it. It will be quite painless.'

'I do not feel well, Capp'en Fitz'oy. Boat Memory feels too sick for his head to be maked into a map.'

'I told you, Boat, you will feel nothing, and it will all be finished in a minute or two. Just a minute or two. That's all.'

Reluctantly the Fuegian signalled his acquiescence, as Morrish produced a variety of sinister-looking measuring devices in metal and polished wood, and proceeded to calculate the size of Boat's head from every conceivable angle. Then he set to work with his fingers, probing smoothly and expertly through the dark thickets of Boat's hair.

'The head is uncommonly small at the top and at the back. There are fewer bumps for the craniologist than one would find in the skull of a civilized man – but that in itself is significant. The forehead is ill-shaped. The propensities are large and full. The sentiments, however, are small, with the exception of cautiousness and firmness. The intellectual organs are small, as one would find with the coloured races or, of course, with the French and the Irish.'

Morrish paused as Boat leaned forward to scratch his ankle. 'Please, Capp'en Fitz'oy, I do not understand.'

'Phrenology is the science of the brain, Boat. The shape of the skull – the bone – corresponds with the shape of the brain. Experts have identified thirty-five areas of the brain, each of which can be read from the outside.' FitzRoy aspired to his most reassuring tone, but privately he was irritated at these medical men who continued to examine the Fuegians as if they were deaf and dumb animals.

'There is cunning here, and indolence, and passive fortitude. A want of energy and a deficient intellect.'

'That is if the physiology can be trusted, Dr Morrish,' said FitzRoy, feeling himself bound to disagree.

'Oh, the physiognomy of man will always reveal its secrets to the trained hand, Commander. You are not to worry: this is anything but an unexpected diagnosis. Savages are entirely different from civilized men, both in outward feature and in mind. They are incapable of progress.'

'But surely, Dr Morrish, all men are equal before God.'

'The presence of the organ of veneration in all men, Commander, is direct proof of the existence of God. But if all men were equal, then all men's skulls would be equally configured. A savage cannot progress into a civilized man.'

Boat scratched his ankle again. 'Am I a savage, Capp'en Fitz'oy?'

FitzRoy did not know what to say.

'Am I a savage, Capp'en Fitz'oy?' parroted Fuegia.

'No, Boat, you are not a savage.'

'Then one day, Capp'en Fitz'oy, I too will be a phrenologist.'

Morrish raised his eyebrows but said nothing. Jemmy, bored, fixed his gaze on his looking-glass, and pushed his nose up to see what it looked like reflected.

'Please, Capp'en Fitz'oy, Boat feels sick.'

'It is almost over now, Boat. The doctor will finish examining your head in a moment.'

'Boat's head does not feel sick. Boat feels sick. Boat's ankles hurt.'

'Your ankles, Boat? What is wrong with your ankles?'

Obligingly Boat leaned forward once more and hitched up his left trouser leg. There was a bump as Morrish dropped his measuring-tool in shock, his chair and its occupant clattering back into the table. FitzRoy stood rooted to the spot, and thought for sure that his heart had stopped. The red rash about Boat's ankle was unmistakable. The first spots were already beginning their transition into the clear pustules, which – within a week or two – would signify the onset of full-blown smallpox.

If he dies, I will have robbed him of his life as surely as if I had allowed Davis to pull the trigger. Yet if he lives I will have robbed him of his handsome features, and of his innocence.

FitzRoy paced his side of the quarterdeck bitterly, left alone by the crew, who knew better than to trouble him. The fresh grey air of the Channel ballooned the *Beagle's* sails and flung FitzRoy's hair hither and thither till it stung his cheeks, but could not shift the weight of putrefying fear that sat heavy in his stomach.

Why had Boat not properly imbibed the vaccine? Was the whole batch bad? Or had that damned fool Figueira botched the inoculation – had he drawn too much blood with his lancet? Would the others catch the disease? Please, God, do not let the others catch the disease.

He had called in the Admiralty's offer of assistance – *how* he had called it in – by arranging for the Fuegians to be admitted to the Royal Naval Hospital at Plymouth, quarantined in a whole ward of their own, under the care of the eminent specialist Dr David Dickson. He had ordered Bennet and Murray to remain at Castle Farm to monitor Boat's progress.

FitzRoy thought keenly of the Fuegians now, bewildered and alone in their empty ward, watching the disease take hold, watching Boat's open, friendly features becoming increasingly and hideously disfigured before their eyes. The cavernous Royal Naval Hospital, so packed with the wounded in wartime, boasted few patients now: just the odd pneumonia case, and one or two sailors driven out of their senses by syphilis. The corridors echoed only to the clacking footsteps of the doctors and orderlies. Or would they be echoing now to the screams of Boat Memory? FitzRoy shuddered and pulled his coat about him.

The *Beagle* swung to westward at the Isle of Thanet, beating up the Thames estuary against the previously friendly breeze. The river traffic thickened as the banks came in sight of each other: elegant frigates with uniformed crews, dark barges swarming with silhouetted figures in coal-dirty smocks, tiny skiffs scurrying to avoid being run down, all went about their business oblivious to the little brig that had travelled to the far end of the world and had returned with such an unusual cargo. There were East Indiamen loaded with cotton and pepper, West Indiamen bearing coffee, rum and sugar, and tobacco ships from the United States, awaiting clearance to enter the mighty fortress gates of the new dockyards. This was the throbbing, filthy hub of the greatest modern commercial city in the world: the newly constructed tobacco warehouse at Wapping, it was said, was the largest building to be constructed since the Egyptian pyramids. The *Beagle* picked its way through a converging winter forest of bare masts, sidestepping shoal after shoal of struggling oars, the water by turns stained purple with wine and white with flour. A clangorous noise, half-familiar but its sheer intensity forgotten, assaulted the eardrums of the crew; the unflinching stench of stale herrings and weak beer insinuated itself into their nostrils.

They berthed their vessel at the Naval Dockyard at Woolwich, there to be paid off, stripped and cleared out, her pendant hauled down, her company dispersed, never – in all probability – to meet again. *All of us who have passed so many rough hours together, scattered like chaff on the wind.* They were expected at Woolwich, their berth already prepared, the Admiralty as always aware of the exact movements of each and every one of its ships; the precision with which their lordships gathered each vessel in at the end of its voyage matched only by the careless abandon with which each and every crewman was tossed aside. It should have been a proud, emotional time, of farewells and handclaspings and promises to meet again, when old shipmates' virtues loomed large and their vices were generously set aside, to be diminished for ever by the sentimental glow of memory. But FitzRoy could think of nothing except the young man who lay fighting for his life in the Royal Naval Hospital, beset by a strange disease in a strange land, a young man who had put his trust in him, a young man to whom he had given his word that he would become an English gentleman. Oh, there were handclaspings all right, for Kempe and King and Stokes and Wilson and Boatswain Sorrell and all the others, but these were uncommonly muted farewells on both sides. Eventually, his duty of care towards the *Beagle* finally discharged, FitzRoy said his own silent farewell to her, and stepped on to the wharf. He adjusted his watch by twenty minutes, from Plymouth time to London time, signalled to the waiting coachman, carefully supervised the loading of his trunk, climbed aboard his carriage and set off for London.

'I may – ah – I may be able to be of assistance to you.'

The Reverend Joseph Wigram, a young man prone to slight, mannered hesitations, tapped out his pipe and lit it anew. The smoke curled upward, searching for an escape route from the study, but the heavy moreen curtains that stood guard against the daylight forced it to circle restlessly above his head. Really, Wigram was too young even for a post of such uncertain status as the secretaryship of the National Society for Providing the Education of the Poor in the Principles of the Established Church. Without doubt, it was an appointment that owed much to the good offices of his father, Sir Robert Wigram of Walthamstow House. But the younger Wigram's earnest countenance and his obvious eagerness to be of assistance betokened well. The clergyman smoothed his hair down for the third or fourth time: the presence of such a distinguished visitor as Commander FitzRoy of HMS *Beagle* had obviously unnerved him. He maintained the air of a man who had arrived late for an important appointment.

'I have the – ah – the honour to be the governor of Walthamstow School. I share the honour with the rector of Walthamstow, William Wilson. Are you familiar with Walthamstow? It is – ah – a small village to the north-east of London. Most agreeable. I am sure it would be possible to enter the – ah – the four savages as boarders and pupils. They can start as soon as they are ready.'

'I am most indebted to you, sir, for your kindness. You are more than generous.'

'Not a bit of it, sir, not a bit of it. We are all as one before God. But I must own that ours is only a small and ill-funded institution, ill-equipped for all but the most basic instruction. As I am sure you are aware, sir, these are straitened times.'

'The most basic instruction, Mr Wigram, is all that could be wished for in the present circumstances. I would desire the Fuegians to become fluent in English and the plainer truths of Christianity, as the first object, and in the use of common tools, a slight acquaintance with husbandry, gardening and mechanism as the second, all areas of instruction which you have convinced me are well within your capabilities.'

'Absolutely – absolutely. And may I enquire as to their – ah – their present whereabouts?'

'They are currently residing at Plymouth.'

FitzRoy paused. Should he convey the full, awful circumstances to Mr Wigram, that one of the Fuegians – and perhaps before long all of them – was engaged in a desperate struggle for life? His hesitation was brief. He had no right to withhold the truth from anyone, particularly not a man of the cloth who had so generously answered his prayers.

'They are at the Royal Naval Hospital. Tragically, one of them has contracted smallpox. I had them inoculated, but it was not properly imbibed. I am, however, confident that he will make a full recovery.'

'Indeed – indeed. So I have read in the *Morning Post*.'

FitzRoy was exceedingly glad that he had not sought to dissemble. The young man's question, it seemed, had been disingenuous.

'We must hope, Commander FitzRoy, that the good Lord in His infinite mercy will spare them the ultimate punishment for their formerly base lives. Might I enquire the – ah – ages of the four savages?'

'York Minster, the oldest' – the Reverend Wigram raised one eyebrow at York's unusual name – 'appears to be about twenty-six. Boat Memory, the, ah, patient' – FitzRoy discovered Wigram's verbal tic to be infectious – 'is of some twenty summers. The boy Jemmy Button is perhaps sixteen or seventeen, while the little girl Fuegia Basket is, I would guess, eleven or twelve.'

'Excellent, excellent. I am sure that the – ah – age gap will not present a problem. It is, after all, a uniform level of ability that determines the homogeneous composition of any classroom.'

'The age gap, Mr Wigram?'

'Did I not say, Commander FitzRoy? Walthamstow is an infants' school. The average age of our pupils is between four and seven.'

FitzRoy emerged into broken sunshine, walked down the rectory steps and turned through the wrought-iron gateway. He hired a hackney coach at the stand on Piccadilly, tipping the waterman a penny. Judging by the faded coat of arms, the deep, comfortable seats and the exhausted suspension, the vehicle had once belonged to a nobleman. He felt like an infant, swaddled and jiggled helplessly by its nurse, as the coach shuddered its way through the London traffic. He paid off the driver outside the Admiralty, where he was to begin the task of supervising the final drafting of several hundred charts and plans.

A familiar figure was waiting for him on the Admiralty steps, but the extreme unfamiliarity of the context led him to hesitate for a moment, trying to place the apparition. It was a figure he was better used to seeing at the wheel of the *Beagle* as she bucked into a head-on gale.

'Mr Murray?'

Murray said nothing, and FitzRoy ran the whole gamut of emotions in an instant, from fearing the worst to believing that events must have come to a satisfactory conclusion. The Scotsman simply handed him a letter, his face a blank canvas on which FitzRoy had painted a thousand imaginary expressions before he had even broken the wafer and unfolded the wrapper.

The letter was signed by Dr Dickson, of the Royal Naval Hospital.

Sir

I am sorry to inform you that Boat Memory died this afternoon in the eruptive stage of smallpox. He was perfectly covered with the eruption; but the pustules did not advance to maturation as they should have done, and as the breathing was much impeded, I had little or no expectation of his recovery. He has been saved much suffering – and those about him from attending a loathsome Disease. In the boy Button the appearance of the vaccine bacilli is satisfactory – and as the others have been revaccinated, I am in hope they will be saved from the fate of their countryman.

I beg to remain

Sir

Yours faithfully

D.H. Dickson

FitzRoy looked up from the letter, and realized that the expression on Murray's face had not been a vacant one; it was the look of a man whose heart has been scoured out from the inside.

PART TWO

CHAPTER NINE

The Mount, Shrewsbury, 29 August 1831

The mail coach from Oswestry disgorged Charles Darwin and three other passengers into the crowded inn-yard of the Lion, where he stretched his cramped legs and waited for his pack to be unloaded from the roof. Post-boys in smart red jackets and pedlars in smock frocks swarmed around to see to the horses and passengers respectively, most persistent of all being an urchin claiming to possess a trained bullfinch that would whistle 'The White Cockade' for a penny. Although the afternoon was grey and faintly sticky, Darwin decided to make his way to the Mount on foot. The trip from North Wales on macadamized roads had hardly taxed his muscles; the milestones had ticked rapidly by, although the relentless quickset hedges that arrowed into the distance had quickly become monotonous. Both his limbs and his senses were in need of exercise. Piqued as his curiosity was by the prospect of a singing bullfinch, he was keen to be home and marched off up Wyle Cop at a good pace. His long legs covered the ground with rapid strides, leaving the disappointed little boy – who thought he had sensed a business deal – to give up the chase some thirty yards beyond the inn gates.

Before long the streets and houses had given way to stands of acacia and copper beech, which in turn receded to reveal the great red-brick mansion that his father had built. It was an impassive rectangle boasting of solid provincial prosperity, its clean lines broken only by the classical portico at its base, put there to remind the visitor of the culture and learning that had literally elevated the Darwin family to this comfortable spot. Charles could see the servants going about their business on the lawn, and a tall, willowy shape – his sister Caroline, to judge from the brown mass of curls escaping from under the bonnet – compiling a bouquet of flowers. Before long, one of the housemaids spotted the dusty figure striding vigorously through the gates and sounded the alert. Maids scurried to check that Master Charles's room was properly prepared, while the waterman rushed to fill a bucket with hot water. By the time he had reached the sitting room, the whole house was aware that its youngest son had returned.

'Charley!'

His sister Susan put down her embroidery, pitter-pattered across the room and threw her arms round him. 'You look uncommon well.'

'Hello, Susan. Hello, Catty.'

His younger sister Catherine also rose to embrace him, but not before she had finished her paragraph in the *Weekly Magazine of the Society for the Diffusion of Useful Knowledge.*

'Charley dear. We thought you were never coming back.'

'If you thought I would forgo the start of the partridge season, then you do not know your beloved brother.'

'Have you had any sport in Wales?'

'After a fashion – I have been hunting old red sandstone, which is the next best thing. Professor Sedgwick and I walked all the way from Llangollen to Great Orme's Head, looking for a band of sandstone that is on Greenough's map. Well, it is there on the map right enough, but by the Lord Harry there is none in the ground. Old Greenough's map is pure fiction!' His face flushed with exhilaration at the memory of his and Sedgwick's discovery.

'How exciting,' said Susan brightly.

'How I should love to go geologizing,' said Catherine, quietly.

'Oh, you wouldn't like it, Catty, really you wouldn't. It's the most fearful slog, all that tramping and hiking through rocks and mud and gorse – it's really no hobby for a gentlewoman. It's all frightfully boring – just measuring and collecting samples. Although I was able to make use of the clinometer that Professor Henslow gave me.'

'What's a clinometer?'

'It measures the inclination of rock beds. It really is the most splendid instrument, in brass and wood. I must write to thank Henslow once more.

Oh, but this is all I, I, I! I see your sister has begun another embroidery.'

'It is to be "Fame Scattering Flowers on Shakespeare's Tomb"' explained Susan. 'Why, you may have it when it is finished, if you approve.' She gave him another kiss.

Caroline, the eldest of the three sisters, now made an entrance from the garden, having demurely exchanged her bonnet for an indoor cap.

'The wanderer returns,' she beamed, hugging her brother and joining in the fuss. 'Have you told him about the letter yet?'

'The letter, of course,' cried Susan with excitement, and went to fetch it from the hallway, too flustered to call for a servant.

'A most urgent letter,' Caroline explained conspiratorially. 'Express delivery, at treble the cost. There were two shillings and fourpence to pay. We had to send Edward to the inn twice, as he had insufficient coin with him the first time.'

'Papa had to tip up for it, so of course he grumbled for a good half-hour,' confided Catherine. 'He said you could hire a man to ride to Cambridge and back for less.'

'It's from Cambridge? Where is Papa?' A hint of trepidation crept into Darwin's voice.

'In his study, with window-curtains drawn as usual. Papa has not been able to get about much these last few weeks – even less so than usual.'

'I am sorry to hear it.'

Susan returned bearing the letter, and the three women formed a tall white palisade about their brother. Each was eager for news, hungry for anything out of the ordinary.

'Talk of the very devil – it's from Professor Henslow himself,' said Darwin, glancing at the superscription. He broke open the wafer and unwrapped the brown paper.

'Well?'

'What does it say?'

'It is about a certain Captain FitzRoy.'

'Read it out.'

' "Captain FitzRoy is undertaking a second voyage to survey the coast

of Tierra del Fuego, and afterwards to visit many of the South Sea
Islands, to return by the Indian Archipelago. The vessel is fitted out
expressly for scientific purposes, combined with the survey; it will
furnish, therefore, a rare opportunity for a Naturalist. An offer has
been made to me by the Hydrographer's office, to recommend a
proper person to go out with this expedition; he will be treated with
every consideration. The Captain is a young man of very pleasing
manners, of great zeal in his profession, and who is very highly
spoken of. I have stated that I consider you the best qualified person
I know of who is likely to undertake such a situation. I state this
not on the supposition of your being a finished Naturalist, but as
amply qualified for collecting, observing and noting anything worthy
to be noted on Natural History." '

Darwin broke off. 'A voyage around the world,' he breathed. 'What
would I forfeit to go on such a journey? Imagine it!'

'Oh, Charles,' squeaked Susan. 'I can't.'

'I can,' said Catherine.

'He admits I am not the first candidate – the Reverend Mr Jenyns has
turned it down, and Henslow has too – "Mrs Henslow looked so miser-
able that I at once settled the point." And he writes a word or two as to
the cost...it will be thirty guineas per annum to mess, plus some six
hundred guineas in the way of equipment. Well, there, I think, will be the
stumbling block. It is a pretty sum.' His mind turned once more to the
forbidding prospect of his father, awaiting him in the darkened study.

'If he grumbled about two shillings and fourpence, think what he will
say to six hundred guineas,' murmured Caroline, whose thoughts had
strayed in the same direction.

'*Do* go on,' said Catherine, impatiently.

' "Captain FitzRoy wants a man (I understand) more as a companion
than a mere collector, and would not take anyone, however good a
Naturalist, who was not recommended to him likewise as a
gentleman. Don't put on any modest doubts or fears about your

disqualifications, for I assure you I think you are the very man they are in search of.

So conceive yourself to be tapped on the shoulder by your affectionate friend, Professor John Henslow." '

Susan exhaled, and Caroline looked faintly anxious.

'Well,' breathed Catherine finally, 'it sounds to me like a pretty desperate way of avoiding having to pay your tailor.'

The first thing Charles saw upon entering the study was the shape of an inverted crescent moon, where the daylight, split into shafts by the heavy drapes, illuminated the bald rim of his father's head. As his eyes struggled against the twilight his father's colossal silhouette took form, all six foot two and twenty-three stone of it. Dr Darwin was wedged into his favourite stiff-backed armchair or, rather, he seemed to grow from it, as if man and chair were hewn from the same enormous slab of rock. Charles could barely make out his father's features, but memory filled the void: the heavy black brows angled severely in to the bridge of the nose, contrasting with the neatly trimmed white tufts over each ear; the defiant bulldog jowls; the pursed, unsmiling mouth, the lower lip curled contemptuously against the world as a matter of routine. Any resolve he had felt upon entering his father's study evaporated in an instant.

'You have returned, Charles.'

'Yes, sir.'

'Your trip was satisfactory?'

'Most satisfactory, sir.'

'I have received an account, Charles, from Christ's College, Cambridge. An account for two hundred and three guineas, seven shillings and sixpence in unpaid battels. An account which I have settled.'

Charles's heart sank. He had quietly prayed for that particular chicken to refrain from coming home to roost just yet.

'Thank you, sir.'

'Do you have anything to say for yourself, Charles?'

'I'm sorry, sir.'

'You have an allowance, Charles. A most generous allowance. And yet you have exceeded it importunately. Have I not been generous, Charles?'

'You have been most generous, sir.'

'I have also had to part with the sum of two shillings and fourpence for an express letter from Cambridge. Does it contain another account in need of settlement?'

'No sir. It contains an offer from Professor Henslow, the professor of botany at the university. He has recommended me for the post of super-numerary naturalist, sir, on a Royal Naval expedition travelling around the world.'

Charles awaited the expected explosion, but it did not come. Yet. Instead, the doctor's eyes remained hooded in the darkness; his head lifted from his shoulders like a cobra's, his already broad neck seeming to thicken as it did so.

'And is it your intention to accept this offer, Charles?'

Charles took a deep breath, and stuck out his own neck. 'I do consider it to be an invaluable opportunity, sir, for one of my lowly standing in the scientific community.'

'Indeed. I was not aware that you were a member of the *scientific community*. I was under the impression that you were taking instruction in theology as a preliminary to entering the curacy. Is it now the business of a priest to encircle the globe? Does the route to heaven go via Cape Horn?'

'Professor Henslow is a priest, sir. As is Professor Sedgwick, with whom I have been studying geology in North Wales.'

'Then why does not *the Reverend* Professor Henslow apply for this exalted position himself?'

'He is...indisposed, sir, on account of his family. And the Reverend Mr Jenyns, sir, who was offered the position before me, would have travelled but for his duty to his parishioners at Bottisham.'

'It is to be wondered, then, that the parishes of England are not wholly vacant. And how, pray, do you intend to maintain yourself on this voyage of – forgive me, for I omitted to enquire of its duration.'

'Two years, sir. Possibly three.'

'Two years, possibly three. How, then, do you intend to maintain yourself during this considerable length of time?'

'I had very much hoped, sir, to lay claim to your generosity in this matter.'

'You had hoped to lay claim to my generosity in this matter.'

'You have been generous enough, sir, to defray the cost of my brother Erasmus's year in Switzerland and Germany.'

'Your brother Erasmus has completed his medical studies at Edinburgh University, and now furthers them on the continent. Your brother Erasmus did not leave off his studies after spending two years riding to hounds and collecting rocks when he should have been studying medicine. Your brother Erasmus did not exceed *his* most generous allowance.'

'I should be deuced clever to spend more than my allowance while cooped on board a naval vessel, sir,' chuckled Charles, in an unwise attempt at levity.

'But they all tell me you are very clever, Charles, not, I must confess, that I can discern any trace of it in this instant. So, to the crux. What, pray, is the expected cost of this adventure?'

The young man swallowed. 'Approximately...approximately seven hundred guineas all told, sir.'

There was silence. Charles had hoped that his eyesight would have better accustomed itself to the gloom, but his father's study seemed darker than ever. He could barely make out Dr Darwin's face, but instinct, coupled with a gradual change in the doctor's breathing, told him that it had turned a shade of purple he knew all too well. And then the explosion came.

'You care for nothing, do you hear me? You care for nothing but shooting, dogs and rat-catching, and you will be a disgrace to yourself and all your family! You dare to suggest that I pay for you to alter your profession for the third time in six years! And not, indeed, for the sake of any respectable position but for the sake of a wild scheme – a thoroughly useless undertaking – that would be entirely disreputable to your character as a clergyman hereafter! How should you ever settle down to a steady, respectable existence after such a – a jaunt? Clearly, nobody else can be found who will take on this utterly discreditable enterprise; many others have obviously turned down this – this *escapade* before you. From its not being previously accepted, one can only surmise that there is some serious objection to this vessel or expedition. Sailing ships are like gaols – brutal discipline, filthy conditions, with the additional disadvantage of being drowned!'

Even in the midst of a rage, Dr Darwin was not averse to quoting Johnson.

'What was the name of the vessel that went down with all hands not a few months back? The *Thetis*, was it? I cannot permit you, Charles, to involve yourself in such a foolish and costly undertaking. Whatever would your mother have said?'

Charles's train of thought diverted automatically to the inadequate framework of memories he had constructed to represent his mother. The edge of her work-table, seen from below. The rustle of her black velvet gown. Her white face on her deathbed, on a July afternoon. The smell in the room. Not once since that bewildering and frightening day had his father even mentioned his mother, still less invoked her name. *He's frightened of me dying too*, Charles realized. *Behind all that thunderous rage at unpaid accounts lies genuine fear at the prospect of losing another member of his family.*

'I understand, sir. Thank you, sir.'

'If you find any man of common sense – *any* man – who advises you to go, I shall give my consent. Otherwise, I suggest in the strongest terms that you write to Professor Henslow, declining his offer.'

'Yes sir.'

And with that, Charles left the study and emerged blinking into the hallway, heading for the front door and escape. Hearing his footsteps, Catherine came out of the sitting room, the obvious question framed upon her lips, but as soon as she saw her brother's burning cheeks and corrugated brow she had her answer.

Charles strode around to the back of the house, tactfully left to himself by his sisters, and halted at the edge of the terrace. In the distance, the river Severn curled through a lush, inviting panorama of soft green meadows. Below him the ramshackle dwellings of Frankwell, Shrewsbury's poorest suburb, lapped against the foot of the hill like a dull grey sea. Resentfully, he turned on his heel and headed inside to compose his letter of refusal to John Henslow.

The first day of the partridge season saw Darwin rise early and take the curricle over to Maer to go shooting with his uncle Jos. He had opted for that particular vehicle as it was light and fast, but even in the early morning the road to Stoke-on-Trent seemed unusually littered with obstacles. A sleeping tollman. A gang of navvies macadamizing the road. A flock of sheep on their uncomplaining way to Market Drayton. A ridiculously slow cartload of pulverized stone pulled by a single donkey that looked fit only for cartwheel grease. Waggonloads of bleak-faced agricultural labourers, who had in all probability lost their homes, roaming the countryside in search of late harvest-work threshing oats or barley.

Darwin sat up on the box with the coachman, as if stealing an extra foot or two would get him to Maer sooner. His mood had not improved: the past couple of days at the Mount had been made awkward by the business of Henslow's letter, and he was glad to get away. A labourer seated outside his cottage waved a respectful good morning, his breakfast of bread, onions and donkey milk spread out before him in the sunshine, but Darwin was in no mood to return the greeting. There were endless such cottages bordering the road, the crude, single-roomed lath-and-plaster constructions of the rural poor. Was he expected to salute every single occupant? They passed a crowd of women lining a stream, beating their threadbare laundry with wooden paddles. It seemed incredible that the countryside could support so many people in such squalor. Surely, in this age of mechanization and modernization, somebody could do something for them?

After Market Drayton the traffic thinned out somewhat, but his father's coachman kept a careful course between the whitethorn hedgerows, anxious not to scratch Dr Darwin's paintwork. Six miles south-west of Stoke they turned off on the rough track towards Maer, whereupon Charles's new stock, which he had put on for the benefit of his female cousins, chafed at his neck with every bounce of the curricle. It was with an enormous sense of relief that he finally spied the gates of Maer thrown welcomingly open, and beyond them the warm, ancient stone of Maer Hall itself amid the trees. The thirty-mile journey had taken more than four hours.

As he expected, he found the Wedgwood family on the garden side, out on their picturesque porch, gathered adoringly around Uncle Jos and Aunt Bessie. A great shout of excitement rose up as he marched round the corner. How friendly, how informal, he thought, how different from the rigid courtesies of life at the Mount. Uncle Jos strode forward and extended all five fingers, rather than the polite double digit, for his favourite nephew to shake. 'Charles. I had a feeling we might see you today.'

Darwin laughed. 'You could not keep me away, sir. Good morning, Aunt Bessie. Good morning, everybody!'

Uncle Jos's eyes shone with pleasure as greetings and embraces were exchanged. An obsessive hunter and shooter, he had suffered the misfortune of siring four sons, not one of whom had ever shown the slightest sporting interest. His nephew, on the other hand, lived for the hunt as he did.

'Oh Charles,' teased Fanny Wedgwood, 'would you not like to come boating with us on the pool? We should *so* love you to come.'

'Oh yes *please*,' echoed Emma, who sat with her arm round her elder sister's waist.

Beyond the flower garden, a steep wooded slope ran down to the sparkling mere that had given the hall its name in the seventeenth century. Fed by clear springs, its marshy end, adjoining the house, had been cleared by Capability Brown and transformed at great expense into a fishtail-shaped landscape feature. Water-birds now paddled in the shallows, or flapped lazily across the surface, scanning the reeds for insects.

'Ladies, that would be a high treat indeed,' affirmed Darwin, his bad mood swiftly evaporating. 'But I fear your father and I have business at hand.'

'Oh Charles,' protested Emma with mock reproach. 'I am sure that you would prefer to go boating if Fanny Owen were present.'

'Ladies, you are making a game of me,' mumbled Darwin, but he knew that he was blushing. It was not merely the mention of the infuriatingly flirtatious and delightful Fanny Owen that had embarrassed him so, but that he appreciated the quietly competing charms of Emma herself just as keenly.

'Come on, my lad. Out with it. Something disturbs you, I can tell.'

Unlike Etruria, the family's former home, which sat grandly on a ridge above Stoke-on-Trent, overlooking the pottery factories that had yielded the vast wealth of the Wedgwoods, Maer Hall nestled amid woods and wild heathland. Walking its sandy paths in search of partridge, one might never imagine that the hustle and bustle of the nineteenth century lay so close by.

'It is nothing, sir. I have been offered a place as a naturalist on a naval expedition around the world – I was recommended by Henslow, the professor of botany at Cambridge – but my father, I suppose under-standably, is reluctant to allow it. He says it is a wild scheme, which will be disreputable to my future character as a clergyman. And it will be costly, too. I think he fears I will end up in the sponging-house.'

Uncle Jos smiled. 'You have felt the rough edge of his tongue, I do not doubt.'

'Yes, sir.'

'Your father cares for your safety, Charles. I saw this with Susannah when she was alive. Although a casual observer might have thought him unduly formal, I could see that he loved your mother very much. But as to this being a wild scheme, and disreputable to a clergyman's character, well, with all due respect to your father, I am bound to disagree. I should think the offer is extremely honourable to you. The pursuit of natural history, though certainly not professional, is very suitable to a clergyman.'

'My father also thought the vessel must be uncomfortable – that there must be some objection to it, as I am not the first to be offered the post.'

'Well, I am no naval expert, but I cannot conceive that the Admiralty would send out a bad vessel on such a service. And if you were appointed by the Admiralty, you would have a claim to be as well accommodated as the vessel would allow. Did your father entertain any other objections?'

'He considered that I was once again changing my profession.'

Uncle Jos laughed. 'Well, you have not been the most steadfast appren-tice to the professions that have been selected for you. If you were presently absorbed in professional studies, then I should probably agree that it would be inadvisable to interrupt them, but this is not the case. Admit-tedly, this journey would be of no use as regards a curacy, but looking upon you as a man of enlarged curiosity, it would afford you such an opportunity of seeing the world as happens to very few.'

'Those are my very own thoughts on the subject – my own thoughts exactly, sir.'

A tiny spark of hope ignited somewhere deep in the young man's heart.

As the last rays of the summer sun flared through the trees, Fanny Wedg-wood sat on the porch, working on a rolled-paperwork decoration for a tea canister, while her sister Emma read out passages from the *Ladies' Pocket Magazine*.

'There is a delightful walking-dress pictured, of striped sarcenet, sea-green on a white ground. The border has a double flounce, the sleeves have mancherons of three points bound round with green satin, the hat has a white veil, and it is ornamented in front with three yellow garden poppies. It says here that all the most distinguished ladies in Kensington Gardens are wearing coloured skirts and dresses this year, trimmed with fine lace. "Silk pelisses are generally seen on our matrons", apparently.'

'You have a silk pelisse or two, Fan,' cut in Hensleigh Wedgwood. 'Does that make you a matron? After all, you are twenty-five.'

Fanny threw a handful of rolled-paperwork trimmings at her brother. 'The canister will be next if you utter another word.'

'Really, Hen. You must learn to be more courteous with your sister,' chided Bessie Wedgwood maternally.

Just then Charles and Jos appeared through the trees bordering the mere, and trudged up between lines of geraniums towards the house. Charles held forth a solitary partridge by its neck, looking curiously pleased with himself for a man with such a paltry bag. 'Just the one,' he called in confirmation.

'A good job we were not expecting partridge pie for supper,' laughed Fanny.

'All the more left over for the poachers,' scoffed Hen.

'And there are certainly enough of those, if the last quarter-sessions are anything to go by,' grumbled Jos.

'Still, even a solitary partridge is one in the eye for the Duke of Wellington!' Charles's comment was deliberately intended to flatter his uncle who, as Whig MP for Shropshire, had helped win the battle to make game licences available outside the squirearchy for the first time.

'Very true,' beamed Jos. 'Mind you, with only one partridge in the bag that's a devilish dear game licence I've shelled out for.'

'Never mind, dear,' said his wife. 'I'm sure you will have better luck on the morrow.'

'On the morrow? Ah, but we shall not be shooting on the morrow.'

'On the second day of the partridge season? Why ever not, dear?'

Jos grinned at Charles conspiratorially. 'Because Charles and I shall go off tomorrow to return Robert Darwin's curricle to its owner.'

The door to Dr Darwin's study was pushed warily open. The silent dust motes, unexpectedly disturbed, whirled about in panic-stricken eddies. Charles moved forward cautiously into the darkened room.

'Charles?'

'Father.'

'I thought you were at Maer, for the partridge.'

'I have just returned from there, sir. Father...would you consider Uncle Jos to be a "man of common sense"?'

Dr Darwin could just make out a stiff-backed figure silhouetted in the doorway behind his son, a pair of neatly trimmed grey sideburns illuminated by the daylight from the hallway. 'Your uncle Josiah?...But of course. That goes without saying. What an absurd question. Why ever do you ask?'

Josiah Wedgwood stepped forward into the study.

'Good morning, Robert,' he said.

*

'I am the devil of a fellow at hunting – the best shot in my family, sir. One day I intend to be an admiral. The best way for me to arrive at that position, it seems, will be for me to serve on the *Beagle*. The arrangement will benefit you and it will also benefit me.'

Charles Musters looked FitzRoy squarely in the eye. Coolly, FitzRoy returned his gaze. They were sitting facing each other across a desk in a borrowed Admiralty office, where FitzRoy was recruiting the few remaining officers required for the second surveying voyage of the *Beagle*. At the back of the room, Musters's mother raised her eyes despairingly to heaven. Charles Musters was eleven years old.

'I could have gone to the Royal Naval College in Portsmouth, but my father says it is better to learn seamanship on a ship than in a class-room. My father says that college volunteers are all soft-handed whelps, sir.'

'Your father may well have a point,' conceded FitzRoy gravely, 'but I'm sure he would be the first to stress the importance of practical knowl-edge as well.' He opened a desk drawer, took out a copy of *The Young Sea Officer's Sheet Anchor* by Darcy Lever, and passed it to the boy. 'Now, Mr Musters. If you can learn the entire contents of this book, by rote, by the time the *Beagle* sails in October – and no slacking, for I shall test you on it – then I may just have a place for you as a volunteer. You will need to bring your own south-wester, two pairs of canvas trousers, two flannel shirts, a blanket, a straw mattress—'

'A donkey's breakfast, sir.'

'A donkey's breakfast indeed. One pair of shoes – without nails – a panikin, a spoon and, most important of all, your own knife.'

'A sailor without a knife is like a woman without a tongue, sir.'

'You certainly know a fair amount about seamanship for one who has never sailed, Mr Musters,' conceded FitzRoy, giving silent thanks that the boy's father had not taught his son the full unexpurgated version of the quip. 'Your salary will be ten shillings a month. I look forward to seeing you at Devonport in October, Mr Musters.'

'The pleasure is all mine, sir.'

The interview over, FitzRoy stood up and formally shook the boy's hand.

'You will take care of him, won't you?' breathed Musters's mother.

'As if he were my own son, madam. There will be another volunteer aboard – my new clerk, Edward Hellyer, who is an altogether...quieter boy, who writes a good hand, so Charles will not go short of company his own age. I am sure they will get on famously. Rest assured, madam, I will do everything in my power to ensure your son's safe return.'

FitzRoy ushered Mrs Musters and Charles into the corridor, where he was surprised to find a large, bleary-eyed, unshorn youth in a chair, surrounded by vast piles of luggage, his huge, knitted brows buried deep in a copy of the *Edinburgh Review*. As the Musterses bade him farewell, the youth looked up.

'Captain FitzRoy?'

'Yes?'

'I'm so sorry I am late. I came as soon as I could. I caught the Wonder – the lightning coach from Shrewsbury. It makes the journey up to London overnight, non-stop. It's remarkable – they sound a bugle, and the turnpike opens up, and you thunder straight through like a mail coach.'

'Remarkable,' assented FitzRoy. 'But there is not the least occasion for any apology.'

The youth rose to his feet, revealing the crumpled wreckage of a gentleman's woollen country suit, which contrasted sharply with FitzRoy's own immaculate buckskin tights. The stranger was extremely tall – at least six feet in height, thickset and shambling, with long arms, a pleasant round face and friendly grey eyes. His bulbous unsightly nose was squashed against his face like that of a farmer recently defeated in a tavern brawl. All in all, it struck FitzRoy that there was something vaguely simian about the young man's appearance.

'Please excuse my apparel. I have come directly from the inn by hackney coach. I have not slept at all.'

'I beg you won't mention it,' murmured FitzRoy.

'I hope I am not too late. Did you receive a copy of my letter?'

'It seems not,' advanced FitzRoy, cautiously, now utterly bewildered as to the stranger's identity.

'Thank goodness for that. You must disregard it if you do. Everything has changed. I say, would you mind awfully helping me move my bags into your office?'

FitzRoy, who felt in no position to refuse such an urgent request, complied politely.

'I believe I have brought everything I need. A hand-magnifier, a portable dissecting microscope, equipment for blow-pipe analysis, a contact goniometer for measuring the angles of crystals – that's bound to be useful –'

'Bound to be,' acknowledged FitzRoy.

'– a magnet, beeswax, several jars with cork lids, preserving-papers for specimens, a clinometer, dinner drawers and shirt – do you dress for dinner? – thick worsted stockings, several shirts – I've had them all marked "Darwin" – a cotton nightcap—'

The stranger broke off, for FitzRoy had begun to laugh.

'I'm sorry, is my inventory at fault? I did my best to conceive of every-thing that might be needed, but what with the shortage of time…'

'My dear sir, you must forgive me. My manners are atrocious. But I do believe you have omitted to tell me your name. Although I must thank your shirts for furnishing me with a clue.'

'By the Lord Harry, what a buffoon I am! I am Charles Darwin,' explained the stranger, as if that settled the matter.

'Charles Darwin,' repeated FitzRoy blankly.

'I am the naturalist invited on your voyage by Professor Henslow.'

'Ah!' FitzRoy exhaled, beginning to understand. 'I am delighted to make your acquaintance, Mr Darwin. Please forgive my inexcusable confusion. I did enquire of the hydrographer, Captain Beaufort, some weeks back, as to finding me a naturalist and companion for this voyage, but I had heard nothing by return. In the meantime I have also pursued other avenues. I fear I must own' – here FitzRoy improvised hastily – 'that the position is already taken, by a Mr Chester. Do you know Harry Chester?'

'No,' said Darwin bleakly, his face a picture of misery.

'He is the son of Sir Robert Chester. He works in the Privy Council office.' It was true that FitzRoy had offered the post to Harry Chester, who, fearing for his life, had turned him down flat inside five minutes. But now that he had lied about Chester's acceptance, FitzRoy began to feel like a thorough scoundrel.

'I suppose I had better leave, then.' The young man addressed the remark unhappily to his own oversized knees.

'No, wait. Please tell me about yourself. Who knows? Perhaps Mr Chester will change his mind. You are a botanist? A stratigrapher?'

'I do a little in that way. I am a parson. A parson-to-be, at any rate. That is to say, I am a student. I am doing an ordinary arts degree, preparatory to a career in orders. But I am fascinated by all branches of natural philosophy. I always have been. Even when I was at Mr Case's school, aged eight, I used to fish for newts in the quarry pool. And I collected pebbles – I wanted to know about each and every stone in front of the hall door. My nickname at Shrewsbury School was Gas. My brother Erasmus and I had our own laboratory. It was in an old scullery in the garden. We used to determine the composition of commonplace substances, coins and so forth, by producing calxes – you know, oxides. And we used to buy compounds and purify them into their constituent elements. We naïvely thought we might isolate a new element of our own. We had an argand lamp for heating the chemicals, an industrial thermometer from my uncle Jos, and a goniometer – the same one that's in my bag.' The young man's enthusiasm, which had nostalgically begun to pick up speed, came to an abrupt halt at the thought of all the useless equipment gathered about his feet.

What on earth was Beaufort thinking about? wondered FitzRoy. *Sending me an enthusiastic student – a typical country gentleman in orders, who rides to hounds and fancies himself a philosopher. And not even a finished one at that. And if he reads the* Edinburgh Review, *it's ten to a penny he's a Whig.*

'We used to heat everything over an open flame,' Darwin went on, aimlessly filling the silence in the room. 'More often than not the substances exploded.'

'Is that how you came by the scar on your hand?'

'Oh, no, that was done by my sister Caroline when I was but a few months old. I was on her lap, and she was cutting an orange for me, when a cow ran by the window, which made me jump, and the knife went into my hand. I remember it vividly.'

'If it happened to you as a baby, then surely you have been told what happened since and have visualized the incident in your mind.'

'Oh no, because I clearly remember which way the cow ran, and that would not have been told me subsequently.'

For the first time, FitzRoy sat up and took notice. Something in that one act of analysis told him that here was a mind worthy of further investigation, however unpromising the state of the individual that housed it.

'How are you on stratigraphy, Mr Darwin? For I fear there is not much call for a chemist on a naval survey vessel.'

'Oh, but we must now call it geology, Captain FitzRoy. I am fascinated about it. After hunting, it is my second love. I have recently returned from surveying the Llangollen area with Professor Sedgwick – the professor of geology at Cambridge University. He is a marvellous man, sir – a visionary, in my notion. He says that our knowledge of the structure of the earth is much like what an old hen would know of a hundred-acre field, were she scratching in one corner of it. But he says that were we to expand our knowledge sufficiently, we might arrive at the all-embracing hypothesis that would explain the earth's history – the scientific truths that would finally reveal God's intention.'

'I must say, I find myself in complete agreement with your Professor Sedgwick. Not that I am much in the way of geology. Does he have anything to say about the flood?'

'Absolutely. He believes that the investigations of geology can prove that the deluge left traces in diluvial detritus, spread out over all the strata of the world.'

'Proof of the sacred record, in the strata of the rocks?'

'Exactly.'

'Tell me, have you read Buckland's *Reliquiae Diluvianae*?' FitzRoy's enthusiasm was all fired up now.

'About Kirkdale Cave?'

'The very same – hyena and tiger bones, elephant, rhino, hippo and mastodon remains, all in the same North Yorkshire cave. Proof that such beasts once lived and breathed here in Britain. Beasts that must have drowned in the great Biblical deluge.'

'I have been to Whitby to see the incredible fossils exposed by the alum mining there. Have you read William Smith? Professor Sedgwick calls him the father of English geology. He was surveying the digging of canals when he realized that red marl was always to be found over coal deposits. As the strata were angled upwards to the east, one only had to find red marl at the surface, then look to the east to find coal. Such a simple observation, but brilliant nonetheless.'

'Mr Darwin, I often feel there is an underlying simplicity to God's plan that continues to elude us all.'

'But our understanding of it changes every day. Those who pause even for a moment are liable to be swept away by the waters of progress.'

'We are making intellectual progress indeed, but is there such a thing as stratigraphic – I mean, geological progress? I have been reading Lyell's *Principles of Geology Volume One*. Lyell himself has asked me to send him a report from South America. He believes that geological changes are not progressive but random.'

'How can that be? Surely all God's works could be said to advance mankind and the world we live in. Hence the development of modern man from his primitive ancestors.'

'Lyell believes that the idea of geological progress plays into the hands of the transmutationists. That to allow for progress in nature allows for the profane possibility that beasts might gradually have been transmuted into men.'

'Ah. Always an awkward subject in my family, Captain FitzRoy.'

'But of course!' replied FitzRoy, thunderstruck at his own slow-wittedness. 'You must be related to Erasmus Darwin, the transmutationist poet.'

'He was my grandfather. A remarkable man, too, in many ways. But rest assured – I have not the least doubt of the strict and literal truth of every word in the scriptures. Otherwise, how could I lead men to heaven in later life?'

'I am glad to hear it, Mr Darwin. Very glad indeed. Here – I shall make you a present of Lyell.'

He handed his copy of Lyell's book across to Darwin, who leafed through the first few pages. The volume, Darwin observed, had been inscribed by its author. 'But, Captain FitzRoy, I cannot possibly accept this. It is personally dedicated.'

'On the contrary, sir, it is my great privilege to make you a present of it. In due course I beg to make you known to the author himself.'

'You are too kind, sir – too kind.'

'But tell me, Mr Darwin, why a country parsonage for such an enquiring mind?'

'Oh, I was all set to be a physician, sir, like my father. I studied medicine at Edinburgh University but I am afraid I did not come up to the scratch. I was too squeamish. I saw the amputation of a child's leg as part of my studies. It was a very bad operation – the poor thing was screaming fit to burst and lost a sight of blood. So I quitted, and transferred to marine biology under Professor Grant. We collected invertebrates together in Leith harbour. And I read up for natural history under Jameson – zoology, botany, palaeontology, mineralogy and geology. When my father found out he was furious, and withdrew me from the university. Although I have since wondered whether he was not simply worried that I might fall into the clutches of Burke and Hare.'

FitzRoy chuckled.

Darwin went on, in full flow now: 'Jameson was a quite dreadful speaker, but I think you will be in accord with the principles governing his philosophy, as I was. He believes that the very aim of science is to prove God's natural law. To obtain a detailed view of the animal creation, which affords striking proofs and illustrations of the wisdom and power of its author. He believes that nature is governed by laws laid down by God, laws that are difficult to discern or capture in mathematical terms, but to understand which is the highest aim of all natural philosophy.'

'But that is one of the very purposes of my voyage, Mr Darwin, to advance such knowledge as best we are able! But, tell me, what did you do when you left Edinburgh?'

'My father entered me for Christ's College, Cambridge, to train as a priest. But theology is a broad church, Captain FitzRoy! I studied Paley's natural theology. Do you know of William Paley? He believed that the Creator has designed the universe as a watchmaker would fashion a watch. I must say, sir, I found his logic irresistible. The rest of the time I spent hunting, or collecting beetles with my cousin Fox. We discovered several new species in the fields outside Cambridge. They are all in Stephens's *Illustrations of British Insects*. I tell you, sir, no poet ever felt more delight at seeing his first poem published than I did at seeing the magic words "Captured by C. Darwin Esquire". On one day, I found three new species under the same piece of bark. I put one in each hand and popped the third into my mouth. Alas, it ejected some intensely acid fluid that burnt my tongue. So I was forced to spit out the beetle and all three were lost.'

FitzRoy roared with laughter. 'Well, Mr Darwin, I have had one or two unusual meals in my time, but nothing to match that.'

'Oh, we formed a club at Cambridge, the Glutton Club, with the sole intention of consuming strange flesh. We tried hawk, and bittern, and a stringy old brown owl, which tasted quite disgusting. All consumed with claret over a game of *vingt-et-un*. Anything we could shoot, really. I stuffed the skins myself and divided them between my own and Fox's rooms. I was taught to stuff birds in Edinburgh by a blackamoor servant.'

'My dear Mr Darwin, will you excuse me for a minute?'

FitzRoy stepped outside and stood in the corridor, his back against the wall, pondering his dilemma. Really, this was not the sort of person he had envisaged taking around the world. Phrenologically speaking, the man's squashed nose spoke of insufficient energy and determination. But his sheer enthusiasm, his quick mind and his training in natural theology had combined to win over FitzRoy. Furthermore, the young man had made him laugh. He had not been able to laugh, not once, since Boat Memory's death. The news of the loss of the *Thetis*, sunk with all hands off Cabo Frio, had compounded his misery. All those close friends drowned. Hamond, Purkis, de Courcy, even Captain Bingham; indecisive, fussy, well-meaning Captain Bingham, who had once nursed him through a potentially fatal bout of cholera. Only he, Murray and Sulivan had escaped, by virtue of transferring to the *Beagle*. All the others were dead. There but for the grace of God. And now God had sent this ridiculous young man to resurrect his spirits. FitzRoy made up his mind, turned, and went back into the room.

'It seems you are in luck, Mr Darwin. I have just heard from my friend Mr Chester. He has sent a note to say that he is in office, and will not be able to travel.'

'But – but this is wonderful news!' stammered Darwin. 'You – you are sure?'

'Never more so. But I want you to be aware that there are certain conditions attached to your acceptance of my offer. The voyage may take at least two years. I make no guarantee that we will be able to visit every place stipulated on our route. Your accommodations, I must make clear, shall not be numerous. There shall be seventy souls or more aboard the *Beagle*, so the want of room on such a vessel shall be considerable. We must live poorly – as my companion, you will have no wine and the plainest of dinners. And most important of all: shall you bear being told that I want the cabin to myself? If not, probably we should wish each other at the devil.' *I am hoping that you will save me from the devil,* thought FitzRoy. *But if you cannot – if he comes for me once more – then nobody can see me in the midst of that struggle. Not you. Not anybody.*

'I understand completely, Captain FitzRoy. As long as I have the freedom to make whatever shore excursions I require – I have been reading Humboldt on the tropics, you see, and am eager to explore – then everything you describe shall be to my satisfaction. If you can suffer me, then I shall accept with the greatest delight.'

'Excellent. You will be borne on the ship's books for provisions. I have already fixed this matter with the Admiralty.'

'My dear FitzRoy, I insist that I pay a fair share of the expenses of your table. My father is a rich man, having made a considerable fortune from funds and consolidated annuities, and a most generous individual. I assure you that it will not present any problem for me to pay my share.' A terrifying vision of Dr Darwin in his darkened study loomed into his son's thoughts, but he resolved to face this obstacle at a later date.

'My dear Darwin, as long as you are comfortable according to your own terms, we shall co-exist happily. I am sure we shall suit. Tell me, are you a Whig?'

'All my life and proud of it, sir. My uncle is the Whig MP for Shropshire.'

'Well, you are to room with a stalwart Tory, from a family positively riddled with Tory MPs. So I suggest that we give the subject of politics a wide berth.'

'As my friends say, who can touch pitch and not become a Tory?'

FitzRoy laughed. 'Your friends will also tell you that a sea captain is the greatest brute on the face of the Creation. I do not know how to help you in this, except by hoping that you will give me a fair trial.'

Darwin laughed too, and realized in that moment that he was intoxicated with the captain's perfect manners, his understanding nature and his quiet authority.

'By the bye, Mr Darwin, do you believe in phrenology?'

'Of course.'

'Well, then, I must confess that when you first came into this office, I deduced that the shape of your forehead, and of your nose, might make us ill-suited as companions for a long sea voyage. I must now admit, sir, that your nose spoke falsely.'

And the pair leaned back in their chairs and rocked with laughter.

'Hang me if I shall give sixty guineas for pistols!'

Darwin could hardly believe his eyes.

FitzRoy, having scheduled no further interviews for the rest of the day, and being in such an enthusiastic state regarding the learned discussions he was to have with his new-found friend that he wished to commence them straight away, had dragged Darwin with him on a spending spree that very afternoon. Normally the West End would have been deserted at this time of year, but the coronation procession of William IV was due in three days' time: the pavements were bedecked with flags, gas illuminations, crowns, anchors and little decorative WRs, and the streets were packed with gigs, phaetons and carriages of every shape and size. FitzRoy's own gig had positively crawled past Regent Street's shiny colonnades, before eventually depositing the pair on the steps of Collier's gunshop at number forty-five the Strand. It was, as FitzRoy pointed out, the most expensive gunshop in London, but indubitably the best.

'Mr Collier may be an American but, by Jove, he knows his stuff,' he exclaimed, raising a Brunswick rifle to the light from the window. 'See? The bullet has a raised band on it. It engages with spiral grooves inside the barrel, which imparts spin.'

'My dear Captain FitzRoy—'

'Call me FitzRoy, please.'

'My dear FitzRoy, these rifles are two hundred guineas apiece.'

'I'm all for economy, Darwin, except on one point. The point where one's life, or the life of a fellow crew member, is jeopardized. Besides, I suspect the silver filigree work does not come cheap.'

Once again, the image of an oversized purple parent swam into Darwin's mind.

'Well, I suppose I might give sixty guineas for the pistols,' he conceded, trying hard to convince himself that this would be regarded as a safety measure back at the Mount. 'They are good strong weapons, double-barrelled with top-spring bayonets. They should keep the natives quiet. I dare say we shall have plenty of fighting with those damned cannibals, what? It would be something to shoot the King of the Cannibal Islands!'

Notwithstanding Darwin's enthusiasm for intellectual enquiry, there was a youthful quality to his manner that reminded FitzRoy irresistibly of Midshipman King. 'Actually, Darwin, I shall introduce to you some cannibal friends of mine. That is to say, they are ex-cannibals, of course. They really are quite charming – at least, two of them are. They are presently staying at Walthamstow, and we shall be returning them to their homeland in Tierra del Fuego. I am sure they will be delighted to make your acquaintance. If you like,' he added mischievously, 'I shall invite them to dine with us. I can assure you that their manners are immaculate. Although you can bring your new pistols if you are worried.'

Three days later, Darwin and FitzRoy bought jellies at Dutton's, gave a guinea each for front-row seats to see the coronation procession, and allowed themselves to be childishly swept away by patriotic fervour. Their places were located right opposite the mansion of the Duke of Northumberland, which lit up as dusk fell like the palace of an eastern potentate.

'I was in London for the illumination to launch the Reform Bill, and this is much grander,' marvelled Darwin.

'A comment, perhaps, on his lordship's successful resistance to reform.'

'Well, he has certainly compensated for it this time. The little gas-jets in the windows are almost painfully brilliant.'

'Were not the Life Guards magnificent this afternoon?' exclaimed FitzRoy. 'And prodigious tall. They do say that each of those fellows is over six feet.'

Darwin grinned. 'Then there is hope for me finding yet another profession! I say, when the crowd spilled into the roadway I thought that the captain on the black horse would kill a score at least. One would suppose men were made of sponge, to see them shrink away so.'

'I have never seen so many human beings in one place. Even now it is like a raceground.'

The crowds gathered for the evening's fireworks were, if anything, thicker than those that had lined the route during the day.

'One wonders what the poor of London must make of so much gilt and show. I mean, I'm none of your radicals, but with all the riots and hangings and transportations of late, I cannot imagine their humour will be much improved by such a display. Even you as a Tory, FitzRoy, must concede the point. To subsist on bread and coffee, and then to have to witness a bejewelled buffoon like that fellow accompanying the King's regalia – who was it again?'

'The Duke of Grafton.'

'The Duke of Grafton. It must put them in mind to pain. Do you not concede the point?' Darwin, a rosy flush seeping across his face, looked every inch the eager student.

'On this occasion, my dear Darwin, I shall concede the point,' replied FitzRoy with extreme gravity. 'But not as a Tory.'

'Indeed, sir? Then how so?'

'I shall concede the point from personal acquaintance. The Duke of Grafton is my uncle.'

Darwin's face, frozen in horror, was a perfect picture. FitzRoy's features, by contrast, showed no expression. The young man endeavoured to stammer an apology.

'M-my dear FitzRoy, I must beg – no, I must crave your forgiveness. I have behaved like an absolute blackguard. My conduct has been inexcusable – quite inexcusable. I offer you my most sincere, heartfelt apologies. I really do not know what—'

FitzRoy could keep a straight face no longer. He threw back his head and roared with helpless laughter, revelling in the sensation of enjoying himself for the first time in months.

Captain Francis Beaufort, the distinguished hydrographer of His Majesty's Navy, hobbled painfully across the turkey-carpet to his chair. His femur had been shattered just below the hip by a musket-ball, fired at him by pirates in the Eastern Mediterranean in 1812; a catastrophic event undoubtedly, but one that had initiated perhaps the most distinguished naval career ever to unfold from behind a desk. Wiry and energetic of mind, if not body, Beaufort gave no hint of his invalidity when seated behind a solid block of mahogany, at the heart of his empire. As a fellow 'scientific' sailor, FitzRoy regarded him with the deepest respect.

'I must extend the most profound thanks to you, sir, for finding me such a suitable companion. Mr Darwin is young, extremely so at times, but any rough edges will be well and truly polished after two years at sea. I am in a thoroughly good cue at the prospect of his company.'

'You may not thank me when you hear what I have to say.' Beaufort's normally gentle Irish tones sounded unexpectedly gruff and awkward.

'If it is the chronometers, sir, then the Admiralty board have already written to me to explain their reasoning in limiting me to five instruments. I shall ensure that the other four are returned to stores immediately. Meanwhile I have taken the liberty, sir, of purchasing a further six chronometers at my own expense, for a total outlay of three hundred pounds. I feel that for absolute accuracy of observation, one cannot have enough—'

Abruptly, Beaufort waved FitzRoy to silence. His tone was unhappy. 'You're not going.'

'I beg your pardon, sir?'

'I said, you're not going. For reasons of economy, their lordships have decided that the previous survey undertaken by yourself and Captain King will be "entirely sufficient in compiling first-rate navigational charts of Tierra del Fuego and the surrounding waters".'

Stunned, FitzRoy fought to clear his head. He felt, suddenly, as if he were drowning. 'With all due respect, sir, that is wholly untrue. Their lordships appear to be unconscious of the fact that the previous survey barely scratched the surface.'

'You have no need of convincing me, FitzRoy. I have already argued your case, without success. Their lordships' decision is final. Their intention is to prosecute no further surveys of the South American coast.'

'But – but there must be other avenues. I have relatives. Lord Londonderry. The Duke of Grafton.'

'That is a dangerous course to pursue, FitzRoy, and I would strongly advise against it. Your journey might indeed go forward on this occasion, but you will make dangerous enemies of those who are overruled. They will bide their time, mark my words. And the Tories are no longer in power.'

'Indeed not, sir. But I have given my word to the three Fuegians that they will be returned to their homeland before long. I cannot go back on that.'

'Your word, FitzRoy? Your standing will hardly be diminished if you are unable to fulfil your obligations to three natives. They can simply remain here – I am sure they will find an existence wholly preferable to their former lives. They can enter domestic service or somesuch – I gather their grasp of English is reasonably advanced.'

'Sir, I have given my word as a gentleman that they shall be educated as gentlemen – and gentlewoman – and returned to the country of their birth.'

'Well, I am sorry, FitzRoy, but short of taking them back at your own expense, that is not a pledge you will be able to fulfil.'

'In that case, sir, I beg your permission to request a year's leave of absence.'

'I beg your pardon, FitzRoy?'

'I request, sir, that I be allowed to take my leave of the Royal Navy.'

CHAPTER TEN

St Mary's Infants' School, Walthamstow, 17 September 1831

'This is the way we wash our hands
Wash our hands
Wash our hands
This is the way we wash our hands
Early in the morning.'

Jenkins felt his customary warm glow of pride as the children sang, sweetly and harmoniously, making the appropriate hand gestures that accompanied each line. The Indian girl was perhaps the most enthusiastic contributor of all: she wriggled with pleasure on her fat little thighs, a wide beam curving from one ear to the other. As the class moved on to 'This is the way we wash our face', the schoolmaster allowed his gaze to drift benevolently across the heads of his charges, until it came to a rude stop, as it always did, at the hulking form of the big Indian. He alone was not joining in, as he never did. His face wore the same brutal sneer it always wore. He loomed threateningly over the tiny children to either side, as always. What on earth had prompted the Reverend Mr Wilson to invite him here? And who in God's name had thought to christen this remnant of base creation with the title of one of England's finest cathedrals? The Lord did indeed move in a mysterious way that he should test his loyal servant Edward Jenkins so. Jenkins fingered the smallpox scars that had pitted his cheeks since childhood. There had been sterner tests before, and there would be others to come. It was up to him to rise to this challenge.

'Now, children, there are seven things that are an abomination unto the Lord. Can we remember all seven?'

Several hands shot up.

'Alice?' He chose the most tentative.

'A lying tongue, sir.'

Alice, a quiet, undernourished waif who walked in every day from a farm labourer's cottage a few miles south of Walthamstow, had barely spoken a word during her first few months at the school. She ranked as one of Jenkins's proudest achievements.

'Very good, Alice,' he smiled. 'William?'

William, a rake-thin five-year-old lost in a large, ragged smock, let his answer slip out shyly. 'A proud look, sir.'

'Excellent, William.' Such was the Lord's way, he thought: to reproach him gently for his pride, through the mouth of a child.

It was Jenkins's practice to disregard the claims of his more insistent pupils, but the other Indian, the one who was always gazing at his reflection in a looking-glass, had his arm so far in the air it was in danger of popping out of its socket. Like a scarlet balloon tethered to his front row seat, he appeared ready to burst.

'Yes, Jemmy?'

'Hands that shed innocent blood, sir!' exclaimed Jemmy Button, savouring each syllable with undue relish.

'Very good, Jemmy. The Lord abominates hands that shed innocent blood.'

Why couldn't the big one be as keen as this one, as willing to please? Not for the first time, he decided to tackle York Minster's brooding presence head on. 'York. Can you think of anything that is an abomination unto the Lord?'

The big Indian simply stared at him, a look of surly contempt on his face.

'Do you have an answer for me, York?'

Silence.

Jenkins opted to provoke his adversary.

'Do you all see this little boy?' he asked the class.

An affirmative chorus responded.

'I am very sorry for him for he does not allow the Lord into his heart.

Are you not sorry for him, boys and girls?'

'Yes, sir,' chorused the class.

'Let us all try to make him a good boy, for if he is a good boy, we shall all love him, and the Lord shall love him too. Remember, York, "A child is known by his doings" – Proverbs chapter twenty, verse eleven.'

Nothing. The barbarian simply did not react at all, but continued to stare intently in his direction. Jenkins admitted defeat, and moved behind him to the girl, the poor creature who had the misfortune to be betrothed to the brute.

'And you, Fuegia, do you have something to tell the class? Can you think of anything that is an abomination unto the Lord?'

Fuegia smiled her biggest, most appealing smile.

'Feet that be swift,' she replied, in her thickly accented English.

'Feet that be swift...' He waited in vain for her to finish the quotation, before supplying the remainder himself: '...in running to mischief, Fuegia. Feet that be swift in running to mischief.'

Really, the contrast between this delightful child and the feral savage seated in front of her could not have been greater. He reached out an avuncular hand and stroked Fuegia's hair.

And then, he felt it again – that strangest of feelings. The tiny hairs on the nape of his neck rose as if charged with an electric current. His every instinct told him to run for cover, as if there had been a tiger in the room. He glanced round wildly at York, but all he could see was the back of his square, brutal head. It was as if the animal could *sense* his affectionate gesture towards the girl. He tensed, and withdrew his hand abruptly. A flustered pause ensued. A sea of eager faces was looking expectantly up at him, all except one. Jenkins pulled himself together.

'An heart that deviseth wicked imaginations, York. You could have said, an heart that deviseth wicked imaginations.'

'How utterly delightful is the countryside hereabouts!' exclaimed Mrs Rice-Trevor. 'And so close to the city.'

As the carriage clattered across the new metal bridge spanning the river Lea, the surrounding woodlands parted to reveal a marvellous vista of

London beyond the marshes, distant clouds of kites wheeling above the city in the late-summer sunshine.

'Why, all that smog and filth and wretchedness is rendered almost tranquil at such a distance, Mr Wilson. You are fortunate indeed to minister to such a peaceful parish.'

'Sadly, Mrs Rice-Trevor, I rarely see it in the summertime. You see, I have a plural living.' The Reverend William Wilson, who had become utterly entranced by Mrs Rice-Trevor, flushed with the sheer exertion of trying to impress her. 'In winter, I minister to the people of Walthamstow. In summer I minister to the parish of Worton, near Woodstock, itself a place of rare beauty; but not even the considerable beauty of Worton, madam, would stand comparison with your own. We are most honoured that you are able to bless us with your society.'

'Why, Mr Wilson, you are too kind.' Fanny Rice-Trevor blessed the clergyman with a smile that flowed through his bloodstream like a tot of warm whisky, stirring every doubt he had ever nurtured as to his calling. 'I am sure that the three Indians in your charge could not be more fortunate, Mr Wilson. Is that not the case, Bob?'

Suppressing a smile, FitzRoy took the hint and came to his sister's rescue. 'I think there can be no doubt that fortune smiled upon them when the Reverend Mr Wilson consented to admit them to his school. I trust they are advancing well?'

'Oh, there has been considerable progress, Captain FitzRoy, considerable progress. That is, by the boy and the girl. The man is harder to teach, except mechanically. He is interested in carpentry and smithying and animal husbandry, but he is a reluctant gardener – apparently he considers it to be a woman's work.' Wilson smirked in what he hoped was a man-of-the-world fashion at Fanny. 'Jenkins tells me that he quite refuses to learn to read. But in general I must report that they are well disposed, quiet and cleanly people, and not at all fierce and dirty savages. You have done a remarkable job in civilizing them, Captain FitzRoy.'

FitzRoy demurred. 'I am sure that the credit is entirely yours, Mr Wilson.'

'And what about the one who died, Mr Wilson?' Fanny enquired. 'Boat

Memory – do they ever mention him?'

'Never, madam, to my knowledge.'

'Bennet tells the same story,' added FitzRoy. 'But he reports that when Boat died, the other three blackened their faces with a mixture of grease and charcoal from the grate.'

'Remarkable,' said Wilson.

'Perhaps not so remarkable, Mr Wilson,' suggested Fanny. 'Do we not mourn the death of a loved one by dressing in black? In their society they have no clothing but animal skins, so they must decorate themselves in black instead. Perhaps they are not so very different from ourselves, after all.'

'Perhaps not,' murmured Wilson, unconvinced.

Coxswain Bennet watched as the carriage rattled into the centre of Walthamstow village. He tapped out his pipe on the old flint wall of St Mary's Church and straightened his posture. He would be glad to see the skipper again. His paid billet in Walthamstow had been a welcome rest to begin with – keeping an eye on the three Fuegians had hardly been an arduous detail – but the inactivity had begun to pall, and he was eager to return to sea once more, to man the *Beagle*'s boats and ride the waves.

A pair of watchmen moved to challenge the carriage – day patrols had been instituted in the light of the reform riots sweeping the countryside – but almost immediately relaxed again as they recognized Wilson's rubicund visage at the window. The vehicle swept to a halt outside the Squires' Almshouses, from where a little path ran up through the graveyard to the church. Bennet made his way between two lines of jumbled headstones. As the coachman jumped down to open the door for Fanny, he sprang forward to assist her. FitzRoy followed and pumped the coxswain's hand.

'It's good to see you, sir.'

'And you, Mr Bennet, and you. Mrs Rice-Trevor, may I introduce to your acquaintance Coxswain Bennet? Mrs Rice-Trevor is my sister.'

'I'm delighted to make your acquaintance, Mr Bennet. My brother tells me that he might not be here today, if it were not for your courage and resolution.'

'It's quite the other way round, ma'am, I'm sure. It's an honour to make your acquaintance, ma'am.'

Bennet's features had reddened under his flaxen mop. Fanny had that effect on people.

'All's well in Walthamstow, Mr Bennet?'

'All's well, sir – no sign of any rioters or revolutionaries. To be honest, sir, it's been a little dull. I've sometimes found myself hoping for a baying mob to come round the corner.'

'I'm not sure I'd fancy your chances, Mr Bennet. The mobs are getting bigger. I read in the *Morning Post* that three thousand people have demolished fifty miles of fencing at the Forest of Dean. And the army have shot and killed several iron-workers at Merthyr Tydfil.'

'The French have a lot to answer for,' grumbled Wilson, coming round from the other side of the carriage where he had been attending to his luggage. 'All of this is their doing. Good afternoon, Bennet.'

'Afternoon, sir.'

'Rest assured, Mrs Rice-Trevor, we'll have none of that sort of thing in Walthamstow. The extra day patrols of watchmen will see to that.'

'How very comforting, Mr Wilson.'

Bennet struggled without success to picture the two portly, middle-aged watchmen in their greatcoats and broad-brimmed hats, beating off a three-thousand-strong mob of starving farm-workers. Wilson, meanwhile, marched the party across to the infants' school.

'St Mary's, Mrs Rice-Trevor, was the country's first Church of England infants' school, constructed and paid for entirely by myself.'

'How very generous of you, Mr Wilson.'

'My father made a considerable fortune, madam, from the manufacture of silk. The school has been established according to the principles of the great educator Mr Samuel Wilderspin. Are you familiar with Mr Wilderspin's teachings, Mrs Rice-Trevor?'

'I admit that I cannot say so.'

'Wilderspin believes that the years between two and seven are a wasted opportunity. That the early period in a child's life is vital for impressing those Christian values and teachings that might otherwise be debased by the beliefs and actions of crudely educated parents. By the time each of our children starts national school they have attained a religious and moral excellence, an understanding of personal cleanliness, as well as a basic standard of reading and arithmetic.'

'How very laudable.'

'Our children learn by singing and clapping. They are encouraged to learn, Mrs Rice-Trevor, and never beaten or punished physically. I can think of no better environment for the education of three members of a primitive race, whose mental development is akin to that of an English child.'

FitzRoy kept his counsel at this.

Bennet's mind swam at the thought of the carnage that would ensue if Schoolmaster Jenkins ever tried to beat York Minster.

The party made its way into the school and through to the school-room that occupied the majority of the building.

It really was an impressive construction – light and airy, with arching ecclesiastical windows – quite unlike the gloomy workhouse conditions of the national school across the road. However self-regarding Mr Wilson might be, FitzRoy could only admire the generosity with which he had built and endowed St Mary's.

Jenkins was midway through an arithmetic lesson when the school-room door opened. Every member of the class, except York, shot to his or her feet. After a brisk 'Carry on, Jenkins,' from Wilson, he continued to teach in that slightly stilted manner common to all schoolmasters under scrutiny.

'We shall take our rhymes from *Marmaduke Multiply's Merry Method of Making Minor Mathematicians*,' he announced, brandishing the book for all to see. Tiny beads of sweat formed visibly upon his upper lip. The dignitaries were there to see the savages perform, he knew that.

'Four times five are twenty – Fuegia Basket?'

'Jack Tar say – his purse is empty!' beamed the little girl.

'Very good, Fuegia. Seven times ten are seventy – Jemmy?'

'Now we're sailing very pleasantly!' Jemmy grinned across at FitzRoy, seeking approval, and won an answering smile.

'Excellent, Jemmy, well done. Nine times twelve are a hundred and eight...'

York's eyes bored into the schoolmaster's. The brute seemed to grow in his seat. Surely there was no chance of a response from that quarter?

'...Peter?'

'See what a noble, fine first-rate!' chimed Peter.

I don't blame you, thought FitzRoy.

'Well done, Peter. All our rhymes today have a nautical theme, Captain FitzRoy, in honour of your visit.'

'I am indeed honoured, Mr Jenkins.'

'Thank you, Jenkins, that will do,' interrupted Wilson. 'Now, children, you all know Captain FitzRoy. What do we say?'

'Good afternoon, Captain FitzRoy,' chorused the school.

'And this is the captain's sister, Mrs Rice-Trevor.'

The school said its good-afternoons.

'Mrs Rice-Trevor has an important announcement to make, regarding our three Fuegian friends.'

Fanny swept to the head of the room, graceful and gorgeous in a carriage dress of Indian red satin, with a cloak and bonnet of black velvet; she appeared to the children as a dark, mysterious princess. *What a beauty,* thought Bennet.

'Children, I have an invitation here, from Colonel John Wood, the extra messenger in His Majesty's Household. Our friends Jemmy, Fuegia and York have been invited to London, to St James's Palace, for a private audience with King William and Queen Adelaide. They are to have tea with the King!'

A gasp ran round the room. Jenkins's glance darted instinctively to York Minster. Was that the ghost of a smile passing across the barbarian's features?

'What do you say, Captain FitzRoy? Is it not a pretty scheme?'

The party had adjourned to the Vestry House, adjoining the school, where Mrs Jenkins afforded refreshments, each serving accompanied by a little paean of praise to the all-round charm and sweet nature of that 'good little creature' Fuegia Basket. The Reverend William Wilson, inbetweentimes, continued to hold forth.

'Two missionary volunteers to return to Tierra del Fuego with your Fuegians. That way, the savages may be taught such useful arts as will be suited to their gradual civilization. The Fuegians who have learned God's truth here can provide assistance in establishing a friendly intercourse with the natives, and establishing a missionary settlement among them. I hope you will not think me forward, Captain FitzRoy, but a subscription has already been set on foot. What do you say? Will you take them in the *Beagle*?'

'I will not be returning to the south in the *Beagle* – the Admiralty has other plans for her. The journey is to be a private undertaking. But—'

'Not in the *Beagle*?' interjected Bennet, stunned. Unsure of his manners in such company, he had chosen – despite being invited to take a seat – to hover by the door like a sentry standing easy. And now he had let himself down.

'I shall explain later, Mr Bennet.'

'I'm sorry, sir.'

'I must own, Mr Wilson, that your proposition takes me by surprise. Of course, any such venture would have to receive the blessing of the Admiralty, as they have sponsored the education of the Fuegians. Provided that you can find two brave souls willing to habit that Godforsaken coast, I see no reason why I should not be of assistance, but that is a considerable provision. Tierra del Fuego has claimed many European lives. I would not consign any man to those wild shores without his being fully cognizant of the dangers involved.'

'The modern evangelist is a muscular Christian, Captain FitzRoy. He has tamed the cannibal islands of the South Seas and has made inroads into darkest Africa. We cannot exempt any part of God's earth from receiving the light of His love.'

Any further discussion on the matter was postponed by the return of Mrs Jenkins, with the news that classes were over, and that Jemmy, York and Fuegia were waiting to receive their visitors in their lodgings above the school.

The boarders' rooms in the eaves proved surprisingly attractive and spacious, with exposed beams and simple wooden furniture. As the party climbed the creaking staircase to the upper floor, they were intercepted by a little yellow blur, as Fuegia Basket launched herself like a cannonball into Fanny's skirts. 'Capp'en Sisser! Capp'en Sisser!' she squealed delightedly.

'Why, Bob, she's the *sweetest* little girl,' Fanny exclaimed, giving her a hug.

'Good afternoon, Fuegia. York.'

York Minster, a burly shadow standing sentinel in the corridor ahead, nodded in acknowledgement to FitzRoy.

'Where's Jemmy?'

'I – am – *here!*'

Jemmy stepped smartly out of his room on cue, and struck a dandyish pose in the corridor. The visitors could only gape. He was attired in skintight white buckskins, tucked into knee-length boots that had been polished to a mirror finish, an extravagant neckcloth of Flemish lace, and, topping off the whole ensemble, a long-tailed, double-breasted dress riding coat of the brightest pink, its gathered waist straining gallantly across its owner's pot belly. His hair had been plastered down with pomatum. FitzRoy murmured under his breath to Bennet, 'When I said, "Take him to the tailor's to purchase a suit of clothes," Mr Bennet—'

'He absolutely insisted, sir,' whispered Bennet unhappily. 'You know what he's like. The minute he saw the cloth, wild horses could not have diverted him.'

'I think it looks *marvellous*,' announced Fanny loudly. 'You have the appearance of a real English gentleman, Jemmy.'

Jemmy's face lit up with pleasure.

'You've certainly taken my breath away, Jemmy,' confessed FitzRoy. 'Are you well?'

'Hearty sir, never better!'

'You are pleased with your accommodations?'

'By Jove, indeed I am. We are given many presents! People are very kind.'

'And you, York? I gather you have been your usual quiet self in class.'
A half laugh, half snort from York.

'All those months of divine study, York – is there not one lesson from
the scriptures that you have taken to heart?'

York grunted. 'Too much study is weariness of the flesh,' he said
pointedly.

Early on the Monday afternoon, FitzRoy left Messrs Walker & Co. of
Castle Street in Holborn, where the last of the charts drawn up by the
Hydrographic Office from his surveys had been committed to copper
plate, and called for his carriage. He drove east, out of the city proper
and down the Commercial Road, thick as it always was with empty
waggons heading out to the docks and loaded ones struggling back in.
Where the road divided he took the southern fork, past the moated fortress
of the West India Dock, down Old Street to the South Dock, the old City
Canal on Limehouse Reach. It was high water, so the river had flooded
the marshes on the Isle of Dogs, and despite the lateness of the season
the air was thick with mosquitoes. Only the Deptford and Greenwich
Road on its newly elevated embankment remained above the water,
cutting the silver sheen of the Thames in two as it curved to the ferry
landing at the end of the peninsula. This was one of the poorest parts of
the river: narrow lanes lined with mean slums ran down from the road,
straight into thick Thames mud. Sickly, half-starved children, their limbs
bowed with rickets, foraged in the treacly silt for driftwood or rotten fruit
discarded from passing cargo ships.

The *John* was berthed about half-way along. Its owner, John Mawman,
was waiting for him on the quayside. A taciturn Stepney merchant,
Mawman kept his manners to a minimum. This suited FitzRoy. In the
light of the transaction he was about to undertake, he was in no mood
for pleasantries.

'There she is, sir. That's my brig. John Davey is her master.'

FitzRoy climbed aboard and had a look round. At two hundred tons
she was of roughly the same dimensions as the *Beagle*, and the same
colour – black, with a white stripe running round her rail – but there the

resemblance ended. Her paintwork was dirtied where the crew had thrown slops over the side, rather than lowering buckets. Ropes lay untidy and uncoiled about her deck, like the back of a chandler's shop. Her blocks were in need of oiling, her pitch was cracked and in need of re-paying. The bilges stank for lack of pumping. But all this was not uncommon in the merchant service, where naval discipline did not apply. She was basically sound and seaworthy, he could see that. Her timbers were solid. She would do.

'You choose an opportune moment to depart the country, sir. If there is not reform soon, I do not doubt we shall all have our throats slit in our beds.'

FitzRoy ignored him. 'There shall be seven passengers, Mr Mawman – myself, Mr Bennet my coxswain, the three Fuegians and two volunteer missionaries.'

'You said five passengers.'

'As our provisions are accounted for separately I take it that this does not amount to a problem.'

'No, it does not. I believe the sum agreed was one thousand pounds?'

'It was.'

'Pilotage fees will also be extra.'

'As we discussed.'

He could have negotiated the sum down a little, FitzRoy knew, but haggling invariably made him feel sordid. He produced his pocket-book and took out the cheque for a thousand pounds, drawn on his London bank. It was a huge amount: enough to buy a sizeable townhouse in the city. The hire of a brig and her crew to voyage into perilous waters for six months was no small undertaking. But he had given his word to the Fuegians. He handed the cheque to the merchant, and signed Mawman's fourteen-page contract.

'You realize, Commander, that if you abandon the trip for any reason you will forfeit the entire sum?'

'I am fully aware of the conditions binding our agreement, Mr Mawman.'

They shook hands on the deal. FitzRoy stepped back into his carriage, and joined the laden cart-stream heading back towards the city.

'I've done the deed, Fan.'

'Oh, Bob, I do hope you know what you're doing. How much has it cost you?'

'One thousand pounds.'

A faint, high-pitched whistle of breath escaped Fanny Rice-Trevor's lips. 'Do you have so much to spare?'

'If I did not, I should have to find it. I cannot go back on my word.'

'Of course not. I understand.'

His sister's tone was soothing, but the candlelight from the chandelier illuminated a wet gleam in her eyes. A hundred tiny flames shimmered in her concerned gaze.

The occasion was a private coronation ball, at the house of Mrs Beauchamp in Park Lane. Of course the ball season normally ended in late July, when the evenings began to draw in, but the coronation had made 1831 an unusual year. At one end of the ballroom, a small orchestra had begun the opening quadrille, and black-and-white-clad dancers whirled past in stately formations. Their hostess wove her way through the chattering crowds at the dancers' edge to where the FitzRoys stood, a quiet island amid all the activity. 'Are you young people enjoying yourselves?'

'Quite so, Mrs Beauchamp. Your hospitality is always generous, but this year you have surpassed yourself.'

'My, you look dashing, Commander FitzRoy. And what a wonderful dress, my dear. I adore the white lace over the blue satin. How very wise of you to wear blue to offset the orange of the candlelight. Now, if either of you finds that your appetites are in need of recruitment, I have placed refreshments in the small room at the far end. There will be a proper supper downstairs, of course, but we can't have you catching a chill passing down that draughty staircase for lemonade and biscuits. Or something stronger if you prefer, Commander.'

'You are as thoughtful as ever, Mrs Beauchamp.'

FitzRoy's imagination could not help but compare the potential draughts on Mrs Beauchamp's staircase with the 'draughts' he could expect on the exposed bridge of the *John*: South Atlantic gales screaming into his face, icing the rigging and raising surging walls of grey water thirty or forty feet high. Mrs Beauchamp wove away again, her heavy skirts shouldering aside the flimsier creations of the younger ladies.

'She's right, Bob. You do look dashing,' Fanny said, adjusting her brother's already immaculate white tie. 'We must find you a dancing partner. It really would be most unfair to a multitude of ladies if such a fine catch were not to be made available.'

'Really, Fan, there is no need—'

She waved away his protests. 'Come with me. I shall play master of the ceremonies. I shall present you to Miss Mary O'Brien. She is the daughter of Major-General O'Brien, of County Wicklow. I would mark her card for you, except that Miss O'Brien is not the sort to carry a dance-card. She is a rather serious and devout young woman – just the sort for you, if you are to spend six months arm in arm with a brace of missionaries.'

Still protesting feebly, FitzRoy allowed himself to be dragged in the direction of Miss O'Brien; and so it was that, five minutes later, he found himself bowing to her, and she curtsying in reply, as they lined up facing one another for the commencement of the Sir Roger de Coverley. They were the third pair in line, so they had time to exchange a few words before they were called upon to promenade between the two lines of dancers. Their conversation was formal: friendly enough, but stilted. FitzRoy preferred the silence of the dance, which he found not at all awkward but serene. Miss O'Brien wore a plain dress of white satin, slender-waisted and decorated only with three narrow rouleaux at the base. Her hair, unlike that of the other ladies present, was not arranged in clusters of curls about her face, or tied up in a swirling Apollo-knot: rather, it was parted in the centre, swept back and secured simply at the neck by a cameo. It was raven-coloured, and FitzRoy thought that she looked like a Catholic saint from Madrid or Andalucía. There was a beatific quality to her: the overall effect was pure, not severe. She gazed at him intently when they danced.

As they whirled under the giant chandelier that dominated the centre of the ballroom, a fat drop of hot wax fell from the wrought iron and splattered on to the upper slope of her breast, at the place where it disappeared into the V of her dress. Miss O'Brien did not react; there was no indication that she had even noticed. FitzRoy watched the hot liquid congeal instantly against her cool, white skin, and knew at once it was an image that would never leave him.

FitzRoy's carriage, curtains drawn, made staccato progress up the Strand. Jemmy, once more attired in his alarming pink coat (he had refused point-blank to leave Walthamstow unless permitted to wear it), peered in wide-eyed astonishment through the narrow ruler of light at the street outside. A scene of wonder revealed itself. Two giant boots, all of eight feet tall, were trying to negotiate their way past a seven-foot hat. Three enormous tin canisters with human feet, each marked 'Warren's Blacking – 30 Strand', walked alongside the carriage in single file. A man carrying a vast pair of teeth on a long pole met Jemmy's eye and glared at him. There were men with picture placards advertising single-exhibit museums – a stuffed croc-odile here, a civet cat there – dioramas of the Emperor Napoleon's funeral, and paddle-steamer crossings to Rotterdam. There were milkmaids, grape-sellers, cane-chair menders, butchers' and bakers' carts and men offering hunting prints from upturned umbrellas. Towering above the whole seething, shouting, yelling mass was a monstrous four-storey advertise-ment for Lardner's blacking factory, comprising a number of enormous three-dimensional plaster models of hessian boots, Oriental slippers, and inverted blacking bottles suspended over boot-jacks.

'Goliath's boots! Goliath's hat!' shouted Jemmy excitedly. 'They kill Goliath, bring his boots and hat!'

'No, Jemmy,' laughed FitzRoy. 'It's called "advertising". They want you to buy their hats, or their boots, so they build big ones to attract your attention. The Strand is London's main shopping street. One cannot escape it, these days.'

Jemmy's astonishment gave way, at least partly, to confusion.

'Big teeth! Very big teeth!' he said hopefully.

'Another advertisement,' FitzRoy reassured him.

York and Fuegia were peering between the frame and the curtain now, both wriggling uncomfortably in their Sunday best, a demure pair of pantalettes poking out beneath Fuegia's Christian frock.

'I suppose they have not seen the city before,' said FitzRoy to Bennet.

'Well, no sir. They came up from Plymouth to Walthamstow by inside stage. I was wondering, sir, but should you permit it – might I take them up to London for the day, before they go home?'

'Oh *yes please*, Capp'en Fitz'oy! *Yes please!*' begged Jemmy, his gaze now distracted by the extravagant window displays of a row of clothes shops.

'I don't know, Jemmy. There is jeopardy in travel, these days.'

'There are police in London now, sir. It's safer in town than out in the countryside, and safer than when I was a lad.'

'Of course, Mr Bennet – I had forgotten that you are a Londoner.'

'In my notion it's safer than Tierra del Fuego too, sir.'

'*Yes please*, Capp'en Fitz'oy!'

FitzRoy found himself outvoted. 'Very well, Jemmy. You may all travel up to London with Mr Bennet. On a different day.'

They emerged from the chaos of the Strand into the wide empty space of Trafalgar Square, that eternally unfinished building site so brutally carved out of the teeming city. Then west along Pall Mall to St James's Palace, the home of the Royal Family, a mere stone's throw away from another great building site, the New King's Palace that George IV had ordered to be constructed in Green Park. A phalanx of red-jacketed soldiery had been posted outside St James's to protect His Majesty from any rioting mobs, but their presence was largely superfluous. King Billy, after all, had celebrated his accession by throwing a party for the poor of Windsor, all three thousand of them. Earlier in the summer he had eschewed the tiresome job of swearing in privy councillors and had climbed out of a palace window instead, preferring to take a stroll down Pall Mall alone; he had eventually been rescued from the attentions of an adoring crowd by the members of White's, just as a prostitute was about to kiss him on the lips. This was one monarch who was safe from having his throat cut in the night.

Coxswain Bennet was left in a palace anteroom, where Fanny Rice-Trevor had been waiting for them. Today she wore a satin dress shot with gold and a train of black velvet. Together they were escorted to the state apartments and into the presence of the King and Queen.

'Your Majesty. Your Royal Highness.'

FitzRoy acknowledged both in turn and introduced his party, who bowed and curtsied, according to sex. The three Fuegians having been carefully schooled in the correct etiquette, even York managed a little bow, sensing perhaps that it would not do to antagonize the most powerful man in the world; Jemmy, meanwhile, performed the most extravagant of scrapes, reaching almost to the ground.

'How do? Come in, come in.'

All signs of protocol absent, King William beckoned them to a little table, surrounded by Louis XIV chairs, where tea and fancy biscuits had been laid out. His Majesty proved to be a plump, florid man in his mid-sixties, his immensely high forehead surmounted by a ridge of white hair standing neatly to attention. Although squeezed into a formal crimson dress uniform, his manner was informal and jocular in the extreme. Queen Adelaide, a small, round, quiet German with sad eyes, was already seated. The royal couple, it was said, had little to do with each other outside their official duties.

'D'ye take tea? A cup of tea for my friends here. That's a splendid coat, young man.'

Jemmy preened. 'Thank you, Your Majesty.'

'Tell me, how d'ye like London?'

'London is best city in the world! Better than Rio. One day I will build city like London in my own country.'

'Capital, capital! Tell me about your own country.'

'My country is good country. It is called Woollya. Plenty of trees. There is no devil in my land. Plenty of guanaco. My people hunt many guanaco. No guanaco in York's country.'

'Guanaco?'

'It is a type of llama, Your Majesty,' explained FitzRoy.

And so, for the next half-hour, the King continued to question Jemmy

Button – rather intelligently, FitzRoy considered. York sat in inscrutable silence while Fuegia beamed enchantingly at Queen Adelaide, who occasionally prompted the little girl with a supplementary question.

'They do you credit, Commander. They do you prodigious credit. They are uncommonly well conducted.'

'Your Majesty is most kind. I have taken the liberty of bringing Your Majesty and Your Royal Highness a chart of Tierra del Fuego, prepared from the survey expedition commanded by Captain King. It is the first one off the Navy's copper press, sir.'

'Capital, Commander, capital!'

FitzRoy unrolled the chart and spread it before the King and Queen, pointing out Woollya, Desolate Bay and York Minster, the homes of the three Fuegians.

'And these blank spaces – I dare say you'll fill them in when you take these three back in the *Beagle*?'

FitzRoy seized his chance. 'No sir. The Admiralty has decided to prosecute no further surveys of the area. Although I understand that the French have sent an expedition to that quarter under the direction of the naturalist Captain du Petit Thouars.'

'The French? The devil take 'em. What are those damned fools in the Admiralty playing at?'

'I understand there are economic limitations, Your Majesty.'

'Economic limitations be hanged. We can't be outdone by the French. What about all those uncles of yours? Do not the dukes Grafton and Richmond interest themselves about you?'

'Unfortunately, sir, I have had to request a year's leave from the Service to enable me to keep my faith with the natives using my own means. I hope to see our friends here become useful as interpreters, sir, and to be the means of establishing a friendly disposition towards Englishmen on the part of their countrymen.'

'Absolutely. Any fool can see that's a capital idea.'

Fanny looked across at her brother, a worried expression stealing across her face. He was taking an enormous risk, manipulating the conversation like this.

'We can't have good men like you lost to the Service, Commander. You leave their lordships to me. Economic limitations, indeed!'

His Majesty levered his portly frame from his chair, grunting with the exertion involved, indicating that the interview was over. Queen Adelaide, meanwhile, left the room for a moment, then returned with one of her own bonnets, a gold ring and a small purse of coins, which she gave to Fuegia Basket. She tied the bonnet under the little girl's chin and slipped the ring on to her finger. 'The money is for you, my dear, to buy travelling clothes.'

'What must you say, Fuegia?'

'Thank you, Your Royal Highness.'

The ring alone, FitzRoy realized, was valuable enough to keep a working man's family in food for a year.

Bennet rose before dawn, in the little room that discreetly separated Fuegia Basket's quarters from York Minster's, and woke the three Fuegians. Jemmy donned his pink coat and Fuegia her new bonnet, from which she utterly refused to be parted. They assembled in the shivering half-dark of the schoolyard, where they boarded Wilson's carriage, which the clergyman had kindly donated for the day. They took the road for Islington, a cold grey light at their backs. Half-lit brick kilns, orchards, cow-yards, tea-gardens and tenter grounds rattled past, allotments rising as islands from sodden, misty fields. On either side of Hackney village there were bare strawberry allotments, where early-risen women with rough clay pipes in their mouths were potting runners from the summer's exhausted plants.

At first, theirs had been the only carriage on the road, but as they neared Islington the traffic thickened. Milkmaids from the outlying farms took to the road, bowed under the weight of their heavy iron churns. Boys with sticks drove massive herds of cattle and pigs uncomprehendingly forward into the maw of the metropolis, to feed the insatiable appetites of the one and a half million citizens who teemed and sweated in the cramped lattice of streets and alleyways. After Islington, where the new tenements lining the Lower Road disgorged an anthill of clerks, the City Road, St John's Street and the Angel Terrace heading downhill towards

Battlebridge became a veritable swarm of commuters, mounting their inexorable morning assault on London. No one, it seemed, had occasion to pause, even for a few seconds: passers-by grabbed buns and biscuits from pastry shops *en route*, tossing their pennies through the open doorway. Floating serenely above the jostling river of humanity in their opulent carriage, Bennet and his three charges felt as if they were being carried shoulder-high into the very heart of the city. They could see London below them now, drifts of yellow smog lining its alleys like mucus, the ever-present kites soaring and wheeling high above.

At Battlebridge came the first of the city's great sights.

'A mountain!' exclaimed Jemmy.

'A mountain of rubbish,' clarified Bennet, inviting them to look again. It was indeed a mighty triangular summit of ordure, cinders and rags, its secondary hillocks of horse-bones swarming with ravenous pigs. Cinder-sifters and scavengers combed the upper slopes, ragged panting children and women with short pipes and muscled forearms, more wretched than their Hackney sisters, with strawboard gaiters and torn bonnet-boxes for pinafores.

'All of London's rubbish, all her waste, is piled up here,' said Bennet, by way of explanation.

'What for do they want rubbish?' asked Jemmy.

'Tin canisters are re-usable as luggage clamps, old shoes go for Prussian blue dye. Everything is re-usable.'

'These are low people,' said Jemmy. 'Not gentlemen.'

'That they are not, Jemmy. All of this is to be flattened, they say, to make way for a great cross, in memory of His Late Majesty King George IV. Take it all in, for you will never see its like again.'

At the top of Tottenham Court Road they had to queue for their second turnpike. 'This area,' explained Bennet, 'belongs to Captain FitzRoy's family. Not to the captain himself, but to his family. It's called Fitzrovia.' Grand terraces and squares rose behind allotments and smallholdings to the west.

'If it belongs to capp'en's family, it belong to capp'en.'

'Not quite, Jemmy. It doesn't really work like that.'

'All family not live together?'

'They don't live here at all.'

Jemmy subsided into his seat, completely baffled.

'I love Capp'en Sisser,' offered Fuegia.

At the bottom of Tottenham Court Road, the rush-hour traffic finally congealed. A hundred stationary horses tossed their heads and blew steam from their nostrils, while the drivers bellowed greetings and friendly obscenities at each other. Bennet invited the Fuegians to step down from the carriage, and arranged to rendezvous with their driver at the same spot that evening. They pressed through the crowds and turned right into Oxford Street.

After his years of exile in the Southern Ocean and the many long, quiet months in Walthamstow, even James Bennet, a Londoner, was momentarily stunned by the sudden assault on his senses that ensued. It was as if they had stepped not into a main thoroughfare but into the middle of Bartholomew Fair. The street seethed with activity. The rattle of coach-wheels competed with the buzz of flies. There were German bands clashing with bagpipes, who clashed in turn with Italian mechanical organs mounted on carts. Dustmen rang their bells. News vendors blew their tin horns and bragged of 'Bloody News!' and 'Horrible Murder!', their head-lines screaming loudest of all. One side of the street was plastered with song-sheets, as if some unseen authority were orchestrating the cacophony.

Everyone, it seemed, had something to sell. There were knife-grinders and pot-welders and women selling huge blocks of cocoa. There were toy theatres with hand-drawn characters cut and pasted on to cardboard, their owners peddling seats in the street at a penny a ticket. There were jugglers, conjurors and microscope exhibitors. There were men offering tickets to dogfights, cockfights, even ratfights. There were dancing bears, performing apes, and a model of the battle of Waterloo pulled by a donkey. There were baked-potato men, men offering plum duff 'just up', pudding stalls, egg stalls, shoe-cleaners and beggars by the score. Starving lynch mobs might well have been roaming the fields of southern England demanding reform, but here within its heavily policed boundaries,

London pursued its pushing, shoving, shouting commercial life without shame, without hindrance, without distraction.

And then there were the children. Literally hundreds upon hundreds of them, begging, offering themselves up for work holding horses, fetching taxis, opening doors, or simply performing cartwheels for a halfpenny. 'D'you want me, Jack? Want a boy?' came the clamour of shrill voices as every passer-by was besieged. There were black, unwashed climbing boys, their brushes standing to attention against their shoulders like rifles. There were silent, diseased children curled in corners, the ones who would not live long, wasting away in pale misery. There were proud, red-jacketed boys chasing after carriages, collecting fresh horse manure as it fell and placing it in roadside bins; bunters, scooping up dog excrement for the tanning trade; and crossing sweepers, clearing paths through the ordure for gentlemen wishing to cross the street. There were nimble children easing silently between the crowds, risking the gallows by picking pockets. There were drunken children, leaning against the long mahogany bars of the myriad gin palaces, slumped beneath serried ranks of green-and-gold casks, fumbling with their pipes, or challenging each other to meaningless, swaying punch-ups. These people are multiplying, thought Bennet. They are multiplying indefinitely.

Surprisingly, it was York who spoke first. 'So many people,' he said simply.

'So many *people*,' echoed Fuegia.

'There are one and a half million people in London. When I was a boy it was just over one million.' *These figures mean nothing to them,* he realized. *I must find another way to express it.* 'There are more people in this street, now, than in the whole of Tierra del Fuego. In this one street. Do you understand me? That is why this is the biggest city in the world.'

The colours of Oxford Street's inhabitants were so vibrant, so dazzlingly, tastelessly lurid: there were scarlet breeches, candy-striped waistcoats, lime green petticoats and lemon yellow riding jackets. The races that sported these extravagant clothes came in all shades as well: there were Africans and Indians and Spaniards and Chinese and Jews and Malays and West Indians. Any fears he might have entertained as to the conspicuousness of his charges, Bennet realized, were groundless; a Fuegian Indian in a pink coat, even though he might stop the traffic in Walthamstow, would not merit a backward glance on Oxford Street.

The palette on which this kaleidoscopic array had been daubed was jet-black. The buildings on either side were thick with soot and grease. Fallen soot had blended with horse manure to create a three-inch layer of soft black mud in the middle of the road, through which the crowds surged heedlessly. The air was thick with a cloying yellow mixture of seacoal dust and water vapour, which insinuated itself into eyes, ears and noses, and worked relentlessly to dampen the garish extremes of colour in its clammy shroud. Jemmy kept to the new raised wooden pavement until it ran out, then hopped carefully from one dry patch to another, in a vain attempt to keep his shining boots unspattered. He dabbed at his increasingly sooty pink sleeves with a crisp white handkerchief, faintly distressed mewling sounds coming from under his breath.

'Don't worry, Jemmy, it will wash off,' Bennet reassured him.

Blackest of all were the narrow alleys that led off Oxford Street, from which no light at all seemed to emanate. There were only glimpses to be had of the subterranean creatures who inhabited these worlds: painted women with swollen features, ragged Irishmen with uncombed, waist-length hair, canine children, wolfish dogs. Round white eyes peered from desperate black faces. Windows were stuffed with rags or paper, the window-frames themselves loose and rotten.

'Is it a cave?' said Fuegia, transfixed.

'Don't go in there,' said Bennet, grabbing her arm to hold her back, a gesture that sensibly went unchallenged by York Minster. 'Those are the rookeries. Where the St Giles blackbirds live. The black men. And the Irish. It's dangerous. You must not go down any of the bye-streets.'

To distract her, he shelled out fourpence for four tickets to see 'The Smallest Man in the World', with his fellow exhibit 'An Enormous Fat Woman'; followed by a further tuppence to look through the viewfinder of a kaleidoscope, a contrivance that sent Jemmy into raptures.

Finally, in the centre of Oxford Street, the narrow overhanging buildings and patchwork windowpanes of the last century opened out into a wide circle of pale, graceful stone.

'This is Oxford Circus. This is modern London,' Bennet explained. 'And that is Regent Street.'

To the south ran two elegant lines of white pillars, so new as to be barely stained by coal dust, in a curving Doric colonnade. The buildings behind them soared skywards in blinding white stucco.

'It is a new construction, built by Mr Nash, running from Regent's Park at the north of London, down to Waterloo Place at the far south. It is lit up by gas at night, like a starry sky. It is said to be the most beautiful street in the world. On the west are the streets of the nobility and the gentry. On the east is Soho, where the mechanics and traders reside. They had to knock down a hundred lanes and alleys, and a thousand shops and homes, to build it. And there will be other grand streets like it. Old London is being torn down, the London I was born in. In its place they are building a new, modern city, a beautiful city of wide roads and circuses and parks. London will become the most beautiful city in the world.'

'The most beautiful city in the world,' breathed Jemmy. York looked blank. Fuegia stared at a crimson dress in a nearby shop window. Jemmy was the only one of the three to have taken Bennet's little speech to heart.

By some unspoken common consent, the crowds promenading up and down Regent Street were of a different class from those who thronged Oxford Street. There was money on display, both in the shop windows and on the customers' backs. Two men whose blue swallow-tail coats and top hats gave them away as policemen no doubt had a part to play in keeping the pickpockets away, but that could not have been the only factor: it was as if old London had been fenced in by the new street, as if all that gaily coloured squalor was slowly being squeezed by the advancing metropolis, with its stern, clean, white lines.

They walked down to Waterloo Place, keeping a block to the west of the Haymarket's prostitutes and litter, then headed east to Charing Cross, where another huge construction site marked the final remains of the old Hungerford Market. A low growl from York indicated that something was amiss. Jemmy and Fuegia looked confused. Bennet turned to see what had agitated his companion so, but he could see nothing. York was frozen in the same pose he had adopted back in Plymouth Sound, to signal his aggressive intent towards the paddle-steamer. One or two passers-by were starting to stare. Finally, Bennet looked up, and located the source of the challenge: a stone lion atop Northumberland House. He placed a gentle hand on York's forearm, just as it dawned upon the Fuegian that the creature had not moved for several seconds. He relaxed.

They went to see the new market at Covent Garden, where classical colonnades had once again marched across acres of ramshackle sheds and flimsy stalls; they saw pineapples that had been brought from overseas by fast ships; they joined the crowds staring at daffodils and roses out of season, and fuchsia plants from the other side of the world. Then they went down to the river to see the new London Bridge, five elegant arches confidently spanning the river, overlooking its shamed predecessor, which sat rotting and disused a hundred feet downriver.

'King William and Queen Adelaide opened this bridge only last month,' explained Bennet, leaning over the parapet. 'There used to be houses on the old bridge. And they used to put bad men's heads on spikes there. They don't do that any more.' His mind leafed back to the day when his father had taken him, as a child, to see the heads of the Cato Street Conspirators. His father was dead now.

'They're building a tunnel under the Thames as well. Do you see over there, to the right?' He indicated the Southwark side of the river. 'Look. New factories. There's a steam flour mill. And there's the Barclay's Brewery – there are giant steam engines in there, and vats of beer, each one as big as a house. And there's a factory where meat and soup are sealed into tin canisters.'

He looked down at the rickety, lopsided warehouses beneath the bridge, the crowded pubs almost spilling into the water, the flocks of ragged mudlarks and the foul-mouthed watermen in their numberless ferryboats; then across once more at the factories advancing inexorably up the Surrey shore, black smoke trailing eastward in their wake; and he felt a pang of regret for the London of his childhood, mingled with a surge of pride for the new metropolis rising all around him.

'Some people say they shouldn't spend so much money on building the new city. They say it should be given to the poor people instead. But the more money they give to the poor people, the more children the poor people have, and the more poor people there are.'

'London is the most beautiful city in the world, Mister Bennet,' said Jemmy gravely. 'One day I will build some city like London in my country. There will be big streets, and factories making canisters. I will call this city New London.'

'Cities like London don't just spring up overnight, Jemmy,' said Bennet. 'It takes thousands of years of gradual change. The old London that they're knocking down – once that was new London, and it swept away what went before it. Now it is old London, and it is weak and rotten, and it will lose its mortal fight. Perhaps I shouldn't say this, but the people down there in the mud with their rushlights and their sailboats will get weaker, little by little. And the people over there, with their gas lamps and their steam engines, will get stronger, little by little. And slowly, with each succeeding year, the people over there will encroach towards the heart of the city, and the people in the mud will give way, and London herself will end up bigger and stronger as a result. That is how great cities are created.'

'But, Mister Bennet,' said Jemmy, 'I do not want to be in mud. I want to be one of the people with steam engine. You can teach me.'

They ate at a little dining house on the Strand, for discretion's sake in a curtained booth lit by an oil lamp, where Bennet's natural cheeriness reasserted itself over a plate of chops, devils, bread and pickles. The Fuegians wolfed everything they could lay their hands on, as they always did, as if their lives depended on it. After dinner they bought outside shilling seats on the new omnibus to Vauxhall Gardens, where Bennet took them to see the iceberg. This proved to be something of a damp squib, as the three seemed not in the least surprised to find a large iceberg adrift in the middle of a South London park.

'Go ahead and touch it,' said Bennet, prompting.

'Big ice,' said Fuegia.

'Mister Bennet, we have many big ice in my country,' said Jemmy.

'No, but it's not real. It's made of wood. Go and touch it.'

Jemmy walked over and touched the iceberg. It was warm. Jemmy looked confused.

'Sir John Ross has sailed to the Arctic, to find the North West Passage. That's at the other end of the world from Tierra del Fuego, but just as cold. So they have built an iceberg here to give people an idea of what the North Pole looks like.'

Jemmy appeared none the wiser.

It was at this inopportune moment that Black Billy, the celebrated black street violinist who had lost one leg to a French cannonball in his Navy days, approached to offer the party a tune. Pink feathers bobbled from his jester's hat, his good leg was encased in aggressively blue-and-white striped breeches, and a nautical jacket completed the ensemble. Fuegia, taking fright, screamed and grabbed York's leg. The three began to hoot, hiss and make faces. The appearance of a painted clown on stilts behind Black Billy merely added to the Fuegians' trepidation; Bennet thought it best to beat a hasty retreat.

'They were entertainers. Street entertainers,' he grumbled, as they sat on the omnibus clattering back towards Regent Circus. 'They aim for you to enjoy yourself. The Vauxhall Gardens are *pleasure* gardens.'

Jemmy could not rid his mind of the spectre of the black man in the woods. Bennet shook his head in theatrical resignation.

On the way they passed yet further trenches and construction sites, where the innards of the city had been laid open for all to see. Exposed wooden pipes criss-crossed each other in the moist earth, like a decayed forest of fallen trees.

'They are building pipes to bring gas light and washing water into gentlemen's homes.'

'Light and water? In a pipe?'

Jemmy tried hard to take it all in. He tried to remember his own family home back at Woollya, but it all seemed so long ago.

As dusk gathered they found themselves back on Oxford Street, where they ate a supper of fried fish in oily paper, with ginger beer. A gentle drizzle was falling, and Jemmy stared with undisguised envy at the clinking metal pattens under the ladies' shoes, which protected the blacking from the mud and the wet. Carts splashed by, bearing huge advertisements for theatres and shows; women sang maudlin ballads on street corners, collecting tins at their feet. The square gas lamps on their wrought-iron posts had been lit, and every shop window was illuminated by a hundred candles. The ever-present coal-damp mist settled on London for the night, flaring yellow in the lamps' buttery glaze and softening the pinpricks of candlelight. It was a gorgeous effect, as if all the stars in a black velvet sky were overlaid with the golden halo of the setting sun. Fuegia, wide-eyed and entranced, began to dance in the street with slow, intense, happy movements, her arms twirling out and away from her body.

'When it is dark, London not sleeps.'

'No, Jemmy, it never does. The chop-houses and beef-houses and public-houses will stay open half the night. The oyster-rooms by the theatres in the Strand will still be packed at three o'clock in the morning.'

'Not like Walthamstow.'

'No, Jemmy, not like Walthamstow.'

Fuegia had danced away from them now, fifty yards up the street, bathing herself in the candlelight, immersing herself in its glow. And then she stopped by the coal-black entrance to a side alley, like a mouse trans-fixed by an aperture that it feels compelled to enter. Suddenly, she was gone, sucked by curiosity into the dark hole of the rookeries. Bennet shouted a warning, but it was too late. He began to run, his feet slipping on the cobbles. Something streaked past him and he knew it was York, his immense, muscular frame devouring the intervening distance at an inhuman speed. Somewhere behind them, picking his way delicately between the mounds of horse dung, a little cry indicated that Jemmy was falling behind. They were becoming separated. It was the worst thing that could happen, but Bennet did not have time to think what to do. He reached the entrance to the passage that had consumed Fuegia and York. There was no sign of them. Panic iced through his stomach. He plunged in.

He found himself in a rabbit warren thick with urine and human faeces, the stench strong enough to stop a horse in its tracks. A maze of filthy, ill-constructed courts and alleys led away in all directions. As his eyes became accustomed to the gloom, he became aware of faces staring at him: wan children crouched in filthy staircases, their eyes filled with futility and despair. He chose a passageway randomly, and ran down it: another junction. A rushlight glowing in a glassless window provided the only glimmer. He took the right fork, between crumbling masonry and mildewed fencing, disturbing a prostitute and her client, her ragged, greasy skirts gathered about her waist, a momentary glimpse of pink flesh. Then, down another dark court, a flash of yellow told him that he had found Fuegia. And there was York; thank God, he had found Fuegia as well. But they were not alone. Even as Bennet arrived at the passageway leading to the courtyard, dark shapes detached themselves from the surrounding buildings and uncoiled from the shadows.

'What 'ave we 'ere, boys?' said a voice.

'A werry respectable gen'leman to be aht on a night like this, an' in St Giles an' all,' said another.

'For why's you fetched your doxy down our way, mister gentleman?' said another, Irish-accented this time.

York did not speak.

'My mate arksed you a question. Wot's-a-do, cully, someone put a turd in yer mouth?'

Bennet never even saw the knife as it flashed from its owner's pocket towards York's kidneys. But York did; or, rather, he sensed it. As York spun round, Bennet saw that the Irishman's wrist was pinioned fast in his vice-like grip. He heard the blade skitter harmlessly away across the cobbles.

Still York did not speak. He simply increased the pressure of his grasp, forcing his attacker on to his knees. Bennet could see the whites of the Irishman's eyes, and the fear ringed therein. The man let out a cry of pain, but it did not sound like a human cry, more the whimper of a terrified animal come face to face with its own death. York took the Irishman's windpipe carefully between the finger and thumb of his right hand; he looked straight through, into his victim's soul, with cruel, hooded eyes. The other assailants were backing away now, their most primitive instincts beseeching them to turn and flee, any bravery they might have summoned up on their friend's behalf long since evaporated. York's finger and thumb began to close on each other like heavy machinery, twin cogwheels engaging with industrial precision. A faint gargle escaped from the Irishman's throat.

'York!' commanded Bennet.

York froze.

'We must leave.'

For a moment, York did not move, and Bennet feared that he might disobey. Eventually, however, the Fuegian released his grasp, and the Irishman slumped to the ground.

'Come.'

Bennet tried to keep the quaver out of his voice. York took Fuegia gently by the hand and led her out of the courtyard, the little girl still beaming as if nothing had happened. As he moved forward, so the dark shapes fell back, deferentially, to let him pass.

CHAPTER ELEVEN

Plymouth, 25 October 1831

FitzRoy reached the inn-yard of the Royal Hotel a mere half-hour after the arrival of the Portsmouth stage, to find a familiar, oversized, crumpled figure waiting for him.

'My dear Darwin.'

'My dear FitzRoy, please excuse my tardiness – but what a journey I have had! All London's in a panic – there is a cholera outbreak in the city.'

'My dear fellow, your lateness is of no account. You are safe and sound, that is all that matters.'

'I say, would you mind...?' Darwin patted his pockets. 'I find myself a trifle short of cash at present.'

'Of course, of course.'

FitzRoy distributed a few coins among the upturned palms of the attendant post-boys.

'But what a terrible business! When I got to the Swan With Two Necks in Cheapside, all coaches to the West Country had been suspended. They said that rioters in Bristol had burned the Bishop's Palace and the Mansion House, and a score of merchants' stores, and had thrown open the gates of the prison!'

'It is worse. Lieutenant-Colonel Brereton, the governor, has taken his own life – he shot himself through the heart – to avoid court-martial for failing to arrest the progress of the riot. And his deputy, Captain Warrington, is to be court-martialled for failing to order his troop to kill the rioters.'

'Good God! The country is close to collapse! Luckily I managed to secure an outside seat by the Chaplin's coach to Portsmouth, but I was made to sit up-a-top next to a stone-faced guard with a blunderbuss.

Then I have been on this dreadful little rattly chaise for the last two days. Of course there isn't a turnpike road between Portsmouth and Plymouth. In some of the hamlets we went through, we afforded so much excitement, one would think they had never seen a stage coach before. The road was a disgrace, and the wind was in the horses' faces all the way. Between Wool and Wareham I thought my stomach was about to spill its contents. Heavens, it was a damnable place: flat, open heathland with one or two hovels and not a scrap of shelter. God knows how the residents live off such land.'

'It sounds as if you have had the very devil of a time. Now that you are to be a seafaring man, perhaps you will take the steamer in the future.'

They took a hackney to the Royal Dockyard at Devonport, the clip-clop of the horse's hoofs echoing down the regimented lines of deserted barracks, the wheels crunching on the marble chips of the approach road. Eventually three statuesque masts hove in sight. They alighted and FitzRoy paid off the coachman.

'Wait until you see the *Beagle*. She looks magnificent. She has been completely rebuilt, with mahogany and brass fittings. She has an entirely new upper deck, raised by eight inches aft and twelve inches for'ard. It has added materially to the comfort below decks – at last, one no longer has to bend double at all times.'

FitzRoy glowed with pride. The loss of the considerable sum he had laid out on the *John* seemed as nothing, now that he had the *Beagle* back.

'I must say, FitzRoy, I was thrilled to hear that the voyage was reinstated, and doubly thrilled to hear that you had secured such a luxurious refit. Forgive my landsman's ignorance, but surely she is a long way from being ready for sea? Is she normally painted bright yellow?'

FitzRoy burst out laughing.

'My dear Darwin, that is not the *Beagle*. That is the hulk of the *Active*. That is the *Beagle*, moored alongside.'

'*That* is the *Beagle*? I thought it a tender, or a tug-boat.'

'That is the *Beagle*.'

'But she is the length of a cricket pitch!'

'Come, come, my dear fellow, one must not insult a lady. She is a full eight yards longer than a cricket pitch – she is ninety feet long.'

Still taken aback, Darwin allowed himself to be led on board.

'Here, let me show you your quarters. I have put you in the poop cabin, behind the wheel at the rear of the maindeck.'

FitzRoy threw open the door, to reveal a cabin some five foot six inches wide, some five foot six inches deep, and some five foot six inches high. The starboard and stern walls were lined with books from floor to ceiling. Just inside the door was the thick tree trunk of the mizzen-mast. Behind that was a large chart-table, and behind that, in the narrow gap between the table and the bookshelves, stood a thin, balding figure, blinking through a pair of bottle-glass spectacles.

'Ah. Mr Darwin, may I introduce to your acquaintance Stebbing, our librarian? Stebbing is the son of the mathematical instrument-maker at Portsmouth. Mr Darwin is to be our natural philosopher. I should have explained that your cabin doubles as the library.'

Stebbing extended a limp finger for Darwin to shake, but the young man was too stunned to remember his manners.

'See, Darwin – we have Byron, Cook, Milton, Humboldt, Lyell, Euclid's *Geometry*, Paley's *Evidence of Christianity*, all twenty volumes of the *'Cyclopaedia Britannica*, even Lamarck!'

'My dear FitzRoy...the want of room...'

'My dear fellow, this is one of the largest cabins on board. Even with the bookshelves, I am sure you will all fit into it most comfortably.'

'All?'

'Did I not say? You are to room with Mr King and Mr Stokes, whom I have promoted to mate and assistant surveyor. Stokes will need to share the chart-table with you. I should have said that your cabin also doubles as the chartroom. And as the locker for the steering-gear, which is under the table. But do not worry – Mr Stokes will dress and sleep outside under the companionway.'

'And where am I to dress?' Darwin managed to gasp.

'Here.'

'And where am I to sleep?'

'Here.'

'But, FitzRoy, I see no bed.'

'You and King are to sleep in hammocks, slung above the table.'

'But I am taller than the room is long.'

'Ah – not so. The wonders of modern naval design – observe.' FitzRoy pulled out the top drawer from a chest built against the forward bulkhead, and indicated a brass hook in the shadows within. 'The foot-clew of your hammock attaches here,' he smiled.

Darwin gaped like a landed sturgeon. Midshipman King chose this exact moment to cross the deck, so FitzRoy hailed him and made the necessary introductions.

'Ah, my cabin-mate,' said King. 'It's good to have you aboard, Mr Philosopher. I'm sure we shall rub along just fine. I shall be happy to show you the ropes, of course, or answer any questions that may arise. You'll pick it up in no time, I'm sure. Now, you must excuse me, for there is work to do.'

'Er, quite,' gurgled Darwin, and King made a businesslike exit.

'FitzRoy,' whispered Darwin under his breath, 'I am sharing my cabin with a small boy.'

'Well, of course you are. Surely you would not rather share with our burly coxswain? This way you shall have all the more room.'

'All the more room? I have just room to turn round and that is all.'

'My dear fellow, why on earth should you wish to turn round? If you did so, you should be facing the wall. I promise you, I shall take the utmost care to ensure that this corner of the ship is so fitted up that you will be comfortable, and will consider it your home. Besides, you will have the run of my cabin as well. Come, I shall show you.'

They descended the companionway to FitzRoy's cabin, which proved to be no bigger: another work-table, with a narrow cot to starboard doubling as seating and an even narrower sofa to port. A marine sentry stood guard outside.

'This stout fellow protects the magazine hatch and the locker containing the chronometers. There are twenty-two in all, hanging in gimbals and bedded in sawdust. Eleven belong to His Majesty, six I have purchased myself, four were lent by the makers, and one has been lent by Lord

Ashburnham.'

He threw open the door to the narrow locker. A thin, balding figure with bottle-glass spectacles had somehow succeeded in squeezing himself inside.

'Stebbing winds them all at nine every morning. Only he and I are allowed to touch them.'

'But how did he...?'

'Oh, there are many routes about a ship. I have no doubt you shall learn them all in due course. Come, let me show you all my improvements. The canals of England have been overloaded with naval supplies these last few weeks!'

They headed back to the maindeck, Darwin feeling big and clumsy behind the wiry FitzRoy, who sprang exuberantly from one deck to another like a young deer.

'I must confess myself thoroughly delighted that so many of the officers and men chose to return from our first voyage. Almost everybody volunteered for another tour, excepting Wilson, my surgeon, who has retired, and Mr Murray, the master, who sadly accepted another berth when he thought our trip cancelled. I had a positive herd of lieutenants to choose from. In the end I went for my old friend Mr Sulivan, recently qualified, and Mr Wickham, who was first lieutenant on the *Adventure* last time out, under Captain King. A splendid fellow all round – let me introduce you.'

A cheerful, hearty officer with a stentorian voice was directing refitting operations from the centre of the maindeck. Darwin found himself greeted with a warm, friendly smile: Wickham, who looked to be in his early thirties, had an open, round face, surmounted by a mass of short, dark curls.

'So you're the philosopher, eh? Excellent. Well, Mr Darwin, I run a neat and tidy ship here, so if you can keep your messier specimens out of my way, you and I shall be the best of friends. *Entiende?*'

'Of course, of course.'

'Glad to hear it!' said Wickham, pumping Darwin's hand before going on his way.

'Of course, they would not do for St James's,' admitted FitzRoy, discreetly, 'but a more dedicated, intelligent, active and determined set of fellows you will not find anywhere. Wickham's a top-notch botanist, by the way.'

'Who is *that*?' asked Darwin. A harassed-looking individual in shirt-sleeves and shapeless woollen breeches was supervising work on a mast.

'That is William Snow Harris, the inventor. He has devised a lightning-conductor. That is, he invented the device some seven years ago, but so far nobody had dared to use it.'

'A lightning-conductor?'

'Lightning is one of the mariner's greatest adversaries. Not only are a ship's masts a hundred feet higher than any other point for miles around but during a storm they are soaked with salt water – an excellent conductor of electricity. Harris has devised a copper strip that is let into the masts and grounded at the keel, which will actually attract the lightning to the ship.'

'But surely that would be suicidal?'

'No, no – think of it! The copper strip is *grounded*. It attracts the lightning *away* from the combustible wood, and tar, and pitch, and disperses it harmlessly into the water. Simple physics, one would think, but apparently I am the first to put my faith in Harris. I am having conductors installed in every mast, in the bowsprit, even in the flying jib-boom.'

'What an ingenious idea,' enthused Darwin, momentarily forgetting his concerns about his own size relative to that of his cabin.

'One of the many on board. I have spared neither expense nor trouble in making our little expedition as complete with respect to material and preparation as my means will allow. We have a new Frazer's closed galley stove, which does not have to be put out in rough weather. All the cannons are of brass, not iron, so as not to have a deleterious effect on the magnetism of the ship's compasses. We have a patent windlass instead of the old capstan. The rudder is of a new type. All the boats are new, and have been constructed on the diagonal principle—'

'Forgive me, FitzRoy. Did you say *your* means?'

'I did.'

'But surely the Admiralty pays for the fitting-out and manning of its own expeditions?'

'Well, the Admiralty and the Navy board between them, but only up to a point. The *Beagle*'s refit has cost seven and a half thousand pounds, and for that they could have had an entirely new brig. I have chosen to supplement the Admiralty's most generous allowance with a contribution from my own funds.'

Darwin's imagination reeled at the scale of the sums involved, but he said no more on the subject.

Meanwhile, FitzRoy's eyes lit up. 'Come, let me show you the scientific instruments. We have a sympiesometer – it is like a barometer only there is gas above the quicksilver to measure radiation – a pluviometer for the rain and an anemometer for the wind. They are all from Worthington and Allan. I ordered the ship's telescope, though, from Fullerscopes in Victoria Street. Do you know them? I think their instruments superior to Dollond's.'

'I have brought my own telescope, FitzRoy. And my own aneroid barometer and microscope – it is a Coddington's folding microscope. I must show you when my luggage arrives – it is most ingenious.'

'My dear fellow, you must indeed.'

And so the pair spent a happy hour discussing scientific instruments, until Darwin, fired with enthusiasm, realized that an all-consuming naval fervour had come over him.

'I tell you, FitzRoy, I shall become a seafarer yet. With my pistols in my belt and my geological hammer in hand, shall I not look like a pirate at the very least?'

'The key to seafaring, my dear fellow, is to think like a seaman, not a landsman.'

'How does one think like a seaman?'

'It is a state of mind. For instance, the east, the west, the north and south – are they places or directions? The moon – is it a flat disc of light in the sky, put there by the good Lord in order to illuminate the trysts of lovers? Or is it a celestial body of such overwhelming power that it can pull thunderous tonnages of water from one side of the world to the other – a body deserving of careful study and immense respect?'

FitzRoy's reference to trysts with the opposite sex had set Darwin thinking of Fanny Owen.

'Ah, I see that I have distracted you. May I ask, is there a particular lady who will lament your absence?'

'I – well – that is…' Darwin, flustered, dissolved into incoherence.

'My dear fellow, please excuse my question. It was unforgivable.'

'No, no, not at all. There is one young lady – well, I will tell you, FitzRoy, she is the prettiest, plumpest, most charming personage that Shropshire possesses. The want of her company is certainly something that shall try me sorely. But as to whether she shall lament my absence, I cannot tell.'

He brought to mind her letters, so forward, so flirtatious, referring to him archly as 'Dr Postillion' and herself as 'The Housemaid'. 'You cannot imagine how I have *missed* you already,' she had written to him in London. And yet, and yet – at the Forresters' midsummer ball she had seemed to have eyes only for Robert Biddulph, whose father was an aristocrat and a Member of Parliament. She played him, he knew, like a musical instrument, but to what tune?

FitzRoy could sense the troubled journey of his friend's thoughts, and left the subject there. 'Now, my dear fellow, it is time to go ashore. I have taken a room for you at Weakley's Hotel until such time as the *Beagle* is ready for departure.'

'Ashore? Then I am not to sleep aboard when she is in harbour?'

'Forgive me, Darwin, but I would have imagined that the less time you spend in that ridiculously small cabin, the more comfortable you will be – do you not think?'

FitzRoy grinned at him conspiratorially.

The flotilla of small boats bounced around to Devonport from the steamer dock in line abreast, dancing upon the waves like the participants in a drunken late-night quadrille. Jemmy Button, in the bow of the lead boat, gave a shout of excitement as they rounded Devil's Point and turned a-starboard into the dockyard.

'The *Beagle*! Look, Mister Bennet, the *Beagle*!'

'So it is, Jemmy. But there's something different about her. There are more trysails. The skipper's had the deck raised too, and the rail lowered.'

'The *Beagle*! The *Beagle*!' squealed Fuegia Basket.

By the time they had moored alongside, a small reception party had assembled to meet them, headed by a puzzled FitzRoy. He could see Jemmy, York, Fuegia and the coxswain, but where were the two missionaries they were expecting – the two 'muscular' Christians? He could see only a pale, wispy youth of about seventeen, sitting alongside Bennet. And what was in all those boats?

'I love Capp'en Fitz'oy!' shouted Fuegia, levering her increasingly spherical frame on to the quayside with surprising agility and hurtling into his arms. Finally, he extracted himself from a series of high-spirited reunions and said his how-dos to Bennet.

'Commander FitzRoy, may I introduce the Reverend Richard Matthews, of the Church Missionary Society?'

'Welcome to Devonport, Mr Matthews.'

'It is an honour to meet you, Commander.'

FitzRoy extended a hand to assist Matthews, who was labouring to clamber out of the boat, and simultaneously flashed Bennet a what-the-hell-is-going-on? look behind the missionary's back. Bennet responded with a grimace that – he hoped – conveyed his powerlessness with regard to any decisions taken at Walthamstow, however ill-judged.

'Forgive me, Mr Matthews, but I was under the impression that you were to be accompanied by a colleague.'

'Unfortunately not. I have with me a letter from Mr Wilson that explains the situation.'

FitzRoy took the letter and unfolded it.

My dear Sir
I write to introduce the Reverend Richard Matthews, who is to be the permanent representative of the Church Missionary Society in Tierra del Fuego. He is possessed of such knowledge and information as seem calculated to promote the present and eternal welfare

of the savages of that region. I very much regret that we could not meet with a suitable companion for him. However, we have provided Mr Matthews with all such articles as appear to be necessary for him, and which could most advantageously be supplied from this country. I hope that they will not be found to amount to a quantity to occasion you inconvenience; and I think you will be of the opinion that no part of his outfit could, with propriety, be dispensed with.

Believe me, my dear Sir,

Yours faithfully

The Reverend William Wilson

FitzRoy refolded the letter. *With propriety?* What did he mean, *with propriety?* What were these articles?

Under Wickham's direction, crewmen pulled back the tarpaulins on the boats to reveal a series of enormous packing cases.

'Some kind Christian friends have supplied these most essential articles, Commander. I trust that space will be found for them in your hold.'

FitzRoy found himself transfixed by Matthews's moustache or, rather, the lack of it. A few downy hairs were struggling against all odds to take hold on the slopes of his upper lip.

Lieutenant Wickham cut in: 'Mr Matthews, the hold of the *Beagle* is packed to the gunwales with six thousand canisters of Kilner and Moorsom's preserved meat, vegetables and soup. There is absolutely no chance on God's earth of fitting these crates below decks.'

'We must break them open – it is our only course of action,' ordered FitzRoy. 'Distribute the contents about the ship as best you can, Lieutenant. Anywhere there is space.'

'Sir.'

And so, under Matthews's forlorn gaze, the packing cases were shouldered on to the quay and levered open one by one. Gradually, the contents came to light: an astonishing assortment of wine-glasses, butter-bolts, tea-trays, soup tureens and fine white linen, as if someone had transplanted the entire window display of a fashionable Bond Street store to the Devonport quayside. The sniggers and guffaws of the crew were entirely audible, and FitzRoy could see Wickham trying to suppress a smile. One crewman produced an earthenware chamber pot and cracked a joke under his breath. Laughter rippled through the company.

'I am not entirely sure that I see any occasion for levity,' observed Matthews, coldly.

'Quite so,' said FitzRoy, trying to compose his features as best he could.

'Look!' shouted Jemmy, who had found an elegant silver looking-glass with a delicate tracery of filigree-work on the back.

'That's him happy,' said Bennet.

Fuegia was prancing around the quayside in a beaver hat. York had uncovered a cut-glass decanter set, and was holding each piece skyward to catch the glint of daylight as refracted through the glass. Several complete sets of crockery were beginning to stack up, not to mention an entire mahogany dressing-table and a set of French doilies.

'Mr Matthews, are you entirely cognizant of the conditions prevailing in Tierra del Fuego?' FitzRoy asked gently.

'I have not previously left these shores myself, sir, but my elder brother is a missionary near Kororareka in New Zealand. Like him, I will make it my study and endeavour to do these poor creatures all the good in my power, in every practicable way. I shall promise the glory of God and the good of my fellow creatures, and I shall be strong in the grace that is Jesus Christ.'

'Good heavens, sir, an entire packing case of Bibles,' reported Wickham.

'I intend to make the scriptures the basis of all my teaching, Commander. Let us not forget the great theological principle laid down in the sixth article of the Church of England – that Holy Scripture containeth all things necessary to salvation.'

'Absolutely, Mr Matthews. It is a principle I adhere to faithfully myself.'

'By the deuce!' exclaimed Midshipman King. 'Someone's only been and bought up the whole of Swan and Edgar!'

FitzRoy half turned away. As fiercely as he struggled to keep his facial muscles from creasing and his shoulders from heaving, he was losing the battle. Silent tears of laughter trickled down his cheeks.

The rhythmic clump of heavy footsteps, as lines of men tramped on board carrying table-linen and expensive glassware, was counterpointed by high-pitched shrieks of pleasure from above, as Musters and Hellyer chased Fuegia Basket up the rigging and around the crosstrees.

'Really. The *Beagle* is becoming a nursery, with all these deuced kids running about the place,' grumbled King.

FitzRoy had half a mind to let them continue, as it kept Fuegia happy and occupied, but the last thing he needed now was a child with a broken neck. 'Mr Musters! Mr Hellyer! Get down here this instant.'

'Sir!'

The two boys scrambled obediently to the deck.

'Mr Hellyer, I presume by all this foolery that there are no more invoices or pay-tickets to be checked and signed. Have you completed your work?'

'Yes, sir.'

'Have you signed off the inventory from the victualling department?'

'Yes, sir.'

'Good lad. Now, this is Midshipman King. I am going to place you both in his charge.'

King rolled his eyes in despair.

'Over the next few months, I expect you to hang by his every word, after which I hope you will both know everything there is to know about seamanship.'

'I expect I shall know most of it already, sir,' averred Musters, stoutly.

'Quite possibly. But if I hear that you have missed even one nugget of useful information, Mr Musters, you will feel the business end of Mr Sorrell's rattan. Is that clear?'

'Yes, sir.'

'Now go about the business of learning to be a sailor.'

FitzRoy was glad, a moment or two later, that he had put an end to the two boys' larking, when a well-appointed scarlet carriage with livery servants made its way down the approach road towards the *Beagle*. When it drew to a halt, no less a person than Captain Francis Beaufort, His Majesty's hydrographer, climbed down. *Any more visitors*, thought FitzRoy, *and I shall have to employ a footman to collect calling cards on a salver.* He hissed at Wickham and the sailors present to look lively, but he need not have worried. The carriage was sufficiently distinguished that the entire crew had stood to attention even before it had disgorged its occupant. Beaufort limped up the accommodation-ladder, disregarding offers of assistance, and nodded a greeting.

'FitzRoy.'

'This is a most unexpected honour, sir.'

'No need to flatter yourself unduly, FitzRoy, my presence in Plymouth is on Admiralty business. But while I am here I have good reason to pay you a visit.'

His practised eye took in the new trysails between the masts, the brass cannon, the gleaming whaleboats and the hand-painted figure of Neptune on the ship's wheel, with the motto 'England expects that every man will do his duty' circled elegantly around it.

'My, you have dug deep into your capital,' he observed. 'The rail is lower than in an everyday coffin brig, am I right?'

'You are, sir. The deck is raised but not the bulwarks, so as to make her less deep-waisted. It also means that more air will be trapped inside her hull to resist a capsize if she goes over on her beam-ends.'

'You are a marvel, FitzRoy. Although I fear you will bankrupt yourself at this rate – we don't wish to see your name printed in the *London Gazette*, I'm sure. Shall we speak in your cabin?'

They repaired to the cubby-hole that would be FitzRoy's home for the next couple of years.

'So, it seems you have interest enough to get the *Beagle* sent on whatever track you like.'

'My uncle, Lord Londonderry, was kind enough to be interested about me.' FitzRoy though it best to avoid mentioning His Majesty.

'Well, I for one am glad of it. Let us sincerely hope that you have not made enemies in the process. Now, to business. How many chronometers, ultimately, were you able to withdraw from stores?'

'Eleven. I have procured a further eleven myself.'

'Excellent. So the *Beagle* will be better equipped to calculate longitude than any previous vessel to sail from these shores. I want you, FitzRoy, to run a chronometric line around the world. To fix accurately the known points on the surface of the globe *in relation to each other*. Isolated observations are all very well but no one has ever made a complete chain of measurements around the globe before.'

'That's wonderful, sir, but that is to be in addition to the South American survey?'

'Nothing has changed on that account. Use the southern winters to survey the Patagonian coast between Buenos Ayres and Port Desire. Complete the survey of Tierra del Fuego during the summers. And you will be required to provide a full survey of the Falkland Islands as well.'

'The Falklands as well?'

'It is not strictly necessary for the Admiralty's navigational needs, but Buenos Ayres is making noises about inheriting the Spanish claim to the islands. Your presence may act as a deterrent. All ships in the area have been ordered to make a stop there.'

'All of this is to be completed with the one vessel, sir, in two years?'

'You will be wasting your time, FitzRoy, if you pursue the infinite number of bays, openings and roads of Tierra del Fuego. Yet I cannot stress sufficiently that no good harbour should be omitted.'

Do not enter every bay. But do not miss a good harbour on any account. A contrary instruction if ever there was one.

'There will be no time to waste on elaborate maps, Commander. Plain, distinct roughs with explanatory notes shall suffice. After all, you can hardly fail to improve upon the Spanish charts, which are the product merely of a running view of the shore.'

'And if it is discovered that I have omitted a navigable harbour?'

'Then – not to put too fine a point on it – the blame will attach to you. Remember that you are the one who has pursued this commission. There are those who will not be unhappy to see you fail. I suggest that your best course is not to omit one.'

So I shall be damned if I undertake the task properly, and damned if I do not.

'I also desire you to pursue another enquiry for me, in the Pacific. A modern and very plausible theory has arisen regarding coral: that reefs do not ascend from the sea bed, but are raised from the summits of extinct volcanoes. I want you to exert every means that ingenuity can devise of discovering at what depth the coral formation begins.'

Under normal circumstances, a fascinating enquiry. Under normal circumstances.

'Finally, are you familiar with Alexander Dalrymple's proposed numerical scale for the recording of weather conditions? Well, I have long considered that wind and weather should be logged on some intelligible scale, right across the Service. Terms such as "fresh" and "moderate" are ambiguous. I have devised two scales, based upon Dalrymple's, which I should like you to pilot for me. There is a letter code for meteorological observations, and a numerical code for wind strength. Here.'

Beaufort passed a sheet of papers across the table.

'It ranges from nought – dead calm – to twelve, that which no canvas could withstand. Hurricane strength. Although I doubt very much that you would be in a position to report anything back to me, were you to encounter force twelve winds. Let us hope, God willing, that the eventuality shall not arise.'

FitzRoy thought back to the storm at Maldonado Bay, which had nearly cost them all their lives. Would that have counted as a twelve on Beaufort's new scale?

'It will not incommode us, sir.'

'Oh, one more thing, FitzRoy. Do you have a surgeon on the *Beagle*?'

'There is Bynoe, sir, the assistant surgeon. He has acted as surgeon before. He is young, sir, but a regular trump.'

'Well, I am afraid he will have to remain assistant surgeon for the duration of the voyage. A surgeon named Robert McCormick shall be joining you. He was in the Arctic with Parry, but was invalided home. I should warn you that he has been invalided home from overseas a further three times.'

FitzRoy's heart sank. 'Invalided home', both men knew, was a euphemism for 'sacked'. McCormick's previous captains had clearly found him intolerable.

'I have met him, and he seems a sound, good fellow at the bottom.

Perhaps a trifle brusque – he would have made a fine Army man.'

FitzRoy smiled.

'He studied natural philosophy at Edinburgh, so he is well qualified to carry out the job of ship's naturalist.'

'I already have a naturalist aboard, sir.'

'Ah, yes, young Mr Darwin. Well, I am afraid that Mr McCormick must take precedence – it is his right, as surgeon. But I am sure that they can rub along together. Perhaps they can be encouraged to concentrate on different areas. Natural philosophy is a wide discipline, is it not?'

'It is indeed, sir.'

'I'm sorry, FitzRoy, but it is the price you pay for their lordships' consent to your commission. You are not the only man in the Service with influence in high places.'

'And if Mr McCormick were to be invalided home once again, sir?'

'I should not advise it.'

It was a rueful FitzRoy that followed the hydrographer's limping progress up the companionway and out into the glare of the maindeck. As their eyes adjusted to the light, they found themselves standing behind Midshipman King, who was crouched mid-instruction with his new charges.

'Remember to show willing by tailing on to any ropes that are being pulled. Ropes are always coiled out of the way – the way the sun goes round. Right toe, left toe, out in front of you – see? Now, if you're sent up to loose the sails, be sure to take hold of the shrouds and not the ratlines. When the sails are loosed and set, you will hear the orders given for backing and filling them. It is to keep control of the ship's course. The orders will sound like Greek at first, I expect.'

'Not to me they won't,' said Musters.

Beaufort smiled indulgently, and turned to FitzRoy. 'That's the age at which I started. You, too, I expect.'

'Near enough, sir.'

Hearing the officers' voices behind them, the three boys jumped to their feet and saluted smartly.

'You two younkers – what are your names?'

'Volunteer First Class Musters, sir!'
'Volunteer First Class Hellyer, sir!'
'How old are you?'
'Eleven, sir!'
'Twelve, sir!'
'Is this to be your first voyage?'
'Yes sir!'
'Excellent, excellent,' chuckled Beaufort. 'Take good care of these two in the south, Commander, for lads like these are the future of the service.'
'I intend to, sir.'
'Here – not strictly naval procedure, but I think we might stretch a point, seeing as this is your first trip.' Beaufort reached into his pocket and extracted a handful of loose change. 'Hold out your hands.'
He pressed a shiny half-sovereign into each of the two boys' palms.
'That's not fair,' grumbled King, as Beaufort hobbled off the ship.

'I had hoped to be posted to a frigate, sir, or some other desirable ship,' said Robert McCormick, his dark moustache bristling. 'I am, frankly, wearied and tired out with all the buffeting about one has to endure in a small craft. Ofttimes I've had to put up with uncomfortable little vessels on unhealthy stations. But I intend to make my name as a naturalist, sir, which is why I have decided to accept the surgeon's commission on the *Beagle*.'
'I am much obliged to you, Mr McCormick,' said FitzRoy, drily.
'Don't mention it, sir,' said McCormick, entirely missing the sarcasm.
There was a woodenness about the man, thought FitzRoy, an immobility to his bovine features, which was entirely offset by his waxed military moustache. McCormick's moustache quivered animatedly when he spoke, and shuddered in time to his every emphatic declaration. It was as if the moustache spoke for him, in some queer disembodied fashion. The contrast with Matthews's sparse growth struck FitzRoy as faintly ludicrous.
'Captain Beaufort tells me you have voyaged to the Arctic with Parry in the *Hecla*.'

'I did, sir, for my sins, and a more damn-fool expedition was never mounted on the surface of God's earth. Parry's plan was to get to the Pole in wheeled boats pulled by trained reindeer. Of course the damned things were too heavy, and the reindeer couldn't shift 'em. Parry was a fool,' he said scornfully.

FitzRoy wondered what terms his new surgeon would find to describe him behind his back.

'The axles were buried under a foot of snow. So there we all stood in raccoon-skin caps, hooded jackets, blue breeches and white canvas gaiters, straining like idiots to shift 'em even an inch. We must have looked like a party of elves!' McCormick suddenly roared with laughter at the memory.

He has a sense of humour at least, thought FitzRoy. 'So, tell me, Mr McCormick, how have you occupied your time more recently?'

'Well, I have been without a ship since ten months. I've been having a monstrous good time in London, though – boxing, rat-hunting, fives and four-in-hand driving. I've been lodging at my father's place – the old man has lots of tin. But all good things must come to an end, what? Oh, I say, sir, what's that?'

The two men were strolling through the lofty white rectangles of the Royal Dockyard, towards quay number two, where the *Beagle* and the *Active* were moored.

'What's what?'

'On your deck, sir. Looks like a gang of Hottentots.'

'They are Fuegians, Mr McCormick. They have been educated in England at Admiralty expense, and are being returned to their home country to establish a mission.'

'Extraordinary. Wish I'd known – there's a feller of my acquaintance runs the Egyptian Hall in Piccadilly. We could have made a pretty penny exhibiting your savages to the general public.'

'In fact, Mr McCormick, they are very far from the savage state. Three better-mannered and more agreeable souls it would be difficult to find.'

'Wonders will never cease.'

They went aboard, McCormick's brisk, stiff military bearing at variance with FitzRoy's lithe informality. Introductions were made to those officers present on deck, before FitzRoy decided to show the new surgeon the library. They found Stebbing within, entering book titles in a catalogue.

'I say, sir, there must be over three hundred volumes here,' enthused McCormick.

'There are in excess of four hundred.'

'I must say, though, sir, I'm surprised to see Lamarck here. Should we really be giving house-room to a transmutationist? Beasts evolving into men? Typical of a Frenchman to espouse the most atrocious revolutionary principles and the most dangerous Godless doctrines.'

'I hold no more with transmutationism than you do, Mr McCormick, but is it not preferable to understand the arguments of one's enemy than to dismiss them out of hand?'

'Well,' snorted McCormick, 'if there is a halfway house between man and beast, then it's your Frenchy, and no mistake. Personally, I'd chuck the whole beastly nonsense overboard. Ah, I see you have a copy of Lyell. Another damned fool.'

'Mr Lyell is one of our foremost geologists. He has expressed an interest in the results of our expedition.'

'Has he, by Jove? Lyell's the fellow who devised all that gammon about the world's geology being the result of internal heat. Well, I studied under Jameson at Edinburgh – a genius, sir – and he has proved conclusively that both granite and basalt are formed by crystallization from a watery soup. The earth's core is an underground sea – that's where the flood came from.'

'Now you are interesting me, Mr McCormick. We must discuss this with Mr Darwin, the – ah – my companion.'

'Your what, sir?'

'I have engaged a gentleman companion for the voyage, a Mr Charles Darwin. He too is interested in natural philosophy, and intends to make a collection.'

'Well, as long as it doesn't interfere with my official work as surgeon and naturalist.'

'I gather that he, too, studied under Jameson at Edinburgh.'

'Did he? Splendid.'

Although I seem to recall that he was not as complimentary in his assessment of the professor.

'He is presently in the Atheneum Gardens assisting Stokes, my assistant surveyor. He is to mark the time and take observations on the dipping needle, while Stokes calibrates the chronometers for their initial readings. We have selected the Atheneum as the starting point for a chain of chronometric measurements around the globe.'

'Is that usual, sir, for a civilian to assist with naval surveying matters?' McCormick looked decidedly piqued to hear of Darwin's involvement in the scientific life of the ship.

'It may not be usual, Mr McCormick, but the arrangement is most satisfactory to all concerned.'

'Of course, sir.' McCormick took the hint. 'I say, you there.' The surgeon indicated Stebbing. 'I'm absolutely gasping for a drink. Fetch me a glass of wine, will you, well qualified with brandy and spice.'

Stebbing looked bewildered.

'There is no alcohol on the *Beagle*, Mr McCormick,' cut in FitzRoy. 'This is to be an alcohol-free voyage. Shall I show you to your cabin?'

'No alcohol! Good Lord. Belay that. And I felt just like swallowing off a glass.' McCormick wore a bleak expression. 'It's going to be a deuced long two years, sir.'

The officers' cabins were forward of FitzRoy's own cabin on the lower deck, leading off the old messroom, which had been converted into a well-appointed gunroom. McCormick flung open his cabin door: a cot, a washstand and a cramped chest of drawers consumed almost all the meagre space available.

'The cabins in these coffin brigs are so damned poky,' he complained. 'Are they all painted white?'

'It affords some reflected light, given the paucity of natural light below decks.'

'I'm not sure I wouldn't prefer French grey. It's more restful. On second thoughts, it is a French colour. Hmm. I shall give the matter due consideration.'

Shall you indeed? thought FitzRoy, who was beginning to wonder how he would last two hours in McCormick's company, let alone two years. McCormick, he realized, had now fallen silent, for the first time that afternoon. The surgeon had pulled open the cabin drawers one by one, and stood open-mouthed before them.

'Excuse me, sir,' he said finally.

'Yes, Mr McCormick?'

'My cabin appears to be full of French lace, sir.'

FitzRoy marched up George Street in a disturbed frame of mind, a silent Darwin trailing a yard behind. The impossibility of completing his commission in the time available bore down heavily upon him; the callow inexperience of Matthews, and the imposition of McCormick upon what had been a close-knit group of colleagues only made matters worse. He felt a vague sense of urgency as a physical need, an itch he could not scratch, a strange discomfort for which there was no relief. Anxiety had made him tired through lack of sleep; a sense of the pointlessness of all his meticulous preparations was creeping over him, even though his mind was too filled with thoughts to be still. The wider panorama of problems that assailed him was for the most part impossible to address; but on a more intimate scale he could, at least, remedy the ludicrous surfeit of crockery aboard the *Beagle*. So it was that he marched through the doorway of Addison's china shop in combative mood, Darwin – bringing up the rear – wondering all the time what had happened to his *beau idéal* of a sea-captain.

'Commander FitzRoy, is it not? May I be of assistance, sir?' The proprietor – presumably Addison himself – glided from behind the counter to greet his distinguished visitor.

'You may indeed. I have recently had occasion to purchase several complete sets of crockery from this very shop.'

'I remember the occasion well, sir.'

'It seems I have over-ordered. I will have to return them.'

'The items in question have provided every satisfaction, I trust?'

'I told you, I have over-ordered.'

'Then forgive me, Commander' – here Addison indicated a sign – 'but goods may not be returned unless they are found to be faulty.'

'I beg your pardon?' said FitzRoy, taking a step forward with sufficient intent that the proprietor was forced to take a step back.

'G-goods may not be returned, Commander, unless they are found to be faulty.'

'Do you see this, sir? And this, and this?' FitzRoy indicated the most expensive items on display. 'I would have purchased these – all of these – had you not been so disobliging. You are a blackguard, sir!'

'Really, Commander, I must—'

'I said, you are a blackguard, sir!' FitzRoy seized the principal teapot from the nearest crockery display, and dashed it to the floor. Darwin stood, stunned. Addison, unable to believe his eyes, remained rooted to the spot, shaking and confused. FitzRoy swept out of the shop.

With only a brief, panic-stricken glance of sympathy at the proprietor, Darwin followed him into the street. 'My dear FitzRoy, what the deuce—'

'You do not believe me? You do not believe that I would have purchased those items?' His nostrils flared; his features were contorted with rage.

It was, thought Darwin, as if a complete personality change had suddenly overwhelmed the captain. 'But the *Beagle* already has a surfeit of crockery,' he pointed out.

'I tell you sir, I – I – I...' FitzRoy tailed off, and stood there on the cobbles, outwardly silent; but Darwin could see that a superhuman struggle was taking place inside his friend's mind.

FitzRoy could see Darwin now, a ghostly grey shape embodying calm and reason, superimposed against that other Darwin who had inexplicably driven him to anger just a moment before. It was as if another, different reality was showing through, a palimpsest behind the reality that currently intensified each and every one of his senses, that stretched his every nerve-ending like india-rubber. A surge of panic threatened to overwhelm him, as he felt himself on the edge of an abyss, a terrifying black hole of enveloping hopelessness and despair. But he was also conscious of the fact that, for the first time, an alternative course presented itself, if he could only find the strength to reach for it.

'FitzRoy?'

'Darwin, I – I…I'm sorry, but I…'

He wanted to complete the sentence, but he realized that he could not recall the start of it. Big tears, huge dollops of salt water, began to roll helplessly down his face. *I'm all right,* he realized. *I'm all right. Whatever it was, it went away.*

He had come back from the brink. But was his sudden salvation anything to do with his friend's presence? Had the very fact of Darwin's companionship driven the demons of loneliness away? Or was his recovery mere coincidence, another unpredictable fluctuation in the electric current that seemed to course unchecked and undirected through his mind?

'FitzRoy? Are you all right?'

'Yes…yes, I'm fine. I am most terribly sorry…Please, let us leave now.'

And he led his friend back down George Street towards Devonport.

CHAPTER TWELVE

Barnet Pool, Devonport, 24 December 1831

'Deep in wide caverns and their shadowy aisles
Daughter of Earth, the chaste Truffelia smiles;
On silvery beds of soft asbestos wove,
Meets her gnome-husband, and avows her love.'

Darwin giggled when he reached the end of the verse, and shot FitzRoy an I-told-you-so look.

'And you are seriously informing me,' repeated FitzRoy, 'that these lines were written about two truffles mating underground?'

'I do not jest.'

'Extraordinary.'

'It is not the finest verse ever composed.'

'It is certainly the best entertainment I have had this last month.'

The *Beagle* had received Admiralty permission to leave in late November, and had moved to the holding area at Barnet Pool beneath Mount Edgcumbe, ready for departure. No sooner had she done so than a persistent gale had set in, flinging squall after squall up the Channel from the west; there had been no break in the weather for nigh on a month. Bucking and dipping and bouncing where she stood, the little brig strained continually at anchor like an impatient dog trying to break free of its lead. Attempting to tack a square-rigger into such a head-on gale, as FitzRoy explained to Darwin, would be a waste of all their efforts; a point made emphatically on 17 December, when the *Persephone*, a brig that had set out for the Bay of Biscay two days before the storm broke, was driven unceremoniously back into Devonport.

It was Christmas Eve. FitzRoy and Darwin had taken refuge in the library; the other occupants of the cabin, King and Stokes, were part of the last dog-watch from six to eight, and so were hunched in their thick woollen surtouts outside, the elements at their backs. Sleeting winds and rain swept mercilessly across the decks, and inside the library, beat their muffled tattoo against the skylight. The oil lamp swung from side to side in its gimbal, bathing the cabin in its warm yellow glow, and tossing out little parabolas of smoke with every rise and fall of the ship. As the lamp swung back and forth, the two men's shadows alternately grew and shrank against the cabin walls, like pugilists advancing and retreating.

Darwin, who had been feeling queasy for a whole month, was endeavouring to distract himself and entertain FitzRoy by reading aloud from a book of his grandfather Erasmus's scientific verse.

'I say, listen to this. It's about the reproductive process of the *Gloriosa* flower:

'"Then breath'd from quivering lips a whisper'd vow,
And bent on heaven his pale repentant brow;
'Thus, thus!' he cried, and plung'd the furious dart,
And life and love gush'd mingled from his heart."'

'By the deuce, that's racy stuff!'

'My grandfather did sire a prodigious number of children.'

As their conversation dissolved into laughter the cabin door banged open, and the outside world roared in. The lantern flame guttered, sending their shadows boxing each other crazily across the walls. Pages of poetry flickered past at high speed, as a gust of wind raced dismissively through their contents. McCormick ducked into the cabin, shook himself like a wet spaniel, and shut the door. 'Deuced filthy night, sir,' he observed.

'Good evening, Mr McCormick,' said FitzRoy, finding manners, as so often, a useful cloak for his feelings.

'Poetry,' remarked McCormick suspiciously, picking up the volume on the chart table and leafing through it.

'"Organic life beneath the shoreless waves

Was born and nurs'd in Ocean's pearly caves
First forms minute, unseen by spheric glass,
Move on the mud, or pierce the watery mass;
These as successive generations bloom,
New powers acquire, and larger limbs assume."

'I say, who wrote this bosh?'

'My grandfather did.'

'Sorry,' grunted McCormick, in a tone more or less devoid of apology.

'It is his volume of "scientific" verse.'

'Forgive me, Darwin, but I don't see that the mystery of creation is within the range of legitimate scientific territory.'

'Do you believe so?' asked FitzRoy. 'Surely the purpose of philosophic enquiry is to illuminate all God's works, and to understand the laws by which He has created the universe?'

'Yes, sir, but to suggest that man is just another creature crawling out of the slime, well, it's a beastly and damnable creed that has no place for honour, or generosity, or beauty of the spirit, or any of the qualities given by God to man alone.'

'I'm inclined to agree with you, Mr McCormick. But, if Darwin will forgive me –'

'Please carry on.'

'– my principal objection to the theories of Erasmus Darwin, and Lamarck, and their fellow transmutationists, would be a scientific one. Their contention that living beings can develop useful characteristics and somehow pass them on to the next generation allows no mechanism for doing so. A farm labourer may develop muscles, but he cannot pass them on to his son through inheritance. How can mere matter generate its own variations? It is a question that they cannot answer. I'm afraid, my dear Darwin, that your grandfather undermines the distinction between mind and matter by endowing matter with inherent vitality.'

'Yes, absolutely, of course, that too, sir,' agreed McCormick, his brows knitted. 'But hang it, sir, life comes from God, not from the mind or from matter, for that matter. That is, I didn't mean...' McCormick became momentarily confused. 'I mean, all this nonsense about new species developing. It's been scientifically established that God created every single species of plant and land animal on the same day – Saturday, the thirtieth of October 4004 BC.'

FitzRoy allowed McCormick the debatable contention that Bishop Ussher's dating had been 'scientific'.

'The French Philosophical Anatomists would disagree with you.'

'With all due respect, sir, they *are* French.'

'Not all of them,' said Darwin. 'Professor Grant at Edinburgh was as Scottish as oatcakes.'

'With all due respect, Darwin, Professor Grant is a damned scoundrel.'

'When I was at Cambridge,' persevered Darwin, 'Professor Henslow made a very good case for incorporating philosophical anatomy into the theory of natural theology. He believed that God's laws of creation did allow for new species to occur.'

'Damned scientific Whiggery,' snorted McCormick.

Darwin gave him a supercilious stare. 'I, too, am a Whig, Mr McCormick. As is my father, and as was my grandfather, who – however misguided his scientific principles may have been – believed in liberty, social advancement, industrialization and cultural improvement.'

'So he was a Jacobin, sir, in both his politics and his chemistry,' McCormick shot back.

'If you will forgive me, gentlemen, I have an appointment for supper in the gunroom.' Darwin rose stiffly, taking care not to bang his head on the ceiling, pulled on his benjamin and disappeared through the dark rectangle of the doorway. Once more a flurry of lashing rain and gusting wind disrupted the equilibrium of the cabin, before calm reasserted itself. FitzRoy was left facing McCormick across the chart table.

Finally, the surgeon broke the silence.

'Deuced filthy night, sir,' he said.

'Well, if it isn't the Philosopher!'

'Come in, Philosopher, and make yourself at home!'

'Hello there, Philos!'

The fug of pipe-tobacco in the gunroom was warm, friendly and cosseting. Sulivan stood up, clapped Darwin on the back and offered up his seat.

'Supper won't be long, Philos. We've some rare tackle – a nice bowl of warm soup, boiled duck and onions, with hot duff to follow. How will that suit?'

'Wonderful, thank you.' The idea of filling his stomach with hot food appealed to Darwin, but he was aware that his stomach might take its usual contrary view. He squeezed in between Bynoe and Usborne, the new master's assistant.

'So, Philos, how are you liking your new life on the rolling deep?'

'I dare say I shall like it a deal more, gentlemen, when this fearful storm abates.'

A thunderclap of laughter rolled round the table.

'Fearful storm? This is barely a stiff breeze!'

'Wait 'til Tierra del Fuego, Philosopher, then you'll see a blow or two!'

'It's when the bulkhead's under your feet and the deck's by your left ear that you should start to fret, old man!'

'So, how is your study of the art of seamanship advancing, Philos?' enquired Wickham. 'Have you mastered all the technical terms yet?'

'I feel I have made some progress. I have learned the names of all the sails, and the masts and the parts of the ship. So while not quite a seafarer yet, I am beginning to hold my own.'

'Capital, capital. These are exactly the areas of knowledge that will save your life, when you are atop the mast in a howling gale in the Southern Ocean.'

'When I— My dear Lieutenant Wickham, I do not propose to climb the mast at any time, still less during a howling gale.'

'But Philos,' said Bynoe, a worried look on his face, 'did you not realize? When the order is given for all hands on deck, that means all hands. Even the civilians.'

'In a gale we all pull together,' confirmed Bennet.

'Did the skipper not mention it?' said Usborne.

'Do not worry yourself unduly, Philos,' said Wickham. 'As a passenger, you will be asked to reeve the halliards through the block at the peak of the driver, or something like that.'

Darwin's face wore a worried look. 'The driver? That's a…temporary sail, if I recollect, hoisted up the mizzen-mast?'

'Spot on,' said Bynoe. 'You do know your stuff. I presume you know your halliards also – outer halliards, middle halliards, inner halliards, throat halliards?'

'Well, I…throat halliards?'

'Oh, it's perfectly simple,' Wickham reassured him. 'The throat halliards are reeved through a block lashed at the mizzen-mast head. But when the sail is large – and it is important you remember this – the lower block of a luff tackle is hooked to a thimble in the throat cringle or nock, and the upper one is hooked to a strap round the mizzen-mast head. The sheet rope is reeved through a sheave-hole in the boom, and clinched to an iron traveller; in the other end, a thimble is spliced, the outer block of a luff tackle is hooked to it, and the inner one to a bolt on the boom. I say, Philosopher, are you all right?'

Panic-stricken, Darwin scanned the room. A circle of grave, concerned faces met his gaze.

'It's just that I…'

There was a worried silence. Sulivan, still standing behind him, ended it by breaking into laughter.

'Enough! Enough, you rotters, you have had your sport.'

The table erupted in hilarity.

'My dear Philosopher, they are having a game with you,' said Sulivan, throwing an arm good-naturedly around Darwin's shoulders. 'If we find ourselves at the mercy of a gale in the Southern Ocean, you will be tucked up like a babe in your hammock, as sure as eggs is eggs!'

The grave faces of a moment before had been replaced by a sea of merriment. Bennet, right before him, was literally weeping with laughter, tears rolling down his rosy cheeks. 'Jimmy' Usborne, to his left, was clutching his ribs as if in pain. Darwin, still stunned, sat in silence for a moment; and then, gradually, a smile stole over his features, and he began to chuckle too. Just a cautious chuckle at first, then a full-throated guffaw, until he was laughing with the best of them.

Two hours later, the dog-watch over, hammocks piped down, all the lights and fires out except for a yellow glow from the gunroom skylight, Darwin stood at the rail. He stared out at the black, choppy surface of Barnet Pool and tried not to frighten himself with the thought of fifty-yard swells, or mighty walls of water that could crush a three-decker to matchwood, waves that might snap the *Beagle* in two like a twig. He had eaten too well, and had taken snuff for the first time, and he felt queasier than ever, for what seemed an inexhaustible variety of reasons.

An hour later still, FitzRoy knocked at his cabin door, and found him attempting forlornly to climb into his hammock.

'It sounded like an enjoyable evening.'

'It was.'

Darwin did not elaborate.

'You are having trouble?'

'I am having the most ludicrous difficulty. Every time I try to climb in, I only succeed in pushing the deuced thing away, without making any progress inserting my own body.'

'Here. Let me show you. The correct method is to sit accurately in the centre of the hammock, then give yourself a dextrous twist, and your head and your feet will come into their respective places. Like so.'

FitzRoy swung easily into the hammock, then hopped down again. Darwin carefully replicated his movements, and succeeded, finally, in wedging himself between the folds of cloth.

'Pray let me tuck you in.'

'Really, FitzRoy, there is no need.'

'My dear fellow. If you will suffer me...' And he arranged the blankets tenderly about Darwin, and pulled them up to his chin. 'I am sure you will feel better on the morrow.'

'My dear preserver, I do hope so.'

FitzRoy extinguished the light. 'Happy Christmas, Darwin,' he said.

'Happy Christmas, FitzRoy.'

The officers took their Christmas dinner ashore at Weakley's Hotel. They ate mutton chops washed down with champagne, followed by plum-dough with raisins, and watched the rain lash into the window-panes, the streets of Plymouth rendered as grey watercolour smears by the streams cascading down the glass. FitzRoy, though, was optimistic: whatever the despondency engendered among his men by the weather, the barometer told a different story. It was on the turn, indicating that they would in all likelihood be able to set sail the next day. He had given most of the crew Christmas Day off as a consequence, and had left charge of the *Beagle* to a small party of men notionally commanded by Midshipman King – partly to give the boy a taste of responsibility, and partly to keep him away from the champagne. Sulivan, who had worked like a Trojan during the preceding months, was in a cheery mood, like his captain, despite his exertions, for such was his nature. Theirs was a merry end of the table. Fuegia Basket hurtled about, admiring the ribbons and the candles, teasing Musters and Hellyer, and playing with a model boat that the captain had given her. FitzRoy felt gladdened to be in such happy company.

Darwin found himself in mid-table, seated opposite Augustus Earle, the new ship's artist, who had been employed by the captain in a private capacity to provide a visual record of the trip. He found Earle an odd fish: nearly twice his age, the man sported a stubbly beard, wore a shabby top-coat and a filthy stock.

'I apprehend that you are an American, Mr Earle.'

'I was born there, Mr Darwin, but I am a man of the world. I have not seen the States since 1815. I have lived in Chili, Peru, Brazil, Madras, India, and Tristan da Cunha. Lately I have spent three years in Australia, employed upon the portraits of colonial governors. When the supply of subjects was exhausted, I passed nine months in New Zealand, painting the natives.'

'I am sorry to hear of your disappointment. I imagine the Australian commission was a lucrative one.'

'Oh, there was no disappointment, Mr Darwin. Producing identical portraits of minor officials to hang before their families is no appointment worth speaking of. It merely paid my way. The New Zealander, by contrast, is a challenging subject for any painter. I like to think I captured something of his vitality, his athleticism. But there ain't many as want to buy a portrait of a New Zealander. It's why I moved on.'

'Do forgive me, Mr Earle, but I cannot imagine who would wish to purchase a portrait of a black man.'

'Well, our own Captain FitzRoy is an admirer, sir. He said I had a sympathetic eye, along with a capacity for detailed observation. It is how I have found myself in his employ. I have also written a book about New Zealand, which is to be published in Port Jackson, Australia, next year.'

'Is there no end to your talents, Mr Earle? May I know the substance of your narrative?'

'The substance of my narrative, Mr Darwin, is that the New Zealanders are an intelligent, spirited people whose way of life is threatened with destruction by what we term Christian civilization.'

'But how can Christian civilization be a destructive force? Is that not a contradiction?'

'You are a parson-in-waiting, Mr Darwin. If you had seen Christian civilization from the other side of the fence, as I have, then you would have a different appreciation. I lived with a native woman for nine months, and saw first-hand what Christian civilization is doing to her people.'

Darwin was horror-struck. 'You mean you were *familiar* with a black savage for nine months? Unwed?'

'Yes, sir, I was.'

'Was she...well, was she *clean*?'

'Cleaner 'n me, that's for sure.'

Darwin sat back, stunned, unsure what to say. There were some things in this world simply beyond his comprehension. Clearly, the voyage would have a lot to teach him.

'Tell me, FitzRoy...tell me about your home.'

'My home? My home is in the *Beagle*.'

FitzRoy and Darwin sat before the fire in the smoking room at Weakley's. The younger man felt emboldened, drawn by the embers' intimate glow into making the kind of personal enquiries that can only be conducted between two gentlemen who are well known to each other.

'I mean, your family home.'

'I was brought up at Wakefield Lodge, which is by the village of Potters-bury in Northamptonshire. But since as long as I can remember I wanted to go to sea. My uncle was an admiral, which put him on a par with Nelson in my eye. I dare say my father was not best pleased. He was a general, and had me down for a career in soldiering, but I badgered him and badgered him until he put me down for the Service.'

Mentally he saluted his father's generosity in giving way to an insistent six-year-old son.

'I was quite the explorer even then. Once, during the servants' dinner hour, I took a laundry tub and slipped out of the house. I was determined to sail the uncharted waters of the large pond, to discover what lay upon the far shore. I could have walked round, I suppose, but that would have been too prosaic a solution. I even took with me a pile of bricks, to act as ballast – I had heard of ballast from my uncle, I think. Sadly I had not thought to anchor my ballast, so when I stood up halfway across to survey the way ahead, all the bricks slid to one side and my little craft capsized. I was saved from a watery grave by one of the gardeners, who dived in and swam out to rescue me. It was an early lesson in nautical mechanics.'

FitzRoy laughed at the memory.

'My word, I'll wager you suffered the most fearful thrashing. What did your mother and father say?'

'I'm afraid my mother died when I was five years old.'

'Just like my own. I'm sorry.'

'My father never found out about my escapade. He was never there. As I'm sure you can imagine, the French were keeping him rather busy in those days. On top of which he was the MP for Bury St Edmunds.'

'Your father is a Member of Parliament? But, my dear FitzRoy, when I told you my uncle was an MP you said nothing.'

'One does not like to boast of such things,' said FitzRoy, abashed. Somehow, he felt reluctant to share his precious memories of his father, so few and far between were they. 'My father is no longer with us either.

He died…he died some time ago.'

'My friend, I am sorry.'

'I have an older brother, George, who has the house, I suppose, but I hardly know him. He was sent away to school when I was but one. It was my sister Fanny who brought me up. Then I, too, was sent to school at six. First Rottingdean, then Harrow, then the Royal Naval College when I was twelve. Everything you see before you was fashioned there. They do not simply teach seamanship, or the classics like a normal school. I learned everything from foreign languages to fencing and dancing. It is the most advanced of educational establishments. It was also my first ship, if you like – certainly, that was how we were encouraged to see it.'

'I attended Shrewsbury School, down in the town, learning nothing but Latin and Greek. It was cold and brutal, and I abhorred it, but at least I had the consolation of returning home to my sisters each night.'

FitzRoy gave a little nod of accord. How he had once longed to return home to his sister's affection and love of an evening.

'But the sea is my home now, and the officers and men my family. With the exception of Fanny, I do not believe I have a close friend ashore. I keep rooms in Onslow Square, but they feel to me like an hotel. I am never truly at ease on dry land. I think you will catch the feeling during the voyage, when you journey ashore yourself. You will start to think of the *Beagle* as your home.'

Darwin was too appalled by FitzRoy's circumstances to consider the notion. 'My dear friend! There is no one, here in England, awaiting your return? Apart from your sister, I mean – you have no one?'

FitzRoy thought of Mary O'Brien, and the splash of hot wax falling from the chandelier on to her pale skin.

'No…there is no one.'

Concern was etched into Darwin's face. FitzRoy was touched, but hurried them through the moment with a sympathetic smile. 'It does not signify. Come, you are to be my guest, in my house, for the next two years or more. Let us make it a voyage to remember.'

'Here's to that! And let us make it a voyage that shall be remembered by others. I have a suggestion, FitzRoy. What say we publish a book, you and I, an account of our voyage together?'

'Well, I must write a journal of the expedition as part of my official duties, and I have Captain King's journal of the first voyage. We could publish them as two volumes, and you could append a third of your geological and natural observations.'

'What a capital idea!'

'We are agreed, then?'

'Most certainly!'

It was drawing late, so the pot-boy came through to dampen the fire with slack and put up the fire-guard. The two would-be authors retired to bed, aglow with excitement about the voyage to come.

Just as the barometer had predicted, Boxing Day dawned calm, the sun glowing red through an early mist. By the time it had lifted the officers had washed and dressed, and had emerged from the hotel to discover a glorious morning in progress. There were mare's tails in the east, and the smoke from the early-morning chimneys was streaming westward into a crisp blue sky, signalling the way ahead. When they reached the quayside at Devonport, however, there was no sign of the cutter, and they had to endure the embarrassment of borrowing another vessel's craft to get across to Barnet Pool. As they rowed themselves nearer to the *Beagle*, it was clear that something was amiss. Even at a distance, her decks were deathly quiet. There was only one sentry on duty, a diminutive sailor lost in a large, shapeless coat, whom FitzRoy did not at first recognize; although there was something familiar, he thought, about the man's bearing. As they made their boat fast to the *Beagle's* flank, the mystery of the sentry's identity became clear. Inside the coat, shaking with cold and fear, his fingers, nose and ears an icy purple, was Midshipman King.

'Mr King? What on earth...?'

'I'm s-sorry, sir. Th-they wouldn't listen to me, sir.'

'Who wouldn't? Where is the sentry?'

King's eyes pricked with tears. 'He said he would no longer stand on duty, sir. He told me to...he told me to go to the devil, sir. There is not a sober man in the ship, sir.'

As FitzRoy hauled himself up the battens and over the rail, the chaos of the maindeck told its own story: the uncoiled and jumbled ropes, the smashed bottles, the wet slick of vomit by the scuttle-butt. 'How long have you been standing sentry, Mr King?'

'Since yesterday afternoon sir. Fourteen hours, sir.'

'I think you had better go below and get some rest, beneath as many warm blankets as you can muster.'

'Am I to be c-court-martialled, sir?'

'No, Mr King, you will not be court-martialled. I must take much of the responsibility for what has happened myself. Now, hurry along. And thank you, Mr King, for your devotion to duty.'

'Aye aye sir.'

'Mr Wickham, I want this deck shipshape and clean as a shirtfront within the hour. Mr Sorrell, Mr Usborne, Mr Chaffers, I want everyone who is below standing to attention on deck in five minutes. Any who are insolent or who are too drunk to stand will be thrown in irons in the hold. Mr Stokes, Mr Bennet, you will search every tavern and gin-palace in Plymouth, and you will find and bring back every single one of our people. And then there will be hell to pay.'

As the officers went about their allotted tasks, the last of the civilian members of the party climbed aboard. Jemmy Button gingerly prodded the very edge of the vomit slick with an immaculately buffed toecap.

'Too much skylark. Far too much skylark,' he observed.

Fuegia poked a finger into the yellow stew, held it up to her face, and wrinkled her nose in disgust. Augustus Earle grinned.

'All of you who are not members of the ship's company have my most sincere apologies,' announced FitzRoy, his quiet anger condensing into white clouds on the morning air. 'To say that these events are unacceptable would be the most prodigious understatement. I give you my word that nothing of this like shall happen again for the duration of the voyage.'

Darwin was not listening, but had wandered up the maindeck towards the prow. Indeed, he had paid little heed to anything that had occurred since their departure from the hotel, when a letter had arrived for him in that morning's post. He had opened it, discreetly, in the boat. It was from his sister, Catherine, announcing Fanny Owen's betrothal to Robert Biddulph. He unfolded it now and scanned the last page for the third time.

...I hope it won't be too great a grief to you, dearest Charley. You will find her a motherly old married woman when you come back. You may be perfectly sure that Fanny will always continue as friendly and affectionate to you as ever, and as rejoiced to see you again, though I fear that will be but poor comfort to you, my dear Charles. God bless you, Charles,
Yours most affectionately,
Catherine Darwin

He did not know whether to cry, or break into bitter laughter. His heart felt fit to break in two. He was torn between a desire to abandon the voyage there and then, take the next stage to Shrewsbury and confront the pair in righteous anger; and a mad urge to dash about the deck, slashing ropes and cutting cables, to free the *Beagle*, to see her dart forward on her way, to see the shores of England recede as quickly as possible. Perhaps he should leave the ship in New Zealand, and take a black savage for a lover, as Earle had done? That would show her – that would show Fanny Owen the disastrous error of her ways. But even as luridly vengeful images of a distraught Fanny flashed into his brain, he knew them for the fantasies they were, and banished them from his imagination. He screwed Catherine's letter into a tight white ball and tossed it over the side, where it sat upon the indigo surface of Barnet Pool, bobbing and mocking.

'Man the windlass!'
Carpenter May knocked the chocks out from beneath the bars, and the men began the back-breaking work of pulling up the main bower anchor.
'Heave, lads! Heave 'n' she must come!' commanded Boatswain Sorrell.
It was the morning of the twenty-seventh, which, fortunately for all,

had dawned bright and gusty, not that the blue skies had taken the edge off FitzRoy's temper. He had elected to save all punishments until the *Beagle* was out to sea: fear of what was to follow would galvanize the men, he knew, whereas the aftermath of the mass floggings that must result from such an act of near-mutiny would leave many in no state to get the *Beagle* under way, least of all an exhausted Bos'n Sorrell.

Every man at the windlass was putting in every last drop of effort, desperate to impress, straining to drag the anchor up from its stubborn, slimy resting-place. Slowly, the ship inched towards that part of Barnet Pool where she was hooked, until she lay directly above it; then the chain clanked vertically upwards into the ship, where the anchor was catted and fished, until it was lashed fast to the fo'c'slehead.

'Up jib.'

The *Beagle's* masts blossomed white and the stiff easterly breeze filled every sail.

'Muster all the officers on the poop deck.'

'Aye aye sir.'

Where the devil was Sulivan? FitzRoy wondered angrily. So hard had his second lieutenant worked, running himself into the ground over the preceding weeks, then combing almost every street in Plymouth the previous day, that he had been given leave to attend a ball with Miss Young on his last night ashore. Sulivan had not been seen since. After the drunken desertions of Boxing Day, it would be just too much if one of his officers had committed the same crime.

Down on the starboard side of the lower deck, in the cramped wooden cot that constituted most of his tiny cabin, a confused Bartholomew Sulivan was woken by the ship's sudden leap forward as the wind caught her sails. He shouted for the officers' steward, who put his head round the door.

'What is the time, if you please, Sutton?'

'Eight o'clock in the morning, sir.'

'What? I have missed the ball? I was only to have a short rest! Why did you not call me to gunroom tea yesterday evening as bidden?'

'I did, sir.'

'Then, when I did not appear at tea, why in heaven's name did you not call me again? I was to go ashore and dress thereafter!'

'You did appear at tea, sir.'

'What?'

Frantically, Sulivan clambered into his uniform. In the passageway outside, still fumbling with his buttons, he ran into Wickham, heading for the captain's muster on the poop deck.

'Wickham, old man. Am I going mad? Did I appear at gunroom tea last evening?'

Wickham laughed heartily. 'You could say that, dear fellow. In fact, "appeared" is quite the word for it. You appeared at half past seven, in your nightshirt and nightcap, with a large duck gun at your shoulder. You placed the gun in the corner, went to your place at table, drank the tea put before you, then rose, shouldered the gun again and marched off to bed. My dear chap, we thought you plainly overwrought, and we did not wish to awaken the somnambulist.'

'But – but – Miss Young!'

FitzRoy, gathering his officers about him on the poop deck, was relieved to see the face of Lieutenant Sulivan appear at the top of the companionway; but less impressed when he realized that his second lieutenant was not only unshaven but that the buttons of his uniform were misaligned; and even less so when the officer in question hared past him to the rail, and began screaming at two distant female figures on the Devonport dock, two tiny specks in distinctive turquoise skirts. Was one of them waving? It was near-impossible to tell.

'Miss Young!' yelled Sulivan, but his words were blown back past him, for'ard of the ship, in the direction in which the *Beagle* was headed. Even had their recipient been standing fifty yards astern, it was doubtful that she would have been able to make them out.

'Mr Sulivan.' FitzRoy's icy tones sliced through the sea breeze like a sabre thrust. 'I suggest that it would be most strongly in your interest to join us forthwith.'

Reluctantly, Sulivan relinquished his place at the rail and said a mental farewell to the tiny turquoise speck.

'Let me make matters clear in the outset of our departure,' emphasized
FitzRoy. There was steel in his voice. 'The events of the last twenty-four
hours are beyond the pale. We are all of us, officers and men, culpable.
There will be no repetition of these events. Furthermore, I put all of you
on notice that it is my intention not to lose one crewman, one boat, one
mast or even one spar during this voyage. If any man falls overboard –
if we even ship a single sea – I shall punish the officer of the watch. Is
that clear?'

There were nods all round.

'No one is to go out of sight of the ship except in company with at
least two others. Thereby if one man is hurt, one comrade may stay with
him while the third goes for assistance. There are to be no exceptions to
this rule. Is that clear?'

Once more the officers gave their assent.

'Now. All hands will be mustered aft.'

Within five minutes, Boatswain Sorrell had assembled the men to await
the reading of the punishment log.

FitzRoy addressed them in a firm, clear voice. 'Able Seaman William
Bruce: disrated to landsman for breaking his leave and drunkenness.
Bos'n's mate Thos Henderson: disrated to able seaman for breaking his
leave and drunkenness. Captain of the foretop John Wasterham: disrated
to able seaman for breaking his leave and drunkenness. Carpenter's mate
David Russell: a dozen lashes for breaking his leave, drunkenness and
disobedience of orders. Elias Davis: a dozen lashes for breaking his leave,
drunkenness and insolence...'

And so the list went on, seemingly interminably. A forlorn Darwin
made his way to the prow, sickened by the roll of the ship and the catalogue of impending violence. As the *Beagle* nudged past the breakwater
and stood out of the harbour, she pitched into short, steep seas, where
her roll was quick, deep, and awkward; at least the spray freshened his
face and countered his giddiness. After an interval a similarly forlorn
Sulivan joined him at the rail, fresh from a severe dressing-down.

'Good day, Philosopher,' said Sulivan, in an attempt to be of good cheer.
'How does it feel to be heading south in one of His Majesty's bathing

machines?'

'Does he have to flog so many men?'

'Philosopher, the skipper hates corporal punishment. He abhors it. But the lives of every one of us aboard ship depend upon immediate decisions and instant obedience. If he is decisive now, then with good fortune he will obtain that obedience, and will have no occasion to flog anyone else for the rest of the voyage.'

'But why floggings? Why not this "disrating"?'

'Oh, many a man would prefer the flogging. A disrating involves less pay. But they will get their rates back, and the scars of the floggings will heal. They knew what they were doing, Philos. Drunkenness is the sole and never-failing pleasure to which a sailor always looks forward. They expect to see floggings, and if the skipper does not deliver, why, they will lose all respect for him. They have sown the wind, and they shall reap the whirlwind.'

Darwin was silent.

'There isn't such a fine captain in all the world, Philos. He would not take this course were it not absolutely necessary.'

The *Beagle* swung out into the Channel, and as her crew prepared to bring her nose round to starboard, the men began to sing:

'Scrub the mud off the dead man's face
An' haul or ye'll be damned;
For there blow some cold nor'westers, on
The Banks of Newfoundland.'

Darwin shuddered. *What is this antiquated world of peremptory justice and sadistic medieval vengeance that I have joined of my own will?* he asked himself. *A world where men take floggings with equanimity and are as like as not to end their lives drowned in soft brown mud? I must have taken leave of my senses.*

Sulivan guessed what sentiments lay behind the expression on Darwin's face, and smiled. 'It's only a piece of metal, Philos.'

'What is?'

'The dead man's face. It's a triangular piece of metal with three holes in it, used when the ship is moored for long periods, to connect the two anchor chains and prevent them twisting round each other. Ofttimes, it gets muddy. That's why it needs scrubbing.'

Darwin felt small, and stupid, and pale and giddy and sick. He went to his cabin, and climbed with recently acquired expertise into his hammock. As he lay there, he felt waves of nausea undulate through him, so he shut his eyes and listened as the screams of the first of the flogged men echoed through the ship.

Acknowledgments

I should like to thank my father, Gordon Thompson, for his tireless and invaluable assistance, both in the researching and the plotting of this book; the indefatigable Pippa Brown, for coming to the rescue of an abysmal index-finger typist, and typing out the entire manuscript; Martin Fletcher and Bill Hamilton, for all their helpful suggestions, and the wonderful Lisa Whadcock for the benefit of her wisdom and insight; Peter Ackroyd, for pointing me in the direction of George Scharf; the staff of the London Library, for their assistance in locating long-forgotten electoral results and ancient guides to Durham; Robert and Faanya Rose, for graciously inviting me into FitzRoy's old home in Chester Street; the Norwood Historical Society, for its help in locating FitzRoy's latterday whereabouts; John Morrish, for allowing me access to his unpublished manuscript about living with manic depression; Tom Russell and Paul Daniels (no, not that one) for slogging up to the fort in Montevideo Bay with me; Patrick Watts (he won't remember, it was so long ago) for giving me a guided tour of Stanley harbour; the staff of the Fazenda Bananal Engenho de Murycana in Brazil, for showing me round their property; and the penguins of Dungeness Point in Patagonia, for taking care of me when I was the only human being for miles and miles around.

Bibliography

I am, of course, indebted to the various biographers of Robert FitzRoy: H. E. L. Mellersh (*FitzRoy of the Beagle*, Rupert Hart-Davis, 1968), Paul Moon (*FitzRoy, Governor in Crisis 1843–1845*, David Ling Publishing, Auckland, 2000), Peter Nichols (*Evolution's Captain*, Profile, 2003) and those exceptional scholars John and Mary Gribbin (*FitzRoy*, Review Books, 2003). These last two works were suddenly published in the middle of my writing this novel, and afforded me considerable assistance. There are, of course, Darwin biographies by the score, but it would be difficult to better Janet Browne's *Charles Darwin* (2 vols, Jonathan Cape, 1995), Adrian Desmond and James Moore's *Darwin* (Michael Joseph, 1991), Randal Keynes's *Annie's Box: Charles Darwin, His Daughter and Human Evolution* (Fourth Estate, 2001), Ronald W. Clark's *The Survival of Charles Darwin* (Random House, 1984), and covering this area alone, Richard Keynes' exceptional and infallible *Fossils, Finches and Fuegians* (Harper-Collins, 2002). Keynes was also responsible for *The Beagle Record* (Cambridge University Press, 1979). From a pictorial point of view, Alan Moorehead's *Darwin and the Beagle* (Hamish Hamilton 1969) and John Chancellor's *Charles Darwin* (Weidenfeld & Nicolson 1973) were especially valuable.

Jemmy Button has been the subject of one excellent biography, Nick Hazlewood's *Savage* (Hodder & Stoughton, 2000), as indeed has the *Beagle* herself (*HMS Beagle*, Keith S. Thomson, W. W. Norton & Co., New York, 1995). Then, of course, there are FitzRoy and Darwin's own works. Darwin's *The Voyage of the Beagle* and *The Origin of Species* are available in many editions. By contrast, FitzRoy's *Weather Book, Remarks on New Zealand* and *Narrative of the Voyage of HMS Beagle* are hard to find outside the Bodleian (the library's copy of the latter volume still had its pages uncut – nobody had bothered to read it in 165 years); extracts from his

Narrative were, however, published by the Folio Society of London in 1977. Charles Darwin's correspondence has been edited for publication over many disparate volumes by his granddaughter Nora Barlow. Bartholomew Sulivan's letters were edited by his son, Henry Norton Sulivan (published by Murray, 1896), although they too are long out of print; as is Augustus Earle's *A Narrative of Nine Months' Residence in New Zealand*, which was published by Longman & Co. in 1832. *The Journal of Syms Covington* has only been published on the Internet, by the Australian Science Archives Project, on ASAPWeb, 23 August 1995. Among other contemporary documents, the report of the 1860 British Association meeting in Oxford was published in the *Athenaeum* magazine. The British Government Select Committee reports on New Zealand are also available for scrutiny, at the House of Lords Record Office, London.

For technical maritime information, I used the book that FitzRoy himself always recommended to his subordinates: *The Young Sea Officer's Sheet Anchor* by Darcy Lever (John Richardson, 1819, miraculously reprinted by Dover Maritime Books, Toronto, 1998). But I am also indebted to Christopher Lloyd (*The British Seaman 1200–1860*, Collins, 1968), Michael Lewis (*England's Sea-Officers*, Allen & Unwin, 1939), Henry Baynham (*Before the Mast*, Hutchinson & Co., 1971), Stan Hugill (*Shanties and Sailors' Songs*, Barrie & Jenkins, 1969), Lew Lind (*Sea Jargon*, Kangaroo Press, 1982), Nicholas Blake and Richard Lawrence (*The Illustrated Companion to Nelson's Navy*, Chatham Publishing, 2000), Peter Kemp (*The Oxford Companion to Ships and the Sea*, Oxford University Press, 1976), Tristan Jones (*Yarns*, Adlard Coles Nautical, 1983), W. E. May (*The Boats of Men of War*, National Maritime Museum/Chatham Publishing, 1974 and 1979), the long-deceased Captain Charles Chapman (*All About Ships*, Ward Lock, 1866), Frederick Wilkinson (*Antique Guns and Gun Collecting*, Hamlyn, 1974), and Colonel H. C. B. Rogers (*Weapons of the British Soldier*, Seeley, Service & Co., 1960); and, of course, I must not forget the contemporary works of Captain Marryat, Sir Francis Beaufort and Sir Home Popham, and the considerable later writings of C. S. Forester, Patrick O'Brian and Dudley Pope.

For help with the descriptions of London, I should like to thank Peter Ackroyd (*London – the Biography*, Chatto & Windus, 2000), Peter Jackson (*George Scharf's London 1820–50*, John Murray, 1987), Eric de Maré (*London 1851*, The Folio Society, 1972), and Felix Barker and Peter Jackson once more for *London* (Cassell, 1974). The parliamentary scenes came courtesy of *The Houses of Parliament – History, Art and Architecture* (ed. Christine and Jacqueline Ridley, Merrell, 2000) and *The London Journal of Flora Tristan* (first published in France, 1842; modern edition trans. Jean Hawkes, Virago, 1982). Another contemporary perspective came from George Cruikshank (*Sunday in London*, Effingham Wilson, 1833). More general historical information came courtesy of comtemporary issues of *The Ladies' Magazine*, as well as Elizabeth Burton's *The Early Victorians at Home* (Longman, 1972), A. N. Wilson's *The Victorians* (Hutchinson, 2002), J. F. C. Harrison's *Early Victorian Britain* (Fontana, 1988), G. M. Trevelyan's *English Social History* (Longman, 1944), Christopher Hibbert's *Social History of Victorian Britain* (Illustrated London News, 1975), Leith McGrandle's *The Cost of Living in Britain* (Wayland, 1973), D. J. Smith's *Horse Drawn Carriages* (Shire Publications, 1974), Henny Harald Hansen's *Costume Cavalcade* (Eyre Methuen, 1972), and Daniel Pool's *What Jane Austen Ate and Charles Dickens Knew* (Simon & Schuster Inc., USA, 1994). Dickens himself was shamelessly plundered for much of the vocabulary, as were Thackeray, Hughes and Captain Marryat.

For the Durham scenes, I consulted *A Historical, Topographical and Descriptive View of the County Palatine of Durham* by E. Mackenzie and M. Ross (Mackenzie & Dent, 1834), *The History & Antiquities of the County Palatine of Durham* by William Fordyce (Thomas Fordyce, 1855), *Cathedral City* by Thomas Sharp (The Architectural Press, 1945), *In and Around Durham* by Frank H. Rushford (Durham County Press, 1946) and *Durham* by Sir Timothy Eden (Robert Hale, 1952).

Among the various scientific books and articles consulted during the preparation of this novel, I should like to mention *Bones of Contention* by Paul Chambers (John Murray, 2003), *Return to the Wilberforce-Huxley Debate* by J. Vernon Jensen (British Journal for the History of Science,

21, pp. 161–79, 1988), *A Journey to a Birth – William Smith at the birth of Stratigraphy* by L. R. Cox (International Geological Congress, 1948), *The Pony Fish's Glow, and Other Clues to Plan and Purpose in Nature* by George C. Williams (Basic Books, 1997), *Darwinism – A Crumbling Theory and Evidence for Creation by Outside Intervention* by Lloyd Pye (*Nexus Magazine*, volume 10, number 1, December 2002–January 2003 and volume 9, number 4, June–July 2002), *FitzRoy's Foxes and Darwin's Finches* by W. R. P. Bourne (Archives of Natural History, 1992, 19 (1)), *Noah's Flood – the Genesis Story in Western Thought* by Norman Cohn (Yale University Press, 1996), *The Weather Prophets: Science and Reputation in Victorian Meteorology* by Katharine Anderson (*History of Science*, 37, June 1999), *Matthew Fontaine Maury – Scientist of the Sea* by Francis Leigh Williams (Rutgers University Press, New Brunswick, NJ, 1963), *From Wind Stars to Weather Forecasts: The Last Voyage of Admiral Robert FitzRoy* by Derek Barlow (Weather London, 1994, volume 49, number 4), *Not in our Genes* by Steven Rose, Leon J. Kamin and Richard C. Lewontin (Penguin, 1984), *The Biblical Flood – A Case Study of the Church's Response to Extra-biblical Evidence* by Davis A. Young (Paternoster Press, 1995), and of course many, many fine articles by the inimitable Stephen Jay Gould. For their insights into the processes of manic depression, I am utterly indebted to the work of Andrew Solomon, Dr Irene Whitehill, Sally Brampton and John Morrish.

As to the geographical descriptions, the vast majority were obtained by personal visits to the actual locations. FitzRoy and Darwin themselves provided plenty of supplementary assistance, as did *A Journey in Brazil* by Louis Agassiz (1868, modern ed. by Praeger, Westport, CT, 1970), *Giants of Patagonia* by Captain Bourne (Ingram, Cooke & Co., 1853), and *The Narrative of the Honourable John Byron* (Baker & Leitch, 1778). John Campbell's *In Darwin's Wake* (Waterline, 1997) provided specific information regarding the *Beagle's* South American anchorages.

ABOUT THE AUTHOR

To the Edge of the World, originally published in the U.K. as *This Thing of Darkness*, was Harry Thompson's first novel. In 2005, it was long-listed for the Man Booker Prize and short-listed for the Pendleton First Novel Award. Thompson died in 2005 after a battle with cancer.

Thompson was the producer of *Have I Got News for You, They Think It's All Over, Never Mind the Buzzcocks*, and *Da Ali G Show*. He was the author of numerous nonfiction best sellers, including *Peter Cook: A Biography*. He wrote for several U.K. national newspapers, especially on travel, and was nominated for Travel Journalist of the Year.